D1396140

WHAT KATY DID AT SCHOOL
and
WHAT KATY DID NEXT

What Katy Did at School
&
What Katy Did Next

SUSAN COOLIDGE

WORDSWORTH CLASSICS

In loving memory of
MICHAEL TRAYLER
the founder of Wordsworth Editions

2

Readers who are interested in other titles from
Wordsworth Editions are invited to visit our website at
www.wordsworth-editions.com

For our latest list and a full mail-order service, contact
Bibliophile Books, 5 Thomas Road, London E14 7BN
TEL: +44 (0)20 7515 9222 FAX: +44 (0)20 7538 4115
E-MAIL: orders@bibliophilebooks.com

This edition published 2001 by Wordsworth Editions Limited
8B East Street, Ware, Hertfordshire SG12 9HJ

ISBN   978 1 84022 437 5

Typeset in Great Britain by Antony Gray
Printed and bound by Clays Ltd, St Ives plc

CONTENTS

WHAT KATY DID AT SCHOOL

CHAPTER ONE

Conic Section

It was just after that happy visit of which I told at the end of *What Katy Did*, that Elsie and John made their famous excursion to Conic Section; an excursion which neither of them ever forgot, and about which the family teased them for a long time afterward.

The summer had been cool; but, as often happens after cool summers, the autumn proved unusually hot. It seemed as if the months had been playing a game, and had 'changed places' all round; and as if September were determined to show that he knew how to make himself just as disagreeable as August, if only he chose to do so. All the last half of Cousin Helen's stay, the weather was excessively sultry. She felt it very much, though the children did all they could to make her comfortable, with shaded rooms, and iced water, and fans. Every evening the boys would wheel her sofa out on the porch, in hopes of coolness, but it was of no use: the evenings were as warm as the days, and the yellow dust hanging in the air made the sunshine look thick and hot. A few bright leaves appeared on the trees, but they were wrinkled, and of an ugly colour. Clover said she thought they had been boiled red like lobsters. Altogether, the month was a trying one, and the coming of October made little or no difference: still the dust continued, and the heat; and the wind, when it blew, had no refreshment in it, but seemed to have passed over some great furnace which had burned out of it all life and flavour.

In spite of this, however, it was wonderful to see how Katy

gained and improved. Every day added to her powers. First she came down to dinner, then to breakfast. She sat on the porch in the afternoons; she poured the tea. It was like a miracle to the others, in the beginning, to watch her going about the house; but they got used to it surprisingly soon – one does to pleasant things. One person, however, never got used to it, never took it as a matter of course; and that was Katy herself. She could not run downstairs, or out into the garden; she could not open the kitchen door to give an order, without a sense of gladness and exultation which was beyond words. The wider and more active life stimulated her in every way. Her cheeks grew round and pink, her eyes bright. Cousin Helen and papa watched this change with indescribable pleasure; and Mrs Worrett, who dropped in to lunch one day, fairly screamed with surprise at the sight of it.

'To think of it!' she cried; 'why, the last time I was here you looked as if you had took root in that chair of yours for the rest of your days, and here you are stepping about as lively as I be. Well, well! wonders will never cease. It does my eyes good to see you, Katherine. I wish your poor aunt were here today; that I do. How pleased she'd be!'

It is doubtful whether Aunt Izzie would have been so pleased, for the lived-in look of the best parlour would have horrified her extremely; but Katy did not recollect that just then. She was touched at the genuine kindness of Mrs Worrett's voice, and took very willingly her offered kiss. Clover brought lemonade and grapes, and they all devoted themselves to making the poor lady comfortable. Just before she went away she said: 'How is it that I can't never get any of you to come out to Conic Section? I'm sure I've asked you often enough. There's Elsie, now, and John, they're just the age to enjoy being in the country. Why won't you send 'em out for a week? Johnnie can feed chickens, and chase 'em too, if she likes,' she added, as Johnnie dashed just then into view, pursuing one of Phil's bantams round the house. 'Tell her so, won't you, Katherine? There is lots of chickens on the farm. She can chase 'em from morning to night, if she's a mind to.'

Katy thanked her, but she didn't think the children would care to go. She gave Johnnie the message, and then the whole matter passed out of her mind. She was surprised, a few days later, by having it brought up again by Elsie. The family were in low spirits that morning because of Cousin Helen's having just gone away; and Elsie was lying on the sofa, fanning herself with a great palm-leaf fan.

'Oh, dear!' she sighed. 'Do you suppose it's ever going to be cool again in this world? It does seem as if I couldn't bear it any longer.'

'Aren't you well, darling?' enquire Katy, anxiously. 'Oh, yes! well enough,' replied Elsie. 'It's only this horrid heat, and never going away to where it's cooler. I keep thinking about the country, and wishing I were there feeling the wind blow. I wonder if Papa wouldn't let John and me go to Conic Section, and see Mrs Worrett. Do you think he would if you asked him?'

'But,' said Katy, amazed, 'Conic Section isn't exactly country, you know. It is just out of the city – only six miles from here. And Mrs Worrett's house is close to the road, Papa said. Do you think you'd like it, dear? It can't be very much cooler than this.'

'Oh, yes! it can,' rejoined Elsie, in a tone which was a little fretful. 'It's quite near woods; Mrs Worrett told me so. Besides, it's always cooler on a farm. There's more room for the wind, and – oh, everything's pleasanter! You can't think how tired I am of this hot house. Last night I hardly slept at all; and, when I did, I dreamed that I was a loaf of brown bread, and Debby was putting me into the oven to bake. It was a horrid dream. I was so glad to wake up. Won't you ask Papa if we may go, Katy?'

'Why, of course I will, if you wish it so much. Only – '

Katy stopped and did not finish her sentence. A vision of fat Mrs Worrett had risen before her, and she could not help doubting if Elsie would find the farm as pleasant as she expected. But sometimes the truest kindness is in giving people their own unwise way, and Elsie's eyes looked so wistful that Katy had no heart to argue or refuse.

Dr Carr looked doubtful when the plan was proposed to him.

'It's too hot,' he said. 'I don't believe the girls will like it.'

'Oh, yes! we will, Papa; indeed we will,' pleaded Elsie and John, who had lingered near the door to learn the fate of their request.

Dr Carr smiled at the imploring faces, but he looked a little quizzical. 'Very well,' he said, 'you may go. Mr Worrett is coming into town tomorrow, on some bank business. I'll send word by him; and in the afternoon, when it is cooler, Alexander can drive you out.'

'Goody! Goody!' cried John, jumping up and down; while Elsie put her arms round Papa's neck and gave him a hug.

'And Thursday I'll send for you,' he continued.

'But, Papa,' expostulated Elsie, 'that's only two days. Mrs Worrett said a week.'

'Yes, she said a week,' chimed in John; 'and she's got ever so many chickens, and I'm to feed them, and chase them about as much as I like. Only it's too hot to run much,' she added reflectively.

'You won't really send for us on Thursday, will you, Papa?' urged Elsie, anxiously. 'I'd like to stay ever and ever so long; but Mrs Worrett said a week.'

'I shall send on Thursday,' repeated Dr Carr, in a decided tone. Then, seeing that Elsie's lip was trembling, and her eyes were full of tears, he continued: 'Don't look so woeful, Pussy. Alexander shall drive out for you; but if you want to stay longer, you may send him back with a note to say what day you would like to have him come again. Will that do?'

'Oh, yes!' said Elsie, wiping her eyes; 'that will do beautifully, Papa. Only, it seems such a pity that Alexander should have to go twice when it's so hot; for we're perfectly sure to want to stay a week.'

Papa only laughed, as he kissed her. All being settled the children began to get ready. It was quite an excitement packing the bags, and deciding what to take and what not to take. Elsie grew bright and gay with the bustle. Just to think of being in the country – the cool green country – made her perfectly happy, she declared. The truth was, she was a little feverish and not quite well, and didn't know exactly how she felt or what she wanted.

The drive out was pleasant, except that Alexander upset John's gravity, and hurt Elsie's dignity very much, by enquiring, as they left the gate, 'Do the little misses know where it is that they want to go?' Part of the way the road ran through woods. They were rather boggy woods; but the dense shade kept off the sun, and there was a spicy smell of evergreens and sweet fern. Elsie felt that the good time had fairly begun, and her spirits rose with every turn of the wheels.

By and by they left the woods, and came out again into the sunshine. The road was dusty, and so were the fields, and the ragged sheaves of cornstalks, which dotted them here and there, looked dusty too. Piles of dusty red apples lay on the grass, under the orchard trees. Some cows going down a lane toward their milking-shed, mooed in a dispirited and thirsty way, which made the children feel thirsty also.

'I want a drink of water awfully,' said John. 'Do you suppose it's much farther? How long will it be before we get to Mrs Worrett's, Alexander?'

'Most there, miss,' replied Alexander, laconically.

Elsie put her head out of the carriage, and looked eagerly round. Where was the delightful farm? She saw a big, pumpkin-coloured house by the roadside, a little farther on;

but surely that couldn't be it. Yes; Alexander drew up at the gate, and jumped down to lift them out. It really was! The surprise quite took away her breath.

She looked about. There were the woods, to be sure, but half a mile away across the fields. Near the house, there were no trees at all; only some lilac bushes at one side; there was no green grass either. A gravel path took up the whole of the narrow front yard; and, what with the blazing colour of the paint and the wide-awake look of the blindless windows, the house had somehow the air of standing on tiptoe and staring hard at something – the dust in the road, perhaps; for there seemed nothing else to stare at.

Elsie's heart sank indescribably, as she and John got very slowly out of the carry-all, and Alexander, putting his arm over the fence, rapped loudly at the front door. It was some minutes before the rap was answered. Then a heavy step was heard creaking through the hall, and somebody began fumbling at an obstinate bolt, which would not move. Next, a voice which they recognised as Mrs Worrett's called: 'Isaphiny! Isaphiny, come and see if you can open this door.'

'How funny!' whispered Johnnie, beginning to giggle.

'Isaphiny, seemed to be upstairs; for presently they heard her running down, after which a fresh rattle began at the obstinate bolt. But still the door did not open, and at length Mrs Worrett put her lips to the keyhole, and asked 'Who is it?'

The voice sounded so hollow and ghostly, that Elsie jumped, as she answered: 'It's I, Mrs Worrett – Elsie Carr. And Johnnie's here too.'

'Ts, ts, ts!' sounded from within, and then came a whispering; after which Mrs Worrett put her mouth again to the keyhole, and called out: 'Go round to the back, children. I can't make this door open anyway. It's all swelled up with the damp.'

'Damp!' whispered Johnnie; 'why, it hasn't rained since the third week in August; Papa said so yesterday.'

'That's nothing, Miss Johnnie,' put in Alexander, over-hearing her. 'Folks hereaway don't open their front doors much – only for weddings and funerals and suchlike. Very likely this has stood shut these five years. I know the last time I drove Miss Carr out, before she died, it was just so; and she had to go round to the back, as you're a-doing now.'

John's eyes grew wide with wonder; but there was no time to say anything, for they had turned the corner of the house, and there was Mrs Worrett waiting at the kitchen door to receive them. She looked fatter than ever, Elsie thought; but she kissed them both, and said she was very glad to see a Carr in her house at last.

'It was too bad,' she went on, 'to keep you waiting so. But the fact is I got asleep; and when you knocked, I waked up all in a daze, and for a minute it didn't come to me who it must be. Take the bags right upstairs, Isaphiny; and put them in the keeping-room chamber. How's your papa, Elsie – and Katy? Not laid up again, I hope.'

'Oh, no! she seems to get better all the time.'

'That's right,' responded Mrs Worrett, heartily. 'I didn't know but what, with hot weather, and company in the house, and all – there's a chicken, Johnnie,' she exclaimed, suddenly interrupting herself, as a long-legged hen ran past the door. 'Want to chase it just now? You can, if you like. Or would you rather go upstairs first?'

'Upstairs, please,' replied John, while Elsie went to the door and watched Alexander driving away down the dusty road. She felt as if their last friend had deserted them. Then she and Johnnie followed Isaphiny upstairs. Mrs Worrett never 'mounted' in hot weather, she told them.

The spare chamber was just under the roof. It was very hot, and smelt as if the windows had never been opened since the house was built. As soon as they were alone, Elsie ran across the room and threw up the sash; but the moment she let go, down it fell again with a crash which shook the floor and made the pitcher dance and rattle in the washbowl. The children were dreadfully frightened, especially when they heard Mrs Worrett at the foot of the stairs calling to ask what was the matter.

'It's only the window,' explained Elsie, going into the hall. 'I'm so sorry; but it won't stay open. Something's the matter with it.'

'Did you stick the nail in?' enquired Mrs Worrett.

'The nail? No, ma'am.'

'Why, how on earth did you expect it to stay up then? You young folks never see what's before your eyes. Look on the windowsill, and you'll find it. It's put there on purpose.'

Elsie returned, much discomfited. She looked and, sure enough, there was a big nail, and there was a hole in the side of the window-frame in which to stick it.

This time she got the window open without accident; but a long blue paper shade caused her much embarrassment. It hung down, and kept the air from coming in. She saw no way of fastening it.

'Roll it up, and put in a pin,' suggested John.

'I'm afraid of tearing the paper. Dear, what a horrid thing it is!' replied Elsie, in a disgusted tone.

However, she stuck in a couple of pins and fastened the shade out of the way. After that, they looked about the room. It was plainly furnished, but very nice and neat. The bureau was covered with a white towel, on which stood a pincushion, with 'Remember Ruth' stuck upon it in pins. John admired this very much, and felt that she could never make up her mind to spoil the pattern by taking out a pin, however great her need of one might be.

'What a high bed!' she exclaimed. 'Elsie, you'll have to climb on a chair to get into it; and so shall I.'

Elsie felt it. 'Feathers!' she cried in a tone of horror. 'Oh John! why did we come? What shall we do?'

'I think we shan't mind it much,' replied John, who was

perfectly well, and considered these little variations on home habits rather as fun than otherwise. But Elsie gave a groan. Two nights on a featherbed! How should she bear it!

Tea was ready in the kitchen when they went downstairs. A small fire had been lit to boil the water. It was almost out, but the room felt stiflingly warm, and the butter was so nearly melted that Mrs Worrett had to help it with a teaspoon. Buzzing flies hovered above the table, and gathered thick on the plate of cake. The bread was excellent, and so were the cottage cheeses and the stewed quince; but Elsie could eat nothing. She was in a fever of heat. Mrs Worrett was distressed at this want of appetite; and so was Mr Worrett, to whom the children had just been introduced. He was a kindly-looking old man, with a bald head, who came to supper in his shirtsleeves, and was as thin as his wife was fat.

'I'm afraid the little girl don't like her supper, Lucinda,' he said. 'You must see about getting her something different tomorrow.'

'Oh, it isn't that! Everything is very nice, only I'm not hungry,' pleaded Elsie, feeling as if she should like to cry. She did cry a little after tea, as they sat in the dusk; Mr Worrett smoking his pipe and slapping mosquitoes outside the door, and Mrs Worrett sleeping rather noisily in a big rocking-chair. But not even Johnnie found out that she was crying; for Elsie felt that she was the naughtiest child in the world to behave so badly when everybody was so kind to her. She repeated this to herself many times, but it didn't do much good. As often as the thought of home and Katy and Papa came, a wild longing to get back to them would rush over her, and her eyes would fill again with sudden tears.

The night was very uncomfortable. Not a breath of wind was stirring, or none found its way to the stifling bed where the little sisters lay. John slept pretty well, in spite of heat and mosquitoes, but Elsie hardly closed her eyes. Once she got up and went to the window, but the blue paper shade had become unfastened, and rattled down upon her head with a sudden bump, which startled her very much. She could find no pins in the dark, so she left it hanging; whereupon it rustled and flapped through the rest of the night, and did its share toward keeping her awake. About three o'clock she fell into a doze; and it seemed only a minute after that before she waked up to find bright sunshine in the room, and half a dozen roosters crowing and calling under the windows. Her head ached violently. She longed to stay in bed, but was afraid it would be thought impolite: so she dressed and went down with Johnnie; but she looked so pale and ate so little breakfast that Mrs Worrett was quite troubled, and said she had better not try to go out, but just lie on the lounge in the best room, and amuse herself with a book.

The lounge in the best room was covered with slippery, purple chintz. It was a high lounge and very narrow. There was nothing at the end to hold the pillow in its place; so the pillow constantly tumbled off and jerked Elsie's head suddenly backward, which was not at all comfortable. Worse – Elsie having dropped into a doze, she herself tumbled to the floor, rolling from the glassy, smooth chintz as if it had been a slope of ice. This adventure made her so nervous that she dared not go to sleep again, though Johnnie fetched two chairs, and placed them beside the sofa to hold her on. So she followed Mrs Worrett's advice, and 'amused herself with a book'. There were not many books in the best room. The one Elsie chose was a fat black volume called *The Complete Works of Mrs Hannah More*. Part of it was prose, and part was poetry. Elsie began with a chapter called 'Hints on the Formation of the Character of a Youthful Princess'. But there were a great many long words in it; so she turned to a story named 'Coelebs in Search of a Wife'. It was about a young gentleman who wanted to get married, but who didn't feel sure that there were any young ladies nice enough for him; so he went about making visits, first to one and then to another; and, when he had stayed a few days at a house, he would always say, 'No, she won't do,' and then he would go away. At last, he found a young lady who seemed the very person, who visited the poor, and got up early in the morning, and always wore white, and never forgot to wind up her watch or do her duty; and Elsie almost thought that now the difficult young gentleman must be satisfied, and say, 'This is the very thing.' When, lo! her attention wandered a little, and the next thing she knew she was rolling off the lounge for the second time, in company with Mrs Hannah More. They landed in the chairs, and Johnnie ran and picked them both up. Altogether, lying on the best parlour sofa was not very restful; and as the day went on, and the sun beating on the blindless windows made the room hotter, Elsie grew continually more and more feverish and homesick and disconsolate.

Meanwhile Johnnie was kept in occupation by Mrs Worrett, who had got the idea firmly fixed in her mind that the chief joy of a child's life was to chase chickens. Whenever a hen fluttered past the kitchen door, which was about once in three minutes, she would cry: 'Here, Johnnie, here's another chicken for you to chase;' and poor Johnnie would feel obliged to dash out into the sun. Being a very polite little girl, she did not like to say to Mrs Worrett that running in the heat was disagreeable: so by dinnertime she was thoroughly tired, and would have been cross if she had known how; but she didn't – Johnnie was never cross. After dinner it was even worse; for the sun was hotter, and the chickens, who didn't mind sun, seemed to be walking all the time. 'Hurry, Johnnie, here's another,' came so constantly, that at last Elsie grew desperate, got up, and went to the kitchen with a languid appeal: 'Please, Mrs Worrett, won't you let Johnnie stay by me, because my head aches so hard?' After that Johnnie had rest; for Mrs Worrett was the kindest of women, and had no idea that she was not amusing her little guest in the most delightful manner.

A little before six, Elsie's head felt better; and she and Johnnie put on their hats, and went for a walk in the garden. There was not much to see: beds of vegetables – a few currant bushes – that was all. Elsie was leaning against a paling, and trying to make out why the Worrett house had that queer tiptoe expression, when a sudden loud grunt startled her, and something touched the top of her head. She turned, and there was an enormous pig, standing on his hind legs, on the other side of the paling. He was taller than Elsie, as he stood thus, and it was his cold nose which had touched her head. Somehow, appearing in this unexpected way, he seemed to the children like some dreadful wild beast. They screamed with fright and fled to the house, from which Elsie never ventured to stir again during their visit. John chased the chickens at intervals, but it was a doubtful pleasure; and all the time she kept a wary eye on the distant pig.

That evening, while Mrs Worrett slept and Mr Worrett smoked outside the door, Elsie felt so very miserable that she broke down altogether. She put her head in Johnnie's lap, as they sat together in the darkest corner of the room, and sobbed and cried, making as little noise as she possibly could. Johnnie comforted her with soft pats and strokings; but did not dare to say a word, for fear Mrs Worrett should wake up and find then out.

When morning came, Elsie's one thought was, Would Alexander come for them in the afternoon? All day she watched the clock and the road with feverish anxiety. Oh! if Papa had changed his mind – had decided to let them stay for a week at Conic Section – what would she do? It was just possible to worry through and keep alive till afternoon, she thought; but if they were forced to spend another night in that featherbed, with these mosquitoes, hearing the blue shade rattle and quiver hour after hour – she should die, she was sure she should die!

But Elsie was not called upon to die, or even to discover how easy it is to survive a little discomfort. About five, her anxious watch was rewarded by the appearance of a cloud of dust, out of which presently emerged old Whitey's ears and the top of the well-known carriage. They stopped at the gate. There was Alexander, brisk and smiling, very glad to see his 'little misses' again, and to find them so glad to go home. Mrs Worrett, however, did not discover that they were glad; no indeed! Elsie and John were much too polite for that. They thanked the old lady, and said goodbye so prettily that, after they were gone, she told Mr Worrett that it hadn't been a bit of trouble having them there, and she hoped they would come again; they enjoyed everything so much; only it was a pity that Elsie looked so peaked. And at that very moment Elsie was sitting on the floor of the carriage, with her head in John's lap, crying and sobbing for joy that the visit was over, and that she was on the way home. 'If only I live to get there,' she said, 'I'll never, no, never, go into the country again!' which was silly enough; but we must forgive her because she was not very well.

Ah, how charming home did look, with the family grouped in the shady porch, Katy in her white dress! Clover with rosebuds in her belt, and everybody ready to welcome and pet the little absentees! There was much hugging and kissing, and much to tell of what had happened in the two days: how a letter had come from Cousin Helen; how Daisy White had had four kittens as white as herself; how Dorry had finished his water-wheel – a wheel which turned in the bathtub, and was 'really ingenious', Papa said; and Phil had 'swapped' one of his bantam chicks for one of Eugene Slack's Brahmapootras. It was not till they were all seated round the tea-table that anybody demanded an account of the visit. Elsie felt this a relief, and was just thinking how delicious everything was, from the sliced peaches to the clinking ice in the milk-pitcher, when Papa put the dreaded question: 'Well, Elsie, so you decided to come back, after all. How was it? Why didn't you stay your week out? You look pale, it seems to me. Have you been enjoying yourself too much? Tell us all about it.'

Elsie looked at Papa, and Papa looked at Elsie. Dr Carr's eyes twinkled just a little, but otherwise he was perfectly grave. Elsie began to speak, then to laugh, then to cry, and the explanation, when it came, was given in a mingled burst of all three.

'Oh Papa, it was horrid! That is, Mrs Worrett was just as kind as could be, but so fat; and oh, such a pig! I never imagined such a pig. And the calico on that horrid sofa was so slippery that I rolled off five times, and once I hurt myself very badly. And we had a featherbed; and I was so homesick that I cried all the evening.'

'That must have been gratifying to Mrs Worrett,' put in Dr Carr.

'Oh! she didn't know it, Papa. She was asleep, and snoring so that nobody could hear. And the flies! – such flies, Katy! – and the mosquitoes, and our window wouldn't open till I put in a nail. I am so glad to get home! I never want to go into the country again, never, never! Oh! if Alexander hadn't come! – why, Clover what are you laughing for? And Dorry – I think it's very unkind,' and Elsie ran to Katy, hid her face, and began to cry.

'Never mind, darling, they didn't mean to be unkind. Papa, her hands are quite hot; you must give her something.' Katy's voice shook a little; but she would not hurt Elsie's feelings by showing that she was amused. Papa gave Elsie 'something' before she went to bed – a very mild dose, I fancy; for doctors' little girls, as a general rule, do not take medicine; and next day she was much better. As the adventures of the Conic Section visit leaked out bit by bit, the family laughed till it seemed as if they would never stop. Phil was forever enacting the pig, standing on his triumphant hind legs, and patting Elsie's head with his nose; and many and many a time, 'It will end like your visit to Mrs Worrett,' proved a useful check when Elsie was in a self-willed mood and bent on some scheme which for the moment struck her as delightful. For one of the good things about our childish mistakes is that each one teaches us something; and so, blundering on, we grow wiser, till, when the time comes, we are ready to take our places among the wonderful grown-up people who never make mistakes.

CHAPTER TWO

A New Year and a New Plan

When summer lingers on into October, it often seems as if winter, anxious to catch a glimpse of her, hurries a little; and so people are cheated out of their autumn. It was so that year. Almost as soon as it ceased to be hot it began to be cold. The leaves, instead of drifting away in soft, dying colours, like sunset clouds, turned yellow all at once, and were whirled off the trees in a single gusty night, leaving everything bare and desolate. Thanksgiving came; and before the smell of the turkey was fairly out of the house, it was time to hang up stockings and dress the Christmas tree. They had a tree that year in honour of Katy's being downstairs. Cecy, who had gone away to boarding-school, came home; and it was all delightful, except that the days flew too fast. Clover said it seemed to her very queer that there was so much less time than usual in the world. She couldn't imagine what had become of it; there used to be plenty. And she was certain that Dorry must have been tinkering with all the clocks – they struck so often.

It was just after New Year that Dr Carr walked in one day with a letter in his hand, and remarked: 'Mr and Mrs Page are coming to stay with us.'

'Mr and Mrs Page!' repeated Katy. 'Who are they, Papa? Did I ever see them?'

'Once, when you were four years old, and Elsie a baby. Of course you don't remember it.'

'But who are they, Papa?'

'Mrs Page was your dear mother's second cousin, and at

one time she lived in your grandfather's family and was like a sister to Mamma and Uncle Charles. It is a good many years since I have seen her. Mr Page is a railroad engineer. He is coming this way on business, and they will stop for a few days with us. Your Cousin Olivia writes that she is anxious to see all you children. Have everything as nice as you can, Katy.'

'Of course I will. What day are they coming?'

'Thursday; no, Friday,' replied Dr Carr, consulting the letter, 'Friday evening, at half-past six. Order something substantial for tea that night, Katy. They'll be hungry after travelling.'

Katy worked with a will for the next two days. Twenty times, at least, she went into the blue-room to make sure that nothing was forgotten; repeating, as if it had been a lesson in geography, 'Bath towels, face towels, matches, soap, candles, cologne, extra blanket, ink.' A nice little fire was lighted in the bedroom on Friday afternoon, and a big, beautiful one in the parlour, which looked very pleasant with the lamp lit and Clover's geraniums and china roses in the window. The tea table was set with the best linen and the pink-and-white china. Debby's muffins were very light. The crab-apple jelly came out of its mould clear and whole, and the cold chicken looked appetising, with its green wreath of parsley. There was stewed potato, too; and of course, oysters. Everybody in Burnet had oysters for tea when company was expected. They were counted a special treat, because they were rather dear, and could not always be procured. Burnet was a thousand miles from the sea, so the oysters were of the tin-can variety. The cans gave the oysters a curious taste – tinny, or was it more like solder? At all events, Burnet people liked it, and always insisted that it was a striking improvement on the flavour which oysters have on their native shores. Everything was as nice as could be when Katy stood in the dining-room to take a last look at her arrangements, and she hoped Papa would be pleased, and that Mamma's cousin would think her a good house-keeper.

'I don't want to have on my other jacket,' observed Phil, putting his head in at the door. 'Need I? This is nice.'

'Let me see,' said Katy, gently turning him round. 'Well, it does pretty well, but I think I'd rather you should put on the other, if you don't mind much. We want everything as nice as possible, you know, because this is Papa's company, and he hardly ever has any.'

'Just one little sticky place isn't much,' said Phil, rather gloomily, wetting his finger and rubbing at a shiny place on his sleeve. 'Do you really think I'd better? Well, then, I will.'

'That's a dear,' kissing him. 'Be quick, Philly, for it's almost time they were here. And please tell Dorry to make haste. It's ever so long since he went upstairs.'

'Dorry's an awful dandy,' remarked Phil, confidentially. 'He looks in the glass, and makes faces if he can't get his parting straight. I wouldn't care so much about my clothes for a good deal. It's like a girl. Jim Slack says a boy who makes his hair shine up like that never'll get to be president, not if he lives a thousand years.'

'Well,' said Katy, laughing, 'it's something to be clean, even if you can't be president.' She was not at all alarmed by Dorry's recent reaction in favour of personal adornment. He came down pretty soon, very spick and span in his best suit, and asked her to fasten the blue ribbon under his collar, which she did most obligingly, though he was very particular as to the size of the bows and length of the ends, and made her tie and re-tie more than once. She had just arranged it to suit him when a carriage stopped.

'There they are,' she cried. 'Run and open the door, Dorry.'

Dorry did so, and Katy, following, found Papa ushering in a tall gentleman, and a lady who was not tall, but whose

Roman nose and long neck, and the general air of style and fashion, made her look so. Katy bent quite over to be kissed, but for all that she felt small and young and unformed, as the eyes of Mamma's cousin looked her over and over and through and through, and Mrs Page said: 'Why, Philip, is it possible that this tall girl is one of yours? Dear me, how time flies! I was thinking of the little creatures I saw when I was here last. And this other great creature can't be Elsie? That mite of a baby? Impossible! I cannot realise it. I really cannot realise it in the least.'

'Won't you come to the fire, Mrs Page?' said Katy, rather timidly.

'Don't call me Mrs Page, my dear. Call me Cousin Olivia.' Then the newcomer rustled into the parlour, where Johnnie and Phil were waiting to be introduced, and again she remarked that she 'couldn't realise it'. I don't know why Mrs Page's not realising it should have made Katy uncomfortable, but it did.

Supper went off well. The guests ate and praised, and Dr Carr looked pleased and said, 'We think Katy an excellent housekeeper for her age;' at which Katy blushed and was delighted, till she caught Mrs Page's eyes fixed upon her, with a look of scrutiny and amusement, whereupon she felt awkward and ill at ease. It was so all the evening. Mamma's cousin was entertaining and bright, and told lively stories; but the children felt that she was watching them, and passing judgement on their ways. Children are very quick to suspect when older people hold within themselves these little private courts of inquiry, and they always resent it.

Next morning, Mrs Page sat by while Katy washed the breakfast things, fed the birds, and did various odd jobs about the room and house. 'My dear,' she said at last, 'what a solemn girl you are! I should think from your face that you were at least five-and-thirty. Don't you ever laugh or frolic, like other girls of your age? Why, my Lilly, who is four months older than you, is a perfect child still; impulsive as a baby, bubbling over with fun from morning till night.'

'I've been shut up a good deal,' said Katy, trying to defend herself; 'but I didn't know I was solemn.'

'My dear, that's the very thing I complain of: you don't know it! You are altogether ahead of your age. It's very bad for you, in my opinion. All this housekeeping and care, for young girls like you and Clover, is wrong and unnatural. I don't like it; indeed I don't.'

'Oh! housekeeping doesn't hurt me a bit,' protested Katy, trying to smile. 'We have lovely times; indeed we do, Cousin Olivia.'

Cousin Olivia only pursed up her mouth, and repeated: 'It's wrong, my dear. It's unnatural. It's not the thing for you. Depend upon it, it's not the thing.'

This was unpleasant; but what was worse, had Katy known it, Mrs Page attacked Dr Carr upon the subject. He was quite troubled to learn that she considered Katy grave and careworn and unlike what girls of her age should be. Katy caught him looking at her with a puzzled expression.

'What is it, dear Papa? Do you want anything?'

'No, child, nothing. What are you doing there? Mending the parlour curtain, eh? Can't old Mary attend to that, and give you a chance to frisk about with the other girls?'

'Papa! As if I wanted to frisk! I declare you're as bad as Cousin Olivia. She's always telling me that I ought to bubble over with mirth. I don't wish to bubble. I don't know how.'

'I'm afraid you don't,' said Dr Carr, with an odd sigh, which set Katy to wondering. What should Papa sigh for? Had she done anything wrong? She began to rack her brains and memory as to whether it could be this or that; or, if not, what could it be? Such needless self-examination does no good. Katy looked more 'solemn' than ever after it.

Altogether, Mrs Page was not a favourite in the family.

She had every intention of being kind to her cousin's children, 'so dreadfully in want of a mother, poor things!' but she could not hide the fact that their ways puzzled and did not please her; and the children detected this, as children always will. She and Mr Page were very polite. They praised the housekeeping, and the excellent order of everything and said there never were better children in the world than John and Dorry and Phil. But, through all, Katy perceived the hidden disapproval; and she couldn't help feeling glad when the visit ended, and they went away.

With their departure, matters went back to their old train, and Katy forgot her disagreeable feelings. Papa seemed a little grave and preoccupied; but doctors often are when they have bad cases to think of, and nobody noticed it particularly, or remarked that several letters came from Mrs Page and nothing was heard of their contents, except that 'Cousin Olivia sent her love'. So it was a shock when one day Papa called Katy into the study to tell her of a new plan. She knew at once that it was something important when she heard his voice: it sounded so grave. Beside, he said 'My daughter' – a phrase he never used except upon the most impressive occasions.

'My daughter,' he began, 'I want to talk to you about something which I have been thinking of. How would you and Clover like going away to school together?'

'To school? To Mrs Knight's?'

'No, not to Mrs Knight's. To a boarding-school in the East, where Lilly Page has been for two years Didn't you hear Cousin Olivia speak of it when she was here?'

'I believe I did. But, Papa, you won't really?'

'Yes, I think so,' said Dr Carr gently. 'Listen, Katy, and don't feel so badly, my dear child. I've thought the plan over carefully; and it seems to me a good one, though I hate to part from you. It is pretty much as your cousin says: these home cares, which I can't take from you while you are at home, are making you old before your time. Heaven knows I don't want to turn you into a silly, giggling miss; but I should like you to enjoy your youth while you have it, and not grow middle-aged before you are twenty.'

'What is the name of the school?' asked Katy. Her voice sounded a good deal like a sob.

'The girls call it the Nunnery. It is at Hillsover, on the Connecticut River, pretty far north. And the winters are pretty cold, I fancy; but the air is sure to be good and bracing. This is one thing which has inclined me to the plan. The climate is just what you need.'

'Hillsover? Isn't there a college there too?'

'Yes: Arrowmouth College. I believe there is always a college where there is a boarding-school: though why, I can't for the life of me imagine. That's neither here nor there, however. I'm not afraid of your getting into silly scrapes, as girls sometimes do.'

'College scrapes? Why, how could I? We don't have anything to do with the college, do we?' said Katy, opening her candid eyes with such a wondering stare that Dr Carr laughed, as he patted her cheek and replied: 'No, my dear, not a thing.'

'The term opens the third week in April,' he went on. 'You must begin to get ready at once. Mrs Hall has just fitted out Cecy: so she can tell you what you will need. You'd better consult her tomorrow.'

'But, Papa,' cried Katy, beginning to realise it, 'what are you going to do? Elsie's a darling, but she's so very little. I don't see how you can possibly manage. I'm sure you'll miss us, and so will the children.'

'I rather think we shall,' said Dr Carr, with a smile, which ended in a sigh; 'but we shall do very well, Katy; never fear. Miss Finch will see to us.'

'Miss Finch? Do you mean Mrs Knight's sister-in-law?'

'Yes. Her mother died in the summer; so she has no

particular home now, and is glad to come for a year and keep house for us. Mrs Knight says she is a good manager; and I dare say she'll fill your place sufficiently well, as far as that goes. We can't expect her to be you, you know; that would be unreasonable.' And Dr Carr put his arm round Katy, and kissed her so fondly that she was quite overcome and clung to him, crying: 'O Papa! don't make us go. I'll frisk, and be as young as I can, and not grow middle-aged or anything disagreeable, if only you'll let us stay. Never mind what Cousin Olivia says; she doesn't know. Cousin Helen wouldn't say so, I'm sure.'

'On the contrary, Helen thinks well of the plan; only she wishes the school were nearer,' said Dr Carr. 'No, Katy, don't coax. My mind is made up. It will do you and Clover both good, and once you are settled at Hillsover, you'll be very happy, I hope.'

When Papa spoke in this decided tone, it was never any use to urge him. Katy knew this, and ceased her pleadings. She went to find Clover and tell her the news, and the two girls had a hearty cry together. A sort of 'clearing-up shower' it turned out to be; for when once they had wiped their eyes, everything looked brighter, and they began to see a pleasant side to the plan.

'The travelling part of it will be very nice,' pronounced Clover. 'We never went so far away from home before.'

Elsie, who was still looking very woeful, burst into tears afresh at this remark.

'Oh, don't, darling!' said Katy. 'Think how pleasant it will be to send letters, and to get them from us. I shall write to you every Saturday. Run for the big atlas – there's a dear, and let us see where we are going.'

Elsie brought the atlas; and the three heads bent eagerly over it as Clover traced the route of the journey with her forefinger. How exciting it looked! There was the railroad, twisting and curving over half a dozen states. The black dots which followed it were towns and villages, all of which they should see. By and by the road made a bend, and swept northward by the side of the Connecticut River and toward the hills. They had heard how beautiful the Connecticut valley is.

'Only think! we shall be close to it,' remarked Clover; 'and we shall see the hills. I suppose they are very high, a great deal higher than the hill at Bolton.'

'I hope so,' laughed Dr Carr, who came into the room just then. The hill at Bolton was one of his favourite jokes. When Mamma first came to Burnet, she had paid a visit to some friends at Bolton, and one day, when they were all out walking, they asked her if she felt strong enough to go to the top of the hill. Mamma was used to hills, so she said yes, and walked on, very glad to find that there was a hill in that flat country, but wondering a little why they did not see it. At last she asked where it was, and, behold, they had just reached the top! The slope had been so gradual that she had never found out that they were going uphill at all. Dr Carr had told this story to the children, but had never been able to make them see the joke very clearly. In fact, when Clover went to Bolton, she was quite struck with the hill: it was so much higher than the sandbank which bordered the lake at Burnet.

There was a great deal to do to make the girls ready for school by the third week in April. Mrs Hall was very kind, and her advice was sensible; though, except for Dr Carr, the girls would hardly have had furs and flannels enough for so cold a place as Hillsover. Everything for winter as well as for summer had to be thought of; for it had been arranged that the girls should not come home for the autumn vacation, but should spend it with Mrs Page. This was the hardest thing about the plan. Katy begged very hard for Christmas; but when she learned that it would take three days to come and three to go, and that the holidays lasted less than a week, she saw it was of no use, and gave up the idea, while Elsie tried to comfort herself by planning a Christmas-box. The preparations kept them so busy that there was no time for anything else. Mrs Hall was always wanting them to go with her to shops, or Miss Petingill demanding that they should try on linings; and so the days flew by. At last all was ready. The nice half-dozens of pretty underclothes came home from the sewing-machine woman's, and were done up by Bridget, who dropped many a tear into the bluing water, at the thought of the young ladies going away. Mrs Hall, who was a good packer, put the things into the new trunks. Everybody gave the girls presents, as if they had been brides starting on a wedding journey.

Papa's was a watch for each. They were not new, but the girls thought them beautiful. Katy's had belonged to her mother. It was large and old-fashioned, with a finely-wrought case. Clover's, which had been her grandmother's, was larger still. It had a quaint ornament on the back – a sort of true-love knot, done in gold of different tints. The girls were excessively pleased with these watches. They wore them with guard-chains of black watered ribbon, and every other minute they looked to see what the time was.

Elsie had been in Papa's confidence, so her presents were watch-cases, embroidered on perforated paper. Johnnie gave Katy a case of pencils, and Clover a penknife with a pearl handle. Dorry and Phil clubbed to buy a box of notepaper and envelopes, which the girls were requested to divide between them. Miss Petingill contributed a bottle of ginger balsam, and a box of opodeldoc salve, to be used in case of possible chilblains. Old Mary's offering was a couple of needle-books, full of bright sharp needles.

'I wouldn't give you scissors,' she said; 'but you can't cut love – or, for the matter of that, anything else with a needle.'

Miss Finch, the new housekeeper, arrived a few days before they started; so Katy had time to take her over the house and explain all the different things she wanted done, and not done, to secure Papa's comfort and the children's. Miss Finch was meek and gentle. She seemed glad of a comfortable home. And Katy felt that she would be kind to the boys, and not fret Debby, and drive her into marrying Alexander and going away – an event which Aunt Izzie had been used to predict. Now that all was settled, she and Clover found themselves looking forward to the change with pleasure. There was something new and interesting about it which excited their imaginations.

The last evening was a melancholy one. Elsie had been too much absorbed in the preparations to realise her loss; but, when it came to locking the trunks, her courage gave way altogether. She was in such a state of affliction that everybody else became afflicted too; and there is no knowing what would have happened, had not a parcel arrived by express and distracted their attention. The parcel was from Cousin Helen, whose things, like herself, had a knack of coming at the moment when most wanted. It contained two pretty silk umbrellas – one brown, and one dark-green, with Katy's initials on one handle and Clover's on the other. Opening these treasures, and exclaiming over them, helped the family through the evening wonderfully; and next morning there was such a bustle of getting off that nobody had time to cry.

After the last kisses had been given, and Philly, who had climbed on the horse-block, was clamouring for 'one more – just one more', Dr Carr, looking at the sober faces, was struck by a bright idea, and, calling Alexander, told him to hurry old Whitey into the carriage, and drive the children down to Willett's Point, that they might wave their handkerchiefs to the boat as she went by This suggestion worked like a charm on the spirits of the party. Phil began to caper, and Elsie and John ran in to get their hats. Half an hour later, when the boat rounded the point, there stood the little crew, radiant with smiles, fluttering their handkerchiefs and kissing their hands as cheerfully as possible. It was a pleasant last look to the two who stood beside Papa on the deck; and, as they waved back their greetings to the little ones, and then looked forward across the blue water to the unknown places they were going to see, Katy and Clover felt that the new life opened well, and promised to be very interesting indeed.

CHAPTER THREE

On the Way

The journey from Burnet to Hillsover was a very long one. It took the greater part of three days, and as Dr Carr was in a hurry to get back to his patients, they travelled without stopping, spending the first night on the boat and the second on a railroad train. Papa found this tiresome; but the girls, to whom everything was new, thought it delightful. They enjoyed their stateroom, with its narrow shelves of beds, as much as if it had been a baby house, and they two children playing in it. To tuck themselves away for the night in a car-section seemed the greatest fun in the world. When older people fretted, they laughed. Everything was interesting, from the telegraph poles by the wayside to the faces of their fellow-passengers. It amused them to watch strange people, and make up stories about them – where they were going, and what relation they could be to each other. The strange people, in their turn, cast curious glances toward the bright, happy-faced sisters; but Katy and Clover did not mind that, or, in fact, notice it. They were too much absorbed to think of themselves, or the impression they were making on others.

It was early on the third morning that the train, puffing and shrieking, ran into the Springfield depot. Other trains stood waiting; and there was such a chorus of snorts and whistles, and such clouds of smoke, that Katy was half frightened. Papa, who was half asleep, jumped up, and told the girls to collect their bags and books; for they were to breakfast here, and to meet Lilly Page, who was going on to Hillsover with them.

'Do you suppose she is here already?' asked Katy, tucking the railway guide into the shawl-trap, and closing her bag with a snap.

'Yes: we shall meet her at the Massasoit. She and her father were to pass the night there.'

The Massasoit was close at hand, and in less than five minutes the girls and Papa were seated at a table in its pleasant dining-room. They were ordering their breakfast, when Mr Page came in, accompanied by his daughter – a pretty girl, with light hair, delicate, rather sharp features, and her mother's stylish ease of manner. Her travelling dress was simple, but had the finish which a French dressmaker knows how to give to a simple thing; and all its appointments – boots, hat, gloves, collar, neck ribbon – were so perfect, each in its way, that Clover, glancing down at her own grey alpaca, and then at Katy's, felt suddenly countrified and shabby.

'Well, Lilly, here they are; here are your cousins,' said Mr Page, giving the girls a cordial greeting. Lilly only said, 'How do you do?' Clover saw her glancing at the grey alpacas, and was conscious of a sudden flush. But perhaps Lilly looked at something beside the alpaca; for after a minute her manner changed, and became more friendly.

'Did you order waffles?' she asked.

'Waffles? no, I think not,' replied Katy.

'Oh! why not? Don't you know how celebrated they are for waffles at this hotel? I thought everybody knew *that.*' Then she tinkled her fork against her glass, and, when the waiter came, said, 'Waffles, please,' with an air which impressed Clover extremely. Lilly seemed to her like a young lady in a story – so elegant and self-possessed. She wondered if all the girls at Hillsover were going to be like her.

The waffles came, crisp and hot, with delicious maple syrup to eat on them; and the party made a satisfactory breakfast. Lilly, in spite of all her elegance, displayed a wonderful appetite. 'You see,' she explained to Clover, 'I don't expect to have another decent thing to eat till next September – not a thing: so I'm making the most of this.' Accordingly she disposed of nine waffles, in quick succession, before she found time to utter anything further, except, 'Butter, please,' or, 'May I trouble you for the molasses?' As she swallowed the last morsel, Dr Carr, looking at his watch, said that it was time to start for the train; and they set off. Mr Page went with them. As they crossed the street, Katy was surprised to see that Lilly, who had seemed quite happy only a minute before, had begun to cry. After they reached the car, her tears increased to sobs: she grew almost hysterical.

'Oh! don't make me go, Papa,' she implored, clinging to her father's arm. 'I shall be so homesick! It will kill me: I know it will. Please let me stay. Please let me go home with you.'

'Now, my darling,' protested Mr Page, 'this is foolish: you know it is.'

'I can't help it,' blubbered Lilly. 'I ca–n't help it. Oh! don't, don't make me go. Don't, Papa dear. I ca–n't bear it.'

Katy and Clover felt embarrassed during this scene. They had always been used to considering tears as things to be rather ashamed of – to be kept back, if possible; or, if not, shed in private corners, in dark closets, or behind the bed in the nursery. To see the stylish Lilly crying like a baby in the midst of a railway carriage with strangers looking on, quite shocked them. It did not last long, however. The whistle sounded; the conductor shouted, 'All aboard!' and Mr Page, giving Lilly a last kiss, disengaged her clinging arms, put her into the seat beside Clover, and hurried out of the car. Lilly sobbed loudly for a few seconds; then she dried her eyes, lifted her head, adjusted her veil and the wrists of her three-buttoned gloves, and remarked: 'I always go on in this way. Mamma says I am a real cry-baby; and I suppose I am. I don't see how people can be calm and composed when they're leaving home, do you? You'll be just as bad tomorrow, when you come to say goodbye to your papa.'

'Oh! I hope not,' said Katy. 'Because Papa would feel so badly.'

Lilly stared. 'I shall think you very cold-hearted if you don't,' she said in an offended tone.

Katy took no notice of the tone; and before long Lilly recovered from her pettishness, and began to talk about the school. Katy and Clover asked eager questions. They were eager to hear all that Lilly could tell.

'You'll adore Mrs Florence,' she said. 'All the girls do. She's the most fascinating woman! She does just what she likes with everybody. Why, even the students think her perfectly splendid; and yet she's just as strict as she can be.'

'Strict with the students?' asked Clover, looking puzzled.

'No; strict with us girls. She never lets anyone call, unless it's a brother or a first cousin; and then you have to have a letter from your parents, asking permission. I wanted Mamma to write and say that George Hickman might call on me. He isn't a first cousin exactly, but his father married Papa's sister-in-law's sister. So it's just as good. But Mamma was very mean about it. She says I'm too young to have gentlemen coming to see me! I can't think why. Ever so many girls have them who are younger than I.

'Which row are you going to room in?' she went on.

'I don't know. Nobody told us that there were any rows.'

'Oh, yes! Shaker Row and Quaker Row and Attic Row. Attic Row is the nicest, because it's highest up, and farthest away from Mrs Florence. My room is in Attic Row. Annie Silsbie and I engaged it last term. You'll be in Quaker Row, I should think. Most of the new girls are.'

'Is that a nice row?' asked Clover, greatly interested.

'Pretty nice. It isn't so good as Attic, but it's ever so much better than Shaker; because there you're close to Mrs Florence, and can't have a bit of fun without her hearing you. I'd try to get the end room, if I were you. Mary Andrews and I had it once. There is a splendid view of Berry Searles's windows.'

'Berry Searles?'

'Yes: President Searles, you know; his youngest son. He's a splendid fellow. All the girls are cracked about him – perfectly cracked! The president's house is next door to the Nunnery, you know; and Berry's room is at the very end of the back building, just opposite Quaker Row. It used to be such fun! He'd sit at his window; and we'd sit at ours, in silent-study hour, you know and he'd pretend to read, and all the time keep looking over the top of his book at us, and trying to make us laugh. Once Mary did laugh right out; and Miss Jane heard her, and came in. But Berry is just as quick as a flash, and he ducked down under the window-sill: so she didn't see him. It was such fun!'

'Who's Miss Jane?' asked Katy.

'The horridest old thing. She's Mrs Florence's niece, and engaged to a missionary. Mrs Florence keeps her on purpose to spy on us girls, and report when we break the rules. Oh, those rules! Just wait till you come to read them over. They're nailed up on all the doors, thirty-two of them, and you can't help breaking them if you try ever so much.'

'What are they? what sort of rules?' cried Katy and Clover in a breath.

'Oh! about being punctual to prayers, and turning your mattress, and smoothing over the undersheet before you leave the room, and never speaking a word in the hall, or in private-study hour, and hanging your towel on your own nail in the washroom, and all that.'

'Washroom? what do you mean?' said Katy, aghast.

'At the head of the Quaker Row, you know. All the girls wash there, except on Saturdays, when they go to the bathhouse. You have your own bowl and soap-dish, and a hook for your towel. Why, what's the matter? How big your eyes are!'

'I never heard anything so horrid!' cried Katy, when she had recovered her breath. 'Do you really mean that the girls don't have washstands in their own rooms?'

'You'll get used to it. All the girls do,' responded Lilly.

'I don't want to get used to it,' said Katy, resolving to appeal to Papa; but Papa had gone into the smoking-car, and she had to wait. Meantime Lilly went on talking.

'If you have that end room in Quaker Row, you'll see all the fun that goes on at the commencement time. Mrs Searles always has a big party, and you can look right in, and watch the people and the supper-table, just as if you were there. Last summer Berry and Alpheus Seccomb got a lot of cakes and mottoes from the table, and came out into the backyard and threw them up one by one to Rose Red and her room-mate. They didn't have the end room, though; but the one next to it.'

'What a funny name! – Rose Red,' said Clover.

'Oh! her real name is Rosamond Redding; but the girls call her Rose Red. She's the greatest witch in the school; not exactly pretty, you know, but sort of killing and fascinating. She's always getting into the most awful scrapes. Mrs Florence would have expelled her long ago, if she hadn't been such a favourite; and Mr Redding's daughter, beside. He's a member of Congress, you know, and all that; and Mrs Florence is quite proud of having Rose in her school.

'Berry Searles is so funny!' she continued. 'His mother is a horrid old thing, and always interfering with him. Sometimes when he has a party of fellows in his room, and they're playing cards, we can see her coming with her candle through the house; and when she gets to his door, she tries it, and then she knocks, and calls out, "Abernethy, my son!" And the fellows whip the cards into their pockets, and stick the bottles under the table, and get out their books and dictionaries like a flash; and when Berry unlocks the door, there they sit, studying away; and Mrs Searles looks so disappointed! I thought I should die one night, Mary Andrews and I laughed so.'

I verily believe that if Dr Carr had been present at this conversation, he would have stopped at the next station, and taken the girls back to Burnet. But he did not return from the smoking-car till the anecdotes about Berry were finished, and Lilly had begun again on Mrs Florence.

'She's a sort of queen, you know. Everybody minds her. She's tall, and always dresses beautifully. Her eyes are lovely; but when she gets angry, they're perfectly awful. Rose Red says she'd rather face a mad bull any day than Mrs Florence in a fury; and Rose ought to know, for she's had more reprimands than any girl in school.'

'How many girls are there?' enquired Dr Carr.

'There were forty-eight last term. I don't know how many there'll be this; for they say Mrs Florence is going to give up. It's she who makes the school so popular.'

All this time the train was moving northward. With every mile the country grew prettier. Spring had not fairly opened; but the grass was green, and the buds on the trees gave a tender mist-like colour to the woods. The road followed the river, which here and there turned upon itself in long links and windings. Ranges of blue hills closed the distance. Now and then a nearer mountain rose, single and alone, from the plain. The air was cool, and full of a brilliant zest, which the Western girls had never before tasted. Katy felt as if she were drinking champagne. She and Clover flew from window to window, exclaiming with such delight that Lilly was surprised.

'I can't see what there is to make such a fuss about,' she remarked. 'That's only Deerfield. It's quite a small place.'

'But how pretty it looks, nestled in among the hills! Hills are lovely, Clover, aren't they?'

'These hills are nothing. You should see the White Mountains,' said the experienced Lilly. 'Mamma and I spent three weeks at the Profile House last vacation. It was perfectly splendid.'

In the course of the afternoon Katy drew Papa away to a distant seat, and confided her distress about the washstands.

'Don't you think it is horrid, Papa? Aunt Izzie always said that it isn't ladylike not to take a sponge-bath every morning; but how can we, with forty-eight girls in the room? I don't see what we are going to do.'

'I fancy we can arrange it; don't be distressed, my dear,' replied Dr Carr. And Katy was satisfied; for when Papa undertook to arrange things, they were very apt to be done.

It was almost evening when they reached their final stopping-place.

'Now, two miles in the stage, and then we're at the horrid old Nunnery,' said Lilly. 'Ugh! look at that snow. It never melts here till long after it's all gone at home. How I do hate this station! I'm going to be awfully homesick; I know I am.'

But just then she caught sight of the stagecoach, which stood waiting; and her mood changed, for the stage was full of girls who had come by the other train.

'Hurrah! there's Mary Edwards and Mary Silver,' she exclaimed; 'and, I declare, Rose Red! Oh, you precious darling! how do you do?' Scrambling up the steps, she plunged at a girl with waving hair, and a rosy, mischievous face; and began kissing her with effusion

Rose Red did not seem equally enchanted. 'Well, Lilly, how are you?' she said, and then went on talking to a girl who had sat by her side, and whose hand she held, while Lilly rushed up and down the line, embracing and being embraced. She did not introduce Katy and Clover; and, as Papa was outside, on the driver's box, they felt a little lonely and strange. All the rest were chatting merrily, and were evidently well acquainted; they were the only ones left out.

Clover watched Rose Red, to whose face she had taken a fancy. It made her think of a pink carnation, or of a twinkling wild rose, with saucy whiskers of brown calyx. Whatever she said or did seemed full of a flavour especially her own. Her eyes, which were blue, and not very large, sparkled with fun and mischief. Her cheeks were round and soft, like a baby's; when she laughed, two dimples broke their pink, and made you want to laugh too. A slender white throat supported this pretty head, as a stem supports a flower; and, altogether, she was like a flower; except that flowers don't talk, and she talked all the time. What she said seemed very droll, for the girls about her were in fits of laughter; but Clover only caught a word now and then, the stage made such a noise.

Suddenly Rose Red leaned forward, and touched Clover's hand.

'What's your name?' she said. 'You've got eyes like my sister's. Are you coming to the Nunnery?'

'Yes,' replied Clover, smiling back. 'My name is Clover – Clover Carr.'

'What a dear little name! It sounds just as you look!'

'So does your name – Rose Red,' said Clover shyly.

'It's a ridiculous name,' protested Rose Red, trying to pout. Just then the stage stopped.

'Why! Who's going to the hotel?' cried the schoolgirls, in a chorus.

'I am,' said Dr Carr, putting his head in at the door, with a smile which captivated every girl there. 'Come, Katy; come, Clover. I've decided that you shan't begin school till tomorrow.'

'Oh, my! Don't I wish he was my father!' cried Rose Red. Then the stage moved on.

'Who are they? What's their name?' asked the girls. 'They look nice.'

'They're sort of cousins of mine, and they come from the

West,' replied Lilly, not unwilling to own the relationship, now that she perceived that Dr Carr had made a favourable impression.

'Why on earth didn't you introduce them, then? I declare that was just like you, Lilly Page,' put in Rose Red, indignantly. 'They looked so lonesome that I wanted to pat and stroke both of them. That little one has the sweetest eyes!'

Meantime Katy and Clover entered the hotel, very glad of the reprieve, and of one more quiet evening alone with Papa. They needed to get their ideas straightened out and put to rights, after the confusions of the day and Lilly's extraordinary talk. It was very evident that the Nunnery was to be quite different from their expectations; but another thing was equally evident – it would not be dull! Rose Red by herself, and without anyone to help her, would be enough to prevent that.

CHAPTER FOUR

The Nunnery

The night seemed short, for the girls, tired by their journey, slept like dormice. About seven o'clock Katy was roused by the click of a blind, and, opening her eyes, saw Clover standing in the window, and peeping out through the half-opened shutters. When she heard Katy move, she cried out: 'Oh, do come! It's so interesting! I can see the colleges and the church, and, I think, the Nunnery; only I am not quite sure, because the houses are all so much alike.'

Katy jumped up and hurried to the window. The hotel stood on one side of a green common, planted with trees. The common had a lead-coloured fence, and gravel paths, which ran across it from corner to corner. Opposite the hotel was a long row of red buildings, broken by one or two brown ones with cupolas. These were evidently the colleges, and a large grey building with a spire was as evidently the church; but which one of the many white, green-blinded houses which filled the other sides of the common was the Nunnery the girls could not tell. Clover thought it was one with a garden at the side, but Katy thought not, because Lilly had said nothing of a garden. They discussed the point so long that the breakfast bell took them by surprise, and they were forced to rush through their dressing as fast as possible, so as not to keep Papa waiting.

When breakfast was over, Dr Carr told them to put on their hats and get ready to walk with him to the school. Clover took one arm and Katy the other, and the three passed between some lead-coloured posts, and took one of the diagonal paths which led across the common.

'That's the house,' said Dr Carr, pointing.

'It isn't the one you picked out, Clover,' said Katy.

'No,' replied Clover, a little disappointed. The house Papa indicated was by no means so pleasant as the one she had chosen.

It was a tall, narrow building, with dormer windows in the roof, and a square porch supported by whitewashed pillars. A pile of trunks stood in the porch. From above came sounds of voices. Girls' heads were popped out of upper windows at the swinging of the gate, and as the door opened more heads appeared looking over the balusters from the hall above.

The parlour into which they were taken was full of heavy, old-fashioned furniture, stiffly arranged. The sofa and chairs were covered with black hair-cloth, and stood closely against the wall. Some books lay upon the table, arranged two by two, each upper book being exactly at a right angle with each lower book. A bunch of dried grasses stood in the fireplace. There were no pictures, except one portrait in oils of a forbidding old gentleman in a wig and glasses, sitting with his middle finger majestically inserted in a half-open Bible. Altogether, it was not a cheerful room, nor one calculated to raise the spirits of newcomers; and Katy, whose long seclusion had made her sensitive on the subject of rooms, shrank instinctively nearer Papa as they went in.

Two ladies rose to receive them. One, a tall, dignified person, was Mrs Florence. The other she introduced as 'my assistant principal, Mrs Nipson'. Mrs Nipson was not tall. She had a round face, pinched lips and half-shut grey eyes.

'This lady is fully associated with me in the management of the school,' explained Mrs Florence. 'When I go, she will assume the entire control.'

'Is that likely to be soon?' enquired Dr Carr, surprised, and not well pleased that the teacher of whom he had heard, and with whom he had proposed to leave his children, was planning to yield her place to a stranger.

'The time is not yet determined,' replied Mrs Florence. Then she changed the subject gracefully, but so decidedly that Dr Carr had no chance for further question. She spoke of classes, and discussed what Katy and Clover were to study. Finally, she proposed to take them upstairs to see their room. Papa might come too, she said.

'I dare say that Lilly Page, who tells me that she is a cousin of yours, has described the arrangements of the house,' she remarked to Katy. 'The room I have assigned to you is in the back building. "Quaker Row", the girls call it.' She smiled as she spoke, and Katy, meeting her eyes for the first time, felt that there was something in what Lilly had said. Mrs Florence *was* a sort of queen.

They went upstairs. Some girls who were peeping over the baluster hurried away at their approach. Mrs Florence shook her head at them.

'The first day is always one of licence,' she said, leading the way along an uncarpeted entry to a door at the end from which, by a couple of steps, they went down into a square room round three sides of which ran a shelf on which stood rows of washbowls and pitchers. Above were hooks for towels. Katy perceived that this was the much-dreaded washroom.

'Our lavatory,' remarked Mrs Florence, blandly.

Opening from the washroom was a very long hall, lighted at each end by a window. The doors on either side were numbered 'one', 'two', 'three', and so on. Some of them were half open. As they went by, Katy and Clover caught glimpses of girls and trunks, and beds strewn with things. At number six, Mrs Florence paused.

'Here is the room which I propose to give you,' she said.

Katy and Clover looked eagerly about. It was a small room, but the sun shone in cheerfully at the window. There was a maple bedstead and table, a couple of chairs, and a row of books; that was all, except that in the wall was set a case of black-handled drawers, with cupboard doors above them.

'These take the place of a bureau, and hold your clothes,' explained Mrs Florence, pulling out one of the drawers. 'I hope, when once you are settled, you will find yourselves comfortable. The rooms are small; but young people do not require so much space as older ones. Though, indeed, your elder daughter, Dr Carr, looks more advanced and grown-up than I was prepared to find her. What did you say was her age?'

'She is past sixteen; but has been so long confined to her room by the illness of which I wrote, you may probably find her behindhand in some respects, which reminds me' (this was very adroit of Papa!) 'I am anxious that she should keep up the system to which she has been accustomed at home – among other things, sponge-baths of cold water every morning; and, as I see that the bedrooms are not furnished with washstands, I will ask your permission to provide one for the use of my little girls. Perhaps you will kindly tell me where I would better look for it.'

Mrs Florence was not pleased, but she could not object; so she mentioned a shop. Katy's heart gave a bound of relief. She thought No. 6, with a washstand, might be very comfortable. Its bareness and simplicity had the charm of novelty. Then there was something very interesting to her in the idea of a whole house full of girls.

They did not stay long after seeing the room, but went off on a shopping excursion. Shops were few and far between at Hillsover; but they found a neat little maple washstand and rocking-chair, and Papa also bought a comfortable low chair, with a slatted back and a cushion. This was for Katy.

'Never study till your back aches,' he told her: 'when you are tired, lie flat on the bed for half an hour, and tell Mrs Florence that it was by my direction.'

'Or Mrs Nipson,' said Katy, laughing rather ruefully. She

had taken no fancy to Mrs Nipson, and did not enjoy the idea of a divided authority.

A hurried lunch at the hotel followed, and then it was time for Dr Carr to go away. They all walked to the school together, and said goodbye upon the steps. The girls did not cry, but they clung very tightly to Papa, and put as much feeling into their last kisses as would have furnished forth half a dozen fits of tears. Lilly might have thought them cold-hearted, but Papa did not; he knew better.

'That's my brave girls!' he said. Then he kissed them once more, and hurried away. Perhaps he did not wish them to see that his eyes too were a little misty.

As the door closed behind them, Katy and Clover realised that they were alone among strangers. The sensation was not pleasant; and they felt forlorn, as they went upstairs, and down Quaker Row, towards No. 6.

'Aha! so you're going to be next door,' said a gay voice, as they passed No. 5, and Rose Red popped her head into the hall. 'Well, I'm glad,' she went on, shaking hands cordially; 'I sort of thought you would, and yet I didn't know, and there are some awful stiffies among the new girls. How do you both do?'

'Oh! are we next door to you?' cried Clover, brightening.

'Yes. It's rather good of me not to hate you; for I wanted the end room myself, and Mrs Florence wouldn't give it to me. Come in, and let me introduce you to my room-mate. It's against the rules, but that's no matter: nobody pretends to keep rules the first day.'

They went in. No. 5 was precisely like No. 6 in shape, size, and furniture; but Rose had unpacked her trunk, and decorated the room with odds and ends of all sorts. The table was covered with books and boxes; coloured lithographs were pinned on the walls; a huge blue rosette ornamented the headboard of the bed; the blinds were tied together with pink ribbon; over the top of the window was a festoon of hemlock boughs, fresh and spicy. The effect was fantastic, but cheery; and Katy and Clover exclaimed, with one voice, 'How pretty!'

The room-mate was a pale, shy girl, with a half-scared look in her eyes, and small hands which twisted uneasily together when she moved and spoke. Her name was Mary Silver. She and Rose were so utterly unlike that Katy thought it odd they should have chosen to be together. Afterwards she understood it better. Rose liked to protect, and Mary to be protected; Rose to talk, and Mary to listen. Mary evidently considered Rose the most entertaining creature in the world; she giggled violently at all her jokes, and then stopped short and covered her mouth with her fingers, in a frightened way, as if giggling were wrong.

'Only think, Mary,' began Rose, after introducing Katy and Clover, 'these young ladies have got the end room. What do you suppose was the reason that Mrs Florence did not give it to us? It's very peculiar.'

Mary laughed her uneasy laugh. She looked as if she could tell the reason, but did not dare.

'Never mind,' continued Rose. 'Trials are good for one, they say. It's something to have nice people in that room, if we can't be there ourselves. You are nice, aren't you?' turning to Clover.

'Very,' replied Clover, laughing.

'I thought so. I can almost always tell without asking; still, it is something to have it on the best authority. We'll be good neighbours, won't we? Look here!' and she pulled one of the black-handled drawers completely out and laid it on the bed. 'Do you see? your drawers are exactly behind ours. Any time in silent-study hour, if I have something I want to say, I'll just rap and pop a note into your drawer, and you can do the same to me. Isn't it fun?'

Clover said, 'Yes;' but Katy, though she laughed, shook her head.

'Don't entice us into mischief,' she said.

'Oh, gracious!' exclaimed Rose. 'Now, are you going to be good – you two? If you are, just break the news at once, and have it over. I can bear it.' She fanned herself in such a comical way that no one could help laughing. Mary Silver joined, but stopped pretty soon in her sudden manner.

'There's Mary, now,' went on Rose: 'she's named Silver, but she's as good as gold. She's a Paragon. It's quite a trial to me, rooming with a Paragon. But if any more are coming into the entry, just give me fair notice, and I pack and move up among the sinners in Attic Row. Somehow, you don't look like Paragons either – you especially,' nodding to Clover. 'Your eyes are like violets; but so are Sylvia's – that's my sister – and she's the greatest witch in Massachusetts. Eyes are dreadfully deceitful things. As for you' – to Katy – 'you're so tall that I can't take you all in at once; but the piece I see doesn't look dreadful a bit.'

Rose was sitting in the window as she made these remarks; and leaning forward suddenly, she gave a pretty, blushing nod to someone below. Katy glanced down, and saw a handsome young man replacing the cap he had lifted from his head.

'That's Berry Searles,' said Rose. 'He's the president's son, you know. He always comes through the side yard to get to his room. That's it – the one with the red curtain. It's exactly opposite your window: don't you see?'

'So it is!' exclaimed Katy, remembering what Lilly had said. 'Oh! was that the reason?' – she stopped, afraid of being rude.

'The reason we wanted the room?' enquired Rose, coolly. 'Well, I don't know. It hadn't occurred to me to look at it in that light. Mary!' with sudden severity, 'is it possible that you had Berry Searles in your mind when you were so pertinacious about that room?'

'Rose! How can you? You know I never thought of such a thing,' protested poor Mary.

'I hope not; otherwise I should feel it my duty to consult with Mrs Florence on the subject,' went on Rose, with an air of dignified admonition. 'I consider myself responsible for you and your morals, Mary. Let us change this painful subject.' She looked gravely at the three girls for a moment; then her lips began to twitch, the irresistible dimples appeared in her cheeks and, throwing herself back in her chair, she burst into a fit of laughter.

'Oh Mary, you blessed goose! Some day or other you'll be the death of me! Dear, dear! how I am behaving! It's perfectly horrid of me. And I didn't mean it. I'm going to be real good this term: I promised Mother. Please forget it, and don't take a dislike to me and never come again,' she added, coaxingly, as Katy and Clover rose to go.

'Indeed we won't,' replied Katy. As for sensible Clover, she was already desperately in love with Rose, on that very first day!

After a couple of hours of hard work, No. 6 was in order, and looked like a different place. Fringed towels were laid over the washstand and the table; Dr Carr's photograph and some pretty chromos ornamented the walls; the rocking-chair and the study-chair stood by the window; the trunks were hidden by chintz covers, made for the purpose by old Mary. On the window-sill stood Cousin Helen's vase, which Katy had brought carefully packed among her clothes.

'Now,' she said, tying the blinds together with a knot of ribbon in imitation of Rose Red's, 'when we get a bunch of wild flowers for my vase, we shall be all right.'

A tap at the door. Rose entered.

'Are you done?' she asked. 'May I come in and see?'

'Oh, this is pretty!' she exclaimed, looking about: 'how you can tell in one minute what sort of a girl one is, just by looking at her room! I should know you had been neat and dainty and housekeepery all your days. And you would see in a minute that I'm a Madge Wildfire, and that Ellen Gray is a saint, and Sally Satterlee a scatterbrain, and Lilly Page an affected little hum – oh, I forgot! she is your cousin, isn't she? How dreadfully rude of me!' dimpling at Clover, who couldn't help dimpling back again.

'Oh, my!' she went on, 'a washstand, I declare! Where did you get it?'

'Papa bought it,' explained Katy: 'he asked Mrs Florence's permission.'

'How delightful of him! I shall just write to my father to ask for permission too.' Which she did; and the result was that it set the fashion for washstands, and so many papas wrote to 'ask permission', that Mrs Florence found it necessary to give up the lavatory system, and provide washstands for the whole house. Katy's request had been the opening wedge. I do not think this fact made her more popular with the principals.

'By the way, where is Lilly?' asked Katy: 'I haven't seen her today.'

'Do you want to know? I can tell you. She's sitting on the edge of one chair, with her feet on the rung of another chair, and her head on the shoulder of her room-mate (who is dying to get away and arrange her drawers); and she's cry – '

'How do you know? Have you been up to see her?'

'Oh! I haven't seen her. It isn't necessary. I saw her last term, and the term before. She always spends the first day at school in that way. I'll take you up, if you'd like to examine for yourselves.'

Katy and Clover, much amused, followed as she led the way upstairs. Sure enough, Lilly was sitting exactly as Rose had predicted. Her face was swollen with crying. When she saw the girls, her sobs redoubled.

'Oh! isn't it dreadful?' she demanded. 'I shall die, I know I shall. Oh! why did Papa make me come?'

'Now, Lilly, don't be an idiot,' said the unsympathising Rose. Then she sat down and proceeded to make a series of the most grotesque faces winking her eyes and twinkling her fingers round the head of 'Niobe', as she called Lilly, till the other girls were in fits of laughter, and Niobe, though she shrugged her shoulders pettishly and said, 'Don't be so ridiculous, Rose Red,' was forced to give way. First she smiled, then a laugh was heard; afterward she announced that she felt better.

'That's right, Niobe,' said Rose. 'Wash your face now, and get ready for tea, for the bell is just going to ring. As for you, Annie, you might as well put your drawers in order,' with a wicked wink. Annie hurried away with a laugh, which she tried in vain to hide.

'You heartless creature!' cried the exasperated Lilly. 'I believe you're made of marble; you haven't one bit of feeling. Nor you either, Katy. You haven't cried a drop.'

'Given this problem,' said the provoking Rose: 'when the nose without is as red as a lobster, what must be the temperature of the heart within, and vice versa?'

The tea-bell rang just in time to avert a fresh flood of tears from Lilly. She brushed her hair in angry haste, and they all hurried down by a side staircase which, as Rose explained, the schoolgirls were expected to use. The dining-room was not large; only part of the girls could be seated at a time; so they took turns at dining at the first table, half one week and half the next.

Mrs Nipson sat at the tea-tray, with Mrs Florence beside her. At the other end of the long board sat a severe-looking person, whom Lilly announced in a whisper as 'that horrid Miss Jane'. The meal was very simple – tea, bread and butter, and dried beef: – it was eaten in silence; the girls were not allowed to speak, except to ask for what they wanted. Rose Red indeed, who sat next to Mrs Florence, talked to her, and even ventured once or twice on daring little jokes, which caused Clover to regard her with admiring astonishment. No one else said anything, except, 'Butter, please,' or, 'Pass the bread.' As they filed upstairs after this cheerless meal, they were met by rows of hungry girls, who were waiting to go down, and who whispered, 'How long you have been! What's for tea?'

The evening passed in making up classes and arranging for recitation-rooms and study-hours. Katy was glad when bedtime came. The day, with all its new impressions and strange faces, seemed to her like a confused dream. She and Clover undressed very quietly. Among the printed rules, which hung on the bedroom door, they read: 'All communication between room-mates, after the retiring bell has rung, is strictly prohibited.' Just then it did not seem difficult to keep this rule. It was only after the candle was blown out that Clover ventured to whisper – very low indeed, for who knew but Miss Jane was listening outside the door? – 'Do you think you're going to like it?' and Katy, in the same cautious whisper, responded, 'I'm not quite sure.' And so ended the first day at the Nunnery.

CHAPTER FIVE

Roses and Thorns

'Oh! what is it? What has happened?' cried Clover, starting up in bed the next morning, as a clanging sound roused her suddenly from sleep. It was only the rising-bell, ringing at the end of Quaker Row.

Katy held her watch up to the dim light. She could just see the hands. Yes: they pointed to six. It was actually morning! She and Clover jumped up, and began to dress as fast as possible.

'We've only got half an hour,' said Clover, unhooking the rules, and carrying them to the window – 'half an hour; and this says that we must turn the mattress, smooth the undersheet over the bolster, and spend five minutes in silent devotion! We'll have to be quick to do all that, besides dressing ourselves!'

It is never easy to be quick when one is in a hurry. Everything sets itself against you. Fingers turn into thumbs; dresses won't button, nor pins keep their place. With all their haste, Katy and Clover were barely ready when the second bell sounded. As they hastened downstairs, Katy fastening her breastpin and Clover her cuffs, they met other girls, some looking half-asleep, some half-dressed; all yawning, rubbing their eyes, and complaining of the early hour.

'Isn't it horrid?' said Lilly Page, hurrying by with no collar on, and her hair hastily tucked into a net. 'I never get up till nine o'clock when I'm at home. Mamma saves my breakfast for me. She says I shall have my sleep out while I have the chance.'

'You don't look quite awake now,' remarked Clover.

'No, because I haven't washed my face. Half the time I don't, before breakfast. There's that old mattress has to be turned; and, when I sleep over, I just do that first, and then scramble my clothes on the best way I can. Anything not to be marked!'

After prayers and breakfast were done, the girls had half an hour for putting their bedrooms to rights, during which interval it is to be hoped that Lilly found time to wash her face. After that, lessons began, and lasted till one o'clock. Dinner followed, with an hour's 'recreation'; then the bell rang for 'silent-study hour', when the girls sat with their books in their bedrooms, but were not allowed to speak to each other. Next came a walk.

'Who are you going to walk with?' asked Rose Red, meeting Clover in Quaker Row.

'I don't know. Katy, I think.'

'Are you really? You and she like each other, don't you? Do you know, you're the first sisters I ever knew at school who did! Generally, they quarrel awfully. The Stearns girls, who were here last term, scarcely spoke to each other. They didn't even room together; and Sarah Stearns was always telling tales against Sue, and Sue against Sarah.'

'How disgusting! I never heard of anything so mean,' cried Clover, indignantly. 'Why, I wouldn't tell tales about Katy if we quarrelled ever so much. We never do, though, Katy is so sweet.'

'I suppose she is,' said Rose, rather doubtfully; 'but, do you know, I'm sort of afraid of her. It's because she's so tall. Tall people always scare me. And then she looks so grave and grown-up! Don't tell her I said so, though; for I want her to like me.'

'Oh, she isn't a bit grave or grown-up! She's the funniest girl in the world. Wait till you know her,' replied loyal Clover.

'I'd give anything if I could walk with you part of this term,' went on Rose, putting her arm round Clover's waist. 'But you see, unluckily, I'm engaged straight through. All of us old girls are. I walk with May Mather this week and next, then Esther Dearborn for a month, then Lilly Page for two weeks, and all the rest of the time with Mary. I can't think why I promised Lilly. I'm sure I don't want to go with her. I'd ask Mary to let me off, only I'm afraid she'd feel bad. I say, suppose we engage now to walk with each other for the first half of next term.'

'Why, that's not till October!' said Clover.

'I know it; but it's nice to be beforehand. Will you?'

'Of course I will; provided that Katy has somebody pleasant to go with,' replied Clover, immensely flattered at being asked by the popular Rose. Then they ran downstairs, and took their places in the long procession of girls, who were ranged two and two, ready to start. Miss Jane walked at the head; and Miss Marsh, another teacher, brought up the rear. Rose Red whispered that it was like a funeral and a caravan mixed – 'as cheerful as hearses at both ends, and wild beasts in the middle'.

The walk was along a wooded road; a mile out and a mile back. The procession was not permitted to stop or straggle, or take any of the liberties which made walking pleasant. Still, Katy and Clover enjoyed it. There was a spring smell in the air, and the woods were beginning to be pretty. They even found a little trailing arbutus blossoming in a sunny hollow. Lilly was just in front of them, and amused them with histories of different girls, whom she pointed out in the long line. That was Esther Dearborn – Rose Red's friend. Handsome, wasn't she? but awfully sarcastic. The two next were Amy Alsop and Ellen Gray. They always walked together, because they were so intimate. Yes; they were nice enough, only so distressingly good. Amy did not get one single mark last term! That child with pigtails was Bella

Arkwright. Why on earth did Katy want to know about her? She was a nasty little thing.

'She's just about Elsie's height,' replied Katy. 'Who's that pretty girl with pink velvet on her hat?'

'Dear me! Do you think she's pretty? I don't. Her name is Louisa Agnew. She lives at Ashburn – quite near us; but we don't know them. Her family are not at all in good society.'

'What a pity! She looks so sweet and ladylike.'

Lilly tossed her head. 'They're quite common people,' she said. 'They live in a little mite of a house, and her father paints portraits.'

'But I should think that would be nice. Doesn't she ever take you to see his pictures?'

'Take me!' cried Lilly, indignantly. 'I should think not. I tell you we don't visit. I just speak when we're here, but I never see her when I'm at home.'

'Move on, young ladies. What are you stopping for?' cried Miss Jane.

'Yes; move on,' muttered Rose Red, from behind. 'Don't you hear Policeman X?'

From walking-hour till teatime was 'recreation' again. Lilly improved this opportunity to call at No. 6. She had waited to see how the girls were likely to take in the school before committing herself to intimacy; but, now that Rose Red had declared in their favour, she was ready to begin to be friendly.

'How lovely!' she said, looking about. 'You got the end room, after all, didn't you? What splendid times you'll have! Oh, how plainly you can see Berry Searles's window! Has he spoken to you yet?'

'Spoken to us – of course not! Why should he?' replied Katy: 'he doesn't know us, and we don't know him.'

'That's nothing; half the girls in the school bow, and speak, and carry on with young men they don't know. You won't have a bit of fun if you're so particular.'

'I don't want that kind of fun,' replied Katy, with energy in her voice; 'neither does Clover. And I can't imagine how the girls can behave so. It isn't ladylike at all.'

Katy was very fond of this word, ladylike. She always laid great stress upon it. It seemed in some way to be connected with Cousin Helen, and to mean everything that was good, and graceful, and sweet.

'Dear me! I'd no idea you were so dreadfully proper,' said Lilly, pouting. 'Mother said you were as prim and precise as your grandmother; but I didn't suppose – '

'How unkind!' broke in Clover, taking fire, as usual, at any affront to Katy. 'Katy prim and precise! She isn't a bit! She's twice as much fun as the rest of you girls; but it's nice fun – not this horrid stuff about students. I wish your mother wouldn't say such things.'

'I didn't – she didn't – I don't mean exactly that,' stammered Lilly, frightened by Clover's indignant eyes. 'All I meant was that Katy is dreadfully dignified for her age, and we bad girls will have to look out. You needn't be so angry, Clover; I'm sure it's very nice to be proper and good, and set an example.'

'I don't want to preach to anybody,' said Katy, colouring, 'and I wasn't thinking about examples. But really and truly, Lilly, wouldn't your mother, and all the girls' mothers, be shocked if they knew about these performances here?'

'Gracious! I should think so; Mamma would kill me. I wouldn't have her know of my goings-on for all the world.'

Just then Rose pulled out a drawer, and called through to ask if Clover would please come in and help her a minute. Lilly took advantage of her absence to say: 'I came on purpose to ask you to walk with me for four weeks. Will you?'

'Thank you; but I'm engaged to Clover.'

'To Clover! But she's your sister; you can get off.'

'I don't want to get off. Clover and I like dearly to go together.'

Lilly stared. 'Well, I never heard of such a thing,' she said; 'you're really romantic. The girls will call you "the Inseparables".'

'I wouldn't mind being inseparable from Clover,' said Katy, laughing.

Next day was Saturday. It was nominally a holiday; but so many tasks were set for it, that it hardly seemed like one. The girls had to practise in the gymnasium, to do their mending and to have all their drawers in apple-pie order before afternoon, when Miss Jane went through the rooms on a tour of inspection. Saturday, also, was the day for writing home letters; so, altogether, it was about the busiest of the week.

Early in the morning Miss Jane appeared in Quaker Row with some slips of paper in her hand, one of which she left at each door. They told the hours at which the girls were to go to the bathhouse.

'You will carry, each, a crash towel, a sponge and soap,' she announced to Katy, 'and will be in the entry at the foot of the stairs at twenty-five minutes after nine precisely. Failures in punctuality will be punished by a mark.' Miss Jane always delivered her words like a machine, and closed her mouth with a snap at the end of the sentences.

'Horrid thing! Don't I wish her missionary would come and carry her off. Not that I blame him for staying away,' remarked Rose Red, from her door; making a face at Miss Jane as she walked down the entry.

'I don't understand about the bathhouse,' said Katy. 'Does it belong to us? And where is it?'

'No, it doesn't belong to us. It belongs to Mr Perrit, and anybody can use it; only on Saturday it is reserved for us nuns. Haven't you ever noticed it when we have been out walking? It's in that street by the bakery, which we pass to take the Lebanon road. We go across the green, and down by Professor Seccomb's, and we are in plain sight from the college all the way; and, of course, those abominable boys sit there with spyglasses, and stare as hard as ever they can. It's perfectly horrid. "A crash towel, a sponge and soap", indeed! I wish I could make Miss Jane eat the pieces of soap which she has forced me to carry across this village.'

'Oh Rose!' remonstrated Mary Silver.

'Well, I do. And the crash towel afterward, by way of a dessert,' replied the incorrigible Rose. 'Never mind! Just wait! A bright idea strikes me!'

'Oh! what?' cried the other three; but Rose only pursed up her mouth, arched her eyebrows and vanished into her own room, locking the door behind her. Mary Silver, finding herself shut out, sat down meekly in the hall till such time as it should please Rose to open the door. This was not till the bath hour. As Katy and Clover went by, Rose put her head out, and called that she would be down in a minute.

The bathing party consisted of eight girls, with Miss Jane for escort. They were halfway across the common before Miss Jane noticed that everybody was shaking with stifled laughter, except Rose, who walked along demurely, apparently unconscious that there was anything to laugh at. Miss Jane looked sharply from one to another for a moment, then stopped short and exclaimed: 'Rosamond Redding! how dare you?'

'What is it, ma'am?' asked Rose, with the face of a lamb.

'Your bath towel! your sponge!' gasped Miss Jane.

'Yes, ma'am, I have them all,' replied the audacious Rose, putting her hand to her hat. There, to be sure, was the long crash towel, hanging down behind like a veil, while the sponge was fastened on one side like a great cockade; and in front appeared a cake of pink soap, neatly pinned into the middle of a black velvet bow.

Miss Jane seized Rose, and removed these ornaments in a twinkling. 'We shall see what Mrs Florence thinks of this conduct,' she grimly remarked. Then, dropping the soap and sponge in her own pocket, she made Rose walk beside her, as if she were a criminal in custody.

The bathhouse was a neat place, with eight small rooms, well supplied with hot and cold water. Katy would have found her bath very nice, had it not been for the thought of the walk home. They must look so absurd, she reflected, with their sponges and damp towels.

Miss Jane was as good as her word. After dinner, Rose was sent for by Mrs Florence, and had an interview of two hours with her: she came out with red eyes, and shut herself into her room with a disconsolate bang. Before long, however, she revived sufficiently to tap on the drawers and push through a note with the following words:

My heart is broken!

R. R.

Clover hastened in to comfort her. Rose was sitting on the floor, with a very clean pocket-handkerchief in her hand. She wept, and put her head against Clover's knee.

'I suppose I'm the nastiest girl in the world,' she said. 'Mrs Florence thinks so. She said I was an evil influence in the school. Wasn't that unkind?' with a little sob.

'I meant to be so good this term,' she went on; 'but what's the use? A codfish might as well try to play the piano! It was always so, when I was a baby. Sylvia says I have got a little fiend inside of me. Do you believe I have? Is it that makes me so horrid?'

Clover purred over her. She could not bear to have Rose feel badly.

'Wasn't Miss Jane funny?' went on Rose, with a sudden twinkle; 'and did you see Berry, and Alfred Seccomb?'

'No; where were they?'

'Close to us, standing by the fence. All the time Miss Jane was unpinning the towel, they were splitting their sides, and Berry made such a face at me that I nearly laughed out. That boy has a perfect genius for faces. He used to frighten Sylvia and me into fits, when we were little tots, up here on visits.'

'Then you knew him before you came to school?'

'Oh dear, yes! I know all the Hillsover boys. We used to make mud-pies together. They're grown up now, most of them, and in college; and when we meet, we're very dignified, and say "Miss Redding", and "Mr Seccomb", and "Mr Searles"; but we're just as good friends as ever. When I go to take tea with Mrs Seccomb, Alfred always invites Berry to drop in, and we have the greatest fun. Mrs Florence won't let me go this term, though, I suppose, she's so angry about the towel.'

Katy was quite relieved when Clover reported this conversation. Rose, for all her wickedness, seemed to be a little lady. Katy did not like to class her among the girls who flirted with students whom they did not know.

It was wonderful how soon they all settled down, and became accustomed to their new life. Before six weeks were over, Katy and Clover felt as if they had lived at Hillsover for years. This was partly because there was so much to do. Nothing makes time fly like having every moment filled, and every hour set apart for a distinct employment.

They made several friends, chief among whom were Ellen Gray and Louisa Agnew. This last intimacy Lilly resented highly, and seemed to consider as an affront to herself. With no one, however, was Katy so intimate as Clover was with Rose Red. This cost Katy some jealous pangs at first. She was so used to considering Clover her own exclusive property that it was not easy to share her with another; and she had occasional fits of feeling resentful, and injured, and left out. These were but momentary, however. Katy was too healthy of mind to let unkind feelings grow, and by and by she grew fond of Rose and Rose of her, so that in the end the sisters shared their friend as they did other nice things, and neither of them was jealous of the other.

But, charming as she was, a certain price had to be paid for the pleasure of intimacy with Rose. Her overflowing spirits, and 'the little fiend inside her', were always provoking scrapes, in which her friends were apt to be more or less involved. She was very penitent and afflicted after these scrapes; but it didn't make a bit of difference: the next time she was just as naughty as ever.

'What are you doing?' said Katy, one day, meeting her in the hall with a heap of black shawls and aprons on her arm.

'Hush!' whispered Rose, mysteriously, 'don't say a word. Senator Brown is dead – our senator, you know. I'm going to put my window into mourning for him, that's all. It's a proper token of respect.'

Two hours later, Mrs Nipson, walking sedately across the common, noticed quite a group of students in the president's side yard, looking up at the Nunnery. She drew nearer. They were admiring Rose's windows, hung with black, and decorated with a photograph of the deceased senator, suspended in the middle of a wreath of weeping-willow. Of course she hurried upstairs, and tore down the shawls and aprons; and, equally of course, Rose had a lecture and a mark; but, dear me! what good did it do? The next day but one, as Katy and Clover sat together in silent-study hour, their lower drawer was pushed open very noiselessly and gently, till it came out entirely, and lay on the floor, and in the aperture thus formed appeared Rose's saucy face flushed with mischief. She was crawling through from her own room!

'Such fun!' she whispered; 'I never thought of this before! We can have parties in study hours, and all sorts of things.'

'Oh, go back, Rosy!' whispered Clover in agonised entreaty, though laughing all the time.

'Go back? Not at all! I'm coming in,' answered Rose, pulling herself through a little farther. But at that moment the door opened: there stood Miss Jane! She had caught the buzz of voices as she passed in the hall, and had entered to see what was going on.

Rose, dreadfully frightened, made a rapid movement to withdraw. But the space was narrow, and she had wedged herself, and could move neither backward nor forward. She had to submit to being helped through by Miss Jane, in a series of pulls, while Katy and Clover sat by, not daring to laugh or to offer assistance. When Rose was on her feet, Miss Jane released her with a final shake which she seemed unable to refrain from giving.

'Go to your room,' she said; 'I shall report all of you young ladies for this flagrant act of disobedience.'

Rose went, and in two minutes the drawer, which Miss Jane had replaced, opened again, and there was this note:

> If I'm never heard of more, give my love to my family, and mention how I died. I forgive my enemies; and leave Clover my band bracelet.
>
> My blessings on you both.
>
> With the deepest regard,
>
> Your afflicted friend, R. R.

Mrs Florence was very angry on this occasion, and would listen to no explanations, but gave Katy and Clover a 'disobedience mark' also. This was very unfair, and Rose felt dreadfully about it. She begged and entreated; but Mrs Florence only replied: 'There is blame on both sides, I have no doubt.'

'She's entirely changed from what she used to be,' declared Rose. 'I don't know what's the matter; I don't like her half so much as I did.'

The truth was that Mrs Florence had secretly determined to give up her connection with the school at midsummer; and, regarding it now rather as Mrs Nipson's school than her own, she took no pains to study character or mete out justice carefully among scholars with whom she was not likely to have much more to do.

CHAPTER SIX

The SSUC

It was Saturday afternoon; and Clover, having finished her practising, dusting and mending, had sealed herself in No. 6 for a couple of hours of quiet enjoyment. Everything was in beautiful order to meet Miss Jane's inspecting eye; and Clover, as she sat in the rocking-chair, writing-case in lap, looked extremely cosy and comfortable.

A half-finished letter to Elsie lay in the writing-case; but Clover felt lazy, and instead of writing was looking out of the window in a dreamy way, to where Berry Searles and some other young men were playing ball in the yard below. She was not thinking of them, or of anything else in particular. A vague sense of pleasant idleness possessed her, and it was like the breaking of a dream when the door opened and Katy came in, not quietly after her wont, but with a certain haste and indignant rustle as if vexed by something.

When she saw Clover at the window, she cried out hastily, 'Oh, Clover, don't!'

'Don't what?' asked Clover, without turning her head.

'Don't sit there looking at those boys.'

'Why? Why not? They can't see me. The blinds are shut.'

'No matter for that. It's just as bad as if they could see you. Don't do it. I can't bear to have you.'

'Well, I won't then,' said Clover good-humouredly, facing round with her back to the window. 'I wasn't looking at them either; not exactly. I was thinking about Elsie and John, and wondering – But what's the matter, Katy? What makes you fire up so about it? You've watched the ball-playing yourself plenty of times.'

'I know I have, and I didn't mean to be cross, Clovy. The truth is, I am all put out. These girls, with their incessant talk about the students, make me absolutely sick. It is so unladylike, and so bad, especially for the little ones. Fancy that mite of a Carrie Steele informing me that she is "in love" with Harry Crosby. In love! A baby like that! She has no business to know that there is such a thing.'

'Yes,' said Clover, laughing, 'she wrote his name on a wintergreen lozenge, and bored a hole and hung it round her neck on a blue ribbon. But it melted and stuck to her frock, and she had to take it off.'

'Whereupon she ate it,' added Rose, who came in at that moment.

The girls shouted, but Katy soon grew grave. 'One can't help laughing,' she said, 'but isn't it a shame to have such things going on? Just fancy our Elsie behaving so, Clover! Why, Papa would have a fit. I declare I've a great mind to get up a society to put down flirting.'

'Do!' said Rose. 'What fun it would be! Call it the Society for the Suppression of Young Men. I'll join.'

'You, indeed!' replied Katy, shaking her head. 'Didn't I see Berry Searles throw a bunch of syringa into your window only this morning?'

'Dear me! Did he? I shall have to speak to Mary again. It's quite shocking to have her go on so. But really and truly, do let us have a society. It would be so jolly. We could meet on Saturday afternoons, and write pieces and have signals and a secret, as Sylvia's society did when she was at school. Get one up, Katy. That's a dear.'

'But,' said Katy, taken aback by having her random idea so suddenly adopted, 'if I did get one up, it would be in real earnest, and it would be a society against flirting. And you know you can't help it, Rosy.'

'Yes, I can. You are doing me great injustice. I don't behave like those girls in Attic Row. I never did. I just bow to Berry and the rest whom I really know; never to anybody else. And you must see, Katherine darling, that it would be the height of ingratitude if I didn't bow to boys who made mud-pies for me when I was little, and lent me their marbles, and did all sorts of kind things. Now, wouldn't it?' coaxingly.

'Per–haps,' admitted Katy, with a smile. 'But you're such a witch.'

'I'm not; indeed I'm not. I'll be a pillar of society if only you'll provide a society for me to be a pillar of. Now, Katy, do – ah, do, do!'

When Rose was in a coaxing mood, few people could resist her. Katy yielded, and between jest and earnest the matter was settled. Katy was to head the plan and invite the members.

'Only a few at first,' suggested Rose. 'When it is proved to be a success and everybody wants to join, we can let in two or three more as a great favour. What shall the name be? We'll keep it a secret, whatever it is. There's no fun in a society without a secret.'

What should the name be? Rose invented half a dozen, each more absurd than the last. The Anti-Jane Society would sound well, she insisted. Or no! – The Put-him-down Club was better yet! Finally they settled upon The Society for the Suppression of Unladylike Conduct.

'Only we'll never use the whole name,' said Rose; 'we'll say the SSUC. That sounds brisk and snappy, and will drive the whole school wild with curiosity. What larks! How I long to begin!'

The next Saturday was fixed upon for the first meeting. During the week Katy proposed the plan to the elect few, all of whom accepted enthusiastically. Lilly Page was the only person who declined. She said it would be stupid; that for her part she didn't set up to be 'proper' or better than she was, and that in any case she shouldn't wish to be mixed up in a society of which 'Miss Agnew' was a member. The girls did not break their hearts over this refusal. They had felt obliged to ask her for relationship's sake, but everybody was a little relieved that she did not wish to join.

No. 6 looked very full indeed that Saturday afternoon when the SSUC came together for the first time. Ten members were present. Mary Silver and Louisa were two; and Rose's crony, Esther Dearborn, another. The remaining four were Sally Alsop and Amy Erskine; Alice Gibbons, one of the new scholars, whom they all liked but did not know very well; and Ellen Gray, a pale, quiet girl, with droll blue eyes, a comical twist to her mouth and a trick of saying funny things in such a demure way that half the people who listened never found out that they were funny. All Rose's chairs had been borrowed for the occasion. Three girls sat on the bed, and three on the floor. With a little squeezing, there was plenty of room for everybody.

Katy was chosen president, and requested to take the rocking-chair as a sign of office. This she did with much dignity, and proceeded to read the constitution and by-laws of the society, which had been drawn up by Rose Red, and copied on an immense sheet of blue paper.

They ran thus:

CONSTITUTION OF THE SOCIETY FOR THE SUPPRESSION OF UNLADYLIKE CONDUCT, KNOWN TO THE UNINITIATED AS THE SSUC

ARTICLE I
The object of this society is twofold: it combines having a good time with the pursuit of virtue.

ARTICLE 2
The good time is to take place once a week in No. 6 Quaker Row, between the hours of four and six p.m.

ARTICLE 3

The nature of the good time is to be decided upon by a committee to be appointed each Saturday by the members of the society.

ARTICLE 4

Virtue is to be pursued at all times and in all seasons by the members of the society setting their faces against the practices of bowing and speaking to young gentlemen who are not acquaintances, the waving of pocket-handkerchiefs, signals from windows and any species of conduct which would be thought unladylike by nice people anywhere, and especially by the mammas of the society.

ARTICLE 5

The members of the society pledge themselves to use their influence against these practices, both by precept and example.

In witness whereof we sign,

Katherine Carr, *President*
Rosamond Redding, *Secretary*
Clover E. Carr
Mary L. Silver
Esther Dearborn
Sally P. Alsop
Amy W. Erskine
Alice Gibbons
Ellen Whitworth Gray

Next followed the by-laws. Katy had not been able to see the necessity of having any by-laws, but Rose had insisted. She had never heard of a society without them, she said, and she didn't think it would be 'legal' to leave them out. It had cost her some trouble to invent them, but at last they stood thus:

BY-LAW NO. I

The members of the SSUC will observe the following signals:

1st *The Grip* – This is given by inserting the first and middle fingers of the right hand between the thumb and the fourth finger of the respondent's left, and describing a rotatory motion in the air with the little finger.

NB – Much practice is necessary to enable members to exchange this signal in such a manner as not to attract attention.

2nd *The Signal of Danger* – The signal is for use when Miss Jane, or any other foe-woman, heaves in sight. It consists in rubbing the nose violently, and at the same time giving three stamps on the floor with the left foot. It must be done with an air of unconsciousness.

3rd *The Signal for Consultation* – The signal is for use when immediate communication is requisite between members of the society. It consists of a pinch on the back of the right hand, accompanied by the word 'Holofernes' pronounced in a low voice.

BY-LAW NO. 2

The members of the SSUC pledge themselves to inviol able secrecy about all society proceedings.

BY-LAW NO. 3

The members of the SSUC will bring their Saturday corn-balls to swell the common entertainment.

BY-LAW NO. 4

Members having boxes from home are at liberty to contribute such part of the contents as they please to the aforementioned common entertainment.

Here the by-laws ended. There was much laughter over them, especially over the last.

'Why did you put that in, Rosy?' asked Ellen Gray; 'it strikes me as hardly necessary.'

'Oh!' replied Rose, 'I put that in to encourage Silvery Mary there. She's expecting a box soon, and I knew that she would pine to give the society a share, but would be too timid to propose it; so I thought I would just pave the way.'

'How truly kind!' laughed Clover.

'Now,' said the president, 'the entertainment of the meeting will begin by the reading of "Trailing Arbutus", a poem by C.E.C.'

Clover had been very unwilling to read the first piece, and had only yielded after much coaxing from Rose, who had bestowed on her in consequence the name of Quinia Curtia. She felt very shy as she stood up with her paper in her hand, and her voice trembled perceptibly; but after a minute she grew used to the sound of it, and read steadily.

'Trailing Arbutus

I always think, when looking
　　At its mingled rose and white,
Of the pink lips of children
　　Put up to say good-night.

Cuddled its green leaves under,
　　Like babies in their beds,
Its blossoms shy and sunny
　　Conceal their pretty heads.

And when I lift the blanket up
　　And peep inside of it,
They seem to give me smile for smile,
　　Nor be afraid a bit.

Dear little flower, the earliest
　　Of all the flowers that are;
Twinkling upon the bare, brown earth,
　　As on the clouds a star.

How can we fail to love it well,
    Or prize it more and more!
It is the first small signal
    That winter time is o'er.

That spring has not forgotten us,
    Though late and slow she be,
But is upon her flying way,
    And we her face shall see.'

This production caused quite a sensation among the girls. They had never heard any of Clover's verses before and thought these wonderful.

'Why,' cried Sally Alsop, 'it is almost as good as Tupper!' Sally meant this for a great compliment, for she was devoted to the 'Proverbial Philosophy'.

'A Poem by E. D.' was the next thing on the list. Esther Dearborn rose with great pomp and dignity, cleared her throat, put on a pair of eyeglasses, and began.

'Miss Jane

Who ran to catch me on the spot,
If I the slightest rule forgot,
Believing and excusing not?
                Miss Jane.

Who lurked outside my door all day,
In hopes that I would disobey,
And some low whispered word would say?
                Miss Jane.

Who sternly bade me come and go,
Do this, do that, or else forgo
The other thing I longed for so?
                Miss Jane.

Who caught our Rosebud halfway through
The wall which parted her from two
Friends, and that small prank made her rue?
                                        Miss Jane.

Who is our bane, our foe, our fear?
Who's always certain to appear
Just when we do not think her near?
                                        Miss Jane – '

'Who down the hall is creeping now
With stealthy step, but knowing not how
Exactly to discover – '

broke in Rose, improvising rapidly. Next moment came a
knock at the door. It was Miss Jane.

'Your drawers, Miss Carr – your cupboard,' she said,
going across the room and examining each in turn. There
was no fault to be found with either, so she withdrew, giving
the laughing girls a suspicious glance, and remarking that it
was a bad habit to sit on beds – it always injured them.

'Do you suppose she heard?' whispered Mary Silver.

'No, I don't think she did,' replied Rose. 'Of course she
suspected us of being in some mischief or other – she always
does that. Now, Mary, it's you turn to give us an intellectual
treat. Begin.'

Poor Mary shrank back, blushing and protesting.

'You know I can't,' she said, 'I'm too stupid.'

'Rubbish!' cried Rose. 'You're the dearest girl that ever
was.' She gave Mary's shoulder a reassuring pat.

'Mary is excused this time,' put in Katy. 'It is the first
meeting, so I shall be indulgent. But, after this, every
member will he expected to contribute something for each
meeting. I mean to be very strict.'

'Oh, I never, never can!' cried Mary.

Rose was down on her at once. 'Nonsense! hush!' she said.

'Of course you can. You shall, if I have to write it for you myself!'

'Order!' said the president, rapping on the table with a pencil. 'Rose has something to read to us.'

Rose stood up with great gravity. 'I would ask for a moment's delay, that the society may get out its pocket-handkerchiefs,' she said. 'My piece is an affecting one. I didn't mean it, but it came so. We cannot always be cheerful.' Here she heaved a sigh, which set the SSUC to laughing, and began.

'A Scotch Poem

> Wee, crimson-tippet Willie Wink,
> Wae's me, drear, dree and dra,
> A waeful thocht, a fearsome flea,
> A wuthering wind, and a'.
>
> Sair, sair thy mither sabs her lane,
> Her een, her mou are wat;
> Her cauld kail hae the corbies ta'en,
> And grievously she grat.
>
> Ah me, the suthering of the wind!
> Ah me, the waesome mither!
> Ah me, the bairnies left ahind,
> The shither, hither, blither!'

'What does it mean?' cried the girls, as Rose folded up the paper and sat down.

'Mean?' said Rose, 'I'm sure I don't know. It's Scotch, I tell you! It's the kind of thing that people read and then they say, "One of the loveliest gems that Burns ever wrote!" I thought I'd see if I couldn't do one too Anybody can, I find: it's not at all difficult.'

All the poems having been read, Katy now proposed that they should play 'Word and Question'. She and Clover were accustomed to the game at home, but to some of the others it was quite new.

Each girl was furnished with a slip of paper and a pencil, and was told to write a word at the top of the paper, fold it over, and pass it to her next left-hand neighbour.

'Dear me! I don't know what to write,' said Mary Silver.

'Oh, write anything!' said Clover. So Mary obediently wrote 'Anything', and folded it over.

'What next?' asked Alice Gibbons.

'Now a question,' said Katy. 'Write it under the word, and fold over again. No, Amy, not on the fold. Don't you see, if you do, the writing will be on the wrong side of the paper when we come to read?'

The questions were more troublesome than the words, and the girls sat frowning and biting their pencil-tops for some minutes before all were done. As the slips were handed in, Katy dropped them into the lid of her work-basket, and thoroughly mixed and stirred them up.

'Now,' she said, passing it about, 'each draw one, read, and write a rhyme in which the word is introduced and the question answered. It needn't be more than two lines, unless you like. Here, Rose, it's you turn first.'

'Oh, what a hard game!' cried some of the girls; but pretty soon they grew interested, and began to work over their verses.

'I should uncommonly like to know who wrote this abominable word,' said Rose, in a tone of despair 'Clover, you rascal, I believe it was you.'

Clover peeped over her shoulder, nodded, and laughed.

'Very well then!' snatching up Clover's slip, and putting her own in its place, 'you can just write on it yourself – I shan't! I never heard of such a word in my life! You made it up for the occasion, you know you did!'

'I didn't! it's in the Bible,' replied Clover, setting to work composedly on the fresh paper. But when Rose opened Clover's slip she groaned again.

'It's just as bad as the other!' she cried. 'Do change back again, Clovy – that's a dear.'

'No, indeed!' said Clover, guarding her paper; 'you've changed once, and now you must keep what you have.'

Rose made a face, chewed her pencil awhile, and then began to write rapidly. For some minutes not a word was spoken.

'I've done!' said Esther Dearborn at last, flinging her paper into the basket-lid.

'So have I!' said Katy.

One by one the papers were collected and jumbled into a heap. Then Katy, giving all a final shake, drew out one, opened it and read.

> '*Word* – Radishes.
> *Question* – How do you like your clergymen done?
>
> How do I like them done? Well, that depends.
>   I like them *done* on sleepy, drowsy Sundays;
> I like them underdone on other days;
>   Perhaps a little *over*done on Mondays.
> But always I prefer them old as pa,
>   And not like radishes, all red and raw.'

'Oh, what a rhyme!' cried Clover.

'Well – what is one to do?' said Ellen Gray. Then she stopped and bit her lip, remembering that no one was supposed to know who wrote the separate papers.

'Aha! it's yours, Ellen?' said Rose. 'You're an awfully clever girl, and an ornament to the SSUC. Go on Katy.'

Katy opened the second slip.

> '*Word* – Anything.
> *Question* – Would you rather be a greater fool than you seem, or seem a greater fool than you are?

I wouldn't seem a fool for anything, my dear,
If I could help it; but I can't, I fear.'

'Not bad,' said Rose, nodding her head at Sally Alsop, who blushed crimson.

The third paper ran:

'*Word* – Maharshalalhashbaz.
Question – Does your mother know you're out?'

Rose and Clover exchanged looks.

'Why, of course my mother knows it,
    For she sent me out herself, and
She told me to run quickly, for
    It wasn't but a mile;
But I found it was much farther,
    And my feet grew tired and weary,
And I couldn't hurry greatly,
    So it took a long, long while.
Beside, I stopped to read your word,
    A stranger one I never heard!
I've met with *Pa*-pistical,
                    That's pat;
But *Ma*-harshalalhashbaz,
                    What's that?'

'Oh, Clovy, you bright little thing!' cried Rose, in fits of laughter. But Mary Silver looked quite pale.

'I never heard of anything so awful!' she said. 'If that word had come to me, I should have fainted away on the spot – I know I should!'

Next came:

'*Word* – Buttons.
Question – What is the best way to make home happy?

To me 'tis quite clear I can answer this right:
Sew on the buttons, and sew them on tight.'

'I suspect that is Amy's,' said Esther: 'she's such a model for mending and keeping things in order.'

'It's not fair, guessing aloud in this way,' said Sally Alsop. Sally always spoke for Amy, and Amy for Sally. 'Voice and Echo' Rose called them: only, as she remarked, nobody could tell which was Echo and which was Voice.

The next word was 'Mrs Nipson', and the question, 'Do you like flowers?'

> 'Do I like flowers? I will not write a sonnet,
>   Singing their beauty as a poet might do:
> I just detest those on Aunt Nipson's bonnet,
>   Because they are like her – all grey and blue,
>   Dusty and pinched, and fastened on askew!
> And as for heaven's own buttercups and daisies,
> I am not good enough to sing their praises.'

Nobody knew who wrote this verse. Katy suspected Louisa, and Rose suspected Katy.

The sixth slip was a very brief one.

> *Word* – When?
> *Question* – Are you willing?

>> If I wasn't willing, I would tell you;
>> But when – Oh, dear, I *can't!*'

'What an extraordinary rhyme!' began Clover, but Rose spied poor Mary blushing and looking distressed, and hastily interposed: 'It's very good, I'm sure. I wish I'd written it. Go on, Katy.'

So Katy went on.

> *Word* – Unfeeling.
> *Question* – Which would you rather do, or go fishing?

>> I don't feel up to fishing, or sich;
>> And so, if you please, I'd rather do – which?'

'I don't seem to see the word in that poem,' said Rose. 'The distinguished author will please write another.'

'The distinguished author made no reply to this suggestion; but, after a minute or two, Esther Dearborn, 'quite disinterestedly', as she stated, remarked that, after all, to 'don't feel' was pretty much the same as unfeeling. There was a little chorus of groans at this, and Katy said she should certainly impose a fine if such dodges and evasions were practised again. This was the first meeting, however, and she would be merciful. After this speech she unfolded another paper. It ran:

Word – Flea.
Question – What would you do, love?

> What would I do, love? Well, I do not know.
> How can I tell till you are more explicit?
> If't were a rose you held me, I would smell it;
> If't were a mouth you held me, I would kiss it;
> If't were a frog, I'd scream than furies louder;
> If't were a flea, I'd fetch the Keating's Powder.'

Only two slips remained. One was Katy's own. She knew it by the way in which it was folded, and had almost instinctively avoided and left it for the last. Now, however, she took courage and opened it. The word was 'Measles', and the question, 'Who was the grandmother of Invention?' These were the lines:

> 'The night was horribly dark,
> The measles broke out in the Ark:
> Little Japhet, and Shem, and all the young Hams
> Were screaming at once for potatoes and clams.
> And, "What shall I do," said poor Mrs Noah,
> "All alone by myself in this terrible shower?
> I know what I'll do: I'll step down in the hold,
> And wake up a lioness grim and old,

And tie her close to the children's door,
And give her a ginger-cake to roar
At the top of her voice for an hour or more;
And I'll tell the children to cease their din,
Or I'll let that grim old party in,
To stop their squeazles and likewise their measles."
She practised this with the greatest success.
She was everyone's grandmother, I guess.'

'That's much the best of all!' pronounced Alice Gibbons.
'I wonder who wrote it?'

'Dear me! did you like it so much?' said Rose, simpering,
and doing her best to blush.

'Did you really write it?' said Mary; but Louisa laughed,
and exclaimed, 'No use, Rosy! you can't take us in – we know
better!'

'Now for the last,' said Katy. 'The word is "Buckwheat",
and the question, "What is the origin of dreams?"

When the nuns are sweetly sleeping,
Mrs Nipson comes a-creeping,
Creeping like a kitty-cat from door to door,
And she listens to their slumbers,
And most carefully she numbers,
Counting for every nun a nunlet snore!
And the nuns in sweet forgetfulness who lie,
Dreaming of buckwheat cakes, parental love and – pie,
Moan softly, twist and turn, and see
Black cats and fiends, who frolic in their glee;
And nightmares prancing wildly do abound
While Mrs Nipson makes her nightly round.'

'Who did write that?' exclaimed Rose. Nobody answered.
The girls looked at each other, and Rose scrutinised them all
with sharp glances.

'Well! I never saw such creatures for keeping their

countenances,' she said. 'Somebody is as bold as brass. Didn't you see how I blushed when my piece was read?'

'You monkey!' whispered Clover, who at that moment caught sight of the handwriting on the paper. Rose gave her a warning pinch, and they both subsided into an unseen giggle.

'What! The tea-bell!' cried everybody. 'We wanted to play another game.'

'It's a complete success!' whispered Rose, ecstatically, as they went down the hall. 'The girls all say they never had such a good time in their lives. I'm so glad I didn't die with the measles when I was little!'

'Well,' demanded Lilly, 'so the high and mighty society has had a meeting! How did it go off?'

'Delicious!' replied Rose, smacking her lips as at the recollection of something very nice. 'But you mustn't ask any questions, Lilly. Outsiders have nothing to do with the SSUC. Our proceedings are strictly private.' She ran downstairs with Katy.

'I think you're real mean!' called Lilly after them. Then she said to herself, 'They're just trying to tease. I know it was stupid.'

CHAPTER SEVEN

Injustice

Summer was always slow in getting to Hillsover, but at last she arrived, and woods and hills suddenly put on new colours and became beautiful. The sober village shared in the glorifying process. Vines budded on piazzas. Wistaria purpled whitewashed walls. The brown elm boughs which hung above the common turned into trailing garlands of fresh green. Each walk revealed some change, or ended in some delightful discovery – trilliums, dogtooth violets, apple-trees in blossom or wild strawberries turning red. The wood flowers and mosses, even the birds and bird-songs, were new to our Western girls. Hillsover, in summer, was a great deal prettier than Burnet, and Katy and Clover began to enjoy school very much indeed.

Toward the end of June, however, something took place which gave them quite a different feeling – something so disagreeable that I hate to tell about it; but, as it really happened, I must.

It was on a Saturday morning. They had just come back from the bathhouse, and were going upstairs, laughing and feeling very merry; Clover had written a droll piece for the SSUC meeting, and was telling Katy about it, when, just at the head of the stairs, they met Rose Red. She was evidently in trouble, for she looked flushed and excited, and was under escort of Miss Barnes, who marched before her with the air of a policeman. As she passed the girls, Rose opened her eyes very wide, and made a face expressive of dismay.

'What's the matter?' whispered Clover. Rose only made

another grimace, clawed with her fingers at Miss Barnes's back, and vanished down the entry which led to Mrs Florence's room. They stood looking after her.

'Oh, dear!' sighed Clover, 'I'm so afraid Rose is in a scrape.'

They walked on toward Quaker Row. In the washroom was a knot of girls, with their heads close together, whispering. When they saw Katy and Clover, they became silent, and gazed at them curiously.

'What has Rose Red gone to Mrs Florence about?' asked Clover, too anxious to notice the strange manner of the girls. But at that moment she caught sight of something which so amazed her that she forgot her question. It was nothing less than her own trunk, with 'C.E.C.' at the end, being carried along the entry by two men. Miss Jane followed close behind, with her arms full of clothes and books. Katy's well-known scarlet pincushion topped the pile; in Miss Jane's hand were Clover's comb and brush.

'Why, what does this mean?' gasped Clover, as she and Katy darted after Miss Jane, who had turned into one of the rooms. It was No. 1, at the head of the row – a room which no one had wanted, on account of its smallness and lack of light. The window looked out on a brick wall not ten feet away; there was never a ray of sun to make it cheerful; and Mrs Nipson had converted it into a storeroom for empty trunks. The trunks were taken away now, and the bed was strewn with Katy's and Clover's possessions.

'Miss Jane, what is the matter? What are you moving our things for?' exclaimed the girls in great excitement.

Miss Jane laid down her load of dresses, and looked at them sternly.

'You know the reason as well as I do,' she said icily.

'No, I don't. I haven't the least idea what you mean!' cried Katy. 'Oh, please be careful!' as Miss Jane flung a pair of boots on top of Cousin Helen's vase, 'you'll break it! Dear,

dear! Clover, there's your cologne bottle tipped over, and all the cologne spilt! What does it mean? Is our room going to be painted, or what?'

'Your room,' responded Miss Jane, 'is for the future to be this – No. 1. Miss Benson and Miss James will take No. 6; and, it is to be hoped, will conduct themselves more properly than you have done.'

'Than we have done!' cried Katy, hardly believing her ears.

'Do not repeat my words in that rude way!' said Miss Jane, tartly. 'Yes, than you have done!'

'But what have we done? There is some dreadful mistake. Do tell us what you mean, Miss Jane. We have done nothing wrong, so far as I know.'

'Indeed!' replied Miss Jane, sarcastically. 'Your ideas of right and wrong must be peculiar. I advise you to say no more on the subject, but be thankful that Mrs Florence keeps you in the school at all, instead of dismissing you. Nothing but the fact that your home is at such a distance prevents her from doing so.'

Katy felt as if all the blood in her body were turned to fire, as she heard these words and met Miss Jane's eyes. Her old, hasty temper, which had seemed to die out during years of pain and patience, flashed into sudden life, as a smouldering coal flashes, when you least expect it, into flame. She drew herself up to her full height, gave Miss Jane a look of scorching indignation, and with a rapid impulse darted out of the room and along the hall towards Mrs Florence's door. The girls she met scattered from her path right and left. She looked so tall and moved so impetuously that she absolutely frightened them.

'Come in,' said Mrs Florence, in answer to her sharp, quivering knock. Katy entered. Rose was not there, and Mrs Florence and Mrs Nipson sat together, side by side, in close consultation.

'Mrs Florence,' said Katy, too much excited to feel in the

least afraid, 'will you please tell me why our things are being changed to No. 1?'

Mrs Florence flushed with anger. She looked Katy all over for a minute before she answered; then she said, in a severe voice: 'It is done by my orders, and for good and sufficient reasons. What those reasons are, you know as well as I.'

'No, I don't!' replied Katy, as angry as Mrs Florence. 'I haven't the least idea what they are, and I insist on knowing!'

'I cannot answer questions put in such an improper manner,' said Mrs Florence, with a wave of the hand which meant that Katy was to go. But Katy did not stir.

'I am sorry if my manner was improper,' she said, trying to speak quietly, 'but I think I have a right to ask what this means. If we are accused of doing wrong, it is only fair to tell us what we have done.'

Mrs Florence only waved her hand again; but Mrs Nipson, who had been twisting uneasily in her chair, said: 'Excuse me, Mrs Florence, but perhaps it would be better – would satisfy Miss Carr better – if you were to be explicit.'

'It does not seem to me that Miss Carr can be in need of any explanation,' replied Mrs Florence. 'When a young lady writes underhand notes to young gentlemen, and throws them from her window, and they are discovered, she must naturally expect that persons of correct ideas will be shocked and disgusted. Your note to Mr Abennethy Searles, Miss Carr, was found by his mother while mending his pocket, and was handed by her to me. After this statement, you will hardly be surprised that I do not consider it best to permit you to room longer on that side of the house. I did not suppose I had a girl in my school capable of such conduct.'

For a moment Katy was too much stunned to speak. She took hold of a chair to steady herself, and her colour changed so quickly from red to pale, and back again to red, that Mrs Florence and Mrs Nipson, who sat watching her, might be pardoned for thinking that she looked guilty. As soon as she recovered her voice, she stammered out: 'But I didn't! I never did! I haven't written any note! I wouldn't for the world! Oh, Mrs Florence, please believe me!'

'I prefer to believe the evidence of my eyes,' replied Mrs Florence, as she drew a paper from her pocket.

'Here is the note! I suppose you will hardly deny your own signature.'

Katy seized the note. It was written in a round, unformed hand, and ran thus:

> DEAR BERRY – I saw you last night on the green. I think you are splendid. All the nuns think so. I look at you very often out of my window. If I let down a string, would you tie a cake to it, like that kind which you threw to Mary Andrews last term? Tie two cakes, please; one for me and one for my room-mate. The string will be at the end of the Row.
>
> MISS CARR

In spite of her agitation, Katy could hardly keep back a smile as she read this absurd production. Mrs Florence saw the smile, and her tone was more severe than ever, as she said: 'Give that back to me, if you please. It will be my justification with your father if he objects to your change of room.'

'But, Mrs Florence,' cried Katy, 'I never wrote that note. It isn't my handwriting; it isn't my – Oh, surely you can't think so! It's too ridiculous.'

'Go to your room at once,' said Mrs Florence, 'and be thankful that your punishment is such a mild one. If your home were not so distant, I should write to ask your father to remove you from the school, instead of which I merely put you on the other side of the entry, out of reach of further correspondence of this sort.'

'But I shall write him, and he will take us away immediately,' cried Katy, stung to the quick by this obstinate injustice. 'I will not stay, neither shall Clover, where our word is disbelieved and we are treated like this. Papa knows! Papa will never doubt us a moment when we tell him that this isn't true.'

With these passionate words she left the room. I do not think that either Mrs Florence or Mrs Nipson felt very comfortable after she was gone.

That was a dreadful afternoon. The girls had no heart to arrange No. 1, or do anything toward making it comfortable, but lay on the bed, in the midst of their belongings, crying and receiving visits of condolence from their friends. The SSUC meeting was put off. Katy was in no humour to act as president, or Clover to read her funny poem. Rose and Mary Silver sat by, kissing them at intervals, and declaring that it was a shame, while the other members dropped in one by one to re-echo the same sentiments.

'If it had been anybody else,' said Alice Gibbons; 'but Katy, Katy of all persons! It is too much!'

'So I told Mrs Florence,' sobbed Rose Red. 'Oh, why was I born so bad? If I'd always been good, and a model to the rest of you, perhaps she'd have believed me instead of scolding harder than ever.'

The idea of Rose as a 'model' made Clover smile in the midst of her dolefulness.

'It's an outrageous thing,' said Ellen Gray. 'If Mrs Florence only knew it, you two have done more to keep the rest of us steady than any girls in the school.'

'So they have,' blubbered Rose, whose pretty face was quite swollen with crying. 'I've been getting better and better every day since they came.' She put her arms round Clover as she spoke, and sobbed harder than ever.

It was in the midst of this excitement that Miss Jane thought fit to come in and 'inspect the room'. When she saw the crying girls and the general confusion of everything, she was very angry.

'I shall mark you both for disorder,' she said. 'Get off the bed, Miss Carr. Hang your dresses up at once, Clover, and put your shoes in the shoe-bag. I never saw anything so disgraceful. All these things must be in order when I return, fifteen minutes from now, or I shall report you to Mrs Florence.'

'It's of no consequence what you do. We are not going to stay,' muttered Katy. But soon she was ashamed of having said this. Her anger was melting, and grief taking its place. 'Oh, Papa! Papa! Elsie! Elsie!' she whispered to herself, as she slowly hung up the dresses; and, unseen by the girls, she hid her face in the folds of Clover's grey alpaca, and shed some hot tears. Till then she had been too angry to cry.

This softer mood followed her all through the evening. Clover and Rose sat by, talking over the affair and keeping their wrath warm with discussion. Katy said hardly a word. She felt too weary and depressed to speak.

'Who could have written the note?' asked Clover again and again. It was impossible to guess. It seemed absurd to suspect any of the older girls; but then, as Rose suggested, the absurdity as well as the signature might have been imitated to avoid detection.

'I know one thing,' remarked Rose, 'and that is that I should like to kill Mrs Searles. Horrid old thing! – peeping and prying into pockets. She has no business to be alive at all.'

Rose's ferocious speeches always sounded specially comical when taken in connection with her pink cheeks and her dimples.

'Shall you write to Papa tonight, Katy?' asked Clover.

Katy shook her head. She was too heavy-hearted to talk. Big tears rolled down unseen and fell upon the pillow. After Rose was gone, and the candle out, she cried herself to sleep.

Waking early in the dim dawn, she lay and thought it over, Clover slumbering soundly beside her meanwhile. 'Morning brings counsel,' says the old proverb. In this case it seemed true. Katy, to her surprise, found a train of fresh thoughts filling her mind, which were not there when she fell asleep. She recalled her passionate words and feelings of the day before. Now that the mood had passed, they seemed to her worse than the injury which provoked them. Quick-tempered and generous people often experience this. It was easier for Katy to forgive Mrs Florence, because it was needful also that she should forgive herself.

'I said I would write to Papa to take us away,' she thought. 'Why did I say that? What good would it do? It wouldn't make anybody disbelieve this hateful story. They'd only think I wanted to get away because I was found out. And Papa would be so worried and disappointed. It has cost him a great deal to get us ready and send us here, and he wants us to stay a year. If we went home now, all the money would be wasted. And yet how horrid it is going to be after this! I don't feel as if I could ever bear to see Mrs Florence again. I must write.

'But then,' her thoughts flowed on, 'home wouldn't seem like home if we went away from school in disgrace, and knew that everybody here was believing such things. Suppose, instead, I were to write to Papa to come and make things straight. He'd find out the truth, and force Mrs Florence to see it. It would be very expensive, though; and I know he oughtn't to leave home again so soon. Oh, dear! How hard it is to know what to do!

'What would Cousin Helen say?' she continued, going in imagination to the sofa-side of the dear friend who was to her like a second conscience. She shut her eyes and invented a long talk – her questions, Cousin Helen's replies. But, as everybody knows, it is impossible to play croquet by yourself and be strictly impartial to all the four balls. Katy found that she was making Cousin Helen play (that is, answer) as she herself wished, and not, as something whispered, as she would answer were she really there.

'It is just the "Little Scholar" over again,' she said, half aloud; 'I can't see. I don't know how to act.' She remembered the dream she once had, of a great beautiful Face and a helping hand. 'And it was real,' she murmured, 'and just as real, and just as near, now as then.'

The result of this long meditation was that when Clover woke up she found Katy leaning over, ready to kiss her for good-morning, and looking bright and determined.

'Clovy,' she said, 'I've been thinking; and I'm not going to write to Papa about this affair at all!'

'Aren't you? Why not?' asked Clover, puzzled.

'Because it would worry him, and be of no use. He would come and take us right away, I'm sure; but Mrs Florence and all the teachers, and a great many of the girls, would always believe that this horrid, ridiculous story is true. I can't bear to have them. Let's stay instead, and convince them that it isn't. I think we can.'

'I would a great deal rather go home,' said Clover. 'It won't ever be nice here again. We shall have this dark room, and Miss Jane will be more unkind than ever, and the girls will think you wrote that note, and Lilly Page will say hateful things!' She buttoned her boots with a vindictive air.

'Never mind,' said Katy, trying to feel brave. 'I don't suppose it will be pleasant, but I'm pretty sure it's right. And Rosy and all the girls we really care for know how it is.'

'I can't bear it,' sighed Clover, with tears in her eyes. 'It is so cruel that they should say such things about you.'

'I mean that they shall say something quite different before we go away,' replied Katy, stroking her hair. 'Cousin Helen would tell us to stay, I'm pretty sure. I was thinking about her just now, and I seemed to hear her voice in the air, saying over and over, "Live it down! Live it down! Live it down!"' She half sang this, and took two or three dancing steps across the room.

'What a girl you are!' said Clover, consoled by seeing Katy look so bright.

Mrs Florence was surprised that morning, as she sat in her room, by the appearance of Katy. She looked pale, but perfectly quiet and gentle.

'Mrs Florence,' she said, 'I've come to say that I shall not write to my father to take us away, as I told you I should.'

Mrs Florence bowed stiffly, by way of answer.

'Not,' went on Katy, with a little flash in her eyes, 'that he would hesitate, or doubt my word one moment, if I did. But he wished us to stay here a year, and I don't want to disappoint him. I'd rather stay. And, Mrs Florence, I'm sorry I spoke as I did yesterday. It was not right; but I was angry, and felt that you were unjust.'

'And today you own that I was not?'

'Oh, no!' replied Katy, 'I can't do that. You *were* unjust, because neither Clover nor I wrote that note. We wouldn't do such a horrid thing for the world, and I hope some day you will believe us. But I oughtn't to have spoken so.'

Katy's face and voice were so truthful as she said this that Mrs Florence was almost shaken in her opinion.

'We will say no more about the matter,' she remarked in a kinder tone. 'If your conduct is perfectly correct in future, it will go far to make this forgotten.'

Few things are more aggravating than to be forgiven when one has done no wrong. Katy felt this as she walked away from Mrs Florence's room. But she would not let herself grow angry again. 'Live it down!' she whispered, as she went into the schoolroom.

She and Clover had a good deal to endure for the next two or three weeks. They missed their old room with its sunny window and pleasant outlook. They missed Rose, who, down at the far end of Quaker Row, could not drop in half so often as had been her custom. Miss Jane was specially grim and sharp; and some of the upstairs girls, who resented Katy's plain speaking, and the formation of a society against flirting, improved the chance to be provoking. Lilly Page was one of these. She didn't really believe Katy guilty, but she liked to tease her by pretending to believe it.

'Only to think of the president of the Saintly Stuck-Up Society being caught like this!' she remarked maliciously. 'What are our great reformers coming to? Now if it had been a sinner like me, no one would be surprised!'

All this naturally was vexatious. Even sunny Clover shed many tears in private over her mortifications. But the girls bore their trouble bravely, and never said one syllable about the matter in the letters home. There were consolations, too, mixed with the annoyances. Rose Red clung to her two friends closely, and loyally fought their battles. The SSUC to a girl rallied round its chief. After that sad Saturday the meetings were resumed with as much spirit as ever. Katy's steadiness and uniform politeness and sweet temper impressed even those who would have been glad to believe a tale against her, and in a short time the affair ceased to be a subject for discussion – was almost forgotten, in fact, except for a sore spot in Katy's heart, and one page in Rose Red's album, upon which, under the date of that fatal day, were written these words, headed by an appalling skull and crossbones in pen-and-ink: 'NB – Pay Miss Jane off.'

CHAPTER EIGHT

Changes

'Clover, where's Clover?' cried Rose Red, popping her head into the schoolroom, where Katy sat writing her composition. 'Oh, Katy, there you are! I want you too. Come down to my room at once. I've such a thing to tell you!'

'What is it? Tell me too!' said Bella Arkwright. Bella was a veritable 'little pitcher', of the kind mentioned in the proverb, and had an insatiable curiosity to know everything that other people knew.

'Tell you, miss? I should really like to know why!' replied Rose, who was not at all fond of Bella.

'You're very mean, and very unkind,' whined Bella. 'You think you're a great grown-up lady, and can have secrets. But you are not! You're a little girl too – almost as little as me. So there!'

Rose made a face at her, and a sort of growling rush, which had the effect of sending Bella screaming down the hall. Then, returning to the schoolroom, 'Do come, Katy,' she said; 'find Clover, and hurry! Really and truly I want you. I feel as if I should burst if I don't tell somebody at once what I've found out.'

Katy began to be curious. She went in pursuit of Clover, who was practising in one of the recitation rooms, and the three girls ran together down Quaker Row.

'Now,' said Rose, locking the door, and pushing forward a chair for Katy and another for Clover, 'swear that you won't tell, for this is a real secret – the greatest secret that ever was, and Mrs Florence would flay me alive if she knew that I knew!' She paused to enjoy the effect of her words, and suddenly began to snuff the air in a peculiar manner.

'Girls,' she said solemnly, 'that little wretch of a Bella is in this room. I am sure of it.'

'What makes you think so?' cried the others, surprised.

'I smell that dreadful pomatum that she puts on her hair! Don't you notice it? She's hidden somewhere.' Rose looked sharply about for a minute, then made a pounce, and from under the bed dragged a small kicking heap. It was the guilty Bella.

'What were you doing there, you bad child?' demanded Rose, seizing the kicking feet and holding them fast.

'I don't care,' blubbered Bella, 'you wouldn't tell me your secret. You're just a horrid girl, Rose Red. I don't love you a bit.'

'Your affection is not a thing which I particularly pine for,' retorted Rose, seating herself, and holding the culprit before her by the ends of her short pigtails. 'I don't want little girls, who peep and hide, to love me. I'd rather they wouldn't. Now listen. Do you know what I shall do if you ever come again into my room without leave? First, I shall cut off your hair, pomatum and all, with my penknife' – Bella screamed – 'and then I'll turn myself into a bear – a great brown bear – and eat you up!' Rose pronounced this threat with tremendous energy, and accompanied it with a snarl which showed all her teeth. Bella roared with fright, twitched away her pigtails, unlocked the door and fled, Rose not pursuing her, but sitting comfortably in her chair and growling at intervals, till her victim was out of hearing. Then she rose and bolted the door again.

'How lucky that the imp is so fond of that smelly pomatum!' she remarked: 'one always knows where to look for her. It's as good as a bell round her neck! Now for the secret. You promise not to tell? Well, then, Mrs Florence is going away week after next, and, what's more – she's going to be married!'

'Not really!' cried the others.

'Really and truly. She's going to be married to a clergyman.'

'How did you find that out?'

'Why, it's the most curious thing. You know my blue lawn which Miss James is making. This morning I went to try it on, Miss Barnes with me of course, and while Miss James was fitting the waist Mrs Seccomb came in and sat down on the sofa by Miss Barnes. They began to talk, and pretty soon Mrs Seccomb said, "What day does Mrs Florence go?"

'"Thursday week," said Miss Barnes. She sort of mumbled it, and looked to see if I were listening. I wasn't; but of course after that I did – as hard as I could.

'"And where does the important event take place?" asked Mrs Seccomb. She's so funny with her little bit of a mouth and her long words. She always looks as if each of them was a big pill, and she wanted to swallow it and couldn't.

'"In Lewisberg, at her sister's house," said Miss Barnes. She mumbled more than ever, but I heard.

'"What a deplorable loss she will be to our limited circle!" said Mrs Seccomb. I couldn't imagine what they meant. But what do you think, when I got home there was this letter from Sylvia, and she says, "Your adored Mrs Florence is going to be married. I'm afraid you'll all break your hearts about it. Mother met the gentleman at a party the other night. She says he looks clever, but isn't at all handsome, which is a pity, for Mrs Florence is a raving beauty in my opinion. He's an excellent preacher, we hear; and won't she manage the parish to perfection? How shall you like being left to the tender mercies of Mrs Nipson?" Now did you ever hear anything so droll in your life?' went on Rose, folding up her letter. 'Just think of those two things coming together the same day! It's like a sum in arithmetic, with an answer which "proves" the sum, isn't it?'

Rose had counted on producing an effect, and she certainly was not disappointed. The girls could think and talk of nothing else for the remainder of that afternoon.

It was a singular fact that before two days were over every scholar in the school knew that Mrs Florence was going to be married! How the secret got out, nobody could guess. Rose protested that it wasn't her fault – she had been a miracle of discretion, a perfect sphinx; but there was a guilty laugh in her eyes, and Katy suspected that the sphinx had unbent a little. Nothing so exciting had ever happened at the Nunnery before. Some of the older scholars were quite inconsolable. They bemoaned themselves, and got together in corners to enjoy the luxury of woe. Nothing comforted them but the project of getting up a 'testimonial' for Mrs Florence.

What this testimonial should be caused great discussion in the school. Everybody had a different idea, and everybody was sure that her idea was better than anybody's else. All the school contributed. The money collected amounted to nearly forty dollars, and the question was, What should be bought?

Every sort of thing was proposed. Lilly Page insisted that nothing could possibly be so appropriate as a bouquet of wax flowers and a glass shade to put over it. There was a strong party in favour of spoons. Annie Silsbie suggested 'a statue'; somebody else a clock. Rose Red was for a cabinet piano, and Katy had some trouble in convincing her that forty dollars would not buy one. Bella demanded that they should get 'an organ'.

'You can go along with it as monkey,' said Rose, which remark made Bella caper with indignation.

At last, after long discussion and some quarrelling, a cake-basket was fixed upon. Sylvia Redding happened to be making a visit to Boston, and Rose was commissioned to write and ask her to select the gift and send it up by express. The girls could hardly wait till it came.

'I do hope it will be pretty, don't you?' they said over and over again. When the box arrived, they all gathered to see it opened. Esther Dearborn took out the nails, half a dozen hands lifted the lid, and Rose unwrapped the tissue paper and displayed the basket to general view.

'Oh, what a beauty!' cried everybody. It was woven of twisted silver wire. Two figures of children with wings and garlands supported the handle on either side.

In the middle of the handle was a pair of silver doves, billing and cooing in the most affectionate way, over a tiny shield, on which were engraved Mrs Florence's initials.

'I never saw one like it!' 'Doesn't it look heavy?' 'Rose Red, your sister is splendid!' cried a chorus of voices, as Rose, highly gratified, held up the basket.

'Who shall present it?' asked Louisa Agnew.

'Rose Red,' said some of the girls.

'No, indeed, I'm not tall enough,' protested Rose; 'it must be somebody who'd kind of sweep into the room and be impressive. I vote for Katy.'

'Oh, no!' said Katy, shrinking back. 'I shouldn't do it well at all. Suppose we put it to the vote.'

Ellen Gray cut some slips of paper, and each girl wrote a name and dropped it into a box. When the votes were counted, Katy's name appeared on all but three.

'I propose that we make this vote unanimous,' said Rose, highly delighted. The girls agreed; and Rose, jumping on a chair, exclaimed: 'Three cheers for Katy Carr! keep time, girls – one, two, hip, hip, hurrah!'

The hurrahs were given with enthusiasm, for Katy, almost without knowing it, had become popular. She was too much touched and pleased to speak at first. When she did, it was to protest against her election.

'Esther would do it beautifully,' she said, 'and I think Mrs Florence would like the basket better if she gave it. You know ever since – ' she stopped. Even now she could not refer with composure to the affair of the note.

'Oh!' cried Louisa, 'she's thinking of that ridiculous note Mrs Florence made such a fuss about. As if anybody supposed you wrote it, Katy! I don't believe even Miss Jane is such a goose as that. Anyway, if she is, that's one reason more why you should present the basket, to show that we don't think so.' She gave Katy a kiss by way of period.

'Yes, indeed, you're chosen, and you must give it,' cried the others.

'Very well,' said Katy, extremely gratified, 'what am I to say?'

'We'll compose a speech for you,' replied Rose. 'Sugar your voice, Katy, and whatever you do, stand up straight. Don't crook over, as if you thought you were tall. It's a bad trick you have, child, and I'm always sorry to see it,' concluded Rose, with the air of a wise mamma giving a lecture. It is droll how much can go on in a school unseen and unsuspected by its teachers. Mrs Florence never dreamed that the girls had guessed her secret. Her plan was to go away as if for a visit, and leave Mrs Nipson to explain at her leisure. She was therefore quite unprepared for the appearance of Katy, holding the beautiful basket, which was full of fresh roses, crimson, white and pink. I am afraid the rules of the SSUC had been slightly relaxed to allow of Rose Red's getting these flowers; certainly they grew nowhere in Hillsover except in Professor Seccomb's garden!

'The girls wanted me to give you this, with a great deal of love from us all,' said Katy, feeling strangely embarrassed, and hardly venturing to raise her eyes. She set the basket on the table. 'We hope so much that you will be happy,' she added in a low voice, and moved toward the door. Mrs Florence had been too much surprised to speak, but now she called: 'Wait! Come back a moment.'

Katy came back. Mrs Florence's cheeks were flushed. She looked very handsome. Katy almost thought there were tears in her eyes.

'Tell the girls that I thank them very much. Their present is beautiful. I shall always value it.' She blushed as she spoke, and Katy blushed too. It made her shy to see the usually composed Mrs Florence so confused.

'What did she say? What did she say?' demanded the others, who were collected in groups round the schoolroom door to hear a report of the interview.

Katy repeated her message. Some of the girls were disappointed.

'Is that all?' they said. 'We thought she would stand up and make a speech.'

'Or a short poem,' put in Rose Red – 'a few stanzas thrown off on the spur of the moment; like this, for instance –

> Thank you kindly for your basket,
> Which I didn't mean to ask it;
> But I'll very gladly take it,
> And when 'tis full of cake, it
> Will frequently remind me
> Of the girls I left behind me!'

There was a universal giggle, which brought Miss Jane out of the schoolroom.

'Order!' she said, ringing the bell. 'Young ladies, what are you about? Study hour has begun.'

'We're so sorry Mrs Florence is going away,' said some of the girls.

'How did you know that she is going?' demanded Miss Jane, sharply. Nobody answered.

Next day Mrs Florence left. Katy saw her go with a secret regret. 'If only she would have said that she didn't believe I wrote that note!' she told Clover.

'I don't care what she believes! She's a stupid, unjust woman!' replied independent little Clover.

Mrs Nipson was now in sole charge of the establishment. She had never tried school-keeping before, and had various pet plans and theories of her own, which she had only been waiting on Mrs Florence's departure to put into practice.

One of these was that the school was to dine three times a week on pudding and bread and butter. Mrs Nipson had a theory – very convenient and economical for herself, but highly distasteful to her scholars – that it was injurious for young people to eat meat every day in hot weather.

The puddings were made of batter, with a sprinkling of blackberries or raisins. Now, rising at six, and studying four hours and a half on a light breakfast, has a wonderful effect on the appetite, as all who have tried it will testify. The poor girls would go down to dinner as hungry as wolves, and eye the large, pale slices on their plates with a wrath and dismay which I cannot pretend to describe. Very thick the slices were, and there was plenty of thin, sugared sauce to eat with them, and plenty of bread and butter; but, somehow, the whole was unsatisfying, and the hungry girls would go upstairs almost as ravenous as when they came down. The second-tableites were always hanging over the balusters to receive them, and when to the demand, 'What did you have for dinner?' 'Pudding!' was answered, a low groan would run from one to another, and a general gloom seemed to drop down and envelop the party.

It may have been in consequence of this experience of starvation that the orders for the Fourth of July were that year so unusually large. It was an old custom in the school that the girls should celebrate the National Independence by buying as many goodies as they liked. There was no candy-shop in Hillsover, so Mrs Nipson took the orders, and sent to Boston for the things, which were charged on the bills with other extras. Under these blissful circumstances, the girls felt that they could afford to be extravagant, and made out their lists regardless of expense. Rose Red's, for this Fourth, ran thus:

Two pounds of chocolate caramels
Two pounds of sugar almonds
Two pounds of lemon drops
Two pounds of mixed candy
Two pounds of macaroons
A dozen oranges
A dozen lemons
A drum of figs
A box of French plums
A loaf of almond cake.

The result of this liberal order was that after the great wash-baskets of parcels had been distributed, and the school had rioted for twenty-four hours upon those unaccustomed luxuries, Rose was found lying on her bed, ghastly and pallid.

'Never speak to me of anything sweet again so long as I live!' she gasped. 'Talk of vinegar, or pickles, or sour apples, but don't allude to sugar in any form, if you love me! Oh, why, why did I send for those fatal things?'

In time all the candy was eaten up, and the school went back to its normal condition. Three weeks later came College Commencement.

'Are you and Clover Craters or Symposiums?' demanded Lilly Page, meeting Katy in the hall a few days before this important event.

'What do you mean?'

'Why, has nobody told you about them? They are the two great College Societies. All the girls belong to one or the other, and make the wreaths to dress their halls. We work up in the gymnasium; the Crater girls take the east side, and the Symposium girls the west, and when the wreaths grow too long we hang them out of the windows. It's the greatest fun in the world! Be a Symposium, do! I'm one!'

'I shall have to think about it before deciding,' said Katy, privately resolving to join Rose Red's society, whichever it was. The Crater it proved to be, so Katy and Clover enrolled themselves with the Craters. Three days before Commencement wreath-making began. The afternoons were wholly given up to the work, and, instead of walking or piano practice, the girls sat plaiting oak leaves into garlands many yards long. Baskets of fresh leaves were constantly brought in, and there was a strife between the rival societies as to which should accomplish most.

It was great fun, as Lilly had said, to sit there amid the green boughs and pleasant leafy smells, a buzz of gay voices in the air and a general sense of holiday. The gymnasium would have furnished many a pretty picture for an artist during those three afternoons, only, unfortunately, no artist was let in to see it.

One day, Rose Red, emptying a basket, lighted upon a white parcel, hidden beneath the leaves.

'Lemon drops!' she exclaimed, applying a finger and thumb with all the dexterity of Jack Horner. 'Here, Crater girls, here's something for you! Don't you pity the Symposiums?'

But next day a big package of peppermints appeared in the Symposium basket, so neither society could boast advantage over the other. They were pretty nearly equal, too, in the quantity of wreath made – the Craters' measuring nine hundred yards and the Symposiums' nine hundred and two. As for the halls, which they were taken over to see the evening before Commencement, it was impossible to say which was the more beautifully trimmed. Each faction preferred its own, and President Searles said that both did the young ladies credit.

They all sat in the gallery of the church on Commencement Day, and heard the speeches. It was very hot, and the speeches were not exactly interesting, being on such subjects as 'The Influence of a Republic on Men of Letters' and 'The Abstract Law of Justice, as applied to Human

Affairs'; but the music, and the crowd, and the spectacle of six hundred ladies all fanning themselves at once, were entertaining, and the girls would not have missed them for the world. Later in the day another diversion was afforded them by the throngs of pink and blue ladies and white-gloved gentlemen who passed the house on their way to the president's levee; but they were not allowed to enjoy this amusement long, for Miss Jane, suspecting what was going on, went from room to room, and ordered everybody summarily off to bed.

With the close of Commencement Day, a deep sleep seemed to settle over Hillsover. Most of the professors' families went off to enjoy themselves at the mountains or the seaside, leaving their houses shut up. This gave the village a drowsy and deserted air. There were no boys playing ball on the common, or swinging on the college fence; no look of life in the streets. The weather continued warm, the routine of study and exercise grew dull, and teachers and scholars alike were glad when the middle of September arrived, and with it the opening of the autumn vacation.

CHAPTER NINE

The Autumn Vacation

The last day of the term was one of confusion. Every part of the house was given over to trunks and packing. Mrs Nipson sat at her desk making out bills, and listening to requests about rooms and room-mates. Miss Jane counted books and atlases, taking note of each ink-spot and dog-eared page. The girls ran about, searching for missing articles, deciding what to take home and what to leave, engaging each other for the winter walks. All rules were laid aside. The sober Nunnery seemed turned into a hive of buzzing bees. Bella slid twice down the baluster of the front stairs without being reproved, and Rose Red threw her arm round Katy's waist and waltzed the whole length of Quaker Row.

'I'm so happy that I should like to scream!' she announced, as their last whirl brought them up against the wall. 'Isn't vacation just lovely? Katy, you don't look half glad.'

'We're not going home, you know,' replied Katy, in rather a doleful tone. She and Clover were not so enraptured at the coming of vacation as the rest of the girls. Spending a month with Mrs Page and Lilly was by no means the same thing as spending it with Papa and the children.

Next morning, however, when the big stage drove up, and the girls crowded in; when Mrs Nipson stood in the doorway, blandly waving farewell, and the maids flourished their dusters out of the upper windows, they found themselves sharing the general excitement, and joining heartily in the cheer which arose as the stage moved away. The girls felt so happy and good-natured that some of them even kissed their hands to Miss Jane.

Such a wild company is not often met with on a railroad train. They all went together as far as the Junction; and Mr Gray, Ellen's father, who had been put in charge of the party by Mrs Nipson, had his hands full to keep them in any sort of order. He was a timid old gentleman, and, as Rose suggested, his expression resembled that of a sedate hen who suddenly finds herself responsible for the conduct of a brood of ducklings.

'My dear, my dear!' he feebly remonstrated, 'would you buy any more candy? Do you not think so many peanuts may be bad for you?'

'Oh, no, sir!' replied Rose, 'they never hurt me a bit. I can eat thousands!' Then, as a stout lady entered the car, and made a motion toward the vacant seat beside her, she rolled her eyes wildly, and said. 'Excuse me, but perhaps I had better take the end seat, so as to get out easily in case I have a fit.'

'Fits!' cried the stout lady, and walked away with the utmost dispatch. Rose gave a wicked chuckle, the girls tittered, and Mr Gray visibly trembled.

'Is she really afflicted in this way?' he whispered.

'Oh, no, Papa! it's only Rose's nonsense!' apologised Ellen, who was laughing as hard as the rest. But Mr Gray did not feel comfortable, and he was very glad when they reached the Junction, and half of his troublesome charge departed on the branch road.

At six o'clock they arrived at Springfield. Half a dozen papas were waiting for their daughters, trains stood ready, there was a clamour of goodbyes. Mr Page was absorbed by Lilly, who kissed him incessantly, and chattered so fast that he had no eyes for anyone else. Louisa was borne away by an uncle, with whom she was to pass the night, and Katy and Clover found themselves left alone. They did not like to interrupt Lilly, so they retreated to a bench, and sat down feeling rather left out and homesick; and, though they did not say so, I am sure that each was thinking about Papa.

It was only for a moment. Mr Page spied them, and came up with such a kind greeting that the forlorn feeling fled at once. They were to pass the night at the Massasoit, it seemed; and he collected their bags, and led the way across the street to the hotel, where rooms were already engaged for them.

'Now for waffles,' whispered Lilly, as they went upstairs; and when, after a few minutes of washing and brushing, they came down again into the dining-room, she called for so many things, and announced herself 'starved' in such a tragical tone, that two amused waiters at once flew to the rescue and devoted themselves to supplying her wants. Waffle after waffle – each hotter and crisper than the last – did those long-suffering men produce, till even Lilly's appetite gave out, and she was forced to own that she could not swallow another morsel. This climax reached, they went into the parlour, and the girls sat down in the window to watch the people in the street, which, after quiet Hillsover, looked as brilliant and crowded as Broadway.

There were not many persons in the parlour. A grave-looking couple sat at a table at some distance, and a pretty little boy in a velvet jacket was playing around the room. He seemed about five years old; and Katy, who was fond of children, put out her hand as he went by, caught him, and lifted him into her lap. He did not seem shy, but looked her in the face composedly, like a grown person.

'What is your name, dear?' she asked.

'Daniel d'Aubigny Sparks,' answered the little boy. His voice was prim and distinct.

'Do you live at this hotel?'

'Yes, ma'am. I reside here with my father and mother.'

'And what do you do all day? Are there some other little boys for you to play with?'

'I do not wish to play with any little boys,' replied Daniel d'Aubigny, in a dignified tone: 'I prefer to be with my parents. Today we have taken a walk. We went to see a beautiful conservatory outside the city. There is a Victoria Regia there. I had often heard of this wonderful lily, and in the last number of the London *Musée* there is a picture of it, represented with a small negro child standing upon one of its leaves. My father said that he did not think this possible, but when we saw the plant we perceived that the print was not an exaggeration. Such is the size of the leaf, that a small negro child might very easily be supported upon it.'

'Oh, my!' cried Katy, feeling as if she had accidentally picked up an elderly gentleman or a college professor. 'Pray, how old are you?'

'Nearly nine, ma'am,' replied the little fellow, with a bow.

Katy, too much appalled for further speech, let him slide off her lap. But Mr Page, who was much diverted, continued the conversation; and Daniel, mounting a chair, crossed his short legs, and discoursed with all the gravity of an old man. The talk was principally about himself – his tastes, his adventures, his ideas about art and science. Now and then he alluded to his papa and mamma, and once to his grandfather.

'My maternal grandfather,' he said, 'was a remarkable man. In his youth he spent a great deal of time in France. He was there at the time of the French Revolution, and, as it happened, was present at the execution of the unfortunate Queen Marie Antoinette. This of course was not intentional. It chanced thus. My grandfather was in a barber's shop, having his hair cut. He saw a great crowd going by, and went out to ask what was the cause. The crowd was so immense that he could not extricate himself; he was carried along against his will, and not only so, but was forced to the front and compelled to witness every part of the dreadful scene. He had often told my mother that, after the execution, the executioner held up the queen's head to the people: the eyes were open, and there was in them an expression, not of pain, not of fear, but of great astonishment and surprise.'

This anecdote carried 'great astonishment and surprise' into the company who listened to it. Mr Page gave a short chuckle, and saying, 'By George!' got up and left the room. The girls put their heads out of the window that they might laugh unseen. Daniel gazed at their shaking shoulders with an air of wonder, while the grave couple at the end of the room, who for some moments had been looking disturbed, drew near and informed the youthful prodigy that it was time for him to go to bed.

'Good night, young ladies!' said the small condescending voice. Katy alone had 'presence of countenance' enough to return this salutation. It was a relief to find that Daniel went to bed at all.

Next morning at breakfast they saw him seated between his parents, eating bread and milk. He bowed to them over the edge of the bowl.

'Dreadful little prig! They should bottle him in spirits of wine as a specimen. It's the only thing he'll ever be fit for,' remarked Mr Page, who rarely said so sharp a thing about anybody.

Louisa joined them at the station. She was to travel under Mr Page's care, and Katy was much annoyed at Lilly's manner to her. It grew colder and less polite with every mile. By the time they reached Ashburn it was absolutely rude.

'Come and see me very soon, girls,' said Louisa, as they parted in the station. 'I long to have you know mother and little Daisy. Oh, there's Papa!' and she rushed up to a tall, pleasant-looking man, who kissed her fondly, shook hands with Mr Page, and touched his hat to Lilly, who scarcely bowed in return.

'Boarding-school is so horrid!' she remarked, 'you get all mixed up with people you don't want to know – people not in society at all.'

'How can you talk such nonsense?' said her father: 'the

Agnews are thoroughly respectable, and Mr Agnew is one of the cleverest men I know.'

Katy was pleased when Mr Page said this, but Lilly shrugged her shoulders and looked cross.

'Papa is so democratic,' she whispered to Clover; 'he don't care a bit who people are, so long as they are respectable and clever.'

'Well, why should he?' replied Clover. Lilly was more disgusted than ever.

Ashburn was a large and prosperous town. It was built on the slopes of a picturesque hill, and shaded with fine elms. As they drove through the streets, Katy and Clover caught glimpses of conservatories and shrubberies and beautiful houses with bay-windows and piazzas.

'That's ours,' said Lilly, as the carriage turned in at a gate. It stopped, and Mr Page jumped out.

'Here we are,' he said. 'Gently, Lilly, you'll hurt yourself. Well, my dears, we're very glad to see you in our home at last.'

This was kind and comfortable, and the girls were glad of it, for the size and splendour of the house quite dazzled and made them shy. They had never seen anything like it before. The hall had a marble floor, and busts and statues. Large rooms opened on either side; and Mrs Page, who came forward to receive them, wore a heavy silk with a train and laces, and looked altogether as if she were dressed for a party.

'This is the drawing-room,' said Lilly, delighted to see the girls looking so impressed. 'Isn't it splendid?' And she led the way into a stiff, chilly, magnificent apartment, where all the blinds were closed, and all the shades pulled down, and all the furniture shrouded in linen covers. Even the picture frames and mirrors were sewed up in muslin to keep off flies; and the bronzes and alabaster ornaments on the chimney-piece and *étagère* gleamed through the dim light in a ghostly way. Katy thought it very dismal. She couldn't imagine anybody sitting down there to read or sew, or do anything pleasant, and probably it was not intended that anyone should do so; for Mrs Page showed them out, and led the way into a smaller room at the back of the hall.

'Well, Katy,' she said, 'how do you like Hillsover?'

'Very well, ma'am,' replied Katy; but she did not speak enthusiastically.

'Ah!' said Mrs Page, shaking her head, 'it takes time to shake off home habits, and to learn to get along with young people after living with older ones and catching their ways. You'll like it better as you go on.'

Katy privately doubted whether this was true, but she did not say so. Pretty soon Lilly offered to show them upstairs to their room She took them first into three large and elegant chambers, which she explained were kept for grand company, and then into a much smaller one in the wing.

'Mother always puts my friends in here,' she remarked: 'she says it's plenty good enough for schoolgirls to thrash about in!'

'What does she mean?' cried Clover indignantly, as Lilly closed the door. 'We don't thrash!'

'I can't imagine,' answered Katy, who was vexed too. But pretty soon she began to laugh.

'People are so funny,' she said. 'Never mind, Clovy, this room is good enough, I'm sure.'

'Must we unpack, or will it do to go down in our alpacas?' asked Clover.

'I don't know,' replied Katy in a doubtful tone. 'Perhaps we had better change our gowns. Cousin Olivia always dresses so much! Here's your blue muslin right on the top of the trunk. You might put on that, and I'll wear my purple.'

The girls were glad that they had done this, for it was evidently expected, and Lilly had dressed her hair and donned a fresh white piqué. Mrs Page examined their dresses, and said that Clover's was a lovely blue, but that ruffles were quite gone out, and everything must be made with basques. She supposed they needed quantities of things, and she had already engaged a dressmaker to work for them.

'Thank you,' said Katy, 'but I don't think we need anything, We had our winter dresses made before we left home.'

'Winter dresses! last spring! My dear, what were you thinking of? They must be completely out of fashion!'

'You can't think how little Hillsover people know about fashion,' replied Katy, laughing.

'But, my dear, for your own sake!' exclaimed Mrs Page, distressed by these lax remarks. 'I'll look over your things tomorrow and see what you need.'

Katy did not dare to say no, but she felt rebellious. When they were half through tea, the door opened, and a boy came in.

'You are late, Clarence,' said Mr Page; while Mrs Page frowned and observed: 'Clarence makes a point of being late. He really deserves to be made to go without his supper. Shut the door, Clarence. Oh mercy! don't bang it in that way. I wish you would learn to shut a door properly. Here are your cousins, Katy and Clover Carr. Now let me see if you can shake hands with them like a gentleman, and not like a ploughboy.'

Clarence, a square, freckled boy of thirteen, with reddish hair, and a sort of red sparkle in his eyes, looked very angry at this address. He did not offer to shake hands at all, but elevating his shoulders said, 'How d'you do?' in a sulky voice, and sitting down at the table buried his nose without delay in a glass of milk. His mother gave a disgusted sigh.

'What a boy you are!' she said. 'Your cousins will think that you have never been taught anything, which is not the case; for I'm sure I've taken twice the pains with you that I have with Lilly. Pray excuse him, Katy. It's no use trying to make boys polite!'

'Isn't it?' said Katy, thinking of Phil and Dorry, and wondering what Mrs Page could mean.

'Hullo, Lilly!' broke in Clarence, spying his sister as it seemed for the first time.

'How d'you do?' said Lilly, carelessly. 'I was wondering how long it would be before you would condescend to notice my existence.'

'I didn't see you.'

'I know you didn't. I never knew such a boy. You might as well have no eyes at all.'

Clarence scowled, and went on with his supper. His mother seemed unable to let him alone. 'Clarence, don't take such large mouthfuls! Clarence, pray use your napkin! Clarence, you elbows are on the table, sir! Now, Clarence, don't try to speak until you have swallowed all that bread,' came every other moment. Katy felt very sorry for Clarence. His manners were certainly bad, but it seemed quite dreadful that public attention should be thus constantly called to them.

The evening was rather dull. There was a sort of put-in-order-for-company air about the parlour which made everybody stiff. Mrs Page did not sew or read, but sat in a low chair, looking like a lady in a fashion plate, and asked questions about Hillsover, some of which were not easy to answer, as, for example, 'Have you any other intimate friends among the schoolgirls besides Lilly?' About eight o'clock a couple of young, very young, gentlemen came in, at the sight of whom Lilly, who was half asleep, brightened and became lively and talkative. One of them was the Mr Hickman whose father married Mr Page's sister-in-law's sister, thus making him in some mysterious way a 'first cousin' of Lilly's. He was an Arrowmouth student, and seemed to have so many jokes to laugh over with Lilly that before long they withdrew to a distant sofa where they conversed in whispers. The other youth, introduced as Mr Eels, was left to entertain the other three ladies, which duty he performed by sucking the head of his cane in silence while they talked to him. He too was an Arrowmouth sophomore.

In the midst of the conversation, the door, which stood ajar, opened a little wider, and a dog's head appeared, followed by a tail, which waggled so beseechingly for leave to come farther that Clover, who liked dogs, put out her hand and said: 'Come here, poor fellow!' The dog ran up to her at once. He was not pretty, being of a pepper-and-salt colour, with a blunt nose and no particular sort of a tail, but he looked good-natured, and Clover fondled him cordially, while Mr Eels took his cane out of his mouth to ask: 'What kind of a dog is that, Mrs Page?'

'I'm sure I don't know,' she replied; while Lilly, from the distance, added affectedly: 'Oh, he's the most dreadful dog, Mr Eels. My brother picked him up in the street, and none of us knows the least thing about him, except that he's the commonest kind of dog – a sort of cur, I believe.'

'That's not true,' broke in a stern voice from the hall, which made everybody jump, and Katy, looking that way, was aware of a vengeful eye glaring at Lilly through the crack of the door. 'He's a very valuable dog indeed – half mastiff and half terrier, with a touch of the bulldog; so there, miss!'

The effect of this remark was startling. Lilly gave a scream; Mrs Page rose, and hurried to the door; while the dog, hearing his master's voice, rushed that way also, got before her, and almost threw her down. Katy and Clover could not help laughing, and Mr Eels, meeting their amused eyes, removed the cane from his mouth and grew conversable.

'That Clarence is a droll little chap,' he remarked confidentially. 'Bright, too! He'd be a nice fellow if he wasn't nagged at so much. It never does a fellow any good to be nagged at. Now, does it, Miss Carr?'

'No, I don't think it does.'

'I say,' continued Mr Eels, 'I've seen you young ladies up at Hillsover, haven't I? Aren't you both at the Nunnery?'

'Yes. It's vacation now, you know.'

'I was sure I'd seen you. You had a room on the side next the president's, didn't you? I thought so. We fellows didn't know your names, so we called you "the Real Nuns".'

'Real Nuns?'

'Yes, because you never looked out of the window at us. Real nuns and sham nuns – don't you see? Almost all the young ladies are sham nuns, except you, and two pretty little ones in the storey above, fifth window from the end.'

'Oh, I know!' said Clover, much amused. 'Sally Alsop, you know, Katy, and Amy Erskine. They are such nice girls!'

'Are they?' replied Mr Eels, with the air of one who notes down names for future reference. 'Well, I thought so. Not so much fun in them as some of the others, I guess; but a fellow likes other things as well as fun. I know if my sister was there, I'd rather have her take the dull line than the other.'

Katy treasured up this remark for the benefit of the SSUC Mrs Page came back just then, and Mr Eels resumed his cane. Nothing more was heard of Clarence that night.

Next morning Cousin Olivia fulfilled her threat of inspecting the girls' wardrobe. She shook her head over the simple, untrimmed merinos and thick cloth coats.

'There's no help for it,' she said, 'but it's a great pity. You would much better have waited, and had things fresh. Perhaps it may be possible to match the merino, and have some sort of basque arrangement added on. I will talk to Madame Chonfleur about it. Meantime I shall get one handsome thick dress for each of you, and have it stylishly made. That, at least, you really need.'

Katy was too glad to be so easily let off to raise objections. So that afternoon she and Clover were taken out to 'choose their material', Mrs Page said, but really to sit by while she chose it for them. At the dressmaker's it was the same: they stood passive while the orders were given and everything decided upon.

'Isn't it funny!' whispered Clover; 'but I don't like it a bit. Do you? It's just like Elsie saying how she'll have her doll's things made.'

'Oh, this dress isn't mine; it's Cousin Olivia's,' replied Katy. 'She's welcome to have it trimmed just as she likes.'

But when the suits came home she was forced to be pleased. There was no over-trimming, no look of finery; everything fitted perfectly, and had the air of finish which they had noticed and admired in Lilly's clothes. Katy almost forgot that she had objected to the dresses as unnecessary.

'After all, it is nice to look nice,' she confessed to Clover.

Excepting going to the dressmaker's, there was not much to amuse the girls during the first half of vacation. Mrs Page took them to drive now and then, and Katy found some pleasant books in the library, and read a good deal. Clover meantime made friends with Clarence. I think his heart was won that first evening by her attentions to Guest the dog, that mysterious composite, 'half mastiff and half terrier, with a touch of the bulldog'. Clarence loved Guest dearly, and was gratified that Clover liked him; for the poor animal had few friends in the household. In a little while Clarence became quite sociable with her, and tolerably so with Katy. They found him, as Mr Eels had said, 'a bright fellow', and pleasant and good-humoured enough when taken in the right way. Lilly always seemed to take him wrong, and his treatment of her was most disagreeable, snappish, and quarrelsome to the last degree.

'Much you don't like oranges!' he said one day at dinner, in answer to an innocent remark of hers. 'Much! I've seen you eat two at a time, without stopping. Papa, Lilly says she doesn't like oranges! I've seen her eat two at a time, without stopping! Much she doesn't! I've seen her eat two at a time, without stopping!' He kept this up for five minutes, looking from one person to another, and repeating, 'Much she doesn't! Much!' till Lilly was almost crying from vexation, and even Clover longed to box his ears. Nobody was sorry when Mr Page ordered him to leave the room, which he did with a last vindictive 'Much!' addressed to Lilly.

'How can Clarence behave so?' said Katy, when she and Clover were alone.

'I don't know,' replied Clover. 'He's such a nice boy sometimes; but when he isn't nice, he's the horridest boy I ever saw. I wish you'd talk to him, Katy, and tell him how dreadfully it sounds when he says such things.'

'No, indeed! He'd take it much better from you. You're nearer his age, and could do it nicely and pleasantly, and not make him feel as if he were being scolded. Poor fellow, he gets plenty of that!'

Clover said no more about the subject, but she meditated. She had a good deal of tact for so young a girl, and took care to get Clarence into a specially amicable mood before she began her lecture. 'Look here, you bad boy, how could you tease poor Lilly so yesterday? Guest, speak up, sir, and tell your massa how naughty it was!'

'Oh, dear! now you're going to nag!' growled Clarence, in an injured voice.

'No, I'm not – not the least in the world. I'll promise not to. But just tell me' – and Clover put her hands on the rough, red-brown hair, and stroked it – 'just tell me why you do such things? They're not a bit nice.'

'Lilly's so hateful!' grumbled Clarence.

'Well – she is sometimes, I know,' admitted Clover, candidly. 'But because she is hateful is no reason why you should be unmanly.'

'Unmanly!' cried Clarence, flushing.

'Yes. I call it unmanly to tease and quarrel, and contradict like that. It's like girls. They do it sometimes, but I didn't think a boy would. I thought he'd be ashamed!'

'Doesn't Dorry ever quarrel or tease?' asked Clarence, who liked to hear about Clover's brothers and sisters.

'Not now, and never in that way. He used to sometimes when he was little, but now he's very nice. He wouldn't speak to a girl as you speak to Lilly for anything in the world. He'd think it wasn't being a gentleman.'

'Stuff about gentleman, and all that!' retorted Clarence. 'Mother dings the word in my ears till I hate it.'

'Well, it is rather teasing to be reminded all the time, I admit; but you can't wonder that your mother wants you to be a gentleman, Clarence. It's the best thing in the world, I think. I hope Phil and Dorry will grow up just like Papa, for everybody says he's the most perfect gentleman, and it makes me so proud to hear them.'

'But what does it mean anyway? Mother says it's how you hold your fork, and how you chew, and how you put on your hat. If that's all, I don't think it amounts to much.'

'Oh, that isn't all! It's being gentle, don't you see? Gentle and nice to everybody, and just as polite to poor people as to rich ones,' said Clover, talking fast, in her eagerness to explain her meaning – 'and never being selfish, or noisy, or pushing people out of their place. Forks, and hats, and all that, are only little ways of making oneself more agreeable to other people. A gentleman is a gentleman inside – all through! Oh, I wish I could make you see what I mean!'

'Oh, that's it, is it?' said Clarence. Whether he understood or not, Clover could not tell; or whether she had done any good or not; but she had the discretion to say no more; and certainly Clarence was not offended, for after that day he grew fonder of her than ever. Lilly became absolutely jealous. She had never cared particularly for Clarence's affection, but she did not like to have anyone preferred above herself.

'It's pretty hard, I think,' she told Clover. 'Clare does everything you tell him, and he treats me awfully. It isn't a bit fair! I'm his sister, and you're only a second cousin.'

All this time the girls had seen almost nothing of Louisa Agnew. She called once, but Lilly received the call with them, and was so cool and stiff that Louisa grew cool and stiff also, and made but a short stay; and when the girls returned the visit she was out. A few days before the close of the vacation, however, a note came from her.

> DEAR KATY – I am so sorry not to have seen more of you and Clover. Won't you come and spend Wednesday with us? Mamma sends her love, and hopes you will come early, so as to have a long day, for she wants to know you. I long to show you the baby and everything. Do come. Papa will see you home in the evening. Remember me to Lilly. She has so many friends to see during the vacation that I am sure she will forgive me for stealing you for one day.
>
> Yours affectionately,
>
> LOUISA

Katy thought this message very politely expressed; but Lilly, when she heard it, tossed her head, and said she 'really thought Miss Agnew might let her name alone when she wrote notes'. Mrs Page seemed to pity the girls for having to go. They must, she supposed, as it was a schoolmate; but she feared it would be stupid for them. The Agnews were queer sort of people, not in society at all. Mr Agnew was clever, people said; but, really, she knew very little about the family. Perhaps it would not do to decline.

Katy and Clover had no idea of declining. They sent a warm little note of acceptance, and on the appointed day set off bright and early with a good deal of pleasant anticipation. The vacation had been rather dull at Cousin Olivia's. Lilly was a good deal with her own friends, and Mrs Page with her;

and there never seemed any special place where they might sit, or anything in particular for them to do.

Louisa's home was at some distance from Mr Page's, and in a less fashionable street. It looked pleasant and cosy as the girls opened the gate. There was a small garden in front with gay flower-beds; and on the piazza, which was shaded with vines, sat Mrs Agnew, with a little work-table by her side. She was a pretty and youthful-looking woman, and her voice and smile made them feel at home immediately.

'There is no need for anybody to introduce you,' she said. 'Lulu has described you so often that I know perfectly well which is Katy and which Clover. I am so glad you could come! Won't you go right into my bedroom by that long window and take off your things? Lulu has explained to you that I am lame and never walk, so you won't think it strange that I do not show you the way. She will be here in a moment. She ran upstairs to fetch the baby.'

The girls went into the bedroom. It was a pretty and unusual-looking apartment. The furniture was simple as could be, but bed and toilet and windows were curtained and frilled with white, and the walls were covered thick with pictures, photographs and pen-and-ink sketches, and water-colour drawings, unframed most of them, and just pinned up without regularity, so as to give each the best possible light. It was an odd way of arranging pictures; but Katy liked it, and would gladly have lingered to look at each one, only that she feared Mrs Agnew would expect them and would think it strange that they did not come back.

Just as they went out again to the piazza, Louisa came running downstairs with her little sister in her arms.

'I was curling her hair,' she explained, 'and did not hear you come in. Daisy, give Katy a kiss. Now another for Clover. Isn't she a darling?' embracing the child rapturously herself, 'now isn't she a little beauty?'

'Perfectly lovely!' cried the others, and soon all three were seated on the floor of the piazza, with Daisy in the midst, passing her from hand to hand as if she had been something good to eat. She was used to it, and submitted with perfect good-nature to being kissed, trotted, carried up and down, and generally made love to. Mrs Agnew sat by and laughed at the spectacle. When Baby was taken off for her noonday nap, Louisa took the girls into the parlour, another odd and pretty room, full of prints and sketches, and pictures of all sorts, some with frames, others with a knot of autumn leaves or a twist of ivy around them by way of a finish. There was a bowl of beautiful autumn roses on the table; and, though the price of one of Mrs Page's damask curtains would probably have bought the whole furniture of the room, everything was so bright and homelike and pleasant-looking that Katy's heart warmed at the sight. They were examining a portrait of Louisa with Daisy in her lap, painted by her father, when Mr Agnew came in. The girls liked his face at once. It was fine and frank; and nothing could be prettier than to see him pick up his sweet invalid wife as if she had been a child, and carry her into the dining-room to her place at the head of the table.

Katy and Clover agreed afterward that it was the merriest dinner they had had since they left home. Mr Agnew told stories about painters and painting, and was delightful. No less so was the nice gossip upstairs in Louisa's room which followed dinner, or the afternoon frolic with Daisy, or the long evening spent in looking over books and photographs. Altogether the day seemed only too short. As they went out of the gate at ten o'clock, Mr Agnew following, lo! a dark figure emerged from behind a tree and joined Clover. It was Clarence!

'I thought I'd just walk this way,' he explained; 'the house has been dreadfully dull all day without you.'

Clover was immensely flattered, but Mrs Page's astonishment next day knew no bounds.

'Really,' she said, 'I have hopes of Clarence at last. I never knew him volunteer to escort anybody anywhere before in his life.'

'I say,' remarked Clarence, the evening before the girls went back to school – 'I say, suppose you write to a fellow sometimes, Clover?'

'Do you mean yourself by "a fellow"?' laughed Clover.

'You don't suppose I meant George Hickman or that donkey of an Eels, did you?' retorted Clarence.

'No, I didn't. Well, I've no objection to writing to a fellow, if that fellow is you, provided the fellow answers my letters. Will you?'

'Yes,' gruffly, 'but you mustn't show them to any girls or laugh at my writing, or I'll stop. Lilly says my writing is like beetle tracks. Little she knows about it though! I don't write to her! Promise, Clover!'

'Yes, I promise,' said Clover, pleased at the notion of Clare's proposing a correspondence of his own accord. Next morning they all left for Hillsover. Clarence's friendship and the remembrance of their day with the Agnews were the pleasantest things that the girls carried away with them from their autumn vacation.

CHAPTER TEN

A Budget of Letters

Hillsover, October 21st

DEAREST ELSIE – I didn't write you last Saturday, because that was the day we came back to school, and there hasn't been one minute since when I could. We thought perhaps Miss Jane would let us off from the abstracts on Sunday, because it was the first day, and school was hardly begun; and, if she had, I was going to write to you instead, but she didn't. She said the only way to keep girls out of mischief was to keep them busy. Rose Red is sure that something has gone wrong with Miss Jane's missionary during the vacation – she's so dreadfully cross. Oh, dear, how I do hate to come back and be scolded by her again!

I forget if I told you about the abstracts. They are of the sermons on Sunday, you know, and we have to give the texts, and the heads, and as much as we can remember of the rest. Sometimes Dr Prince begins, 'I shall divide my subject into three parts', and tells what they are going to be. When he does that, most of the girls take out their pencils and note them down, and then they don't listen any more. Katy and I don't, for she says it isn't right not to listen some. Miss Jane pretends that she reads all the abstracts through, but she doesn't; for once, Rose Red, just to try her, wrote in the middle of hers, 'I am sitting by my window at this moment, and a red cow is going down the street. I wonder if she is any relation to Mrs Seccomb's cow?' and Miss Jane never noticed it, but marked her 'perfect' all the same. Wasn't it funny?

But I must tell you about our journey back. Mr Page came all the way with us, and was ever so nice. Clarence rode down in the carriage to the station. He gave me a really pretty india-rubber and gold pencil for a goodbye present. I think you and Dorry would like Clarence, only just as first you might say he was rather rude and cross. I did; but now I like him ever so much. Cousin Olivia gave Katy a worked collar and sleeves, and me an embroidered pocket-handkerchief with clover-leaves in the corner. Wasn't it kind? I'm sorry I said in my last letter that we didn't enjoy our vacation. We didn't, much; but it wasn't exactly Cousin Olivia's fault. She meant we should, but she didn't know how. Some people don't, you know. And don't tell anyone I said so, will you?

Rose Red got here in the train before we did. She was so glad when we came that she cried. It was because she was homesick waiting four hours at the Nunnery without us, she said. Rose is such a darling! She had a splendid vacation, and went to three parties and a picnic. Isn't it queer? her winter bonnet is black velvet trimmed with pink, and so is mine. I wanted blue at first, but Cousin Olivia said pink was more stylish; and now I am glad, because I like to be like Rose.

Katy and I have got No. 2 this term. It's a great deal pleasanter than our old room, and the entry-stove is just outside the door, so we shall keep warm. There is sun, too, only Mrs Nipson has nailed thick cotton over all the window except a little place at the top. Every window in the house is just so. You can't think how mad the girls are about it. The first night we had an indignation meeting, and passed resolutions, and some of the girls said they wouldn't stay – they should write to their fathers to come and take them home. None of them did, though. It's perfectly forlorn, not being able to look out. Oh, dear, how I wish it was spring!

We've got a new dining-room. It's a great deal bigger than the old one, so now we all eat together, and don't have any first and second tables. It's ever so much nicer, for I used to get so dreadfully hungry waiting that I didn't know what to do. One thing is horrid, though, and that is that every girl has to make a remark in French every day at dinner. The remarks are about a subject. Mrs Nipson gives out the subjects. Today the subject was 'Les oiseaux', and Rose Red said, 'J'aime beaucoup les oiseaux, et surtout ceux qui sont rôtis,' which made us all laugh. That ridiculous little Bella Arkwright said, 'J'aime beaucoup les oiseaux qui sing.' She thought sing was French! Every girl in the school began, 'J'aime beaucoup les oiseaux'! Tomorrow the subject is 'Jules César'. I'm sure I don't know what to say. There isn't a word in Ollendorf about him.

'There aren't so many new scholars this term as there were last. The girls think it is because Mrs Nipson isn't so popular as Mrs Florence used to be. Two or three of the new ones look pleasant, but I don't know them yet. Louisa Agnew is the nicest girl here next to Rose. Lilly Page says she is vulgar, because her father paints portraits and they don't know the same people that Cousin Olivia knows, but she isn't a bit. We went to spend the day there just before we left Ashburn, and her father and mother are splendid. Their house is just full of all sorts of queer, interesting things, and pictures; and Mr Agnew told us ever so many stories about painters, and what they did. One was about a boy who used to make figures of lions in butter, and afterward he became famous. I forget his name. We had a lovely time. I wish you could see Lou's little sister Daisy. She's only two, and a perfect little beauty. She has got ten teeth, and hardly ever cries.

Please ask Papa –

Just as Clover had got to this point she was interrupted by Katy, who walked in with her hat on, and a whole handful of letters.

'See here!' she cried. 'Isn't this delightful? Miss Marsh took me with her to the post-office, and we found these. Three for you and two for me, and one for Rose. Wait a minute till I give Rose hers, and we'll read them together.'

In another moment the two were cosily seated with their heads close together, opening their budget. First came one from Papa.

MY DEAREST DAUGHTERS –

'It's for you too, you see,' said Katy.

Last week came your letter of the 31st, and we were glad to hear that you were well and ready to go back to school. By the time this reaches you, you will be in Hillsover, and your winter term begun. Make the most of it, for we all feel as if we could never let you go from home again. Johnny says she shall rub Spalding's Prepared Glue all over your dresses when you come back, so that you cannot stir. I am a little of the same way of thinking myself. Cecy has returned from boarding-school, and set up as a young lady. Elsie is much excited over the party dresses which Mrs Hall is having made for her, and goes over every day to see if anything new has come. I am glad on this account that you are away just now, for it would not be easy to keep steady heads and continue your studies, with so much going on next door. I have sent Cousin Olivia a cheque to pay for the things she bought for you, and am much obliged to her for seeing that you were properly fitted out. Katy was very right to consider expense, but I wish you to have all things needful. I enclose two ten-dollar notes, one for each of you, for pocket-money; and, with much love from the children, am,

Yours affectionately,

P. CARR

PS – Cousin Helen has had a sharp attack, but is better.

'I wish Papa would write longer letters,' said Katy. 'He always sends us money, but he don't send half enough words with it.' She folded the letter, and fondled it affectionately.

'He's always so busy,' replied Clover. 'Don't you remember how he used to sit down at his desk and scrabble off his letters, and how somebody always was sure to ring the bell before he got through? I'm very glad to have some money, for now I can pay the sixty-two cents I owe you. It's my turn to read. This is from Elsie, and a real long one. Put away the notes first, Katy, or they'll be lost. That's right; now we'll begin together.'

DEAR CLOVER – You don't know how glad I am when my turn comes to get a letter all to myself. Of course I read Papa's, and all the rest you write to the family, but it never seems as if you were talking to me unless you begin 'Dear Elsie'. I wish sometime you'd put in a little note marked 'Private', just for me, which nobody else need see. It would be such fun! Please do. I should think you would have hated staying at Cousin Olivia's. When I read what she said about your travelling dresses looking as if they had come out of the Ark, I was too angry for anything. But I shouldn't think you'd want much to go back to school either, though sometimes it must be splendid. John has named her old stockinet doll, which she used to call 'Scratch-face', 'Nippy', after Mrs Nipson; and I made her a muslin cap, and Dorry drew a pair of black spectacles round her eyes. She is a perfect fright, and John plays all the time that dreadful things happen to her. She pricks her with pins, and pretends she has the earache, and lets her tumble down and hurt herself, till sometimes I nearly feel sorry, though it's all make-believe. When you wrote us about only having pudding for dinner, I didn't eat a bit. John put her into the rag-closet that very day, and has been starving her to death ever since, and Phil says it serves her right. You can't think how awfully lonely I sometimes get without you. If it wasn't for Helen Gibbs, that new girl I told you about, I shouldn't know what to do. She is the prettiest girl in Miss M'Crane's school. Her hair curls just like mine, only it is four times as long and a million times as thick, and her waist is really and truly not much bigger round than a bedpost. We're the greatest friends. She says she loves me just exactly as much as if I was her sister, but she never had any real sisters. She was quite angry the other day because I said I couldn't love her quite so well as you and Katy; and all recess-time she wouldn't speak to me, but now we've made up. Dorry is so awfully in love with her that I never can get him to come into the room when she is here, and he blushes when we tease him about her. But this is a great secret. Dorry and I play chess every evening. He almost always beats me unless Papa comes behind and helps me. Phil has learned too, because he always wants to do everything that we do. Dorry gives him a castle, and a bishop, and a knight, and four pawns, and then beats him in six moves. Phil gets so angry that we can't help laughing. Last night he buttoned his king up inside his jacket, and said: 'There! you can't checkmate me now, anyway!'

Cecy has come home. She is a young lady now. She does her hair up quite different, and wears long dresses. This winter she is going to parties, and Mrs Hall is going to have a party for her on Thursday, with real, grown-up young ladies and gentlemen at it. Cecy has got some beautiful new dresses – a white muslin, a blue tarlatan and a pink silk. The pink silk is the prettiest, I think. Cecy is so kind, and lets me see all her things. She has got a lovely breastpin too, and a new fan with ivory sticks, and all sorts of things. I wish I was grown up. It must be so nice. I want to tell you something, only you mustn't tell anybody except Katy. Don't you remember how Cecy used to say that she never was going out to drive with young gentlemen, but was going to stay at home and read the Bible to poor people? Well, she didn't tell the truth, for she has been out three times already with Sylvester Slack in his dogcart. When I told her she oughtn't to do so, because it was breaking a promise, she only laughed, and said I was a silly little girl. Isn't it queer?

I want to tell you what an awful thing I did the other night. Maria Avery invited me to tea, and Papa said I might go. I didn't want to much, but I didn't know what to tell Maria, so I went. You know how poor they are, and how Aunt Izzie used to say that they were 'touchy', so I thought I would take great care not to hurry home right after tea, for fear they would think I wasn't having a good time. So I waited, and waited, and waited, and got so sleepy that I had to pinch my fingers to keep awake. At last I was sure that it must be almost nine, so I asked Mr Avery if he'd please take me home; and you know, when we got there, it was quarter past ten, and Papa was just coming for me! Dorry said he thought I must be enjoying myself to stay so late. I didn't tell anybody about it for three days, because I knew they'd laugh at me, and they did. Wasn't it funny? And old Mrs Avery looked as sleepy as I felt, and kept yawning behind her hand. I told Papa if I had a watch of my own I shouldn't make such mistakes, and he laughed, and said, 'We'll see.' Oh, do you suppose that means that he's going to give me one?

We are so proud of Dorry's having taken two prizes at the examination yesterday. He took the second Latin prize, and the first Mathematics. Dr Pullman says he thinks Dorry is one of the most thorough boys he ever saw. Isn't that nice? The prizes were books; one was the *Life of Benjamin Franklin*, and the other the *Life of General Butler*. Papa says he doesn't think much of the *Life of Butler*. But Dorry has begun it, and says it is splendid. Phil says when he takes a prize he wants candy and a new knife; but he'll have to wait a good while unless he studies harder than he does now. He has just come in to tease me to go up into the garret and help him to get down his sled, because he thinks it is going to snow; but there isn't a sign of it, and the weather is quite warm. I asked him what I should say for him to you, and he said, 'Oh, tell her to come home, and anything you please.' I said, 'Shall I give her your love, and say that you are very well?' and he says, 'Oh, yes, Miss Elsie, I suppose you'd think yourself very well if your head ached as much as mine does every day.' Don't be frightened, however, for he's just as fat and rosy as can be; but almost every day he says he feels sick about school-time. When Papa was at Moorfield, Miss Finch believed him, and let him stay at home two mornings. I don't wonder at it, for you can't think what a face he makes up; but he got well so fast that she pays no attention to him now. The other day, about eleven o'clock, Papa met him coming along the road, shying stones at the birds and making lots of noise. He told Papa he felt so sick that his teacher had let him go home; but Papa noticed that his mouth looked sticky, so he opened his dinner-basket, and found that the little scamp had eaten up all his dinner on the road, corned beef, bread and butter, a great piece of mince-pie and six pears. Papa couldn't help laughing, but he made him turn round and go right back to school again.

I told you in my last about Johnnie's going to school with me now. She is very proud of it, and is always talking about 'Elsie's and my school'. She is twice as smart as the other little girls of her age. Miss M'Crane has put her into the composition class, where they write compositions on their slates. The first subject was, 'A Kitten'; and John's began, 'She's a dear, little, soft, scratching thing, only you'd better not pull her by the tail, but she's very clever.' All the girls laughed, and Johnnie called out, 'Well, it's true, anyhow.'

I can't write any more, for I must study my Latin. Besides, this is the longest letter that ever was. I have been four days writing it. Please send me one just as long. Old Mary and the children send lots of love, and Papa says, 'Tell Katy if a pudding diet sets her to growing again, she must come home at once, for he couldn't afford it.' Oh dear, how I wish I could see you! Please give my love to Rose Red. She must be perfectly splendid.

Your affectionate

ELSIE

'Oh, the dear little duck! Isn't that just like her?' said Clover. 'I think Elsie has a real genius for writing, don't you? She tells all the little things, and is so droll and funny. Nobody writes such nice letters. Who's that from, Katy?'

'Cousin Helen, and it's been such a long time coming. Just look at this date! September 22, a whole month ago!' Then she began to read.

DEAR KATY – It seems a long time since we have had a talk, but I have been less well lately, so that it has been difficult to write. Yesterday I sat up for the first time for several weeks, and today I am dressed and beginning to feel myself. I wish you could see my room this morning – I often wish this – but it is so particularly pretty, for little Helen has been in with a great basketful of leaves and flowers, and together we have dressed it to perfection. There are four vases of roses, a bowl full of chrysanthemums, and red leaves all round my pictures. The leaves are Virginia creeper. It doesn't last long, but is lovely while it lasts. Helen also brought a bird's nest which the gardener found in a hawthorn-tree on the lawn. It hangs on a branch, and she has tied it to one side of my bookshelves. On the opposite side is another nest quite different – a great, grey hornets' nest, as big as a band-box, which came from the mountains a year ago. I wonder if any such grow in the woods about Hillsover. In spite of the red leaves, the day is warm as summer, and the windows stand wide open. I suppose it is cooler with you, but I know it is deliciously cold. Now that I think of it, you must be in Ashburn by this time. I hope you will enjoy every moment of your vacation.

October 19th. I did not finish my letter the day it was begun, dear Katy, and next morning it proved that I was not so strong as I fancied, and I had to go to bed again. I am still there, and, as you see, writing with a pencil; but do not be worried about me, for the doctor says I am mending, and soon I hope to be up and in my chair. The red leaves are gone, but the roses are lovely as ever, for little Helen keeps bringing me fresh ones. She has just been in to read me her composition. The subject was 'Stars', and you can't think how much she found to say about them. She is a bright little creature, and it is a great pleasure to teach her. I am hardly ever so ill that she cannot come for her lessons, and she gets on fast. We have made an arrangement that when she knows more than I do she is to give me lessons, and I am not sure that the time is so very far off.

I must tell you about my Ben. He is a new canary which was given me in the summer, and lately he has grown so delightfully tame that I feel as if he were not a bird at all, but a fairy prince come to live with me and amuse me. The cage door is left open always now, and he flies in and out as he likes. He is a restless, inquisitive fellow, and visits any part of the room, trying each fresh thing with his bill to see if it is good to eat, and then perching on it to see if it is good to sit upon. He mistakes his own reflection in the looking-glass for another canary, and sits on the pincushion twittering and making love to himself for half an hour at a time. To watch him is one of my greatest amusements, especially just now when I am in bed so much. Sometimes he hides and keeps so still that I have not the least idea where he is. But the moment I call 'Ben, Ben,' and hold out my finger, wings begin to rustle, and out he flies and perches on my finger. He isn't the least bit in the world afraid, but sits on my head or shoulders, eats out of my mouth, and kisses me with his beak. He is on the pillow at this moment making runs at my pencil, of which he is mortally jealous. It is just so with my combs and brushes if I attempt to do my hair: he cannot bear to have me do anything but play with him. I do wish I could show him to you and Clover.

'Little Helen, my other pet, has just come in with a sponge-cake which she frosted herself. She sends her love, and says when you come to see me next summer she will frost you each one just like it. Goodbye, my Katy. I had nothing to write about and have written it, but I never like to keep silent too long, or let you feel as if you were forgotten by your loving cousin,

HELEN

PS – Be sure to wear plenty of warm wraps for your winter walks. And, Katy dear, you must eat meat every day. Mrs Nipson will probably give up her favourite puddings now that the cold weather has begun; but if not, write to Papa.

'Isn't that letter Cousin Helen all over?' said Katy; 'so little about her illness, and so bright and merry, and yet she has really been sick. Papa says "a sharp attack". Isn't she the dearest person in the world – next to Papa, I mean?'

'Yes, indeed. There's nobody like her. I do hope we can go to see her next summer. Now it's my turn. I can't think who this letter is from. Oh, Clarence! Katy, I can't let you see this. I promised Clare that I wouldn't show his letters to anybody, not even you!'

'Oh, very well! But you've got another. Dorry, isn't it? Read that first, and I'll go away and leave you in peace.'

So Clover read:

DEAR CLOVER – Elsie says she is going to write you today; but I won't stop, because next Saturday I'm going out fishing with the Slacks. There are a great many trout now in Blue Brook. Eugene caught six the other day – no, five, one was a minnow. Papa has given me a splendid rod, it lets out as tall as a house. I hope I shall catch with it. Alexander says the trout will admire it so much that they won't be able to help biting; but he was only teasing. Elsie and I play chess almost every night. She plays a really good game for a girl. Sometimes Papa helps her, and then she beats me. Miss Finch is well. She doesn't keep house quite as Katy did, and I don't like her so well as I do you, but she's pretty nice. The other day we had a nutting picnic, and she gave me and Phil a loaf of election cake and six quince turnovers to carry. The boys gave three cheers for her when they saw them. Did Elsie tell you that I have invented a new machine? It is called 'The Intellectual Peach Parer'. There is a place to hold a book while you pare the peaches. It is very convenient. I don't think of anything else to tell you. Cecy has got home, and is going to have a party next week. She's grown up now, she says, and she wears her hair quite different. It's a great deal thicker than it used to be. Elsie says it's because there are rats in it; but I don't believe her. Elsie has got a new friend. Her name is Helen Gibbs. She's quite pretty.

    Your affectionate brother,

Dorry

    PS – John wants to put in a note.

John's note was written in a round hand, as easy to read as print.

    Dear Clover – I am well, and hope you are the same. I wish you would write me a letter of my own. I go to school with Elsie now. We write compossizions. They are hard to write. We don't go up into the loft half so much as we used to when you ware at home. Mrs Worrett came to dinner last week. She says she ways two hundred and atey pounds. I should think it would be dredful to way that. I only way 76. My head comes up to the mark on the door where you ware mesured when you ware twelve. Isn't that tal? Goodbye. I send a kiss to Katy.

    Your loving

John

  After they had finished this note, Katy went away, leaving Clover to open Clarence's letter by herself. It was not so well written or spelt as Dorry's, by any means.

    Dear Clover – Don't forget what you promised. I mene about not showing this. And don't tell Lilly I rote. If you do, she'll be as angry as hops. I haven't been doing much since you went away. School begun yesterday, and I am glad, for it's awfully dull now that you girls have gone. Mother says Guest has got flees on him, so she won't let him come into the house any more. I stay out in the barn with him insted. He is well, and sends you a wag of his tail. Jim and me are making him a colar. It is black, with G.P. on it, for Guest Page, you know. A lot of the boys had a camping out last week. I went. It was splendid, but Mama wouldn't let me stay all night, so I lost the best part. They rosted scullpins for supper, and had a bonfire. The camp was on Harstnet Hill. Next time you come I'll take you out there. Papa has gone to Mane on bizness. He said I must take care of the house, so I've borrowed Jim's gun, and if any robers come I mean to shoot them. I always go to sleep with a broom agenst the door, so as to wake up when they open it. This morning I thought they had come, for the broom was gone, and the gun too; but it was only Briget. She opened the door, and it fell down; but I didn't wake up, so she took it away, and put the gun in the closset. I was angry, I can tell you.

This is only a short letter, but I hope you will answer it soon. Give my love to Katy, and tell Dorry that if he likes I'll send him my compas for his machenery, because I've got two.

Your affectionate Cousin,

CLARENCE PAGE

This was the last of the budget. As Clover folded it up, she was dismayed by the tinkle of the tea-bell.

'Oh, dear!' she cried, 'there's tea, and I have not finished my letter to Elsie. Where has the afternoon gone? How splendid it has been! I wish I could have four letters every day as long as I live.'

CHAPTER ELEVEN

Christmas Boxes

October was a delightful month, clear and sparkling; but early in November the weather changed, and became very cold. Thick frosts fell, every leaf vanished from the woods, in the gardens only blackened stalks remained to show where once the summer flowers had been. In spite of the stove outside the door, No. 2 began to be chilly; more than once Katy found her toothbrush stiff with ice in the morning. It was a foretaste of what winter was to be, and the girls shivered at the prospect.

Towards the end of November, Miss Jane caught a heavy cold. Unsparing of herself as of others, she went on hearing her classes as usual, and nobody paid much attention to her hoarseness and flushed cheeks, until she grew so much worse that she was forced to go to bed. There she stayed for nearly four weeks. It made a great change in the school, and the girls found it such a relief to have her sharp voice and eyes taken away that I am afraid they were rather glad of her illness than otherwise.

Katy shared in this feeling of relief. She did not like Miss Jane; it was pleasant not to have to see or hear of her. But as day after day passed, and still she continued ill, Katy's conscience began to prick. One night she lay awake a long time, and heard Miss Jane coughing violently. Katy feared she was very ill, and wondered who took care of her all night and all day. None of the girls went near her. The servants were always busy. And Mrs Nipson, who did not love Miss Jane, was busy too.

In the morning, while studying and practising, Katy caught herself thinking over this question. At last she asked Miss Marsh: 'How is Miss Jane today?'

'About the same. She is not dangerously ill, the doctor says; but she coughs a great deal, and has some fever.'

'Is anybody sitting with her?'

'Oh, no! there's no need of anyone. Susan answers the bell, and she has her medicine on the table within reach.'

It sounded forlorn enough. Katy had lived in a sickroom so long herself that she knew just how dreary it is for an invalid to be left alone with 'medicine within reach', and someone to answer a bell. She began to feel sorry for Miss Jane, and, almost without intending it, went down the entry, and tapped at her door. The 'Come in!' sounded very faint, and Miss Jane, as she lay in bed, looked weak and dismal, and quite unlike the sharp, terrible person whom the girls feared so much. She was amazed at the sight of Katy, and made a feeble attempt to hold up her head and speak as usual.

'What is it, Miss Carr?'

'I only came to see how you are,' said Katy, abashed at her own daring. 'You coughed so much last night that I was afraid you were worse. Isn't there something I could do for you?'

'Thank you,' said Miss Jane, 'you are very kind.'

Think of Miss Jane's thanking anybody, and calling anybody kind!

'I should be very glad. Isn't there anything?' repeated Katy, encouraged.

'Well, I don't know. You might put another stick of wood on the fire,' said Miss Jane, in an ungracious tone. Katy did so; and seeing that the iron cup on top of the stove was empty, she poured some water into it. Then she took a look about the room. Books and papers were scattered over the table; clean clothes from the wash lay on the chairs; nothing was in its place; and Katy, who knew how particular Miss

Jane was on the subject of order, guessed at the discomfort which this untidy state of affairs must have caused her.

'Wouldn't you like to have me put these away?' she asked, touching the pile of clothes.

Miss Jane sighed impatiently, but she did not say no; so Katy, taking silence for consent, opened the drawers, and laid the clothes inside, guessing at the right places with a sort of instinct, and making as little noise and bustle as possible. Next she moved quietly to the table, where she sorted and arranged the papers, piled up the books, and put the pens and pencils in a small tray which stood there for the purpose. Lastly she began to dust the table with her pocket-handkerchief, which proceeding roused Miss Jane at once.

'Don't!' she said, 'there is a duster in the cupboard.'

Katy could not help smiling, but she found the duster, and proceeded to put the rest of the room into nice order, laying a fresh towel over the bedside table, and arranging watch, medicine and spoon within reach.

Miss Jane lay and watched her. I think she was as much surprised at herself for permitting all this as Katy was at being permitted to do it. Sick people often consent because they feel too weak to object. After all, it was comfortable to have someone come in and straighten the things which for ten days past had vexed her neat eyes with their untidiness.

Lastly, smoothing the quilt, Katy asked if Miss Jane wouldn't like to have her pillow shaken up.

'I don't care,' was the answer. It sounded discouraging; but Katy boldly seized the pillow, beat, smoothed, and put it again in place. Then she went out of the room as noiselessly as she could, Miss Jane never saying thank you, or seeming to observe whether she went or stayed.

Rose Red and Clover could hardly believe their ears when told where she had been. They stared at her as people stare at Van Amburgh when he comes safely out of the lion's den.

'My stars!' exclaimed Rose, drawing a long breath. 'You didn't really? And she hasn't bitten your head off?'

'Not a bit,' said Katy, laughing. 'What's more, I'm going again.'

She was as good as her word. After that, she went to see Miss Jane very often. Almost always there was some little thing which she could do – the fire needed mending, or the pitcher to be filled with ice-water, or Miss Jane wanted the blinds opened or shut. Gradually she grew used to seeing Katy about the room. One morning she actually allowed her to brush her hair, and Katy's touch was so light and pleasant that afterwards Miss Jane begged her to do it every day. 'What makes you such a good nurse?' she asked one afternoon, rather abruptly.

'Being ill myself,' replied Katy, gently. Then, in answer to further questioning, she told of her four years' illness, and her life upstairs, keeping house and studying lessons all alone by herself. Miss Jane did not say anything when she got through, but Katy fancied that she looked at her in a new and kinder way.

So time went on till Christmas. It fell on a Friday that year, which shortened the holidays by a day and disappointed many of the girls. Only a few went home; the rest were left to pass the time as best they might till Monday, when lessons were to begin again.

'It isn't much like merry Christmas,' sighed Clover to herself, as she looked up at the uncottoned space at the top of the window, and saw great snowflakes wildly whirling by. No. 2 felt cold and dreary, and she was glad to exchange it for the schoolroom, round whose warm stove a cluster of girls were huddling. Everybody was in bad spirits; there was a tendency to talk about home and the nice time which people were having there, and the very bad time they themselves were having at the Nunnery.

'Isn't it mis–e–ra–ble? I shall cry all night, I know I shall, I am so homesick,' gulped Lilly, who had taken possession of her room-mate's shoulder, and was weeping ostentatiously.

'I declare you're just Mrs Gummidge in *David Copperfield* over again,' said Rose. 'You recollect her, girls, don't you? When the porridge was burnt, you know – "All of us felt the disappointment but Mrs Gummidge felt it the most." Isn't Lilly a real Mrs Gummidge, girls?'

This observation changed Lilly's tears into anger. 'You're as hateful and as horrid as you can be, Rose Red,' she exclaimed angrily. Then she flew out of the room, and shut the door behind her with a bang.

'There! she's gone upstairs to be angry,' said Louisa Agnew.

'I don't care if she has,' replied Rose, who was in a perverse mood.

'I wish you hadn't said that, Rosy,' whispered Clover. 'Lilly really felt badly.'

'Well, what if she did? So do I feel badly, and you, and the rest of us. Lilly hasn't taken out a patent for bad feelings, which nobody must infringe. What business has she to make us feel badder, by setting up to be so much worse off than the rest of the world?'

Clover said nothing, but went on with a book she was reading. In less than ten minutes, Rose, whose sun seldom stayed long behind a cloud, was at her elbow, dimpling and coaxing.

'I forgive you,' she whispered, giving Clover's arm a little pinch.

'What for?'

'For being in the right. About Lilly, I mean. I was rather hateful to her, I confess. Never mind. When she comes downstairs, I'll make up. She's a crocodile, if ever there was one; but, as she's your cousin, I'll be good to her. Kiss me quick to prove that you're not vexed.'

'Vexed, indeed!' said Clover, kissing the middle of the

pink cheek. 'I wonder if anybody ever stayed vexed with you for ten minutes together, you Rosy-Posy, you?'

'Bless you, yes! Miss Jane, for example. She hates me like poison, and all the time – well, what of it? I know she's sick, but I "can't tell a lie, Pa," on that account. Where's Katy?'

'Gone in to see her, I believe.'

'One of these days,' prophesied Rose, solemnly, 'she'll go into that room, and she'll never come out again! Miss Jane is getting back into biting condition. I advise Katy to be careful. What's that noise? Sleighbells, I declare! Girls' – mounting a desk, and peeping out of the window – 'somebody's got a big box – a big one! Here's old Joyce at the door with his sledge. Now, who do you suppose it is?'

'It's for me. I'm sure it's for me,' cried half a dozen voices.

'Bella, my love, peep over the balusters, and see if you can't see the name,' cried Louisa; and Bella, nothing loath, departed at once on this congenial errand.

'No, I can't,' she reported, coming back from the hall. 'The name's tipped up against the wall. There's two boxes! One is big and one is little!'

'Oh, who can they be for?' clamoured the girls. Half the school expected boxes, and had been watching the storm all day, with a dreadful fear that it would block the roads and delay the expected treasures.

At this moment Mrs Nipson came in.

'There will be the usual study-hour this evening,' she announced. 'All of you will prepare lessons for Monday morning. Miss Carr, come here for a moment, if you please.'

Clover, wondering, followed her into the entry.

'A parcel has arrived for you, and a box,' said Mrs Nipson. 'I presume that they contain articles for Christmas. I will have the nails removed, and both of them placed in your room this evening, but I expect you to refrain from examining them until tomorrow. The vacation does not open until after study-hour tonight, and it will then be too late for you to begin.'

'Very well, ma'am,' said Clover, demurely. But the minute Mrs Nipson's back was turned, she gave a jump, and rushed into the schoolroom.

'Oh, girls,' she cried, 'what do you think? Both the boxes are for Katy and me!'

'Both!' cried a disappointed chorus.

'Yes, both. Mrs Nipson said so. I'm so sorry for you. But isn't it nice for us? We've never had a box from home before, you know; and I didn't think we should, it's so far off. It's too lovely! But I do hope yours will come tonight.'

Clover's voice was so sympathising, for all its glee, that nobody could help being glad with her.

'You little darling!' said Louisa, giving her a hug. 'I'm rejoiced that the box is yours. The rest of us are always getting them, and you and Katy never had a thing before. I hope it's a nice one!'

'Oh, it's sure to be nice! It's from home, you know,' responded Clover, with a happy smile. Then she left the room, to find Katy and tell the wonderful news.

Study-hour seemed unusually long that night. The minute it was over, the sisters ran to No. 2. There stood the boxes, a big wooden one, with all the nails taken out of the lid, and a small paper one, carefully tied up and sealed. It was almost more than the girls could do to obey orders and not peep.

'I feel something hard,' announced Clover, inserting a fingertip under the lid.

'Oh, do you?' cried Katy. Then, making an heroic effort, she jumped into bed.

'It's the only way,' she said; 'you'd better come too, Clovy. Blow the candle out, and let's get to sleep as fast as we can, so as to make morning come quicker.'

Katy dreamed of home that night. Perhaps it was that

which made her wake so early. It was not five o'clock, and the room was perfectly dark. She did not like to disturb Clover, so she lay perfectly still, for hours as it seemed, till a faint grey dawn crept in, and revealed the outlines of the big box standing by the window. Then she could wait no longer, but crept out of bed, crossed the floor on tiptoe, and raising the lid put in her hand. Something crumby and sugary met it, and when she drew it out, there, fitting on her finger like a ring, was a round cake with a hole in the middle of it.

'Oh, it's one of Debby's jumbles!' she exclaimed.

'Where? What are you doing? Give me one too!' cried Clover, starting up. Katy rummaged till she found another, then, half frozen, she ran back to bed; and the two lay nibbling the jumbles, and talking about home, till dawn deepened into daylight, and morning was fairly come.

Breakfast was half an hour later than usual, which was comfortable. As soon as it was over, the girls proceeded to unpack their box. The day was so cold that they wrapped themselves in shawls, and Clover put on a hood and thick gloves. Rose Red, passing the door, burst out laughing, and recommended that she should add galoshes and an umbrella.

'Come in,' cried the sisters – 'come in, and help us open our box.'

'Oh, by the way, you have a box, haven't you?' said Rose, who was perfectly aware of the important fact, and had presented herself with the hope of being asked to look on. 'Thank you; but perhaps I would better come some other time. I shall be in your way.'

'You humbug!' said Clover, while Katy seized Rose and pulled her into the room. 'There, sit on the bed, you ridiculous goose, and put on my grey cloak. How can you be so absurd as to say you won't? You know we want you, and you know you came on purpose.'

'Did I? Well, perhaps I did,' laughed Rose. Then Katy lifted off the lid and set it against the door. It was an exciting moment.

'Just look here!' cried Katy.

The top of the box was mostly taken up with four square paper boxes, round which parcels of all shapes and sizes were wedged and fitted. The whole was a miracle of packing. It had taken Miss Finch three mornings, with assistance from old Mary, and much advice from Elsie, to do it so beautifully.

Each box held a different kind of cake. One was full of jumbles, another of ginger-snaps, a third of crullers, and the fourth contained a big square loaf of frosted plum-cake, with a circle of sugar almonds set in the frosting. How the trio exclaimed at this!

'I never imagined anything so nice,' declared Rose, with her mouth full of jumble. 'As for those snaps, they're simply perfect. What can be in all those fascinating bundles? Do hurry and open one, Katy.' Dear little Elsie! The first two bundles opened were hers, a white hood for Katy, and a blue one for Clover, both of her own knitting, and so nicely done. The girls were enchanted.

'How she has improved!' said Katy. 'She knits better than either of us, Clover.'

'There never was such a clever little darling!' responded Clover, and they patted the hoods, tried them on before the glass, and spent so much time in admiring them that Rose grew impatient.

'I declare,' she cried, 'it isn't any of my funeral, I know; but if you don't open another parcel soon, I shall certainly fall to myself. It seems as if, what with cold and curiosity, I couldn't wait.'

'Very well,' said Katy, laying aside her hood, with one final glance. 'Take out a bundle, Clover. It's your turn.'

Clover's bundle was for herself, *Evangeline*, in blue and

gold; and pretty soon the *Golden Legend*, in the same binding, appeared for Katy. Both these were from Dorry. Next came a couple of round packages of exactly the same size. These proved to be inkstands, covered with Russia leather; one marked, 'Katy from Johnnie', and the other, 'Clover from Phil'. It was evident that the children had done their shopping together, for presently two long, narrow parcels revealed carved pen-handles, precisely alike; and these were labelled, 'Katy from Phil', and 'Clover from Johnnie'.

What fun it was opening those bundles! The girls made a long business of it, taking out but one at a time, exclaiming, admiring and exhibiting to Rose before they began upon another. They laughed, they joked, but I do not think it would have taken much to make either of them cry. It was almost too tender a pleasure, these proofs of loving remembrance from the little ones; and each separate article seemed full of the very look and feel of home.

'What can this be?' said Katy, as she unrolled a paper and disclosed a pretty, round box. She opened. Nothing was visible but pink cotton-wool. Katy peeped beneath, and gave a cry.

'Oh Clovy! Such a lovely thing! It's from Papa – of course it's from Papa. How could he? It's a great deal too pretty.'

The 'lovely thing' was a long, slender chain for Katy's watch, worked in fine, yellow gold. Clover admired it extremely; and her joy knew no bounds when further search revealed another box with a precisely similar chain for herself. It was too much. The girls fairly cried with pleasure.

'There never was such a papa in the world!' they said.

'Yes, there is. Mine is just as good,' declared Rose, twinkling away a little teardrop from her own eyes. 'Now don't cry, honeys. Your papa's an angel, there's no doubt about it. I never saw such pretty chains in my life – never. As for the children, they're little ducks. You certainly are a wonderful family. Katy, I'm dying to know what is in that blue parcel.'

The blue parcel was from Cecy, and contained a pretty blue ribbon for Clover. There was a pink one also, with a pink ribbon for Katy. Everybody had thought of the girls. Old Mary sent them each a yard measure; Miss Finch, a thread-case, stocked with differently coloured cottons. Alexander had cracked a bag full of hickory nuts.

'Did you ever!' said Rose, when this last was produced. 'What a thing it is to be popular! Mrs Hall? Who's Mrs Hall?' as Clover unwrapped a tiny carved easel.

'She's Cecy's mother,' explained Clover. 'Wasn't she kind to send me this, Katy? And here's Cecy's photograph in a little frame for you.'

Never was such a wonderful box. It appeared to have no bottom whatever. Under the presents were parcels of figs, prunes, almonds, raisins, candy; under those, apples and pears. There seemed no end to the surprises.

At last all were out.

'Now,' said Katy, 'let's throw back the apples and pears, and then I want you to help me divide the other things, and make up some packages for the girls. They are all so disappointed not to have their boxes. I should like to have them share ours. Wouldn't you, Clover?'

'Yes, indeed. I was just going to propose it.'

So Clover cut twenty-nine squares of white paper, Rose and Katy sorted and divided, and pretty soon ginger-snaps and almonds and sugarplums were walking down all the entries, and a gladsome crunching showed that the girls had found pleasant employment. None of the snowed-up boxes got through till Monday, so except for Katy and Clover the school would have had no Christmas treat at all.

They carried Mrs Nipson a large slice of cake, and a basket full of the beautiful red apples. All the teachers were remembered, and the servants. The SSUC was convened and feasted; and as for Rose, Louisa, and other special cronies, dainties were heaped upon them with such unsparing hand that they finally remonstrated.

'You're giving everything away. You'll have none left for yourselves.'

'Yes, we shall – plenty,' said Clover. 'Oh Rosy! here's such a splendid pear! You must have this.'

'Not no!' protested Rose; but Clover forced it into her pocket.

'The Carrs' Box' was always quoted in the Nunnery afterward as an example of what papas and mammas could accomplish, when they were of the right sort, and really wanted to make schoolgirls happy. Distributing their treasures kept Katy and Clover so busy that it was not until after dinner that they found time to open the smaller box. When they did so, they were sorry for the delay. The box was full of flowers, roses, geranium leaves, heliotrope, beautiful red and white carnations, all so bedded in cotton that the frost had not touched them. But they looked chilled, and Katy hastened to put them in warm water, which she had been told was the best way to revive drooping flowers.

Cousin Helen had sent them; and underneath, sewed to the box, that they might not shake about and do mischief, were two flat parcels, wrapped in tissue paper, and tied with white ribbon, in Cousin Helen's dainty way. They were glove-cases of quilted silk, delicately scented, one white and one lilac; and to each was pinned a loving note, wishing the girls a Merry Christmas.

'How awfully good people are!' said Clover. 'I do think we ought to be the best girls in the world.'

Last of all Katy made a choice little selection from her stores, a splendid apple, a couple of fine pears, a handful of raisins and figs, and, with a few of the freshest flowers in a wineglass, she went down the Row and tapped at Miss Jane's door.

Miss Jane was sitting up for the first time, wrapped in a shawl and looking very thin and pale. Katy, who had almost ceased to be afraid of her, went in cheerily.

'We've had a delicious box from home, Miss Jane, full of all sorts of things. It has been such fun unpacking it! I've brought you an apple, and some pears, and this little bunch of flowers. Wasn't it a nice Christmas for us?'

'Yes,' said Miss Jane, 'very nice indeed. I heard someone saying in the entry that you had a box. Thank you,' as Katy set the basket and glass on the table. 'Those flowers are very sweet. I wish you a Merry Christmas, I'm sure.'

This was much from Miss Jane, who couldn't help speaking shortly, even when she was pleased. Katy withdrew in high glee.

But that night, just before bedtime, something happened so surprising that Katy, telling Clover about it afterward, said she half fancied that she must have dreamed it all. It was about eight o'clock in the evening: she was passing down Quaker Row and Miss Jane called and asked her to come in. Miss Jane's cheeks were flushed, and she spoke fast, as if she had resolved to say something, and thought the sooner it was over the better.

'Miss Carr,' she began, 'I wish to tell you that I made up my mind some time since that we did you an injustice last term. It is not your attentions to me during my illness which have changed my opinion – that was done before I fell ill. It is your general conduct, and the good influence which I have seen you exert over other girls, which convinced me that we must have been wrong about you. That is all. I thought you might like to hear me say this, and I shall say the same to Mrs Nipson.'

'Thank you,' said Katy, 'you don't know how glad I am!' She half thought she would kiss Miss Jane, but somehow it didn't seem possible; so she shook hands very heartily instead, and flew to her room, feeling as if her feet were wings.

'It seems too good to be true. I want to cry, I am so happy,' she told Clover. 'What a lovely day this has been!'

And of all that she had received, I think Katy considered this explanation with Miss Jane as her very best Christmas box.

CHAPTER TWELVE

Waiting for Spring

School was a much happier place after this. Mrs Nipson never alluded to the matter, but her manner altered. Katy felt that she was no longer watched or distrusted, and her heart grew light.

In another week Miss Jane was so much better as to be hearing her classes again. Illness had not changed her materially. It is only in novels that rheumatic fever sweetens tempers, and makes disagreeable people over into agreeable ones. Most of the girls disliked her as much as ever. Her tongue was just as sharp, and her manner as grim. But for Katy, from that time forward there was a difference. Miss Jane was not affectionate to her – it was not in her nature to be that – but she was civil and considerate, and, in a dry way, friendly, and gradually Katy grew to have an odd sort of liking for her.

Do any of you know how incredibly long winter seems in climates where for weeks together the thermometer stands at zero? There is something hopeless in such cold. You think of summer as of a thing read about somewhere in a book, but which has no actual existence. Winter seems the only reality in the world.

Katy and Clover felt this hopelessness growing upon them as the days went on, and the weather became more and more severe. Ten, twenty, even thirty degrees below zero, was no unusual register for the Hillsover thermometers. Such cold half frightened them, but nobody else was frightened or surprised. It was dry, brilliant cold. The December snows

lay unmelted on the ground in March, and the paths cut
then were crisp and hard still, only the white walls on either
side had risen higher and higher, till only a moving line of
hoods and tippets was visible above them when the school
went out for its daily walk. Morning after morning the girls
woke to find thick crusts of frost on their windowpanes, and
every drop of water in washbowl or pitcher turned to solid
ice. Night after night, Clover, who was a chilly little
creature, lay shivering and unable to sleep, notwithstanding
the hot bricks at her feet, and the many wraps which Katy
piled upon her. To Katy herself the cold was more bracing
than depressing. There was something in her blood which
responded to the sharp tingle of frost, and she gained in
strength in a remarkable way during this winter. But the
long storms told upon her spirits. She pined for spring and
home more than she liked to tell, and felt the need of variety
in their monotonous life, where the creeping days appeared
like weeks, and the weeks stretched themselves out, and
seemed as long as months do in other places.

The girls resorted to all sorts of devices to keep themselves alive during this dreary season. They had little
epidemics of occupation. At one time it was 'spattering',
when all faces and fingers had a tendency to smudges of
India ink and there was hardly a fine comb or toothbrush fit
for use in the establishment. Then a rage for tatting set in,
followed by a fever of fancywork, everyone falling in love
with the same pattern at the same time, and copying and
recopying, till nobody could bear the sight of it. At one time
Clover counted eighteen girls all at work on the same bead-
and-canvas pincushion. Later there was a short period of
decalcomanie; and then came the grand album craze, when
thirty-three girls out of the thirty-nine sent for blank books
bound in red morocco, and began to collect signatures and
sentiments. Here, also, there was a tendency towards
repetition.

Sally Austin added to her autograph these lines of her own composition:

> When on this page your beauteous eyes you bend,
> Let it remind you of your absent friend.
>
> SALLIE J. AUSTIN
> Galveston, Texas

The girls found this sentiment charming, at least a dozen borrowed it, and in half the albums in the school you might read: 'When on this page your beauteous eyes', &c.

Esther Dearborn wrote in Clover's book: 'The better part of Valour is Discretion.' Why she wrote it, nobody knew, or why it was more applicable to Clover than to anyone else; but the sentiment proved popular, and was repeated over and over again, above various neatly written signatures. There was a strife as to who should display the largest collection. Some of the girls sent home for autographs of distinguished persons, which they pasted in their books. Rose Red, however, outdid them all.

'Did I ever show you mine?' she asked one day, when most of the girls were together in the schoolroom.

'No, never!' cried a number of voices. 'Have you got one? Oh, do let us see it!'

'Certainly, I'll get it at once, if you like,' said Rose, obligingly.

She went to her room, and returned with a shabby old blank book in her hand. Some of the girls looked disappointed.

'The cover of mine isn't very nice,' explained Rose. 'I'm going to have it rebound one of these days. You see, it's not a new album at all, nor a school album; but it's very valuable to me.' Here she heaved a sentimental sigh. 'All my friends have written in it,' she said.

The girls were quite impressed by the manner in which Rose said this. But, when they turned over the pages of the album, they were even more impressed. Rose had evidently been on intimate terms with a circle of most distinguished persons. Half the autographs in the book were from gentlemen, and they were dated all over the world.

'Just listen to this!' cried Louisa, and she read:

'Thou may'st forget me, but never, never shall I forget thee!

ALPHONSO OF CASTILLE
The Escurial, April 1st.'

'Who's he?' asked a circle of awestruck girls.

'Didn't you ever hear of him? Youngest brother of the King of Spain,' replied Rose, carelessly.

'Oh, my! and just hear this,' exclaimed Annie Silsbie.

'If you ever deign to cast a thought in my direction, Miss Rose, remember me always as
    Thy devoted servitor,

POTEMKIN MONTMORENCY
St Petersburg, July 10th.'

'And this,' shrieked Alice White.

'They say love is a thorn, I say it is a dart,
And yet I cannot tear thee from my heart.

ANTONIO, *Count of Vallambrosa*.'

'Do you really and truly know a count?' asked Bella, backing away from Rose with eyes as big as saucers.

'Know Antonio de Vallambrosa! I should think I did,' replied Rose. 'Nobody in this country knows him so well, I fancy.'

'And he wrote that for you?'

'How else could it get into my book, goosey?'

This was unanswerable; and Rose was installed from that time forward in the minds of Bella and the rest as a heroine of the first water. Katy, however, knew better; and the first time she caught Rose alone she attacked her on the subject.

'Now, Rosy-Posy, confess. Who wrote all those absurd autographs in your book?'

'Absurd autographs! What can you mean?'

'All those counts and things. No, it's no use. You shan't wriggle away till you tell me.'

'Oh, Antonio and dear Potemkin; do you mean them?'

'Yes, of course I do.'

'And you really want to know?'

'Yes.'

'And will swear not to tell?'

'Yes.'

'Well, then,' bursting into a laugh, 'I wrote every one of them myself.'

'Did you really? When?'

'Day before yesterday. I thought Lilly needed taking down, she was so set up with her autographs of Wendell Phillips and Mr Seward, so I just sat down and wrote a book full. It only took me half an hour. I meant to write some more: in fact, I had one all ready:

> I am dead, or pretty near:
> David's done for me I fear.
>
> GOLIATH OF GATH.

But I was afraid even Bella wouldn't swallow that, so I tore out the page. I'm sorry I did now, for I really think the geese would have believed it. Written in his last moments, you know, to oblige an ancestor of my own,' added Rose, in a tone of explanation.

'You monkey!' cried Katy, highly diverted. But she kept Rose's counsel, and I dare say some of the Hillsover girls believe in that wonderful album to this day.

It was not long after that a sad piece of news came for Bella. Her father was dead. Their home was in Iowa, too far to allow of her returning to the funeral; so the poor little girl stayed at school, to bear her trouble as best she might. Katy, who was always kind to children, and had somewhat affected Bella from the first on account of her resemblance to Elsie in height and figure, was especially tender to her now, which Bella repaid with the gift of her whole queer little heart. Her affectionate demonstrations were rather of the monkey order, and not infrequently troublesome; but Katy was never otherwise than patient and gentle with her, though Rose, and even Clover, remonstrated on what they called this 'singular intimacy'.

'Poor little soul! It's so hard for her, and she's only eleven years old,' she told them.

'She has such a funny way of looking at you sometimes,' said Rose, who was very observant. 'It is just the air of a squirrel who has hidden a nut, and doesn't want you to find out where, and yet can hardly help indicating it with his paw. She's got something on her mind, I'm sure.'

'Half a dozen things, very likely,' added Clover; 'she's such a mischief.'

But none of them guessed what this 'something' was.

Early in January, Mrs Nipson announced that in four weeks she proposed to give a 'soirée', to which all young ladies whose records were entirely free from marks during the intervening period would be allowed to come. This announcement created great excitement, and the school set itself to be good; but marks were easy to get, and gradually one girl after another lost her chance, till by the appointed day only a limited party descended to join the festivities, and nearly half the school was left upstairs to sigh over past sins. Katy and Rose were among the unlucky ones. Rose had incurred a mark by writing a note in study-hour, and Katy by being five minutes late for dinner. They consoled themselves by dressing Clover's hair, and making her look as pretty as possible, and then stationed themselves in the upper hall at the head of the stairs to watch her career, and get as much fun out of the occasion as they could.

Pretty soon they saw Clover below on Professor Seccomb's arm. He was a kindly, pleasant man, with a bald head, and it was a fashion among the girls to admire him.

'Doesn't she look pretty?' said Rose. 'Just notice Mrs Searles, Katy. She's grinning at Clover like the Cheshire cat. What a wonderful cap that is of hers! She had it when Sylvia was here at school, eight years ago.'

'Hush! she'll hear you.'

'No, she won't. There's Ellen beginning her piece. I know she's frightened by the way she plays. Hark! how she hurries the time!'

'There, they are going to have refreshments, after all!' cried Esther Dearborn, as trays of lemonade and cake-baskets appeared below on their way to the parlour. 'Isn't it a shame to have to stay up here?'

'Professor Seccomb! Professor!' called Rose in a daring whisper. 'Take pity upon us. We are starving for a piece of cake.'

The professor gave a jump; then retreated, and looked upward. When he saw the circle of hungry faces peering down, he doubled up with laughter. 'Wait a moment,' he whispered back, and vanished into the parlour. Pretty soon the girls saw him making his way through the crowd with an immense slice of pound-cake in each hand.

'Here, Miss Rose,' he said – 'catch it.' But Rose ran halfway downstairs, received the cake, dimpled her thanks, and retreated to the darkness above, whence sounds proceeded which sent the amused professor into the parlour convulsed with suppressed laughter. Pretty soon Clover stole up the back stairs to report.

'Are you having a nice time? Is the lemonade good? Who have you been talking with?' enquired a chorus of voices.

'Pretty nice. Everybody is very old. I haven't been talking to anybody in particular, and the lemonade is only cream-of-tartar water. I think it's jollier up here with you,' replied

Clover. 'I must go now: my turn to play comes next.' Down she ran.

'Except for the glory of the thing, I think we're having more fun than she,' answered Rose.

Next week came St Valentine's Day. Several of the girls received valentines from home, and they wrote them to each other. Katy and Clover both had one from Phil, exactly alike, with the same purple bird in the middle of the page and 'I love you' printed underneath; and they joined in fabricating a gorgeous one for Rose, which was supposed to come from Potemkin de Montmorency, hero of the album. But the most surprising valentine was received by Miss Jane. It came with the others while all the household were at dinner. The girls saw her redden and look angry, but she put the letter in her pocket, and said nothing.

In the afternoon, it came out through Bella that 'Miss Jane's letter was in poetry, and that she was just as angry as fire about it'. Just before tea, Louisa came running down the Row, to No. 5, where Katy was sitting with Rose.

'Girls, what do you think? That letter which Miss Jane got this morning was a valentine, the most dreadful thing, but so funny!' she stopped to laugh.

'How do you know?' cried the other two.

'Miss Marsh told Alice Gibbons. She's a sort of cousin, you know; and Miss Marsh often tells her things. She says Miss Jane and Mrs Nipson are furious, and are determined to find out who sent it. It was from Mr Hardhack, Miss Jane's missionary – or no, not from Mr Hardhack, but from a cannibal who had just eaten Mr Hardhack up; and he sent Miss Jane a lock of his hair and the recipe the tribe cooked him by. They found him "very nice", he said, and "he turned out quite tender". That was one of the lines in the poem. Did you ever hear anything like it? Who do you suppose could have sent it?'

'Who could it have been?' cried the others. Katy had one

moment's awful misgiving; but a glance at Rose's face, calm
and innocent as a baby's, reassured her. It was impossible
that she could have done this mischievous thing. Katy, you
see, was not privy to that entry in Rose's journal, 'Pay Miss
Jane off', nor aware that Rose had just written underneath,
'Did it. February 14, 1869.'

Nobody ever found out the author of this audacious
valentine. Rose kept her own counsel, and Miss Jane
probably concluded that 'the better part of valour was
discretion', for the threatened enquiries were never made.

And now it lacked but six weeks to the end of the term.
The girls counted the days, and practised various devices to
make them pass quickly. Esther Dearborn, who had a turn
for arithmetic, set herself to a careful calculation of how
many hours, minutes and seconds must pass before the
happy time should come. Annie Silsbie strung forty-two
tiny squares of cardboard on a thread, and each night
slipped one off and burned it up in the candle. Others made
diagrams of the time, with a division for each, and every
night blotted one out with a sense of triumph. None of these
devices made the time hasten. It never moved more slowly
than now, when life seemed to consist of a universal waiting.

But though Katy's heart bounded at the thought of home
till she could hardly bear the gladness, she owned to Clover:
'Do you know, much as I long to get away, I am half sorry to
go! It is parting with something which we shall never have
any more. Home is lovely, and I would rather be there than
anywhere else; but, if you and I live to be a hundred, we shall
never be girls at boarding-school again.'

CHAPTER THIRTEEN

Paradise Regained

'Only seven days more to cross off,' said Clover, drawing her pencil through one of the squares on the diagram pinned beside her looking-glass, 'seven more, and then – oh, joy! – Papa will be here, and we shall start for home.'

She was interrupted by the entrance of Katy, holding a letter and looking pale and aggrieved.

'Oh, Clover,' she cried, 'just listen to this. Papa can't come for us. Isn't it too bad?' And she read:

> *Burnet*, March 20th
>
> MY DEAR GIRLS – I find that it will not be possible for me to come for you next week, as I intended. Several people are severely ill, and old Mrs Barlow struck down suddenly with paralysis, so I cannot leave. I am sorry, and so will you be; but there is no help for it. Fortunately, Mrs Hall has just heard that some friends of hers are coming westward with their family, and she has written to ask them to take charge of you. The drawback to this plan is that you will have to travel alone as far as Albany, where Mr Peters (Mrs Hall's friend) will meet you. I have written to ask Mr Page to put you on the train, and under the care of the conductor, on Tuesday morning. I hope you will get through without embarrassment. Mr Peters will be at the station in Albany to receive you; or, if anything should hinder him, you are to drive at once to the Delavan House, where they are staying. I enclose a cheque for your journey. If Dorry were five years older, I should send him after you.

The children are most impatient to have you back. Miss Finch has been suddenly called away by the illness of her sister-in-law, so Elsie is keeping house till your return.

God bless you, my dear daughters, and send you safe!

Yours affectionately,   P. Carr

'Oh, dear!' said Clover, with her lip trembling, 'now Papa won't see Rosy.'

'No,' said Katy, 'and Rosy and Louisa, and the rest, won't see him. That is the worst of all. I wanted them to so much. And just think how dismal it will be to travel with people we don't know. It's too, too bad, I declare.'

'I do think old Mrs Barlow might have put off being ill just one week longer,' grumbled Clover. 'It takes away half the pleasure of going home.'

The girls might be excused for being cross, for this was a great disappointment. There was no help for it, however, as Papa said. They could only sigh and submit. But the journey, to which they had looked forward so much, was no longer thought of as a pleasure, only a disagreeable necessity, something which must be endured in order that they might reach home.

Five, four, three days – the last little square was crossed off, the last dinner was eaten, the last breakfast. There was much mourning over Katy and Clover among the girls who were to return for another year. Louisa and Ellen Gray were inconsolable; and Bella, with a very small pocket-handkerchief held tightly in her hand, clung to Katy every moment, crying, and declaring that she would not let her go. The last evening she followed her into No. 2 (where she was dreadfully in the way of the packing), and after various odd contortions and mysterious, half-spoken sentences, said: 'Say you won't tell if I tell you something?'

'What is it?' asked Katy absently, as she folded and smoothed her best gown.

'Something,' repeated Bella, wagging her head mysteriously, and looking more like a thievish squirrel than ever.

'Well, what is it? Tell me.'

To Katy's surprise, Bella burst into a violent fit of crying.

'I'm very sorry I did it,' she sobbed, 'very sorry! And now
you'll never love me any more.'

'Yes, I will. What is it? Do stop crying, Bella dear, and tell
me,' said Katy, alarmed at the violence of the sobs.

'It was for fun, really and truly it was. But I wanted some
cake too,' protested Bella, sniffing very hard.

'What!'

'And I didn't think anybody would know. Berry Searles
doesn't care a bit for us little girls, only for big ones. And I
knew if I said "Bella", he'd never give me the cake. So I said
"Miss Carr" instead.'

'Bella, did you write that note?' enquired Katy almost too
much surprised to speak.

'Yes. And I tied a string to your blind, because I knew I
could go in and draw it up when you were practising. But I
didn't mean to do any harm, and when Mrs Florence was so
angry and changed your room, I was really sorry,' moaned
Bella, digging her knuckles into her eyes.

'Won't you ever love me any more?' she demanded. Katy
lifted her into her lap, and talked so tenderly and seriously
that her contrition, which was only half genuine, became
real, and she cried in good earnest when Katy kissed her in
token of forgiveness.

'Of course you'll go at once to Mrs Nipson,' said Clover
and Rose, when Katy imparted this surprising discovery.

'No, I think not. Why should I? It would only get poor
little Bella into a dreadful scrape, and she's coming back
again, you know. Mrs Nipson does not believe that story
now – nobody does. We have "lived it down", just as I hoped
we should. That is much better than having it contradicted.'

'I don't think so, and I should enjoy seeing that little

wretch of a Bella well whipped,' persisted Rose. But Katy was not to be shaken.

'To please me, promise that not a word shall be said about it,' she urged; and, to please her, the girls consented.

I think Katy was right in saying that Mrs Nipson no longer believed her guilty in the affair of the note. She had been very friendly to both the girls of late, and when Clover carried in her album and asked for an autograph, she waxed quite sentimental, and wrote, 'I would not exchange the modest Clover for the most brilliant flower in our beautiful parterre, so bring it back, I pray thee, to your affectionate teacher, Marianne Nipson'; which effusion quite overwhelmed 'the modest Clover', and called out the remark from Rose, 'Don't she wish she may get you!' Miss Jane said twice, 'I shall miss you, Katy,' a speech which, to quote Rose again, made Katy look as 'surprised as Balaam'. Rose herself was not coming back to school. She and the girls were half broke-hearted at parting. They lavished tears, kisses, promises of letters and vows of eternal friendship. Neither of them, it was agreed, was ever to love anybody else so well. The final moment would have been almost too tragical had it not been for a last bit of mischief on the part of Rose. It was after the stage was actually at the door, and she had her foot upon the step, that, struck by a happy thought, she rushed upstairs again, collected the girls, and, each taking a window, they tore down the cotton, flung open the sashes, and startled Mrs Nipson, who stood below, by the simultaneous waving therefrom of many white flags. Katy, who was already in the stage, had the full benefit of this performance. Always after that, when she thought of the Nunnery, her memory recalled this scene – Mrs Nipson in the doorway, Bella blubbering behind, and overhead the windows crowded with saucy girls, laughing and triumphantly flapping the long cotton strips which had for so many months obscured the daylight from them all.

At Springfield next morning, she and Clover said goodbye

to Mr Page and Lilly. The ride to Albany was easy and safe. With every mile their spirits rose. At last they were actually on the way home.

At Albany they looked anxiously about the crowded station for 'Mr Peters'. Nobody appeared at first, and they had time to grow nervous before they saw a gentle, careworn, little man coming toward them in company with the conductor.

'I believe you are the young ladies I have come to meet,' he said. 'You must excuse my being late. I was detained by business. There is a great deal to do to move a family out West.' He wiped his forehead in a dispirited way. Then he put the girls into a carriage, and gave the driver a direction.

'We'd better leave your baggage at the office as we pass,' he said, 'because we have to get off so early in the morning.'

'How early?'

'The boat goes at six, but we ought to be on board by half-past five, so as to be well settled before she starts.'

'The boat?' said Katy, opening her eyes.

'Yes. Erie Canal, you know. Our furniture goes that way, so we judged it best to do the same, and keep an eye on it ourselves. Never be separated from your property, if you can help it; that's my maxim. It's the *Prairie Belle*, one of the finest boats on the canal.'

'When do we get to Buffalo?' asked Katy, with an uneasy recollection of having heard that canal boats travel slowly.

'Buffalo? Let me see. This is Tuesday – Wednesday, Thursday – well, if we're lucky, we ought to be there Friday evening; so, if we're not too late to catch the night boat on the lake, you'll reach home Saturday afternoon. Yes, I think we may pretty safely say Saturday afternoon.'

Four days! The girls looked at each other with dismay too deep for words. Elsie was expecting them by Thursday at latest. What should they do?

'Telegraph,' was the only answer that suggested itself. So

Katy scribbled a telegram, 'Coming by canal. Don't expect us till Saturday', which she begged Mr Peters to send, and she and Clover agreed in whispers that it was dreadful, but they must bear it as patiently as they could.

Oh, the patience which is needed on a canal! The motion which is not so much motion as standing still! The crazy impulse to jump out and help the crawling boat along by pushing it from behind! How one grows to hate the slow, monotonous glide, the dull banks, and to envy every swift-moving thing in sight, each man on horseback, each bird flying through the air.

Mrs Peters was a thin, anxious woman, who spent her life anticipating disasters of all sorts. She had her children with her, three little boys and a teething baby; and such a load of bundles, and baskets, and brown-paper parcels, that Katy and Clover privately wondered how she could possibly have got through the journey without their help. Willy, the eldest boy, was always begging leave to go ashore and ride the towing horses; Sammy, the second, could only be kept quiet by means of crooked pins and fish-lines of blue yarn; while Paul, the youngest, was possessed with a curiosity as to the underside of the boat, which resulted in his dropping his new hat overboard five times in three days, Mr Peters and the cabin-boy rowing back in a small boat each time to recover it. Mrs Peters sat on deck with her baby in her lap, and was in a perpetual agony lest the locks should work wrongly, or the boys be drowned, or someone fail to notice the warning cry, 'Bridge!' and have their heads carried off from their shoulders. Nobody did; but the poor lady suffered the anguish of ten accidents in dreading the one which never took place. The berths at night were small and cramped, restless children woke and cried, the cabins were close, the decks cold and windy. There was nothing to see, and nothing to do. Katy and Clover agreed that they never wanted to see a canal boat again.

They were very helpful to Mrs Peters, amused the boys and kept them out of mischief; and she told her husband that she really thought she shouldn't have lived through the journey if it hadn't been for the Miss Carrs, they were such kind girls, and so fond of children. But the three days were terribly long. At last they ended. Buffalo was reached in time for the lake boat; and once established on board, feeling the rapid motion, and knowing that each stroke of the paddles took them nearer home, the girls were rewarded for their long trial of patience.

At four o'clock the next afternoon Burnet was in sight. Long before they touched the wharf Clover discovered old Whitey and the carriage and Alexander waiting for them among the crowd of carriages. Standing on the edge of the dock appeared a well-known figure.

'Papa! Papa!' she shrieked. It seemed as if the girls could not wait for the boat to stop, and the plank to be lowered. How delightful it was to feel Papa again! Such a sense of home and comfort and shelter as came with his touch!

'I'll never go away from you again, never, never!' repeated Clover, keeping tight hold of his hand as they drove up the hill. Dr Carr, as he gazed at his girls, was equally happy – they were so bright, so affectionate and loving. No, he could never spare them again, for boarding-school or anything else, he thought.

'You must be very tired,' he said.

'Not a bit. I'm hardly ever tired now,' replied Katy.

'Oh, dear! I forgot to thank Mr Peters for taking care of us,' said Clover.

'Never mind. I did it for you,' answered her father.

'Oh, that baby!' she continued: 'how glad I am that it has gone to Toledo, and I needn't hear it cry any more! Katy! Katy! there's home. We are at the gate!'

The girls looked eagerly out, but no children were visible. They hurried up the gravel path, under the boughs just beginning to bud. There, over the front door, was an arch of evergreens, with 'Katy' and 'Clover' upon it in scarlet letters; and as they reached the porch, the door flew open, and out poured the children in a tumultuous little crowd. They had been on the roof, looking through a spyglass after the boat.

'We never knew you had come till we heard the gate,' explained John and Dorry; while Elsie hugged Clover, and Phil, locking his arms round Katy's neck, took his feet off the floor, and swung them in an ecstasy of affection, until she begged for mercy.

'How you are grown! Dorry, you're as tall as I am! Elsie, darling, how well you look! Oh, isn't it delicious, delicious, delicious, to be at home again!' There was such a hubbub of endearments and explanations that Dr Carr could hardly make himself heard.

'Clover, your waist has grown as small as a pin. You look just like the beautiful princess in Elsie's story,' said Johnnie.

'Take the girls into the parlour,' repeated Dr Carr: 'it is cold out here, with the door open.'

'Take them upstairs! You don't know what is upstairs!' shouted Phil, whereupon Elsie frowned and shook her head at him.

The parlour was gay with daffodils and hyacinths, and vases of blue violets, which smelt delightfully. Cecy had helped to arrange them, Elsie said. And just at that moment Cecy herself came in. Her hair was arranged in a sort of pincushion of puffs, with a row of curls on top, where no curls used to grow, and her appearance generally was very fine and fashionable; but she was the same affectionate Cecy as ever, and hugged the girls, and danced round them as she used to do at twelve. She had waited until they had had time to kiss once all round, she said, and then she really couldn't wait any longer.

'Now come upstairs,' suggested Elsie, when Clover had

warmed her feet, and the flowers had been admired, and everybody had said ten times over how nice it was to have the girls back, and the girls had replied that it was just as nice to come back.

So they all went upstairs, Elsie leading the way.

'Where are you going?' cried Katy: 'that's the Blue Room.' But Elsie did not pause.

'You see,' she explained, with the doorknob in her hand, 'Papa and I thought you ought to have a bigger room now, because you are grown-up young ladies! So we have arranged this for you, and your old one is going to be the spare room instead.' Then she threw the door open, and led the girls in.

'See, Katy,' she said, 'this is your bureau, and this is Clover's. And look what nice drawers Papa has had put in the closet – two for you, and two for her. Aren't they convenient? Don't you like it? And isn't it a great deal pleasanter than the old room?'

'Oh, a great deal!' cried the girls. 'It is delightful, everything about it.' All Katy's old treasures had been transferred from her old quarters to this. There was her cushioned chair, her table, her bookshelf, the pictures from the walls. There were some new things too – a blue carpet, blue paper on the walls, window curtains of fresh chintz; and Elsie had made a tasteful pincushion for each bureau, and Johnnie crocheted mats for the washstand. Altogether, it was as pretty a bower as two sisters just grown into young ladies could desire.

'What are those lovely things hanging on either side of the bed?' asked Clover.

They were two illuminated texts, sent as a 'welcome home', by Cousin Helen. One was a morning text, and the other an evening text, Elsie explained. The evening text, which bore the words, 'I will lay me down to sleep, and take my rest, for it is Thou, Lord, who only makest me dwell in safety', was painted in soft purples and greys, and among the poppies and silver lilies which wreathed it appeared a cunning little downy bird, fast asleep, with his head under his wing. The morning text, 'When I awake, I am still with Thee', was in bright colours, scarlet and blue and gold, and had a frame of rose garlands and wide-awake-looking butterflies and hummingbirds. The girls thought they had never seen anything so pretty.

Such a gay supper as they had that night! Katy would not take her old place at the tea-tray. She wanted to know how Elsie looked as housekeeper, she said. So she sat on one side of Papa, and Clover on the other, and Elsie poured out the tea, with a mixture of delight and dignity which was worth seeing.

'I'll begin tomorrow,' said Katy.

And with that tomorrow, when she came out of her pretty room and took her place once more as manager of the household, her grown-up life may be said to have begun. So it is time that I should cease to write about her. Grown-up lives may be very interesting, but they have no rightful place in a child's book. If little girls will forget to be little, and take it upon them to become young ladies, they must bear the consequences, one of which is that we can follow their fortunes no longer.

I wrote these last words sitting in the same green meadow where the first words of *What Katy Did* were written. A year had passed, but a cardinal-flower which seemed the same stood looking at itself in the brook, and from the bulrush-bed sounded tiny voices. My little goggle-eyed friends were discussing Katy and her conduct, as they did then, but with less spirit; for one voice came seldom and faintly, while the other, bold and defiant as ever, repeated over and over again, 'Katy didn't! Katy didn't! She didn't, didn't, didn't!'

'Katy did!' sounded faintly from the farther rush.

'She didn't, she didn't!' chirped the undaunted partisan. Silence followed. His opponent was either convinced or tired of the discussion.

'Katy didn't!' The words repeated themselves in my mind as I walked homeward. How much room for 'didn'ts' there is in the world, I thought. What an important part they play! And how glad I am that, with all their own and other people's doings, so many of these very 'didn'ts' were included among the things which my Katy did at school!

WHAT KATY DID NEXT

CHAPTER ONE

An Unexpected Guest

The September sun was glinting cheerfully into a pretty bedroom furnished with blue. It danced on the glossy hair and bright eyes of two girls, who sat together hemming ruffles for a white muslin dress. The half-finished skirt of the dress lay on the bed, and as each crisp ruffle was completed, the girls added it to the snowy heap, which looked like a drift of transparent clouds or a pile of foamy white-of-egg beaten stiff enough to stand alone.

These girls were Clover and Elsie Carr; and it was Clover's first evening-dress for which they were hemming ruffles. It was nearly two years since a certain visit made by Johnnie to Inches Mills, of which some of you have read in *Nine Little Goslings*; and more than three since Clover and Katy had returned home from the boarding-school at Hillsover.

Clover was now eighteen. She was a very small Clover still, but it would have been hard to find anywhere a prettier little maiden than she had grown to be. Her skin was so exquisitely fair that her arms and wrists and shoulders, which were round and dimpled like a baby's, seemed cut out of daisies or white rose leaves. Her thick, brown hair waved and coiled gracefully about her head. Her smile was peculiarly sweet; and the eyes, always Clover's chief beauty, had still that pathetic look which made them irresistible to tender-hearted people.

Elsie, who adored Clover, considered her as beautiful as girls in books, and was proud to be permitted to hem ruffles for the dress in which she was to burst upon the world. Though, as for that, not much 'bursting' was possible in Burnet, where tea-parties of a middle-aged description, and now and then a mild little dance, represented 'gaiety' and 'society'. Girls 'came out' very much as the sun comes out in the morning – by slow degrees and gradual approaches, with no particular one moment which could be fixed upon as having been the crisis of the joyful event.

'There,' said Elsie, adding another ruffle to the pile on the bed – 'there's the fifth done. It's going to be ever so pretty, I think. I'm glad you had it all white; it's a great deal nicer.'

'Cecy wanted me to have a blue bodice and sash,' said Clover, 'but I wouldn't. Then she tried to persuade me to get a long spray of pink roses for the skirt.'

'I'm so glad you didn't! Cecy was always crazy about pink roses. I only wonder she didn't wear them when she was married!'

Yes; the excellent Cecy, who at thirteen had announced her intention to devote her whole life to teaching Sunday School, visiting the poor and setting a good example to her more worldly contemporaries, had actually forgotten these fine resolutions, and before she was twenty had become the wife of Sylvester Slack, a young lawyer in a neighbouring town! Cecy's wedding and wedding-clothes, and Cecy's house-furnishing, had been the great excitement of the preceding year in Burnet; and a fresh excitement had come since in the shape of Cecy's baby, now about two months old and named 'Katherine Clover', after her two friends. This made it natural that Cecy and her affairs should still be of interest in the Carr household; and Johnnie at the time we write of, was making her a week's visit.

'She was rather wedded to them,' went on Clover, pursuing the subject of the pink roses. 'She was almost vexed when I wouldn't buy the spray. But it cost lots, and I didn't want it in the least, so I stood firm. Besides I always said that my first party dress should be plain white. Girls in novels always wear white to their first balls; and fresh flowers are a great deal prettier, anyway, than artificial. Katy says she'll give me some violets to wear.'

'Oh, will she? That will be lovely!' cried the adoring Elsie. 'Violets look just like you, somehow. Oh, Clover, what sort of a dress do you think I shall have when I grow up and go to parties and things? Won't it be awfully interesting when you and I go out to choose it?'

Just then the noise of someone running upstairs quickly made the sisters look up from their work. Footsteps are very significant at times, and these footsteps suggested haste and excitement.

Another moment, the door opened, and Katy dashed in calling out, 'Papa! – Elsie, Clover, where's Papa?'

'He went over the river to see that son of Mr White's who broke his leg. Why, what's the matter?' asked Clover.

'Is somebody hurt?' enquired Elsie, startled at Katy's agitated looks.

'No, not hurt; but poor Mrs Ashe is in such trouble!'

Mrs Ashe, it should be explained, was a widow who had come to Burnet some months previously, and had taken a pleasant house not far from the Carrs'. She was a pretty, ladylike woman, with a particularly graceful, appealing manner, and very fond of her one child, a little girl. Katy and Papa both took a fancy to her at once; and the families had grown neighbourly and intimate in a short time, as people occasionally do when circumstances are favourable.

'I'll tell you all about it in a minute,' went on Katy. 'But first I must find Alexander, and send him off to meet Papa and beg him to hurry home.' She went to the head of the stairs as she spoke, and called 'Debby! Debby!' Debby answered. Katy gave her direction, and then came back again to the room where the other two were sitting.

'Now,' she said, speaking more collectedly, 'I must explain

as fast as I can, for I have got to go back. You know that Mrs Ashe's little nephew is here for a visit, don't you?'

'Yes, he came on Saturday.'

'Well, he was ailing all day yesterday, and today he is worse, and she is afraid it is scarlet fever. Luckily, Amy was spending the day with the Uphams yesterday, so she scarcely saw the boy at all; and as soon as her mother became alarmed, she sent her out into the garden to play, and hasn't let her come indoors since, so she can't have been exposed to any particular danger yet. I went by the house on my way down the street, and there sat the poor little thing all alone in the arbour, with her dolly in her lap, looking so disconsolate. I spoke to her over the fence, and Mrs Ashe heard my voice, and opened the upstairs window and called to me. She said Amy had never had the fever, and that the very idea of her having it frightened her to death. She is such a delicate child, you know.'

'Oh, poor Mrs Ashe!' cried Clover; 'I am so sorry for her! Well, Katy, what did you do?'

'I hope I didn't do wrong, but I offered to bring Amy here. Papa won't object, I am almost sure.'

'Why, of course he won't. Well?'

'I am going back now to fetch Amy. Mrs Ashe is to let Ellen, who hasn't been in the room with the little boy, pack a bagful of clothes and put it out on the steps, and I shall send Alexander for it by and by. You can't think how troubled poor Mrs Ash was. She couldn't help crying when she said that Amy was all she had left in the world. And I nearly cried too, I was so sorry for her. She was so relieved when I said that we would take Amy. You know she has a great deal of confidence in Papa.'

'Yes, and in you, too. Where will you put Amy to sleep, Katy?'

'What do you think would be best? In Dorry's room?'

'I think she'd better come in here with you, and I'll go into

Dorry's room. She is used to sleeping with her mother, you know, and she would be lonely if she were left to herself.'

'Perhaps that will be better, only it is a great bother for you, Clovy dear.'

'I don't mind,' responded Clover cheerfully. 'I rather like to change about and try a new room once in a while. It's as good as going on a journey – almost.'

She pushed aside the half-finished dress as she spoke, opened a drawer, took out its contents, and began to carry them across the entry to Dorry's room, doing everything with the orderly deliberation that was characteristic of whatever Clover did. Her preparations were almost complete before Katy returned, bringing with her little Amy Ashe.

Amy was a tall child of eight, with a frank, happy face, and long light hair hanging down her back. She looked like the pictures of Alice in *Alice in Wonderland*; but just at that moment it was a very woeful little Alice indeed that she resembled, for her cheeks were stained with tears and her eyes swollen with recent crying.

'Why, what is the matter?' cried kind little Clover, taking Amy in her arms, and giving her a great hug. 'Aren't you glad that you are coming to make us a visit? We are.'

'Mamma didn't kiss me goodbye,' sobbed the little girl. 'She didn't come downstairs at all. She just put her head out of the window and said: "Goodbye, Amy! be very good, and don't make Miss Carr any trouble," and then she went away. I never went anywhere before without kissing Mamma goodbye.'

'Mamma was afraid to kiss you for fear she might give you the fever,' explained Katy, taking her turn as a comforter. 'It wasn't because she forgot. She felt worse about it than you did, I imagine. You know the thing she cares most for is that you shall not be ill as your cousin Walter is. She would rather do anything than have that happen. As soon as he gets well she will kiss you dozens of times, see if she doesn't.

Meanwhile, she says in this note that you must write her a little letter every day, and she will hang a basket by a string out of the window, and you and I will go and drop the letters into the basket, and stand by the gate and see her pull it up. That will be funny, won't it? We will play that you are my little girl, and that you have a real mamma and a make-believe mamma.'

'Shall I sleep with you?' demanded Amy.

'Yes, in that bed over there.'

'It's a pretty bed,' pronounced Amy after examining it gravely for a moment. 'Will you tell me a story every morning?'

'If you don't wake me up too early. My stories are always sleepy till seven o'clock. Let us see what Ellen has packed in that bag, and then I'll give you some drawers of your own, and we will put the things away.'

The bag was full of neat little frocks and underclothes stuffed hastily in all together. Katy took them out, smoothing the folds, and crimping the tumbled ruffles with her fingers. As she lifted the last skirt, Amy, with a cry of joy, pounced on something that lay beneath it.

'It is Maria Matilda,' she said; 'I'm glad of that. I thought Ellen would forget her, and poor child wouldn't know what to do, with me and her big sister not coming to see her for so long. She was having the measles on the back shelf of the closet, you know, and nobody would have heard her if she had cried ever so loud.'

'What a pretty face she has!' said Katy, taking the doll out of Amy's hands.

'Yes, but not so pretty as Mabel. Miss Upham says that Mabel is the prettiest child she ever saw. Look, Miss Clover,' lifting the other doll from the table where she had laid it; 'hasn't she got *sweet* eyes? She's older than Maria Matilda, and she knows a great deal more. She's begun on French verbs!'

'Not really! Which ones?'

'Oh! only "J'aime, tu aimes, il aime", you know – the same that our class is learning at school. She hasn't tried any but that. Sometimes she says it quite nicely, but sometimes she's very stupid, and I have to scold her.' Amy had quite recovered her spirits by this time.

'Are these the only dolls you have?'

'Oh, please don't call them that!' urged Amy. 'It hurts their feelings dreadfully. I never let them know that they are dolls. They think that they are real children, only some-times, when they are very bad, I use the word for a punishment. I've got several other children. There's old Ragazza. My uncle named her, and she's made of rag, but she has such bad rheumatism that I don't play with her any longer; I just give her medicine. Then there's Effie Deans, she's only got one leg; and Mopsa the Fairy, she's a tiny one made out of china; and Peg of Linkinvaddy – but she don't count, for she's come all to pieces.'

'What very queer names your children have!' said Elsie, who had come in during the enumeration.

'Yes; Uncle Ned named them. He's a very funny uncle, but he's nice. He's always so much interested in my children.'

'There's Papa now!' cried Katy; and she ran downstairs to meet him.

'Did I do right?' she asked anxiously, after she had told her story.

'Yes, my dear, perfectly right,' replied Dr Carr. 'I only hope Amy was taken away in time. I will go round at once to see Mrs Ashe and the boy; and, Katy, keep away from me when I come back, and keep the others away, till I have changed my coat.'

It is odd how soon and how easily human beings accustom themselves to a new condition of things. When sudden illness comes, or sudden sorrow, or a house is burned down

or blown down by a tornado, there are a few hours or days of
confusion and bewilderment, and then people gather up
their wits and their courage and set to work to repair the
damage. They clear away ruins, plant, rebuild, very much as
ants, whose hill has been trodden upon, after running wildly
about for a little while, begin all together to reconstruct the
tiny cone of sand which is so important in their eyes. In a
very short time the changes which at first seem so sad and
strange become accustomed and matter-of-course things
which no longer surprise us.

It seemed to the Carrs after a few days as if they had always
had Amy in the house with them. Papa's daily visit to the
sickroom, their avoidance of him till after he had 'changed
his coat', Amy's lessons and games of play, her dressing and
undressing, the walks with the make-believe mamma, the
dropping of notes into the little basket, seemed part of a
system of things which had been going on for a long, long
time, and which everybody would miss should they suddenly stop.

But they by no means suddenly stopped. Little Walter
Ashe's case proved to be rather a severe one; and after he had
begun to mend, he caught cold somehow and was taken
worse again. There were some serious symptoms, and for a
few days Dr Carr did not feel sure how things would turn
out. He did not speak of his anxiety at home, but kept silence
and a cheerful face, as doctors know how to do. Only Katy,
who was more intimate with her father than the rest, guessed
that things were going gravely at the other house, and she
was too well trained to ask questions. The threatening
symptoms passed off, however, and little Walter slowly got
better; but it was a long convalescence, and Mrs Ashe grew
thin and pale before he began to look rosy. There was no one
on whom she could devolve the charge of the child. His
mother was dead; his father, an overworked businessman,
had barely time to run up once a week to see about him; there

was no one at his home but a housekeeper, in whom Mrs Ashe had not full confidence. So the good aunt denied herself the sight of her own child, and devoted her strength and time to Walter, and nearly two months passed, and still little Amy remained at Dr Carr's.

She was entirely happy there. She had grown very fond of Katy, and was perfectly at home with the others. Phil and Johnnie, who had returned from her visit to Cecy, were by no means too old or too proud to be playfellows to a child of eight; and with all the older members of the family Amy was a chosen pet. Debby baked turnovers and twisted cinnamon cakes into all sorts of fantastic shapes to please her; Alexander would let her drive if she happened to sit on the front seat of the carry-all; Dr Carr was seldom so tired that he could not tell her a story – and nobody told such nice stories as Dr Carr, Amy thought; Elsie invented all manner of charming games for the hour before bedtime; Clover made wonderful capes and bonnets for Mabel and Maria Matilda; and Katy – Katy did all sorts of things.

Katy had a peculiar gift with children which is not easy to define. Some people possess it, and some do not; it cannot be learned, it comes by nature. She was bright and firm and equable all at once. She both amused and influenced them. There was something about her which excited the childish imagination, and always they felt her sympathy. Amy was a tractable child, and intelligent beyond her age, but she was never quite so good with anyone as with Katy. She followed her about like a little lover; she lavished upon her certain special words and caresses which she gave to no one else; and would kneel on her lap, patting Katy's shoulders with her soft hand, and cooing up into her face like a happy dove, for a half-hour together. Katy laughed at these demonstrations, but they pleased her very much. She loved to be loved, as all affectionate people do, but most of all to be loved by a child.

At last, the long convalescence ended, Walter was carried

away to his father, with every possible precaution against fatigue and exposure, and an army of work people was turned into Mrs Ashe's house. Plaster was scraped and painted, wallpapers torn down, mattresses made over, and clothing burned. At last Dr Carr pronounced the premises in a sanitary condition, and Mrs Ashe sent for her little girl to come home again.

Amy was overjoyed at the prospect of seeing her mother; but at the last moment she clung to Katy and cried as if her heart would break.

'I want you too,' she said. 'Oh, if Dr Carr would only let you come and live with me and Mamma, I should be so happy! I shall be so lone–ly!'

'Nonsense!' cried Clover. 'Lonely with Mamma, and those poor children of yours who have been wondering all these weeks what has become of you! They'll want a great deal of attention at first, I am sure; medicine and new clothes and whippings – all manner of things. You remember I promised to make a dress for Effie Deans out of that blue-and-brown plaid like Johnnie's balmoral. I mean to begin it tomorrow.'

'Oh, will you?' – forgetting her grief – 'that will be lovely. The skirt needn't be *very* full, you know. Effie doesn't walk much, because of only having one leg. She will be *so* pleased, for she hasn't had a new dress I don't know when.'

Consoled by the prospect of Effie's satisfaction, Amy departed quite cheerfully, and Mrs Ashe was spared the pain of seeing her only child in tears on the first evening of their reunion. But Amy talked so constantly of Katy, and seemed to love her so much, that it put a plan into her mother's head which led to important results, as the next chapter will show.

CHAPTER TWO

An Invitation

It is a curious fact, and makes life very interesting, that, generally speaking, none of us have any expectation that things are going to happen till the very moment when they do happen. We wake up some morning with no idea that a great happiness is at hand, and before night it has come, and all the world is changed for us; or we wake bright and cheerful, with never a guess that clouds of sorrow are lowering in our sky, to put all the sunshine out for a while, and before noon all is dark. Nothing whispers of either the joy or the grief. No instinct bids us to delay or to hasten the opening of the letter or telegram, or the lifting of the latch of the door at which stands the messenger of good or ill. And because it may be, and often is, happy tidings that come, and joyful things which happen, each fresh day as it dawns upon us is like an unread story, full of possible interest and adventure, to be made ours as soon as we have cut the pages and begun to read.

Nothing whispered to Katy Carr, as she sat at the window mending a long rent in Johnnie's school coat, and saw Mrs Ashe come in at the side gate and ring the office bell, that the visit had any special significance for her. Mrs Ashe often did come to the office to consult Dr Carr. Amy might not be quite well, Katy thought, or there might be a letter with something about Walter in it, or perhaps matters had gone wrong at the house, where paperers and painters were still at work.

So she went calmly on with her darning, drawing the

'ravelling', with which her needle was threaded, carefully in and out, and taking nice even stitches without one prophetic thrill or tremor, while, if only she could have looked through the two walls and two doors which separated the room in which she sat from the office, and have heard what Mrs Ashe was saying, the school coat would have been thrown to the winds, and for all her tall stature and propriety she would have been skipping with delight and astonishment. For Mrs Ashe was asking Papa to let her do the very thing of all others that she most longed to do; she was asking him to let Katy go with her to Europe!

'I am not very well,' she told the Doctor. 'I got tired and run down while Walter was ill, and I don't seem to throw it off as I hoped I should. I feel as if a change would do me good. Don't you think so yourself?'

'Yes, I do,' Dr Carr admitted.

'This idea of Europe is not altogether a new one,' continued Mrs Ashe. 'I have always meant to go sometime, and have put it off, partly because I dreaded going alone, and didn't know anybody whom I exactly wanted to take with me. But if you will let me have Katy, Dr Carr, it will settle all my difficulties. Amy loves her dearly, and so do I; she is just the companion I need; if I have her with me, I shan't be afraid of anything. I do hope you will consent.'

'How long do you mean to be away?' asked Dr Carr, divided between pleasure at these compliments to Katy and dismay at the idea of losing her.

'About a year, I think. My plans are rather vague as yet; but my idea was to spend a few weeks in Scotland and England first – I have some cousins in London who will be good to us; and an old friend of mine married a gentleman who lives on the Isle of Wight; perhaps we might go there. Then we could cross over to France, and visit Paris and a few other places; and before it gets cold, go down to Nice, and from there to Italy. Katy would like to see Italy. Don't you think so?'

'I dare say she would,' said Dr Carr, with a smile. 'She would be a queer girl if she didn't.'

'There is one reason why I thought Italy would be particularly pleasant this winter for me and for her too,' went on Mrs Ashe; 'and that is, because my brother will be there. He is a lieutenant in the navy, you know, and his ship, the *Natchitoches*, is one of the Mediterranean squadron. They will be in Naples by and by, and if we were there at the same time we should have Ned to go about with; and he would take us to the receptions on the frigate, and all that, which would be a nice chance for Katy. Then towards spring I should like to go to Florence and Venice, and visit the Italian lakes and Switzerland in the early summer. But all this depends on your letting Katy go. If you decide against it, I shall give the whole thing up. But you won't decide against it' – coaxingly – 'you will be kinder than that. I will take the best possible care of her, and do all I can to make her happy, if only you will consent to lend her to me; and I shall consider it *such* a favour. And it is to cost you nothing. You understand, Doctor, she is to be my guest all through. That is a point I want to make clear in the outset; for she goes for my sake, and I cannot take her on any other conditions. Now, Dr Carr, please, please! I am sure you won't deny me, when I have so set my heart upon having her.'

Mrs Ashe was very pretty and persuasive, but still Dr Carr hesitated. To send Katy for a year's pleasuring in Europe was a thing that had never occurred to his mind as possible. The cost alone would have prevented it; for country doctors with six children are not apt to be rich men, even in the limited and old-fashioned construction of the word 'wealth'. It seemed equally impossible to let her go at Mrs Ashe's expense; at the same time, the chance was such a good one, and Mrs Ashe so much in earnest and so urgent, that it was difficult to refuse point-blank. He finally consented to take time for consideration before making his decision.

'I will talk it over with Katy,' he said. 'The child ought to have a say in the matter; and whatever we decide, you must let me thank you in her name as well as my own for your great kindness in proposing it.'

'Doctor, I'm not kind at all, and I don't want to be thanked. My desire to take Katy with me to Europe is purely selfish. I am a lonely person,' she went on; 'I have no mother or sister, and no cousins of my own age. My brother's profession keeps him at sea; I scarcely ever see him. I have no one but a couple of old aunts, too feeble in health to travel with me or to be counted on in case of any emergency. You see, I am a real case for pity.'

Mrs Ashe spoke gaily, but her brown eyes were dim with tears as she ended her little appeal. Dr Carr, who was soft-hearted where women were concerned, was touched. Perhaps his face showed it, for Mrs Ashe added in a more hopeful tone: 'But I won't tease any more. I know you will not refuse me unless you think it right and necessary; and,' she continued mischievously, 'I have great faith in Katy as an ally. I am pretty sure that she will say that she wants to go.'

And indeed Katy's cry of delight when the plan was proposed to her said that sufficiently, without need of further explanation. To go to Europe for a year with Mrs Ashe and Amy seemed simply too delightful to be true. All the things she had heard about and read about – cathedrals, pictures, Alpine peaks, famous places, famous people – came rushing into her mind in a sort of bewildering tide, as dazzling as it was overwhelming. Dr Carr's objections, his reluctance to part with her, melted before the radiance of her satisfaction. He had no idea that Katy would care so much about it. After all, it was a great chance – perhaps the only one of the sort that she would ever have. Mrs Ashe could well afford to give Katy this treat, he knew; and it was quite true what she said, that it was a favour to her as well as to Katy This train of reasoning led to its natural results. Dr Carr began to waver in his mind.

But, the first excitement over, Katy's second thoughts were more sober ones. How could Papa manage without her for a whole year? she asked herself. He would miss her, she well knew; and might not the charge of the house be too much for Clover? The preserves were almost all made, that was one comfort; but there were the winter clothes to be seen to; Dorry needed new flannels, Elsie's dresses must be altered over for Johnnie – there were cucumbers to pickle, the coal to order! A host of housewifely cares began to troop through Katy's mind, and a little pucker came into her forehead, and a worried look across the face which had been so bright a few minutes before.

Strange to say, it was that little pucker and the look of worry which decided Dr Carr.

'She is only twenty-one,' he reflected; 'hardly out of childhood. I don't want her to settle into an anxious drudging state, and lose her youth with caring for us all. She shall go; though how we are to manage without her I don't see. Little Clover will have to come to the fore, and show what sort of stuff there is in her.'

'Little Clover' came gallantly 'to the fore' when the first shock of the surprise was over and she had relieved her mind with one long private cry over having to do without Katy for a year. Then she wiped her eyes, and began to revel unselfishly in the idea of her sister's having so great a treat. Anything and everything seemed possible to secure it for her; and she made light of all Katy's many anxieties and apprehensions.

'My dear child, I know a flannel undershirt when I see one, just as well as you do,' she declared. 'Tucks in Johnnie's dress, forsooth! why, of course. Ripping out a tuck doesn't require any superhuman ingenuity! Give me your scissors, and I'll show you at once. Quince marmalade? Debby can make that. Hers is about as good as yours; and if it wasn't, what should we care, as long as you are ascending Mont

Blanc and hobnobbing with Michelangelo and the crowned heads of Europe? I'll make the spiced peaches! I'll order the kindling! And if there ever comes a time when I feel lost and can't manage without advice, I'll go across to Mrs Hall. Don't worry about us. We shall get on happily and easily; in fact, I shouldn't be surprised if I developed such a turn for housekeeping that when you came back the family refused to change, and you had just to sit for the rest of your life and twirl your thumbs and watch me do it! Wouldn't that be fine?' and Clover laughed merrily. 'So, Katy darling, cast that shadow from your brow, and look as a girl ought to look who's going to Europe. Why, if it were I who were going, I should simply stand on my head every moment of the time!'

'Not a very convenient position for packing,' said Katy smiling.

'Yes it is, if you just turn your trunk upside down! When I think of all the delightful things you are going to do I can hardly sit still. I *love* Mrs Ashe for inviting you.'

'So do I,' said Katy soberly. 'It was the kindest thing. I can't think why she did it.'

'Well, I can,' replied Clover, always ready to defend Katy even against herself. 'She did it because she wanted you, and she wanted you because you are the dearest old thing in the world, and the nicest to have about. You needn't say you're not, for you are! Now, Katy, don't waste another thought on such miserable things as pickles and undershirts. We shall get along perfectly well, I do assure you. Just fix your mind instead on the dome of St Peter's, or try to fancy how you'll feel the first time you step into a gondola or see the Mediterranean. There will be a moment! I feel a forty-horse power of housekeeping developing within me; and what fun it will be to get your letters! We shall fetch out the encyclopaedia and the big atlas and the *History of Modern Europe*, and read all about everything you see and all the places you go to; and it will be as good as a lesson in geography and history and political economy all combined, only a great deal more interesting! We shall stick out all over with knowledge before you come back; and this makes it a plain duty to go, if it were only for our sakes.' With these zealous promises, Katy was forced to be content. Indeed, contentment was not difficult with such a prospect of delight before her. When once her little anxieties had been laid aside, the idea of the coming journey grew in pleasantness every moment. Night after night she and Papa and the children pored over maps and made out schemes for travel and sightseeing, every one of which was likely to be discarded as soon as the real journey began. But they didn't know that, and it made no real difference. Such schemes are the preliminary joys of travel, and it doesn't signify that they come to nothing after they have served their purpose.

Katy learned a great deal while thus talking over what she was to see and do. She read every scrap she could lay her hand on which related to Rome or Florence or Venice or London. The driest details had a charm for her now that she was likely to see the real places. She went about with scraps of paper in her pocket on which were written such things as these: 'Forum. When built? By whom built? More than one?' 'What does *Cenacola* mean?' 'Cecilia Metella. Who was she?' 'Find out about St Catherine of Siena.' 'Who was Beatrice Cenci?' How she wished that she had studied harder and more carefully before this wonderful chance came to her! People always wish this when they are starting for Europe; and they wish it more and more after they get there, and realise of what value exact ideas and information and a fuller knowledge of the foreign languages are to all travellers; how they add to the charm of everything seen, and enhance the ease of everything done.

All Burnet took an interest in Katy's plans, and almost everybody had some sort of advice or help, or some little gift, to offer. Old Mrs Worrett, who, though fatter than

ever, still retained the power of locomotion, drove in from
Conic Section in her roomy carry-all with the present of a
rather obsolete copy of *Murray's Guide*, in faded red covers,
which her father had used in his youth, and which she was
sure Katy would find convenient; also a bottle of Brown's
Jamaica Ginger, in case of seasickness. Debby's sister-in-law
brought a bundle of dried chamomile for the same purpose.
Someone had told her it was the 'handiest thing in the world
to take along with you on them steamboats'. Cecy sent a
wonderful old-gold and scarlet contrivance to hang on the
wall of the stateroom. There were pockets for watches, and
pockets for medicines, and pockets for handkerchiefs and
hairpins – in short, there were pockets for everything,
besides a pincushion with 'Bon Voyage' in rows of shining
pins, a bottle of eau-de-cologne, a cake of soap, and a
hammer and tacks to nail the whole up with. Mrs Hall's gift
was a warm and very pretty woollen wrapper of dark blue
flannel, with a pair of soft knitted slippers to match. Old Mr
Worrett sent a note of advice, recommending Katy to take a
quinine pill every day that she was away, never to stay out
late, because the dews 'over there' were said to be unwhole-
some, and on no account to drink a drop of water which had
not been boiled.

From Cousin Helen came a delightful travelling-bag,
light and strong at once, and fitted up with all manner of
nice little conveniences. Miss Inches sent a *History of Europe*
in five fat volumes, which was so heavy that it had to be left
at home. In fact, a good many of Katy's presents had to be
left at home, including a bronze paperweight in the shape of
a griffin, a large pair of brass screw candlesticks, and an
ormolu inkstand with a pen-rest attached, which weighed at
least a pound and a half. These Katy laid aside to enjoy after
her return. Mrs Ashe and Cousin Helen had both warned
her of the inconvenient consequences of weight in baggage:
and by their advice she had limited herself to a single trunk

of moderate size, besides a little flat valise for use in her stateroom.

Clover's gift was a set of blank books for notes, journals, &c. In one of these Katy made out a list of 'Things I must see', 'Things I must do', 'Things I would like to see', 'Things I would like to do'. Another she devoted to various good shopping addresses which had been given her; for though she did not expect to do any shopping herself, she thought Mrs Ashe might find them useful. Katy's ideas were still so simple and unworldly, and her experience of life so small, that it had not occurred to her how very tantalising it might be to stand in front of shop windows full of delightful things and not be able to buy any of them. She was accordingly overpowered with surprise, gratitude and the sense of sudden wealth when, about a week before the start, her father gave her three little thin strips of paper, which he told her were circular notes, and worth a hundred dollars apiece. He also gave her five English sovereigns.

'Those are for immediate use,' he said. 'Put the notes away carefully, and don't lose them. You had better have them cashed one at a time as you require them. Mrs Ashe will explain how. You will need a gown or so before you come back, and you'll want to buy some photographs and so on, and there will be fees – '

'But, Papa,' protested Katy, opening wide her candid eyes, 'I didn't expect you to give me any money, and I'm afraid you are giving me too much. Do you think you can afford it? Really and truly, I don't want to buy things. I shall see everything, you know, and that's enough.'

Her father only laughed.

'You'll be wiser and greedier before the year is out, my dear,' he replied. 'Three hundred dollars won't go far, as you'll find. But it's all I can spare, and I trust you to keep within it and not come home with any long bills for me to pay.'

'Papa! I should think not!' cried Katy, with unsophisticated horror.

One very interesting thing was to happen before they sailed, the thought of which helped both Katy and Clover through the last hard days, when the preparations were nearly complete and the family had leisure to feel dull and out of spirits. Katy was to make Rose Red a visit.

Rose had by no means been idle during the three years and a half which had elapsed since they all parted at Hillsover, and during which the girls had not seen her. In fact, she had made more out of the time than any of the rest of them, for she had been engaged for eighteen months, had been married, and was now keeping house near Boston with a little Rose of her own, who, she wrote to Clover, was a perfect angel, and more delicious than words could say! Mrs Ashe had taken passage in the *Spartacus*, sailing from Boston; and it was arranged that Katy should spend the last two days before sailing with Rose, while Mrs Ashe and Amy visited an old aunt in Hingham. To see Rose in her own home, and Rose's husband, and Rose's baby, was only next in interest to seeing Europe. None of the changes in her lot seemed to have changed her particularly, to judge by the letter she sent in reply to Katy's announcing her plans, which letter ran as follows:

Longwood, September 20

My dearest Child – Your note made me dance with delight. I stood on my head, waving my heels wildly to the breeze, till Deniston thought I must be taken suddenly mad; but when I explained he did the same. It is too enchanting, the whole of it. I put it at the head of all the nice things that ever happened, except my baby. Write the moment you get this by what train you expect to reach Boston, and when you roll into the station you will behold two forms, one tall and stalwart, the other short and fatsome, waiting for you. They will be those of Deniston and myself. Deniston is not beautiful, but he is good, and he is prepared to *adore* you. The baby is both good and beautiful, and you will adore her. I am neither; but you know all about me, and I always did adore you and always shall. I am going out this moment to the butcher's to order a calf fatted for your special behoof; and he shall be slain and made into cutlets the moment I hear from you. My funny little house, which is quite a dear little house too, assumes a new interest in my eyes from the fact that you so soon are to see it. It is somewhat queer, as you might know my house would be; but I think you will like it.

I saw Silvery Mary the other day and told her you were coming. She is the same mouse as ever. I shall ask her and some of the other girls to come out to lunch on one of your days. Goodbye, with a hundred and fifty kisses to Clovy and the rest.

Your loving

ROSE RED

'She never signs herself Browne, I observe,' said Clover, as she finished the letter.

'Oh, Rose Red Browne would sound too funny! Rose Red she must stay till the end of the chapter; no other name could suit her half so well, and I can't imagine her being called anything else. What fun it will be to see her and little Rose!'

'And Deniston Browne,' put in Clover.

'Somehow I find it rather hard to take in the fact that there is a Deniston Browne,' observed Katy.

'It will be easier after you have seen him, perhaps.' The last day came, as last days will. Katy's trunk, most carefully and exactly packed by the united efforts of the family, stood in the hall, locked and strapped, not to be opened again till

the party reached London. This fact gave it a certain awful
interest in the eyes of Phil and Johnnie, and even Elsie gazed
upon it with respect. The little valise was also ready; and
Dorry, the neat-handed, had painted a red star on both ends
of both it and the trunk, that they might be easily picked
from among a heap of luggage. He now proceeded to
prepare and paste on two square cards, labelled respectively,
'Hold' and 'Stateroom'. Mrs Hall had told them that this
was the correct thing to do.

Mrs Ashe had been full of business likewise in putting her
house to rights for a family who had rented it for the time of
her absence, and Katy and Clover had taken a good many
hours from their own preparations to help her. All was done
at last; and one bright morning in October, Katy stood on
the wharf with her family about her, and a lump in her
throat which made it difficult to speak to any of them. She
stood so very still, and said so very little, that a bystander not
acquainted with the circumstances might have dubbed her
'unfeeling'; while the fact was that she was feeling too much!

The first bell rang. Katy kissed everybody quietly and
went on board with her father. Her parting from him,
hardest of all, took place in the midst of a crowd of people;
then he had to leave her, and as the wheels began to revolve
she went out on the side deck to have a last glimpse of the
home faces. There they were: Elsie, crying tumultuously,
with her head on Papa's coatsleeve; John laughing, or trying
to laugh, with big tears running down her cheeks the while;
and brave little Clover waving her handkerchief encourag-
ingly, but with a very sober look on her face. Katy's heart
went out to the little group with a sudden passion of regret
and yearning. Why had she said she would go? What was all
Europe in comparison with what she was leaving? Life was
so short, how could she take a whole year out of it to spend
away from the people she loved best? If it had been left to
her to choose, I think she would have flown back to the

shore then and there, and given up the journey. I also think she would have been heartily sorry a little later, had she done so.

But it was not left for her to choose. Already the throb of the engines was growing more regular and the distance widening between the great boat and the wharf. Gradually the dear faces faded into distance; and after watching till the flutter of Clover's handkerchief became an indistinguishable speck, Katy went to the cabin with a heavy heart. But there were Mrs Ashe and Amy, inclined to be homesick also, and in need of cheering, and Katy, as she tried to brighten them, gradually grew bright herself, and recovered her hopeful spirits. Burnet pulled less strongly as it got farther away, and Europe beckoned more brilliantly now that they were fairly embarked on their journey. The sun shone, the lake was a beautiful, dazzling blue, and Katy said to herself: 'After all, a year is not very long, and how happy I am going to be!'

CHAPTER THREE

Rose and Rosebud

Thirty-six hours later the Albany train, running smoothly across the green levels beyond the Mill Dam, brought the travellers to Boston.

Katy looked eagerly from the window for her first glimpse of the city of which she had heard so much. 'Dear little Boston! How nice it is to see it again!' she heard a lady behind her say; but why it should be called 'little Boston' she could not imagine. Seen from the train it looked large, imposing and very picturesque after flat Burnet with its one bank down to the edge of the lake. She studied the towers, steeples and red roofs crowding each other up the slopes of the Tri-Mountain, and the big State House dome crowning all, and made up her mind that she liked the looks of it better than any other city she had ever seen.

The train slackened its speed, ran for a few moments between rows of tall, shabby brick walls, and with a long, final screech of its whistle came to halt in the station-house. Everyone made a simultaneous rush for the door; and Katy and Mrs Ashe, waiting to collect their books and bags, found themselves wedged into their seats and unable to get out. It was a confusing moment, and not comfortable; such moments never are.

But the discomfort brightened into a sense of relief as, looking out of the window, Katy caught sight of a face exactly opposite, which had evidently caught sight of her – a fresh, pretty face, with light, waving hair, pink cheeks all a-dimple, and eyes which shone with laughter and welcome. It was Rose herself, not a bit changed during the years since they parted. A tall young man stood beside her, who must, of course, be her husband, Deniston Browne.

'There is Rose Red,' cried Katy to Mrs Ashe. 'Oh, doesn't she look dear and natural? Do wait and let me introduce you. I want you to know her.'

But the train had come in a little behind time, and Mrs Ashe was afraid of missing the Hingham boat; so she only took a hasty peep from the window at Rose, pronounced her to be charming-looking, kissed Katy hurriedly, reminded her that they must be on the steamer punctually at twelve o'clock the following Saturday, and was gone, with Amy beside her, so that Katy, following last of all the slow-moving line of passengers, stepped all alone down from the carriage into the arms of Rose Red.

'You darling!' was Rose's first greeting. 'I began to think you meant to spend the night in the car, you were so long in getting out. Well, how perfectly lovely this is! Deniston, here is Katy; Katy, this is my husband.'

Rose looked about fifteen as she spoke, and so absurdly young to have a 'husband', that Katy could not help laughing as she shook hands with 'Deniston'; and his own eyes twinkled with fun and evident recognition of the same joke. He was a tall young man, with a pleasant, 'steady' face, and seemed to be infinitely amused, in a quiet way, with everything which his wife said and did.

'Let us make haste and get out of this hole,' went on Rose. 'I can scarcely see for the smoke. Deniston, dear, please find the cab, and have Katy's luggage put in it. I am wild to get her home and exhibit baby before she chews up her new sash or does something else that is dreadful to spoil her looks. I left her sitting in state, Katy, with all her best clothes on, waiting to be made known to you.'

'My large trunk is to go straight to the steamer,' explained Katy, as she gave her checks to Mr Browne. 'I only want the little one taken out to Longwood, please.'

'Now, this is cosy,' remarked Rose, when they were seated in the cab with Katy's bag at their feet. 'Deniston, my love, I wish you were going out with us. There's a nice little bench here all ready and vacant, which is just suited to a man of your inches. You won't? Well, come in the early train, then. Don't forget. Now, isn't he just as nice as I told you he was?' she demanded, the moment the cab began to move.

'He looks very nice indeed, as far as I can judge in three minutes and a quarter.'

'My dear, it ought not to take anybody of ordinary discernment a minute and a quarter to perceive that he is simply the dearest fellow that ever lived,' said Rose. 'I discovered it three seconds after I first beheld him, and was desperately in love with him before he had fairly finished his first bow after introduction.'

'And was he equally prompt?' asked Katy.

'He says so,' replied Rose, with a pretty blush. 'But then, you know, he could hardly say less after such a frank confession on my part. It is no more than decent of him to make believe, even if it is not true! Now, Katy, look at Boston, and see if you don't *love* it!'

The cab had now turned into Boylston Street; and on the right hand lay the common, green as summer after the autumn rains, with the elm arches leafy still. Long, slant beams of afternoon sun were filtering through the boughs and falling across the turf and the paths, where people were walking and sitting, and children and babies playing together. It was a delightful scene; and Katy received an impression of space and cheer and air and freshness, which ever after was associated with her recollection of Boston.

Rose was quite satisfied with her raptures as they drove through Charles Street, between the common and the public garden, all ablaze with autumn flowers, and down the length of Beacon Street with the blue bay shining between the handsome houses on the waterside. Every vestibule and bay-window was gay with potted plants and flower-boxes; and a concourse of happy-looking people, on foot, on horseback and in carriages, was surging to and fro like an equal, prosperous tide, while the sunlight glorified all.

' "Boston shows a soft Venetian side," ' quoted Katy, after a while. 'I know now what Mr Lowell meant when he wrote that. I don't believe there is a more beautiful place in the world.'

'Why, of course there isn't,' retorted Rose, who was a most devoted little Bostonian, in spite of the fact that she had lived in Washington nearly all her life. 'I've not seen much beside, to be sure, but that is no matter; I know it is true. It is the dream of my life to come into the city to live. I don't care what part I live in – West End, South End, North End; it's all one to me, so long as it is Boston!'

'But don't you like Longwood?' asked Katy, looking out admiringly at the pretty places set amid vines and shrubberies which they were now passing. 'It looks so very pretty and pleasant.'

'Yes, it's well enough for anyone who has a taste for natural beauties,' replied Rose. 'I haven't; I never had. There is nothing I hate so much as Nature! I'm a born cockney. I'd rather live in one room over Jordan and Marsh's, and see the world wag past, than be the owner of the most romantic villa that ever was built, I don't care where it may be situated.'

The cab now turned in at a gate and followed a curving drive bordered with trees to a pretty stone house with a porch embowered with Virginia creeper, before which it stopped.

'Here we are!' cried Rose, springing out. 'Now, Katy, you mustn't even take time to sit down before I show you the dearest baby that ever was sent to this sinful earth. Here, let me take your bag; come straight upstairs, and I will exhibit her to you.'

They ran up accordingly, and Rose took Katy into a large

sunny nursery, where, tied with pink ribbons into a little basket-chair and watched over by a pretty young nurse, sat a dear, fat, fair baby, so exactly like Rose in miniature that no one could possibly have mistaken the relationship. The baby began to laugh and coo as soon as it caught sight of its gay little mother, and exhibited just such another dimple as hers, in the middle of a pink cheek. Katy was enchanted.

'Oh, you darling!' she said. 'Would she come to me do you think, Rose?'

'Why, of course she shall!' replied Rose, picking up the baby as if she had been a pillow, and stuffing her into Katy's arms head first. 'Now, just look at her, and tell me if you ever saw anything so enchanting in the whole course of your life before? Isn't she big? Isn't she beautiful? Isn't she good? Just see her little hands and her hair! She never cries except when it is clearly her duty to cry. See her turn her head to look at me! Oh, you angel!' And, seizing the long-suffering baby, she smothered it with kisses. 'I never, never, never did see anything so sweet. Smell her, Katy! Doesn't she smell like heaven?'

Little Rose was indeed a delicious baby, all dimples and good-humour and violet powder, with a skin as soft as a lily's leaf, and a happy capacity for allowing herself to be petted and cuddled without remonstrance. Katy wanted to hold her all the time; but this Rose would by no means permit; in fact, I may as well say at once that the two girls spent a great part of their time during the visit in fighting for the possession of the baby, who looked on at the struggle, and smiled on the victor, whichever it happened to be, with all the philosophic composure of Helen of Troy. She was so soft and sunny and equable that it was no more trouble to care for and amuse her than if she had been a bird or a kitten; and, as Rose remarked, it was 'ten times better fun'.

'I was never allowed as much doll as I wanted in my infancy,' she said. 'I suppose I tore them to pieces too soon;

and they couldn't give me tin ones to play with, as they did washbowls, when I broke the china ones.'

'Were you such a very bad child?' asked Katy.

'Oh, utterly depraved, I believe! You wouldn't think so now, would you? I recollect some dreadful occasions at school. Once I had my head pinned up in my apron because I *would* make faces at the other scholars, and they laughed; but I promptly bit a bay window through the apron, and ran my tongue out of it till they laughed worse than ever. The teacher used to send me home with notes fastened to my pinafore with things like this written in them: "Little Frisk has been more troublesome than usual today. She has pinched all the younger children, and bent the bonnets of all the older ones. We hope to see an amendment soon, or we do not know what we shall do." '

'Why did they call you Little Frisk?' enquired Katy, after she had recovered from the laugh which Rose's reminiscences had called forth.

'It was a term of endearment, I suppose; but somehow my family never seemed to enjoy it as they ought. I cannot understand,' she went on reflectively, 'why I had not sense enough to suppress those awful little notes. It would have been so easy to lose them on the way home, but somehow it never occurred to me. Little Rose will be wiser than that; won't you, my angel? She will tear up the horrid notes – mammy will show her how!'

All the time that Katy was washing her face and brushing the dust of the railway from her dress, Rose sat by with the little Rose in her lap, entertaining her thus. When she was ready, the droll little mamma tucked her baby under her arm and led the way downstairs to a large square parlour with a bay-window, through which the westering sun was shining. It was a pretty room, and had a flavour about it 'just like Rose', Katy declared. No one else would have hung the pictures or looped back the curtains in exactly that way, or have hit upon the happy device of filling the grate with a great bunch of marigolds, pale brown, golden and orange, to simulate the fire which would have been quite too warm on so mild an evening. Morris papers and chintzes and 'artistic' shades of colour were in their infancy at that date; but Rose's taste was in advance of her time, and with a foreshadowing of the coming 'reaction', she had chosen a 'greenery, yallery' paper for her walls, against which hung various articles which looked a great deal queerer then than they would today. There was a mandolin, picked up at some Eastern sale, a warming-pan in shining brass from her mother's attic, two old samplers worked in faded silks, and a quantity of gaily-tinted Japanese fans and embroideries. She had also begged from an old aunt at Beverly Farms a couple of droll little armchairs in white painted wood, with covers of antique needlework. One had 'Chit' embroidered on the middle of its cushion; the other, 'Chat'. These stood suggestively at the corners of the hearth.

'Now, Katy,' said Rose, seating herself in 'Chit', 'pull up "Chat", and let us begin.'

So they did begin, and went on, interrupted only by Baby Rose's coos and splutters, till the dusk fell, till appetising smells floated through from the rear of the house, and the click of a latchkey announced Mr Browne, come home just in time for dinner.

The two days' visit went only too quickly. There is nothing more fascinating to a girl than the *ménage* of a young couple of her own age. It is a sort of playing at real life without the cares and the sense of responsibility that real life is sure to bring. Rose was an adventurous house-keeper. She was still new to the position, she found it very entertaining, and she delighted in experiments of all sorts. If they turned out well, it was good fun; if not, that was funnier still! Her husband, for all his serious manner, had a real boy's love of a lark, and he aided and abetted her in all sorts of whimsical devices. They owned a dog who was only less dear than the baby, a cat only less dear than the dog, a parrot whose education required constant supervision, and a hutch of ring-doves whose melancholy little 'whuddering' oos were the delight of Rose the less. The house seemed astir with young life all over. The only elderly thing in it was the cook, who had the reputation of a dreadful temper; only, unfortunately, Rose made her laugh so much that she never found time to be cross.

Katy felt quite an old, experienced person amid all this movement and liveliness and cheer. It seemed to her that nobody in the world could possibly be having such a good time as Rose; but Rose did not take the same view of the situation.

'It's all very well now,' she said, 'while the warm weather lasts; but in winter Longwood is simply gruesome. The wind never stops blowing day nor night. It howls and it roars and it screams, till I feel as if every nerve in my body were on the point of snapping in two. And the snow, ugh! And the wind, ugh! And burglars! Every night of our lives they come – or I think they come – and I lie awake and hear them sharpening their tools and forcing the locks and murdering the cook and kidnapping Baby, till I long to die and have done with them for ever! Oh, Nature is the most unpleasant thing!'

'Burglars are not Nature,' objected Katy.

'What are they, then? Art? High Art? Well, whatever they are, I do not like them. Oh, if ever the happy day comes when Deniston consents to move into town, I never wish to set my eyes on the country again as long as I live, unless – well, yes, I should like to come out just once more in the horse-cars and *kick* that elm tree by the fence! The number of times that I have lain awake at night listening to its creaking!'

'You might kick it without waiting to have a house in town.'

'Oh, I shouldn't dare as long as we are living here! You never know what Nature may do. She has ways of her own of getting even with people,' remarked her friend, solemnly.

No time must be lost in showing Boston to Katy, Rose said. So, the morning after her arrival she was taken in bright and early to see the sights. There were not quite so many sights to be seen then as there are today. The Art Museum had not got much above its foundations; the new Trinity Church was still in the future; but the big organ and the bronze statue of Beethoven were in their glory, and every day at high noon a small straggling audience wandered into Music Hall to hear the instrument played. To this extempore concert Katy was taken, and to Faneuil Hall and the Athenaeum, to Doll and Richards's, where was an exhibition of pictures, to the Granary Graveyard and the Old South. Then the girls did a little shopping; and by that time they were quite tired enough to make the idea of luncheon agreeable, so they took the path across the common to the Joy Street Mall.

Katy was charmed by all she had seen. The delightful nearness of so many interesting things surprised her. She perceived what is one of Boston's chief charms – that the common and its surrounding streets make a natural centre and rallying-point for the whole city; as the heart is the centre of the body and keeps up a quick correspondence and regulates the life of all its extremities. The stately old houses on Beacon Street, with their rounded fronts, deep window-casements, and here and there a mauve or a lilac pane set in the sashes, took her fancy greatly; and so did the State House, whose situation made it sufficiently imposing, even before the gilding of the dome.

Up the steep steps of the Joy Street Mall they went, to the house on Mt Vernon Street which the Reddings had taken on their return from Washington nearly three years before. Rose had previously shown Katy the site of the old family house on Summer Street, where she was born, now given over wholly to warehouses and shops. Their present residence was one of those wide, old-fashioned brick houses on the crest of the hill, whose upper windows command the view across to the Boston Highlands; in the rear was a spacious yard, almost large enough to be called a garden, walled in with ivies and grapevines, under which were long beds full of roses and chrysanthemums and marigolds and mignonette.

Rose carried a latchkey in her pocket, which she said had been one of her wedding-gifts; with this she unlocked the front door and let Katy into a roomy, white-painted hall.

'We will go straight through to the back steps,' she said. 'Mamma is sure to be sitting there; she always sits there till the first frost; she says it makes her think of the country. How different people are! I don't want to think of the country, but I'm never allowed to forget it for a moment. Mamma is so fond of those steps and the garden.'

There, to be sure, Mrs Redding was found sitting in a wickerwork chair under the shade of the grapevines, with a big basket of mending at her side. It looked so homely and country-like to find a person thus occupied in the middle of a busy city that Katy's heart warmed to her at once.

Mrs Redding was a fair little woman, scarcely taller than Rose and very much like her. She gave Katy a kind welcome.

'You do not seem like a stranger,' she said. 'Rose has told us so much about you and your sister. Sylvia will be very disappointed not to see you. She went off to make some visits when we broke up in the country and is not to be home for three weeks yet.'

Katy was disappointed too, for she had heard a great deal about Sylvia and had wished very much to meet her. She was shown her picture, from which she gathered that she did not look in the least like Rose; for, though equally fair, her fairness was of the tall aquiline type, quite different from

Rose's dimpled prettiness. In fact, Rose resembled her mother, and Sylvia her father; they were only alike in little peculiarities of voice and manner, of which a portrait did not enable Katy to judge.

The two girls had a cosy little luncheon with Mrs Redding, after which Rose carried Katy off to see the house and everything in it which was in any way connected with her own personal history – the room where she used to sleep, the highchair in which she sat as a baby and which was presently to be made over to little Rose, the sofa where Deniston offered himself, and the exact spot on the carpet on which she had stood while they were being married! Last of all –

'Now you shall see the best and dearest thing in the whole house,' she said, opening the door of a room on the second storey. 'Grandmamma, here is my friend Katy Carr, whom you have so often heard me tell about.'

It was a large, pleasant room, with a little wood-fire blazing in a grate, by which, in an armchair full of cushions, with a solitaire-board on a little table beside her, sat a sweet old lady. This was Rose's father's mother. She was nearly eighty; but she was beautiful still, and her manner had a gracious old-fashioned courtesy which was full of charm. She had been thrown from a carriage the year before, and had never since been able to come downstairs or to mingle in the family life.

'They come to me instead,' she told Katy. 'There is no lack of pleasant company,' she added; 'everyone is very good to me. I have a reader for two hours a day, and I read to myself a little, and play patience and solitaire, and never lack entertainment.'

There was something restful in the sight of such a lovely specimen of old age. Katy realised, as she looked at her, what a loss it had been to her own life that she had never known either of her grandparents. She sat and gazed at old Mrs Redding with a mixture of regret and fascination. She longed to hold her hand, and kiss her, and play with her beautiful silvery hair, as Rose did. Rose was evidently the old lady's peculiar darling. They were on the most intimate terms; and Rose dimpled and twinkled, and made saucy speeches, and told all her little adventures and the baby's achievements, and made jests, and talked nonsense as freely as to a person of her own age. It was a delightful relation.

'Grandmamma has taken a fancy to you, I can see,' she told Katy, as they drove back to Longwood. 'She always wants to know my friends; and she has her own opinions about them, I can tell you.'

'Do you really think she liked me?' said Katy warmly. 'I am so glad if she did, for I *loved* her. I never saw a really beautiful old person before.'

'Oh, there's nobody like her!' rejoined Rose. 'I can't imagine what it would be not to have her.' Her merry little face was quite sad and serious as she spoke. 'I wish she were not so old,' she added, with a sigh. 'If we could only put her back twenty years! Then, perhaps, she would live as long as I do.'

But, alas! there is no putting back the hands on the dial of time, no matter how much we may desire it.

The second day of Katy's visit was devoted to the luncheon-party of which Rose had written in her letter, and which was meant to be a reunion or 'side chapter' of the SSUC. Rose had asked every old Hillsover girl who was within reach. There was Mary Silver, of course, and Esther Dearborn, both of whom lived in Boston; and by good luck Alice Gibbons happened to be making Esther a visit, and Ellen Gray came in from Waltham, where her father had recently been settled over a parish, so that altogether they made six of the original nine of the society; and Quaker Row itself never heard a merrier confusion of tongues than resounded through Rose's pretty parlour for the first hour after the arrival of the guests.

There was everybody to ask after, and everything to tell. The girls all seemed wonderfully unchanged to Katy, but they professed to find her very grown-up and dignified.

'I wonder if I am,' she said. 'Clover never told me so. But perhaps she has grown dignified too.'

'Nonsense!' cried Rose; 'Clover could no more be dignified than my baby could. Mary Silver, give me that child this moment! I never saw such a greedy thing as you are; you have kept her to yourself at least a quarter of an hour, and it isn't fair.'

'Oh, I beg your pardon!' said Mary, laughing and covering her mouth with her hand exactly in her old, shy, half-frightened way.

'We only need Mrs Nipson to make our little party complete,' went on Rose, 'or dear Miss Jane! What has become of Miss Jane, by the way? Do any of you know?'

'Oh, she is still teaching at Hillsover and waiting for her missionary! He has never come back. Berry Searles says that when he goes out to walk he always walks away from the United States, for fear of diminishing the distance between them.'

'What a shame!' said Katy, though she could not help laughing. 'Miss Jane was really quite nice – no, not *nice* exactly, but she had good things about her.'

'Had she?' remarked Rose satirically. 'I never observed them. It required eyes like yours, real "double million magnifying-glasses of h'extra power", to find them out. She was all teeth and talons as far as I was concerned; but I think she really did have a softish spot in her old heart for you, Katy, and it's the only good thing I ever knew about her.'

'What has become of Lilly Page?' asked Ellen.

'She's in Europe with her mother. I dare say you'll meet, Katy, and what a pleasure that will be! And have you heard about Bella? She's teaching school in the Indian Territory. Just fancy that scrap teaching school!'

'Isn't it dangerous?' asked Mary Silver.

'Dangerous! How? To her scholars, do you mean? Oh, the Indians! Well, her scalp will be easy to identify if she has adhered to her favourite pomatum; that's one comfort,' put in naughty Rose.

It was a merry luncheon indeed, as little Rose seemed to think, for she laughed and cooed incessantly. The girls were enchanted with her, and voted her by acclamation an honorary member of the SSUC. Her health was drunk in Apollinaris water with all the honours and Rose returned thanks in a droll speech. The friends told each other their histories for the past three years; but it was curious how little, on the whole, most of them had to tell. Though perhaps that was because they did not tell all; for Alice Gibbons confided to Katy in a whisper that she strongly suspected Esther of being engaged, and at the same moment Ellen Gray was convulsing Rose by the intelligence that a theological student from Andover was 'very attentive' to Mary Silver.

'My dear, I don't believe it,' Rose said; 'not even a theological student would dare! and if he did, I am quite sure Mary would consider it most improper. You must be mistaken, Ellen.'

'No, I'm not mistaken; for the theological student is my second cousin, and his sister told me all about it. They are not engaged exactly, but she hasn't said no; so he hopes she will say yes.'

'Oh, she'll never say no; but then she will never say yes, either! He would better take silence as consent! Well, I never did think I should live to see Silvery Mary married. I should as soon have expected to find the Thirty-Nine Articles engaged in a flirtation. She's a dear old thing, though, and as good as gold; and I shall consider your second cousin a lucky man if he persuades her.'

'I wonder where we shall all be when you come back,

Katy,' said Esther Dearborn, as they parted at the gate. 'A year is a long time; all sorts of things may happen in a year.'

These words rang in Katy's ears as she fell asleep that night. 'All sorts of things may happen in a year,' she thought, 'and they may not be all happy things, either.' Almost she wished that the journey to Europe had never been thought of!

But when she waked the next morning to the brightest of October suns shining out of a clear blue sky, her misgivings fled. There could not have been a more beautiful day for their start.

She and Rose went early into town, for old Mrs Redding had made Katy promise to come for a few minutes to say goodbye. They found her sitting by the fire as usual, though her windows were open to admit the sun-warmed air. A little basket of grapes stood on the table beside her, with a nosegay of tea-roses on top. These were from Rose's mother, for Katy to take on board the steamer; and there was something else, a small parcel twisted up in thin white paper.

'It is my goodbye gift,' said the dear old lady. 'Don't open it now. Keep it till you are well out at sea, and get some little thing with it as a keepsake from me.'

Grateful and wondering, Katy put the little parcel in her pocket. With kisses and good wishes she parted from these new-made friends, and she and Rose drove to the steamer, stopping for Mr Browne by the way. They were a little late, so there was not much time for farewells after they arrived; but Rose snatched a moment for a private interview with the stewardess, unnoticed by Katy, who was busy with Mrs Ashe and Amy.

The bell rang, and the great steam-vessel slowly backed into the stream. Then her head was turned to sea, and down the bay she went, leaving Rose and her husband still waving their handkerchiefs on the pier. Katy watched them to the last, and when she could no longer distinguish them, felt that her final link with home was broken.

It was not till she had settled her things in the little cabin which was to be her home for the next ten days, had put her bonnet and dress for safekeeping in the upper berth, nailed up her red and yellow bag, and donned the woollen gown, ulster and soft felt hat which were to do service during the voyage, that she found time to examine the mysterious parcel.

Behold, it was a large, beautiful twenty-dollar gold-piece!

'What a darling old lady!' said Katy; and she gave the gold-piece a kiss. 'How did she come to think of such a thing? I wonder if there is anything in Europe good enough to buy with it?'

CHAPTER FOUR

On the Spartacus

The ulster and the felt hat soon came off again, for a head wind lay waiting in the offing, and the *Spartacus* began to pitch and toss in a manner which made all her unseasoned passengers glad to betake themselves to their berths. Mrs Ashe and Amy were among the earliest victims of sea-sickness; and Katy, after helping them to settle in their staterooms, found herself too dizzy and ill to sit up a moment longer, and thankfully resorted to her own.

As the night came on, the wind grew stronger and the motion worse. The *Spartacus* had the reputation of being a dreadful 'roller', and seemed bound to justify it on this particular voyage. Down, down, down the great hull would slide till Katy would hold her breath with fear lest it might never right itself again; then slowly, slowly the turn would be made, and up, up, up it would go, till the cant on the other side was equally alarming. On the whole, Katy preferred to have her own side of the ship the downward one; for it was less difficult to keep herself in the berth, from which she was in continual danger of being thrown. The night seemed endless, for she was too frightened to sleep except in broken snatches; and when day dawned, and she looked through the little round pane of glass in the porthole, only grey sky and grey weltering waves and flying spray and rain met her view.

'Oh, dear, why do people ever go to sea, unless they must?' she thought feebly to herself. She wanted to get up and see how Mrs Ashe had lived through the night, but the attempt to move made her so miserably ill that she was glad to sink again on her pillows.

The stewardess looked in with offers of tea and toast, the very idea of which was simply dreadful, and pronounced the other lady, ' 'orribly ill; worse than you are, miss', and the little girl 'takin' on dreadful in the h'upper berth'. Of this fact Katy soon had audible proof; for as her dizzy senses rallied a little, she could hear Amy in the opposite stateroom crying and sobbing pitifully. She seemed to be angry as well as sick, for she was scolding her poor mother in the most vehement fashion.

'I hate being at sea,' Katy heard her say. 'I won't stay in this nasty old ship. Mamma! Mamma! do you hear me? I won't stay in this ship! It wasn't a bit kind of you to bring me to such a horrid place. It was very un–kind; it was cru–el. I want to go back, Mamma. Tell the captain to take me back to the land. Mamma, why don't you speak to me? Oh, I am so sick and so very un–happy! Don't you wish you were dead? I do!'

And then came another storm of sobs, but never a sound from Mrs Ashe, who, Katy suspected, was too ill to speak. She felt very sorry for poor little Amy, raging there in her high berth like some imprisoned creature, but she was powerless to help her. She could only resign herself to her own discomforts, and try to believe that somehow, some-time, this state of things must mend – either they should all get to land or all go to the bottom and be drowned, and at that moment she didn't care very much which it turned out to be.

The gale increased as the day wore on, and the vessel pitched dreadfully. Twice Katy was thrown out of her berth on to the floor; then the stewardess came and fixed a sort of movable side to the berth, which held her in, but made her feel like a child fastened into a railed crib. At intervals she could still hear Amy crying and scolding her mother, and conjectured that they were having a dreadful time of it in the other stateroom. It was all like a bad dream. 'And they call this travelling for pleasure!' thought poor Katy.

One droll thing happened in the course of the second night – at least it seemed droll afterward; at the time Katy was too uncomfortable to enjoy it. Amid the rush of the wind, the creaking of the ship's timbers, and the shrill buzz of the screw, she heard a sound of queer little footsteps in the entry outside her open door, hopping and leaping together in an odd irregular way, like a regiment of mice or toy soldiers. Nearer and nearer they came; and Katy, opening her eyes, saw a procession of boots and shoes of all sizes and shapes which had evidently been left on the floors or at the doors of various staterooms, and which, in obedience to the lurchings of the vessel, had collected in the cabin. They now seemed to be acting in concert with one another, and really looked alive as they bumped and trotted side by side, and two by two, in at the door and up close to her bedside. There they remained for several moments executing what looked like a dance; then the leading shoe turned on its heel as if giving a signal to the others, and they all hopped slowly again into the passageway and disappeared. It was exactly like one of Hans Christian Andersen's fairy tales, Katy wrote to Clover afterward. She heard them going down the cabin; but how it ended, or whether the owners of the boots and shoes ever got their own particular pairs back again, she never knew.

Toward morning the gale abated, the sea became smoother and she dropped asleep. When she woke the sun was struggling through the clouds, and she felt better.

The stewardess opened the porthole to freshen the air, and helped her to wash her face and smooth her tangled hair; then she produced a little basin of gruel and a triangular piece of toast, and Katy found that her appetite was come again and she could eat.

'And 'ere's a letter, ma'am, which has come for you by post this morning,' said the nice old stewardess, producing an envelope from her pocket, and eyeing her patient with great satisfaction.

'By post!' cried Katy in amazement; 'why, how can that be?' Then, catching sight of Rose's handwriting on the envelope, she understood, and smiled at her own simplicity.

The stewardess beamed at her as she opened it, then saying again, 'Yes, 'm, by post, m'm,' withdrew, and left Katy to enjoy the little surprise.

The letter was not long, but it was very like its writer. Rose drew a picture of what Katy would probably be doing at the time it reached her – a picture so near the truth that Katy felt as if Rose must have the spirit of prophecy, especially as she kindly illustrated the situation with a series of pen-and-ink drawings, in which Katy was depicted as prone in her berth, refusing with horror to go to dinner, looking longingly backward toward the quarter where the United States was supposed to be, and fishing out of her porthole with a crooked pin in hopes of grappling the submarine cable and sending a message to her family to come out at once and take her home. It ended with this short 'poem', over which Katy laughed till Mrs Ashe called feebly across the entry to ask what was the matter?

> Break, break, break,
> And misbehave, O sea,
> And I wish that my tongue could utter
> The hatred I feel for thee!
>
> Oh, well for the fisherman's child
> On the sandy beach at his play;
> Oh, well for all sensible folk
> Who are safe at home today!
>
> But this horrible ship keeps on,
> And is never a moment still,

And I yearn for the touch of the nice dry land,
Where I needn't feel so ill!

Break! break! break!
There is no good left in me;
For the dinner I ate on the shore so late
Has vanished into the sea!'

Laughter is very restorative after the forlornity of seasickness; and Katy was so stimulated by her letter that she managed to struggle into her dressing-gown and slippers and across the entry to Mrs Ashe's stateroom. Amy had fallen asleep at last and must not be waked up, so their interview was conducted in whispers. Mrs Ashe had by no means got to the tea-and-toast stage yet, and was feeling miserable enough.

'I have had the most dreadful time with Amy,' she said. 'All day yesterday, when she wasn't sick, she was raging at me from the upper berth, and I too ill to say a word in reply. I never knew her so naughty! And it seemed very neglectful not to come to see after you, poor dear child! but really I couldn't raise my head.'

'Neither could I, and I felt just as guilty not to be taking care of you,' said Katy. 'Well, the worst is over with all of us, I hope. The vessel doesn't pitch half so much now, and the stewardess says we shall feel a great deal better as soon as we get on deck. She is coming presently to help me up; and when Amy wakes, won't you let her be dressed, and I will take care of her while Mrs Barrett attends to you.'

'I don't think I can be dressed,' sighed poor Mrs Ashe. 'I feel as if I should just lie here till we get to Liverpool.'

'Oh, no, h'indeed, mum – no, you won't,' put in Mrs Barrett, who at that moment appeared, gruel-cup in hand. 'I don't never let my ladies lie in their berths a moment longer than there is need of. I h'always gets them on deck as soon as possible to get the h'air. It's the best medicine you can 'ave, ma'am, the fresh h'air; h'indeed it h'is.'

Stewardesses are all-powerful on board ship, and Mrs Barrett was so persuasive as well as positive that it was not possible to resist her. She got Katy into her dress and wraps, and seated her on deck in a chair with a great rug wrapped about her feet, with very little effort on Katy's part. Then she dived down the companionway again, and in the course of an hour appeared escorting a big, burly steward, who carried poor little pale Amy in his arms as easily as though she had been a kitten. Amy gave a scream of joy at the sight of Katy, and cuddled down in her lap under the warm rug with a sigh of relief and satisfaction.

'I thought I was never going to see you again,' she said, with a little squeeze. 'Oh, Miss Katy, it has been so horrid! I never thought that going to Europe meant such dreadful things as this!'

'This is only the beginning; we shall get across the sea in a few days, and then we shall find out what going to Europe really means. But what made you behave so, Amy, and cry and scold poor Mamma when she was sick? I could hear you all the way across the entry?'

'Could you? Then why didn't you come to me?'

'I wanted to; but I was sick too, so sick that I couldn't move. But why were you so naughty? – you didn't tell me.'

'I didn't mean to be naughty, but I couldn't help crying. You would have cried too, and so would Johnnie, if you had been cooped up in a dreadful old berth at the top of the wall that you couldn't get out of, and hadn't had anything to eat, and nobody to bring you any water when you wanted some. And Mamma wouldn't answer when I called to her.'

'She couldn't answer; she was too ill,' explained Katy. 'Well, my pet, it was pretty hard for you. I hope we shan't have any more such days. The sea is a great deal smoother now.'

'Mabel looks quite pale; she was sick too,' said Amy, regarding the doll in her arms with an anxious air. 'I hope the fresh h'air will do her good.'

'Is she going to have any fresh hair?' asked Katy, wilfully misunderstanding.

'That was what that woman called it – the fat one who made me come up here. But I'm glad she did, for I feel heaps better already; only I keep thinking of poor little Maria Matilda shut up in the trunk in that dark place, and wondering if she's sick. There's nobody to explain to her down there.'

'They say that you don't feel the motion half so much in the bottom of the ship,' said Katy. 'Perhaps she hasn't noticed it at all. Dear me, how good something smells! I wish they would bring us something to eat.'

A good many passengers had come up by this time; and Robert, the deck steward, was going about, tray in hand, taking orders for lunch. Amy and Katy both felt suddenly ravenous; and when Mrs Ashe, a while later, was helped up the stairs, she was amazed to find them eating cold beef and roasted potatoes, with the finest appetites in the world. 'They had served out their apprenticeships,' the kindly old captain told them, 'and were made free of the nautical guild from that time on.' So it proved; for after these two bad days none of the party was sick again during the voyage.

Amy had a clamorous appetite for stories as well as for cold beef; and to appease this craving, Katy started a sort of ocean serial called 'The History of Violet and Emma', which she meant to make last till they got to Liverpool, but which in reality lasted much longer. It might, with equal propriety, have been called 'The Adventures of Two Little Girls Who Didn't Have Any Adventures', for nothing in particular happened to either Emma or Violet during the whole course of their long-drawn-out history. Amy, how-ever, found them perfectly enchanting, and was never weary of hearing how they went to school and came home again, how they got into scrapes and got out of them, how they made good resolutions and broke them, about their

Christmas presents and birthday treats, and what they said and how they felt. The first instalment of this unexciting romance was given that first afternoon on deck; and after that Amy claimed a new chapter daily, and it was a chief ingredient of her pleasure during the voyage.

On the third morning Katy woke and dressed so early that she gained the deck before the sailors had finished their scrubbing and holy-stoning. She took refuge within the companionway, and sat down on the top step of the ladder, to wait till the deck was dry enough to venture upon. There the captain found her and drew near for a talk.

Captain Bryce was exactly the kind of sea-captain that is found in storybooks, but not always in real life. He was stout, and grizzled, and brown, and kind. He had a bluff, weatherbeaten face, lit up by a pair of shrewd blue eyes which twinkled when he was pleased; and his manner, though it was full of the habit of command, was quiet and pleasant. He was a martinet on board his ship. Not a sailor under him would have dared dispute his orders for a moment; but he was very popular with them, notwithstanding; they liked him as much as they feared him, for they knew him to be their best friend if it came to sickness or trouble with any of them.

Katy and he grew quite intimate during their long morning talk. The captain liked girls. He had one of his own, about Katy's age, and was fond of talking about her. Lucy was his mainstay at home, he told Katy. Her mother had been 'weakly' now this long time back, and Bess and Nanny were but children yet, so Lucy had to take command and keep things shipshape when he was away.

'She'll be on the lookout when the steamer comes in,' said the captain. 'There's a signal we've arranged which means "All's well", and when we get up the river a little way I always look to see if it's flying. It's a bit of a towel hung from a particular window; and when I see it I say to myself,

'Thank God! another voyage safely done and no harm come of it.' It's a sad kind of work for a man to go off for a twenty-four days' cruise leaving a sick wife on shore behind him. If it wasn't that I have Lucy to look after things, I should have thrown up my command long ago.'

'Indeed, I am glad you have Lucy; she must be a great comfort to you,' said Katy, sympathetically; for the captain's hearty voice trembled a little as he spoke. She made him tell her the colour of Lucy's hair and eyes, and exactly how tall she was, and what she had studied, and what sort of books she liked. She seemed such a very nice girl and Katy thought she should like to know her.

The deck had dried fast in the fresh sea-wind, and the captain had just arranged Katy in her chair, and was wrapping the rug about her feet in a fatherly way, when Mrs Barrett, all smiles, appeared from below.

'Oh, 'ere you h'are, miss. I couldn't think what 'ad come to you so early; and you're looking ever so well again, I'm pleased to see; and 'ere's a bundle just arrived, miss, by the Parcels Delivery.'

'What!' cried simple Katy. Then she laughed at her own foolishness, and took the 'bundle', which was directed in Rose's unmistakable hand.

It contained a pretty little green-bound copy of Emerson's poems, with Katy's name and 'To be read at sea' written on the flyleaf. Somehow, the little gift seemed to bridge the long misty distance which stretched between the vessel's stern and Boston Bay, and to bring home and friends a great deal nearer. With a half-happy, half-tearful pleasure Katy recognised the fact that distance counts for little if people love one another and that hearts have a telegraph of their own whose messages are as sure and swift as any of those sent over the material lines which link continent to continent and shore with shore.

Later in the morning, Katy, going down to her stateroom

for something, came across a pallid, exhausted-looking lady, who lay stretched on one of the long sofas in the cabin, with a baby in her arms and a little girl sitting at her feet, quite still, with a pair of small hands folded in her lap. The little girl did not seem to be more than four years old. She had two pigtails of thick flaxen hair hanging over her shoulders, and at Katy's approach raised a pair of solemn blue eyes which had so much appeal in them, though she said nothing, that Katy stopped at once.

'Can I do anything for you?' she asked. 'I am afraid you have been very ill.'

At the sound of her voice the lady on the sofa opened her eyes. She tried to speak, but to Katy's dismay began to cry instead; and when the words came they were strangled with sobs.

'You are so kin–d to ask,' she said. 'If you would give my little girl something to eat! She has had nothing since yesterday, and I have been so ill; and no–body has c–ome near us!'

'Oh!' cried Katy, with horror, 'nothing to eat since yesterday! How did it happen?'

'Everybody has been sick on our side of the ship,' explained the poor lady, 'and I suppose the stewardess thought, as I had a maid with me, that I needed her less than the others. But my maid has been sick too; and oh, so selfish! She wouldn't even take the baby into the berth with her; and I have had all I could do to manage with him, when I couldn't lift up my head. Little Gretchen has had to go without anything; and she has been so good and patient!'

Katy lost no time, but ran for Mrs Barrett, whose indignation knew no bounds when she heard how the helpless party had been neglected.

'It's a new person that stewardess h'is, ma'am,' she explained, 'and most h'inefficient! I told the captain when she come aboard that I didn't 'ave much opinion of her, and

now he'll see how it h'is. I'm h'ashamed that such a thing
should 'appen on the *Spartacus*, ma'am – I h'am, h'indeed.
H'it never woul'ave been so h'under h'Eliza, ma'am – she's
the one that went h'off and got herself married the trip
before last when this person came to take her place.'

All the time that she talked Mrs Barrett was busy in making
Mrs Ware – for that, it seemed, was the sick lady's name –
more comfortable; and Katy was feeding Gretchen out of a
big bowl full of bread-and-milk which one of the stewards
had brought. The little uncomplaining thing was evidently
half-starved, but with the mouthfuls, the pink began to steal
back into her cheeks and lips, and the dark circles lessened
under the blue eyes. By the time the bottom of the bowl was
reached she could smile, but still she said not a word except a
whispered *danke schön*. Her mother explained that she had
been born in Germany, and always had till now been cared
for by a German nurse, so that she knew that language better
than English.

Gretchen was a great amusement to Katy and Amy during
the rest of the voyage. They kept her on deck with them a
great deal, and she was perfectly content with them and very
good, though always solemn and quiet. Pleasant people
turned up among the passengers, as always happens on an
ocean steamship, and others not so pleasant, perhaps, who
were rather curious and interesting to watch.

Katy grew to feel as if she knew a great deal about her
fellow-travellers as time went on. There was the young girl
going out to join her parents, under the care of a severe
governess, whom everybody on board rather pitied. There
was the other girl on her way to study art, who was travelling
quite alone and seemed to have nobody to meet her or to go
to except a fellow student of her own age, already in Paris,
but who seemed quite unconscious of her lonely position
and competent to grapple with anything or anybody. There
was the queer old gentleman who had 'crossed' eleven times

before, and had advice and experience to spare for anyone who would listen to them; and the other gentleman, not so old but even more queer, who had 'frozen his stomach', eight years before, by indulging, on a hot summer's day, in sixteen successive ice-creams, alternated with ten glasses of equally cold soda water, and who related this exciting experience in turn to everybody on board. There was the bad little boy, whose parents were powerless to oppose him, and who carried terror to the hearts of all beholders whenever he appeared, and the pretty widow who filled the role of reigning belle; and the other widow, not quite so pretty or so much a belle, who had a good deal to say, in a voice made discreetly low, about what a pity it was that dear Mrs So-and-so should do this or that, and 'Doesn't it strike you as unfortunate that she should not consider, the other thing? A great seagoing steamer is a little world in itself, and gives one a glimpse of all sorts and conditions of people and characters.

On the whole, there was no one on the *Spartacus* whom Katy liked so well as sedate little Gretchen, except the dear old captain with whom she was a prime favourite. He gave Mrs Ashe and herself the seats next to him at table, looked after their comfort in every possible way and each night at dinner sent Katy one of the apple-dumplings made specially for him by the cook, who had gone many voyages with the captain and knew his fancies. Katy did not care particularly for the dumpling, but she valued it as a mark of regard, and always ate it when she could.

Meanwhile, every morning brought a fresh surprise from that dear, painstaking Rose, who had evidently worked hard and thought harder in contriving pleasures for Katy's first voyage at sea. Mrs Barrett was enlisted in the plot, there could be no doubt of that, and enjoyed the joke as much as anyone as she presented herself each day with the invariable formula, 'A letter for you, ma'am,' or, 'A bundle, miss, come by the Parcels Delivery.' On the fourth morning it was a photograph of Baby Rose, in a little flat morocco case. The fifth brought a wonderful epistle, full of startling pieces of news, none of them true. On the sixth appeared a long, narrow box containing a fountain-pen. Then came Mr Howell's *A Foregone Conclusion*, which Katy had never seen; then a box of quinine pills; then a sachet for her trunk; then another burlesque poem; last of all, a cake of delicious violet soap, 'to wash the sea-smell from her hands', the label said. It grew to be one of the little excitements of ship life to watch for the arrival of these daily gifts; and, 'What did the mail bring for you this time, Miss Carr?' was a question frequently asked. Each arrival Katy thought must be the final one; but Rose's forethought had gone so far even as to provide an extra parcel in case the voyage was a day longer than usual, and 'Miss Carr's mail' continued to come in till the very last morning.

Katy never forgot the thrill that went through her when, after so many days of sea, her eyes first caught sight of the dim line of the Irish coast. An exciting and interesting day followed as, after stopping at Queenstown to leave the mails, they sped north-eastward between shores which grew more distinct and beautiful with every hour – on one side Ireland, on the other the bold mountain lines of the Welsh coast. It was late afternoon when they entered the Mersey, and dusk had fallen before the captain got out his glass to look for the white, fluttering speck in his own window which meant so much to him. Long he studied before he made quite sure that it was there. At last he shut the glass with a satisfied air.

'It's all right,' he said to Katy, who stood near, almost as much interested as he. 'Lucy never forgets, bless her! Well, there's another voyage over and done with, thank God, and my Mary is where she was. It's a load taken from my mind.'

The moon had risen and was shining softly on the river as

the crowded tender landed the passengers from the *Spartacus* at the Liverpool docks.

'We shall meet again in London or in Paris,' said one to another, and cards and addresses were exchanged. Then, after a brief delay at the custom house, they separated, each to his own particular destination; and as a general thing, none of them ever saw any of the others again. It is often thus with those who have been fellow-voyagers at sea; and it is always a surprise and perplexity to inexperienced travellers that it can be so, and that those who have been so much to each other for ten days can melt away into space and disappear as though the brief intimacy had never existed.

'Four-wheeler or hansom, ma'am?' said a porter to Mrs Ashe.

'Which, Katy?'

'Oh, let us have a hansom! I never saw one, and they look so nice in *Punch*.'

So a hansom cab was called, the two ladies got in, Amy cuddled down between them, the folding-doors were shut over their knees like a lap-robe, and away they drove up the solidly paved streets to the hotel where they were to pass the night. It was too late to see or do anything but enjoy the sense of being on firm land once more.

'How lovely it will be to sleep in a bed that doesn't tip or roll from side to side!' said Mrs Ashe.

'Yes, and that is wide enough and long enough and soft enough to be comfortable!' replied Katy. 'I feel as if I could sleep for a fortnight to make up for the bad nights at sea.'

Everything seemed delightful to her – the space for undressing, the great tub of fresh water which stood beside the English-looking washstand with its ample basin and ewer, the chintz-curtained bed, the coolness, the silence – and she closed her eyes with the pleasant thought in her mind, 'It is really England, and we are really here!'

CHAPTER FIVE

Storybook England

'Oh, is it raining?' was Katy's first question next morning, when the maid came to call her. The pretty room, with its gaily flowered chintz, and china, and its brass bedstead, did not look half so bright as when lit with gas the night before; and a dim grey light struggled in at the window, which in America would certainly have meant bad weather coming or already come.

'Oh, no, h'indeed, ma'am, it's a very fine day – not bright, ma'am, but very dry,' was the answer.

Katy couldn't imagine what the maid meant, when she peeped between the curtains and saw a thick dull mist lying over everything, and the pavements opposite her window shining with wet. Afterwards, when she understood better the peculiarities of the English climate, she too learned to call days not absolutely rainy 'fine', and to be grateful for them; but on that first morning her sensations were of bewildered surprise, almost vexation.

Mrs Ashe and Amy were waiting in the coffee-room when she went in search of them.

'What shall we have for breakfast,' asked Mrs Ashe – 'our first meal in England? Katy, you order it.'

'Let's have all the things we have read about in books and don't have at home,' said Katy eagerly. But when she came to look over the bill of fare there didn't seem to be many such things. Soles and muffins she finally decided upon, and, as an afterthought, gooseberry jam.

'Muffins sound so very good in Dickens, you know,' she explained to Mrs Ashe; 'and I never saw a sole.'

The soles when they came proved to be nice little pan-fish, not unlike what in New England are called 'scup'. All the party took kindly to them; but the muffins were a great disappointment, tough and tasteless, with a flavour about them as of scorched flannel.

'How queer and disagreeable they are!' said Katy. 'I feel as if I were eating rounds cut from an old ironing-blanket and buttered! Dear me! what did Dickens mean by making such a fuss about them, I wonder? And I don't care for gooseberry jam, either; it isn't half as good as the jams we have at home. Books are very deceptive.'

'I am afraid they are. We must make up our minds to find a great many things not quite so nice as they sound when we read about them,' replied Mrs Ashe.

Mabel was breakfasting with them, of course, and was heard to remark at this juncture that she didn't like muffins either, and would a great deal rather have waffles; where-upon Amy reproved her, and explained that nobody in England knew what waffles were, they were such a stupid nation, and that Mabel must learn to eat whatever was given her and not find fault with it!

After this moral lesson it was found to be dangerously near train-time; and they all hurried to the railroad station which, fortunately, was close by. There was rather a scramble and confusion for a few moments; for Katy, who had undertaken to buy the tickets, was puzzled by the unaccustomed coinage; and Mrs Ashe, whose part was to see after the luggage, found herself perplexed and worried by the absence of checks, and by no means disposed to accept the porter's statement that if she'd only bear in mind that the trunks were in the second van from the engine, and get out to see that they were safe once or twice during the journey, and call for them as soon as they reached London, she'd have no trouble – 'please remember the porter, ma'am!' However, all was happily settled at last; and without any serious inconveniences they found themselves established in a first-class carriage and, presently after, running smoothly at full speed across the rich English Midlands toward London and the eastern coast.

The extreme greenness of the October landscape was what struck them at first, and the wonderfully orderly and trim aspect of the country, with no ragged, stump-dotted fields or reaches of wild untended woods. Late in October as it was, the hedgerows and meadows were still almost summer-like in colour, though the trees were leafless. The delightful-looking old manor-houses and farmhouses of which they had glimpses now and again, were a constant pleasure to Katy, with their mullioned windows, twisted chimney-stacks, porches of quaint build and thick-growing ivy. She contrasted them with the uncompromising ugliness of farmhouses she remembered at home, and wondered whether it could be that at the end of another thousand years or so America would have picturesque buildings like those to show in addition to her picturesque scenery.

Suddenly, into the midst of these reflections there glanced a picture so vivid that it almost took away her breath, as the train steamed past a pack of hounds in full cry, followed by a galloping throng of scarlet-coated huntsmen. One horse and rider were in the air, going over a wall. Another was just rising to the leap. A string of others, headed by a lady, were tearing across a meadow bounded by a little brook, and beyond that streamed the hounds following the invisible fox. It was like one of Muybridge's instantaneous photographs of 'The Horse in Motion' for the moment that it lasted, and Katy put it away in her memory, distinct and brilliant, as she might a real picture.

Their destination in London was Batt's Hotel in Dover Street. The old gentleman on the *Spartacus*, who had 'crossed' so many times, had furnished Mrs Ashe with a number of addresses of hotels and lodging-houses, from among which Katy had chosen Batt's for the reason that it was mentioned in Miss Edgeworth's *Patronage*. 'It was the place,' she explained, 'where Godfrey Percy didn't stay when Lord Oldborough sent him the letter.' It seemed an odd enough reason for going anywhere, that a person in a novel didn't stay there. But Mrs Ashe knew nothing of London, and had no preference of her own; so she was perfectly willing to give Katy hers, and Batt's was decided upon.

'It is just like a dream or a story,' said Katy, as they drove away from the London station in a four-wheeler. 'It is really ourselves, and this is really London. Can you imagine it?'

She looked out. Nothing met her eyes but dingy weather, muddy streets, long rows of ordinary brick or stone houses. It might very well have been New York or Boston on a foggy day, yet to her eyes all things had a subtle difference which made them unlike similar objects at home.

'Wimpole Street!' she cried suddenly, as she caught sight of the name on the corner; 'that is the street where Maria Crawford in *Mansfield Park*, you know, "opened one of the best houses" after she married Mr Rushworth. Think of seeing Wimpole Street! What fun!' She looked eagerly out after the "best houses", but the whole street looked uninteresting and old-fashioned; the best house to be seen was not of a kind, Katy thought, to reconcile an ambitious young woman to a dull husband. Katy had to remind herself that Miss Austen wrote her novels nearly a century ago, that London was a 'growing' place and that things were probably much changed since that day.

More 'fun' awaited them when they arrived at Batt's, and exactly such a landlady sailed forth to welcome them as they had often met with in books – an old landlady, smiling and rubicund, with a towering lace cap on her head, a flowered silk gown, a gold chain, and a pair of fat mittened hands demurely crossed over a black brocade apron. She alone would have been worth crossing the ocean to see, they all declared. Their telegram had been received, and rooms were ready, with a bright, smoky fire of soft coals; the dinner-table was set, and a nice, formal, white-cravatted old waiter, who seemed to have stepped out of the same book with the landlady, was waiting to serve it. Everything was dingy and old-fashioned, but very clean and comfortable; and Katy concluded that on the whole Godfrey Percy would have done wisely to go to Batt's, and could have fared no better at the other hotel where he did stay.

The first of Katy's 'London sights' came to her next morning before she was out of her bedroom. She heard a bell ring and a queer, squeaking little voice utter a speech of which she could not make out a single word. Then came a laugh and a shout, as if several boys were amused at something or other; and altogether her curiosity was roused, so that she finished dressing as fast as she could, and ran to the drawing-room window, which commanded a view of the street. Quite a little crowd was collected under the window, and in their midst was a queer box raised high on poles, with little red curtains tied back on either side to form a miniature stage, on which puppets were moving and vociferating. Katy knew in a moment that she was seeing her first Punch and Judy!

The box and the crowd began to move away. Katy, in despair, ran to Wilkins, the old waiter, who was setting the breakfast table.

'Oh, please stop that man!' she said. 'I want to see him.'

'What man is it, miss?' said Wilkins.

When he reached the window, and realised what Katy meant, his sense of propriety seemed to receive a severe shock. He even ventured on remonstrance.

'H'I wouldn't, miss, h'if h'I was you. Them Punches are a low lot, miss; they h'ought to be put down, really they h'ought. Gentlefolks, h'as a general thing, pays no h'attention to them.'.

But Katy didn't care what 'gentlefolks' did or did not do and insisted upon having Punch called back. So Wilkins was forced to swallow his remonstrances and his dignity, and go in pursuit of the objectionable object. Amy came rushing out, with her hair flying, and Mabel in her arms; and she and Katy had a real treat of Punch and Judy, with all the well-known scenes, and perhaps a few new ones thrown in for their especial behoof; for the showman seemed to be inspired by the rapturous enjoyment of his little audience of three at the first-floor windows. Punch beat Judy and stole the baby, and Judy banged Punch in return, and the constable came in, and Punch outwitted him, and the hangman and the devil made their appearance duly; and it was all perfectly satisfactory, and 'just exactly what she hoped it would be, and it quite made up for the muffins,' Katy declared.

Then, when Punch had gone away, the question arose as to what they should choose out of the many delightful things in London for their first morning.

Like ninety-nine Americans out of a hundred, they decided on Westminster Abbey; and indeed there is nothing in England better worth seeing, or more impressive, in its dim, rich antiquity, to eyes fresh from the world which still calls itself 'new'. So to the Abbey they went, and lingered there till Mrs Ashe declared herself to be absolutely dropping with fatigue.

'If you don't take me home and give me something to eat,' she said, 'I shall drop down on one of these pedestals and stay there and be exhibited for ever after as an "effigy" of somebody belonging to ancient English history.'

So Katy tore herself away from Henry VII and the Poets' Corner, and tore Amy away from a quaint little tomb shaped like a cradle, with the marble image of a baby in it, which had greatly taken her fancy. She could only be consoled by the promise that she should soon come again and stay as long as she liked.

She reminded Katy of this promise the very next morning.

'Mamma has waked up with rather a bad headache and she thinks she will lie still and not come to breakfast,' she reported. 'And she sends her love, and says will you please have a cab and go where you like; and if I won't be a trouble, she would be glad if you would take me with you. And I won't be a trouble, Miss Katy, and I know where I wish you would go.'

'Where is that?'

'To see that cunning little baby again that we saw yesterday. I want to show her to Mabel – she didn't go with us, you know, and I don't like to have her mind not improved; and, darling Miss Katy, mayn't I buy some flowers and put them on the baby? She's so dusty and so old that I don't believe anybody has put any flowers for her for ever so long.'

Katy found this idea rather pretty, and willingly stopped at Covent Garden, where they bought a bunch of late roses for eighteen pence, which entirely satisfied Amy. With them in her hand, and Mabel in her arms, she led the way through the dim aisles of the Abbey, through grates and doors, and up and down steps; the guide following, but not at all needed, for Amy seemed to have a perfectly clear recollection of every turn and winding. When the chapel was reached, she laid the roses on the tomb with gentle fingers, and a pitiful, reverent look in her grey eyes. Then she lifted Mabel up to kiss the odd little baby effigy above the marble quilt; whereupon the guide seemed altogether surprised out of his composure, and remarked to Katy: 'Little miss is an h'American, as is plain to see; no h'English child would be likely to think of doing such a thing.'

'Do not English children take any interest in the tombs of the Abbey?' asked Katy.

'Oh, yes, m'm – h'interest; but they don't take no special notice of one tomb above h'another.'

Katy could scarcely keep from laughing, especially as she heard Amy, who had been listening to the conversation, give an audible sniff, and inform Mabel that she was glad *she* was not an English child who didn't notice things, and liked grown-up graves as much as she did dear little cunning ones like this!

Later in the day, when Mrs Ashe was better, they all drove together to the quaint old keep which has been the scene of so many tragedies and is known as the Tower of London. Here they were shown various rooms and chapels and prisons; and among the rest the apartments where Queen Elizabeth, when a friendless young princess, was shut up for many months by her sister, Queen Mary. Katy had read somewhere, and now told Amy, the pretty legend of the four little children who lived with their parents in the Tower, and used to play with the royal captive; and how one little boy brought her a key which he had picked up from the ground, and said, 'Now you can go out when you will, lady;' and how the Lords of the Council, getting wind of it, sent for the children to question them, and frightened them and their friends almost to death, and forbade them to go near the princess again.

A story about children always brings the past much nearer to a child, and Amy's imagination was so excited by this tale that when they got to the darksome closet which is said to have been the prison of Sir Walter Raleigh, she marched out of it with a pale and wrathful face. 'If this is English history, I never mean to learn any more of it, and neither shall Mabel,' she declared.

But it is not possible for Amy or anyone else not to learn a great deal of history simply by going about London. So many places are associated with people or events, and seeing the places makes one care so much more for the people or the events that one insensibly questions and wonders. Katy, who had 'browsed' all through her childhood in a good old-fashioned library, had her memory stuffed with all manner of little scraps of information and literary allusions, which now came into use. It was like owning the disjointed bits of a puzzle, and suddenly discovering that properly put together they made a pattern. Mrs Ashe, who had never been much of a reader, considered her young friend a prodigy of intelligence; but Katy herself realised how inadequate and inexact her knowledge was, and how many bits were missing from the pattern of her puzzle. She wished with all her heart, as everyone wishes under such circumstances, that she had studied harder and more wisely while the chance was in her power. On a journey you cannot read to advantage. Remember that, dear girls, who are looking forward to travelling someday, and be industrious in time.

October is not a favourable month in which to see England. Water, water is everywhere; you breathe it; you absorb it; it wets your clothes and it dampens your spirits. Mrs Ashe's friends advised her not to think of Scotland at that time of the year. One by one their little intended excursions were given up. A single day and night in Oxford and Stratford-on-Avon; a short visit to the Isle of Wight, where, in a country place which seemed provokingly pretty as far as they could see it for the rain, lived that friend of Mrs Ashe who had married an Englishman and in so doing had, as Katy privately thought, 'renounced the sun'; a peep at Stonehenge from under the shelter of an umbrella, and an hour or two in Salisbury Cathedral – was all that they accomplished, except a brief halt at Winchester, that Katy might have the privilege of seeing the grave of her beloved Miss Austen. Katy had come abroad with a terribly long list of graves to visit, Mrs Ashe declared. They laid a few rain-washed flowers upon the tomb, and listened with edification to the verger, who enquired: 'Whatever was it, ma'am, that lady did which brings so many h'Americans to h'ask about her? Our h'English people don't seem to take the same h'interest.'

'She wrote such delightful stories,' explained Katy: but the old verger shook his head.

'I think h'it must be some other party, miss, you've confused with this here. It stands to reason, miss, that we'd have heard of 'em h'over 'ere in England sooner than you would h'over there in h'America, if the books 'ad been h'anything so h'extraordinary.'

The night after their return to London they were dining for the second time with the cousins of whom Mrs Ashe had spoken to Dr Carr; and as it happened Katy sat next to a quaint elderly American, who had lived for twenty years in London and knew it much better than most Londoners do. This gentleman, Mr Allen Beach, had a hobby for antiquities, old books especially, and passed half his time at the British Museum, and the other half in sale-rooms and the old shops in Wardour Street.

Katy was lamenting over the bad weather which stood in the way of their plans.

'It is so vexatious!' she said. 'Mrs Ashe meant to go to York and Lincoln and all the cathedral towns and to Scotland; and we have had to give it all up because of the rains. We shall go away having seen hardly anything.'

'You can see London.'

'We have – that is, we have seen the things that everybody sees.'

'But there are so many things that people in general do not see. How much longer are you to stay, Miss Carr?'

'A week, I believe.'

'Why don't you make out a list of old buildings which are connected with famous people in history, and visit them in turn? I did that the second year after I came. I gave up three months to it, and it was most interesting. I unearthed all manner of curious stories and traditions.'

'Or,' cried Katy, struck with a sudden bright thought, 'why mightn't I put into the list some of the places I know about in books – novels as well as history – and the places where the people who wrote the books lived?'

'You might do that, and it wouldn't be a bad idea, either,' said Mr Beach, pleased with her enthusiasm. 'I will get a pencil after dinner, and help you with your list if you will allow me.'

Mr Beach was better than his word. He not only suggested places and traced a plan of sightseeing, but on two different mornings he went with them himself; and his intelligent knowledge of London added very much to the interest of the excursions. Under his guidance the little party of four – for Mabel was never left out; it was *such* a chance for her to improve her mind, Amy declared – visited the Charter-House, where Thackeray went to school, and the Home of the Poor Brothers connected with it, in which Colonel Newcome answered 'Adsum' to the roll-call of the angels. They took a look at the small house in Curzon Street, which is supposed to have been in Thackeray's mind when he described the residence of Becky Sharp; and the other house in Russell Square which is unmistakably that where George Osborne courted Amelia Sedley. They went to a service in the delightful old church of St Mary in the Temple, and thought of Ivanhoe and Brian de Bois-Guilbert and Rebecca the Jewess. From there Mr Beach took them to Lamb's Court, where Pendennis and George Warrington dwelt in chambers together; and to Brick Court, where Oliver Goldsmith passed so much of his life, and the little rooms in which Charles and Mary Lamb spent so many sadly happy years. On another day they drove to Whitefriars, for the sake of Lord Glenvarloch and the old privilege of sanctuary in the *Fortunes of Nigel*; and took a peep at Bethnal Green, where the Blind Beggar and his 'Pretty Bessee' lived, and at the old prison of the Marshalsea, made interesting by its associations with *Little Dorrit*. They also went to see Milton's house and St Giles Church, in which he is buried, and stood a long time before St James's Palace, trying to make out which could have been Miss Burney's windows when she was dresser to Queen Charlotte of bitter memory. And they saw Paternoster Row, and No. 5 Cheyne Walk, sacred forevermore to the memory of Thomas Carlyle, and Whitehall, where Queen Elizabeth lay in state and King Charles was beheaded, and the state rooms of Holland House; and by great good luck had a glimpse of George Eliot getting out of a cab. She stood for a moment while she gave her fare to the cabman, and Katy looked as one who might not look again, and carried away a distinct picture of the unbeautiful, interesting, remarkable face.

With all this to see and to do, the last week sped all too swiftly, and the last day came before they were at all ready to leave what Katy called 'Storybook England'. Mrs Ashe had decided to cross from Newhaven to Dieppe, because someone had told her of the beautiful old town of Rouen, and it seemed easy and convenient to take it in on the way to Paris. Just landed from the long voyage across the Atlantic, the little passage of the Channel seemed nothing to our travellers, and they made ready for their night on the Dieppe steamer with the philosophy which is born of ignorance. They were speedily undeceived!

The English Channel has a character of its own, which distinguishes it from other seas and straits. It seems made fractious and difficult by Nature, and set as on purpose to be a barrier between two nations who are too unlike easily to understand each other, and are the safer neighbours for this wholesome difficulty of communication between them. The 'chop' was worse than usual on the night when our travellers crossed; the steamer had to fight her way inch by inch. And oh, such a little steamer! and oh, such a long night!

CHAPTER SIX

Across the Channel

Dawn had given place to day, and day was well advanced toward noon, before the stout little steamer gained her port. It was hours after the usual time for arrival; the train for Paris must long since have started, and Katy felt dejected and forlorn as, making her way out of the terrible ladies' cabin, she crept on deck for her first glimpse of France.

The sun was struggling through the fog with a watery smile, and his faint beams shone on a confusion of stone piers, higher than the vessel's deck, intersected with canal-like waterways, through whose intricate windings the steamer was slowly threading her course to the landing-place. Looking up, Katy could see crowds of people assembled to watch the boat come in – workmen, peasants, women, children, soldiers, custom-house officers, moving to and fro – and all this crowd were talking all at once and all were talking French.

I don't know why this should have startled her as it did. She knew, of course, that people of different countries were liable to be found speaking their own languages; but somehow the spectacle of the chattering multitude, all seeming so perfectly at ease with their preterits and subjunctives and never once having to refer to Ollendorf or a dictionary, filled her with a sense of dismayed surprise.

'Good gracious!' she said to herself, 'even the babies understand it!' She racked her brains to recall what she had once known of French, but very little seemed to have survived the horrors of the night!

'Oh, dear! what is the word for trunk-key?' she asked herself. 'They will all begin to ask questions, and I shall not have a word to say; and Mrs Ashe will be even worse off, I know.' She saw the red-trousered custom-house officers pounce upon the passengers as they landed one by one, and she felt her heart sink within her.

But after all, when the time came, it did not prove so very bad. Katy's pleasant looks and courteous manner stood her in good stead. She did not trust herself to say much; but the officials seemed to understand without saying. They bowed and gestured, whisked the keys in and out, and in a surprisingly short time all was pronounced right, the baggage had 'passed', and it and its owners were free to proceed to the railway station, which fortunately was close at hand.

Enquiry revealed the fact that no train for Paris left till four in the afternoon.

'I am rather glad,' declared poor Mrs Ashe, 'for I feel too used up to move. I will lie here on this sofa; and, Katy dear, please see if there is an eating-place, and get some breakfast for yourself and Amy, and send me a cup of tea.'

'I don't like to leave you alone,' Katy was beginning; but at that moment a nice old woman, who seemed to be in charge of the waiting-room, appeared, and with a flood of French which none of them could follow, but which was evidently sympathetic in its nature, flew at Mrs Ashe and began to make her comfortable. From a cupboard in the wall she produced a pillow, from another cupboard a blanket; in a trice she had one under Mrs Ashe's head and the other wrapped round her feet.

'Pauvre madame,' she said, 'si pâle! si souffrante! Il faut avoir quelque chose à boire et à manger tout de suite.' She trotted across the room and into the restaurant which opened out of it, while Mrs Ashe smiled at Katy and said, 'You see, you can leave me quite safely; I am to be taken care of.' And Katy and Amy passed through the same door into the buffet, and sat down at a little table.

It was a particularly pleasant-looking place to breakfast in. There were many windows with bright polished panes and very clean short muslin curtains, and on the window-sills stood rows of thrifty potted plants in full bloom – marigolds, balsams, nasturtiums and many-coloured geraniums. Two birds in cages were singing loudly; the floor was waxed to a glasslike polish; nothing could have been whiter than the marble of the tables except the napkins laid over them. And such a good breakfast as was presently brought to them – delicious coffee in bowl-like cups, crisp rolls and rusks, an omelette with a delicate flavour of fine herbs, stewed chicken, little pats of freshly-churned butter without salt, shaped like shells and tasting like solidified cream, and a pot of some sort of nice preserve. Amy made great delightful eyes at Katy, and remarking, 'I think France is heaps nicer than that old England,' began to eat with a will; and Katy herself felt that if this railroad meal was a specimen of what they had to expect in the future, they had indeed come to a land of plenty.

Fortified with the satisfactory breakfast, she felt equal to a walk; and after they had made sure that Mrs Ashe had all she needed, she and Amy (and Mabel) set off by themselves to see the sights of Dieppe. I don't know that travellers generally have considered Dieppe an interesting place, but Katy found it so. There was a really old church and some quaint buildings of the style of two centuries back, and even the more modern streets had a novel look to her unaccustomed eyes. At first they only ventured a timid turn or two, marking each corner, and going back now and then to reassure themselves by a look at the station; but after a while, growing bolder, Katy ventured to ask a question or two in French, and was surprised and charmed to find herself understood. After that she grew adventurous, and, no longer fearful of being lost, led Amy straight down a long street lined with shops, almost all of which were for the sale of articles in ivory.

Ivory wares are one of the chief industries of Dieppe. There were cases full, windows full, counters full, of the most exquisite combs and brushes, some with elaborate monograms in silver and colours, others plain; there were boxes and caskets of every size and shape, ornaments, fans, parasol handles, looking-glasses, frames for pictures large and small, napkin-rings.

Katy was particularly smitten with a paperknife in the form of an angel with long, slender wings raised over its head and meeting to form a point. Its price was twenty francs, and she was strongly tempted to buy it for Clover or Rose Red. But she said to herself sensibly: 'This is the first shop I have been into and the first thing I have really wanted to buy, and very likely as we go on I shall see things I like better and want more, so it would be foolish to do it. No, I won't.' And she resolutely turned her back on the ivory angel, and walked away.

The next turn brought them to a gay-looking little marketplace, where old women in white caps were sitting on the ground beside baskets and panniers full of apples, pears and various queer and curly vegetables, none of which Katy recognised as familiar; fish of all shapes and colours were flapping in shallow tubs of sea-water; there were piles of stockings, muffettees and comforters in vivid blue and red worsted, and coarse pottery glazed in bright patterns. The faces of the women were brown and wrinkled; there were no pretty ones among them, but their black eyes were full of life and quickness, and their fingers one and all clicked with knitting-needles, as their tongues flew equally fast in the chatter and the chaffer, which went on without stop or stay, though customers did not seem to be many and sales were few.

Returning to the station they found that Mrs Ashe had been asleep during their absence, and seemed so much better that it was with greatly amended spirits that they took their places in the late afternoon train which was to set them down at Rouen. Katy said they were like the Wise Men of the East, 'following a star', in their choice of a hotel; for, having no better advice, they had decided upon one of those thus distinguished in Baedeker's *Guidebook*.

The star did not betray their confidence; for the Hôtel de la Cloche, to which it led them, proved to be quaint and old, and very pleasant of aspect. The lofty chambers, with their dimly frescoed ceilings, and beds curtained with faded patch, might to all appearances have been furnished about the time when 'Columbus crossed the ocean blue'; but everything was clean, and had an air of old-time respectability. The dining-room, which was evidently of more modern build, opened into a square courtyard, where oleanders and lemon trees in boxes stood round the basin of a little fountain, whose tinkle and plash blended agreeably with the rattle of the knives and forks. In one corner of the room was a raised and railed platform, where, behind a desk, sat the mistress of the house, busy with her account-books, but keeping a eye the while on all that went forward.

Mrs Ashe walked past this personage without taking any notice of her, as Americans are wont to do under such circumstances; but presently the observant Katy noticed that everyone else, as they went in or out of the room, addressed a bow or a civil remark to this lady. She quite blushed at the recollection afterward, as she made ready for bed.

'How rude we must have seemed!' she thought. 'I am afraid the people here think that Americans have *awful* manners, everybody is so polite. They said "Bonsoir", and "Merci", and "Voulez-vous avoir la bonté" to the waiters even! Well, there is one thing – I am going to reform. Tomorrow I will be as polite as anybody. They will think that I am miraculously improved by one night on French soil; but, never mind! I am going to do it.'

She kept her resolution, and astonished Mrs Ashe next morning by bowing to the dame on the platform in the most winning manner and saying, 'Bonjour, madame,' as they went by.

'But, Katy, who is that person? Why do you speak to her?'

'Don't you see that they all do? She is the landlady, I think; at all events, everybody bows to her. And just notice how prettily these ladies at the next table speak to the waiter. They do not order him to do things as we do at home. I noticed it last night, and I liked it so much that I made a resolution to get up and be as polite as the French themselves this morning.'

So all the time that they went about the sumptuous old city, rich in carvings and sculptures and traditions, while they were looking at the cathedral and the wonderful church of St Ouen and the Palace of Justice and the 'Place of the Maid', where poor Jeanne d'Arc was burned and her ashes scattered to the winds, Katy remembered her manners, and smiled and bowed, and used courteous prefixes in a soft, pleasant voice; and as Mrs Ashe and Amy fell in with her example more or less, I think the guides and coachmen and the old women who showed them over the buildings felt that the air of France was very civilising indeed, and that these strangers from savage countries over the sea were in a fair way to be as well bred as if they had been born in a more favoured part of the world!

Paris looked very modern after the peculiar quaint richness and air of the Middle Ages which distinguish Rouen. Rooms had been engaged for Mrs Ashe's party in a *pension* near the Arc de l'Etoile, and there they drove immediately on arriving. The rooms were not in the *pension* itself, but in a house close by – a sitting-room with six mirrors, three clocks, and a pinched little grate about a foot wide, a dining-

room just large enough for a table and four chairs, and two
bedrooms. A maid called Amandine had been detailed to
take charge of these rooms and serve their meals.

Dampness, as Katy afterwards wrote to Clover, was the
first impression they received of 'gay Paris'. The tiny fire in
the tiny grate had only just been lighted, and the walls and
the sheets and even the blankets felt chilly and moist to the
touch. They spent their first evening in hanging the
bedclothes round the grate and piling on fuel; they even set
the mattresses up on edge to warm and dry! It was not very
enlivening, it must be confessed. Amy had taken a cold, Mrs
Ashe looked worried, and Katy thought of Burnet and the
safety and comfort of home with a throb of longing.

The days that ensued were not brilliant enough to remove
this impression. The November fogs seemed to have
followed them across the Channel, and Paris remained
enveloped in a wet blanket which dimmed and hid its usually
brilliant features. Going about in cabs with the windows
drawn up, and now and then making a rush through the drip
into shops, was not exactly delightful, but it seemed pretty
much all that they could do. It was worse for Amy, whose
cold kept her indoors and denied her even the relaxation of
the cab. Mrs Ashe had engaged a well-recommended elderly
English maid to come every morning and take care of Amy
while they were out; and with this respectable functionary,
whose ideas were of a rigidly British type, and who did not
speak a word of any language but her own, poor Amy was
compelled to spend most of her time. Her only consolation
was in persuading this serene attendant to take a part in the
French lessons which she made a daily point of giving to
Mabel out of her own little phrase-book.

'Wilkins is getting on, I think,' she told Katy one night.
'She says "Biscuit glacé" quite nicely now. But I never will
let her look at the book, though she always wants to; for if
once she saw how the words are spelled, she would never in

the world pronounce them right again. They look so very different, you know.'

Katy looked at Amy's pale little face and eager eyes with a real heartache. Her rapture when, at the end of the long dull afternoons, her mother returned to her was touching. Paris was very *triste* to poor Amy, with all her happy facility for amusing herself; and Katy felt that the sooner they got away from it the better it would be. So, in spite of the delight which her brief glimpses at the Louvre gave her, and the fun it was to go about with Mrs Ashe and see her buy pretty things, and the real satisfaction she took in the one perfectly made walking-suit to which she had treated herself, she was glad when the final day came, when the belated dressmakers and artistes in jackets and wraps had sent home their last wares, and the trunks were packed. It had been rather the fault of circumstances than of Paris; but Katy had not learned to love the beautiful capital as most Americans do, and did not feel at all as if she wanted that her 'reward of virtue' should be to go there when she died! There must be more interesting places for live people, and ghosts too, to be found on the map of Europe, she was sure.

Next morning, as they drove slowly down the Champs Elysées, and looked back for a last glimpse of the famous Arch, a bright object met their eyes, moving vaguely against the mist. It was the gay red wagon of the Bon Marché, carrying bundles home to the dwellers of some up-town street.

Katy burst out laughing. 'It is an emblem of Paris,' she said – 'of our Paris, I mean. It has been all Bon Marché and fog!'

'Miss Katy,' interrupted Amy, 'do you like Europe? For my part, I was never so disgusted with any place in my life!'

'Poor little bird, her views of "Europe" are rather dark just now, and no wonder,' said her mother. 'Never mind,

darling, you shall have something pleasanter by and by if I
can find it for you.'

'Burnet is a great deal pleasanter than Paris,' pronounced
Amy, decidedly. 'It doesn't keep always raining there, and I
can take walks, and I understand everything that people say.'

All that day they sped southward, and with every hour
came a change in the aspect of their surroundings.

Now they made brief stops in large busy towns which
seemed humming with industry. Now they whirled through
grape countries with miles of vineyards, where the brown
leaves still hung on the vines. Then again came glimpses of
old Roman ruins, amphitheatres, viaducts, fragments of a
wall or arch; or a sudden chill betokened their approach to
mountains, where snowy peaks could be seen on the far
horizon. And when the long night ended and day roused
them from broken slumbers, behold, the world was made
over! Autumn had vanished, and the summer, which they
thought fled for good, had taken its place. Green woods
waved about them, fresh leaves were blowing in the wind,
roses and hollyhocks beckoned from white-walled gardens;
and before they had done with exclaiming and rejoicing, the
Mediterranean shot into view, intensely blue, with white
fringes of foam, white sails blowing across, white gulls flying
above it, and over all a sky of the same exquisite blue, whose
clouds were white as the drifting sails on the water below,
and they were at Marseilles.

It was like a glimpse of Paradise, to eyes fresh from
autumnal greys and glooms, as they sped along the lovely
coast, every curve and turn showing new combinations of
sea and shore, olive-crowned cliff and shining mountain
peak. With every mile the blue became bluer, the wind
softer, the feathery verdure more dense and summer-like.
Hyères and Cannes and Antibes were passed, and then, as
they rounded a long point, came the view of a sunshiny city
lying on a sunlit shore; the train slackened its speed, and

they knew that their journey's end was come and they were in Nice.

The place seemed to laugh with gaiety as they drove down the Promenade des Anglais and past the English garden, where the band was playing beneath the acacias and palm trees. On one side was a line of bright-windowed hotels and *pensions*, with balconies and striped awnings; on the other, the long reach of yellow sand-beach, where ladies were grouped on shawls and rugs and children ran up and down in the sun, while beyond stretched the waveless sea. The December sun felt as warm as on a late June day at home, and had the same soft caressing touch. The pavements were thronged with groups of leisurely-looking people, all wearing an unmistakable holiday aspect; pretty girls in correct Parisian costumes walked demurely beside their mothers with cavaliers in attendance; and among these young men appeared now and again the well-known uniform of the United States Navy.

'I wonder,' said Mrs Ashe, struck by a sudden thought, 'if by any chance our squadron is here.' She asked the question the moment they entered the hotel; and the porter, who prided himself on understanding 'zose Eenglesh', replied: 'Mais oui, madame, za Americaine fleet it is 'ere; zat is, not 'ere, but at Villefranche, just a leetle four mile away – it is ze same zing exactly.'

'Katy, do you hear that?' cried Mrs Ashe. 'The frigates *are* here, and the *Natchitoches* among them, of course; and we shall have Ned to go about with us everywhere. It is a real piece of good luck for us. Ladies are at such a loss in a place like this, with nobody to escort them. I am perfectly delighted.'

'So am I,' said Katy. 'I never saw a frigate, and I always wanted to see one. Do you suppose they will let us go on board of them?'

'Why, of course they will.' Then to the porter: 'Give me a

sheet of paper and an envelope, please – I must let Ned know that I am here at once.'

Mrs Ashe wrote her note and dispatched it before they went upstairs to take off their bonnets. She seemed to have a half-hope that some bird of the air might carry the news of her arrival to her brother, for she kept running to the window as if in expectation of seeing him. She was too restless to lie down or sleep, and after she and Katy had lunched, proposed that they should go out on the beach for a while.

'Perhaps we may come across Ned,' she remarked. They did not come across Ned, but there was no lack of other delightful objects to engage their attention. The sands were smooth and hard as a floor. Soft pink lights were beginning to tinge the western sky. To the north shone the peaks of the maritime Alps, and the same rosy glow caught them here and there, and warmed their greys and whites into colour.

'I wonder what that can be!' said Katy, indicating the rocky point which bounded the beach to the east, where stood a picturesque building of stone, with massive towers and steep pitches of roof. 'It looks half like a house and half like a castle, but it is quite fascinating, I think. Do you suppose that people live there?'

'We might ask,' suggested Mrs Ashe.

Just then they came to a shallow river, spanned by a bridge, beside whose pebbly bed stood a number of women who seemed to be washing clothes by the simple and primitive process of laying them in the water on top of the stones, and pounding them with a flat wooden paddle till they were white. Katy privately thought that the clothes stood a poor chance of lasting through these cleansing operations; but she did not say so, and made the enquiry which Mrs Ashe had suggested, in her best French.

'Celle-là?' answered the old woman whom she had addressed. 'Mais c'est la Pension Suisse.'

'A *pension*! why, that means a boarding-house!' cried Katy. 'What fun it must be to board there!'

'Well, why shouldn't we board there?' said her friend. 'You know we meant to look for rooms as soon as we were rested and had found out a little about the place. Let us walk on and see what the Pension Suisse is like. If the inside is as pleasant as the outside, we could not do better, I should think.'

'Oh, I do hope all the rooms are not already taken!' said Katy, who had fallen in love at first sight with the Pension Suisse. She felt quite oppressed with anxiety as they rang the bell.

The Pension Suisse proved to be quite as charming inside as out. The thick stone walls made deep sills and embrasures for the casement windows, which were furnished with red cushions to serve as seats and lounging-places. Every window seemed to command a view, for those which did not look toward the sea looked toward the mountains. The house was by no means full either. Several sets of rooms were to be had; and Katy felt as if she had walked straight into the pages of a romance when Mrs Ashe engaged for a month a delightful suite of three, a sitting-room and two sleeping-chambers, in a round tower, with a balcony overhanging the water, and a side window, from which a flight of steps led down into a little walled garden, nestled in among the masonry, where tall laurustinus and lemon trees grew, and orange and brown wallflowers made the air sweet. Her contentment knew no bounds.

'I am so glad that I came!' she told Mrs Ashe. 'I never confessed it to you before, but sometimes – when we were sick at sea, you know, and when it would rain all the time, and after Amy caught that cold in Paris – I have almost wished, just for a minute or two at a time, that I hadn't. But now I wouldn't not have come for the world! This is perfectly delicious. I am glad, glad, glad we are here, and we are going to have a lovely time, I know.'

They were passing out of the rooms into the hall as she said these words, and two ladies who were walking up a cross passage turned their heads at the sound of her voice. To her great surprise Katy recognised Mrs Page and Lilly.

'Why, Cousin Olivia, is it you?' she cried, springing forward with the cordiality one naturally feels in seeing a familiar face in a foreign land.

Mrs Page seemed rather puzzled than cordial. She put up her eyeglass and did not seem to quite make out who Katy was.

'It is Katy Carr, Mamma,' explained Lilly. 'Well, Katy, this *is* a surprise! Who would have thought of meeting you in Nice?'

There was a decided absence of rapture in Lilly's manner. She was prettier than ever, as Katy saw in a moment, and beautifully dressed in soft brown velvet, which exactly suited her complexion and her pale-coloured wavy hair.

'Katy Carr! why, so it is!' admitted Mrs Page. 'It is a surprise indeed. We had no idea that you were abroad. What has brought you so far from Tunket – Burnet, I mean? Who are you with?'

'With my friend Mrs Ashe,' explained Katy, rather chilled by this cool reception. 'Let me introduce you. Mrs Ashe, these are my cousins, Mrs Page and Miss Page. Amy – why, where is Amy?'

Amy had walked back to the door of the garden staircase, and was standing there looking down upon the flowers.

Cousin Olivia bowed rather distantly. Her quick eye took in the details of Mrs Ashe's travelling-dress and Katy's dark-blue ulster.

'Some countrified friend from that dreadful Western town where they live,' she said to herself. 'How foolish of Philip Carr to try to send his girls to Europe! He can't afford it, I know.' Her voice was rather rigid as she enquired: 'And what brings you here – to this house, I mean?'

'Oh, we are coming tomorrow to stay! We have taken rooms for a month,' explained Katy. 'What a delicious-looking old place it is!'

'Have you?' said Lilly, in a voice which did not express any particular pleasure. 'Why, we are staying here too.'

CHAPTER SEVEN

The Pension Suisse

'What do you suppose can have brought Katy Carr to Europe?' enquired Lilly, as she stood in the window watching the three figures walk slowly down the sands. 'She is the last person I expected to turn up here. I supposed she was stuck in that horrid place – what is the name of it? – where they live, for the rest of her life.'

'I confess I am surprised at meeting her myself,' rejoined Mrs Page. 'I had no idea that her father could afford so expensive a journey.'

'And who is this woman that she has got along with her?'

'I have no idea, I'm sure. Some Western friend, I suppose.'

'Dear me! I wish they were going to some other house than this,' said Lilly discontentedly. 'If they were at the Rivoir, for instance, or one of those places at the far end of the beach, we shouldn't need to see anything of them, or even know that they were in town! It's a real nuisance to have people spring upon you this way, people you don't want to meet; and when they happen to be relations it is all the worse. Katy will be hanging on us all the time, I'm afraid.'

'Oh, my dear, there is no fear of that! A little repression on our part will prevent her from being any trouble, I'm quite certain. But we *must* treat her politely, you know, Lilly; her father is my cousin by marriage.'

'That's the saddest part of it! Well, there's one thing, I shall *not* take her with me every time we go to the frigates,' said Lilly decisively. 'I am not going to inflict a country cousin on Lieutenant Worthington and spoil all my own fun beside. So I give you fair warning, Mamma, and you must manage it somehow.'

'Certainly, dear, I will. It would be a great pity to have your visit to Nice spoiled in any way, with the squadron here, too, and that pleasant Mr Worthington so very attentive.'

Unconscious of these plans for her suppression, Katy walked back to the hotel in a mood of pensive pleasure. Europe at last promised to be as delightful as it had seemed when she only knew it from maps and books, and Nice so far appeared to her the most charming place in the world.

Somebody was waiting for them at the Hôtel des Anglais – a tall, bronzed, good-looking somebody in uniform, with pleasant brown eyes beaming from beneath a gold-banded cap; at the sight of whom Amy rushed forward with her long locks flying, and Mrs Ashe uttered an exclamation of pleasure. It was Ned Worthington, Mrs Ashe's only brother, whom she had not met for two years and a half; and you can easily imagine how glad she was to see him.

'You got my note then?' she said, after the first eager greetings were over and she had introduced him to Katy.

'Note? No. Did you write me a note?'

'Yes; to Villefranche.'

'To the ship? I shan't get that till tomorrow. No; finding out that you were here is just a bit of good fortune. I came over to call on some friends who are staying down the beach a little way, and, dropping in to look over the list of arrivals, as I generally do, I saw your names; and the porter not being able to say which way you had gone, I waited for you to come in.'

'We have been looking at such a delightful old place, the Pension Suisse, and have taken rooms.'

'The Pension Suisse, eh? Why, that was where I was going to call. I know some people who are staying there. It seems a pleasant house; I'm glad you are going there, Polly. It's first-rate luck that the ships happen to be here just now. I can see you every day.'

'But, Ned, surely you are not leaving me so soon? Surely you will stay and dine with us?' urged his sister, as he took up his cap.

'I wish I could, but I can't tonight, Polly. You see I had engaged to take some ladies out to drive, and they will expect me. I had no idea that you would be here, or I should have kept myself free,' apologetically. 'Tomorrow I will come over early, and be at your service for whatever you like to do.'

'That's right, dear boy. We shall expect you.' Then the next moment he was gone: 'Now, Katy, isn't he nice?'

'Very nice, I should think,' said Katy, who had watched the brief interview with interest. 'I like his face so much, and how fond he is of you!'

'Dear fellow! so he is. I am seven years older than he, but we have always been intimate. Brothers and sisters are not always intimate, you know – or perhaps you don't know, for all of yours are.'

'Yes, indeed,' said Katy, with a happy smile. 'There is nobody like Clover and Elsie, except perhaps Johnnie and Dorry and Phil,' she added, with a laugh.

The remove to the Pension Suisse was made early the next morning. Mrs Page and Lilly did not appear to welcome them. Katy rather rejoiced in their absence, for she wanted the chance to get into order without interruptions. There was something comfortable in the thought that they were to stay a whole month in these new quarters; for so long a time it seemed worth while to make them pretty and homelike. So, while Mrs Ashe unpacked her own belongings and Amy's, Katy, who had a natural turn for arranging rooms, took possession of the little parlour, pulled the furniture into new positions, laid out portfolios and work-cases and their few books, pinned various photographs which they had bought in Oxford and London on the walls, and tied back the curtains to admit the sunshine. Then she paid a visit to the little garden, and came back with a long branch of laurustinus, which she trained across the mantelpiece, and a bunch of wallflowers for their one little vase. The maid, by her orders, laid a fire of wood and pine cones ready for lighting; and when all was done she called Mrs Ashe to pronounce upon the effect.

'It is lovely,' she said, sinking into a great velvet armchair which Katy had drawn close to the seaward window. 'I haven't seen anything so pleasant since we left home. You are a witch, Katy, and the comfort of my life. I am so glad I brought you! Now, pray go and unpack your own things, and make yourself look nice for the second breakfast. We have been a shabby set enough since we arrived. I saw those cousins of yours looking askance at our old travelling-dresses yesterday. Let us try to make a more respectable impression today.'

So they went down to breakfast, Mrs Ashe in one of her new Paris gowns, Katy in a pretty dress of olive serge, and Amy all smiles and ruffled pinafore, walking hand in hand with her Uncle Ned, who had just arrived, and whose great ally she was; and Mrs Page and Lilly, who were already seated at table, had much ado to conceal their somewhat unflattering surprise at the conjunction. For one moment Lilly's eyes opened into a wild stare of incredulous astonishment; then she remembered herself, nodded as pleasantly as she could to Mrs Ashe and Katy, and favoured Lieutenant Worthington with a pretty blushing smile as he went by, while she murmured: 'Mamma, do you see that? What does it mean?'

'Why, Ned, do you know those people?' asked Mrs Ashe at the same moment.

'Do you know them?'

'Yes, we met yesterday. They are connections of my friend Miss Carr.'

'Really? There is not the least family likeness between them.' And Mr Worthington's eyes travelled deliberately from Lilly's delicate golden prettiness to Katy, who, truth to say, did not shine by the contrast.

'She has a nice, sensible sort of face, ' he thought, 'and she looks like a lady, but for beauty there is no comparison between the two.'

Then he turned to listen to his sister as she replied: 'No, indeed, not the least; no two girls could be less like.' Mrs Ashe had made the same comparison, but with quite a different result. Katy's face was grown dear to her, and she had not taken the smallest fancy to Lilly Page.

Her relationship to the young naval officer, however, made a wonderful difference in the attitude of Mrs Page and Lilly toward the party. Katy became a person to be cultivated rather than repressed, and thenceforward there was no lack of cordiality on their part.

'I want to come in and have a good talk,' said Lilly slipping her arm through Katy's as they left the dining-room. 'Mayn't I come now while Mamma is calling on Mrs Ashe?' This arrangement brought her to the side of Lieutenant Worthington, and she walked between him and Katy down the hall and into the little drawing-room.

'Oh, how perfectly charming! You have been fixing it up ever since you came, haven't you? It looks like home. I wish we had a *salon*, but Mamma thought it wasn't worth while, as we were only to be here such a little time. What a delicious balcony over the water, too! May I go out on it? Oh, Mr Worthington, do see this!'

She pushed open the half-closed window and stepped out as she spoke. Mr Worthington, after hesitating a moment, followed. Katy paused uncertain. There was hardly room for three in the balcony, yet she did not quite like to leave them. But Lilly had turned her back, and was talking in a low tone; it was nothing more in reality than the lightest chitchat, but it had the air of being something confidential; so Katy, after waiting a little while, retreated to the sofa and took up her work, joining now and then in the conversation which Mrs Ashe was keeping up with Cousin Olivia. She did not mind Lilly's ill-breeding, nor was she surprised at it. Mrs Ashe was less tolerant.

'Isn't it rather damp out there, Ned?' she called to her brother; 'you had better throw my shawl round Miss Page's shoulders.'

'Oh, it isn't a bit damp!' said Lilly, recalled to herself by this broad hint. Thank you so much for thinking of it, Mrs Ashe, but I am just coming in.' She seated herself beside Katy, and began to question her rather languidly.

'When did you leave home, and how were they all when you came away?'

'All well, thank you. We sailed from Boston on the 14th of October; and before that I spent two days with Rose Red – you remember her? She is married now, and has the dearest little home and such a darling baby!'

'Yes, I heard of her marriage. It didn't seem much of a match for Mr Redding's daughter to make, did it? I never supposed she would be satisfied with anything less than a member of Congress or a secretary of legation.'

'Rose isn't particularly ambitious, I think, and she seems perfectly happy,' replied Katy flushing.

'Oh, you needn't fire up in her defence! You and Clover always did adore Rose Red, I know, but I never could see what there was about her that was so wonderfully fascinating. She never had the least style, and she was always just as rude to me as she could be.'

'You were not intimate at school, but I am sure Rose was never rude,' said Katy with spirit.

'Well, we won't fight about her at this late day. Tell me

where you have been, and where you are going, and how
long you are to stay in Europe.'

Katy, glad to change the subject, complied, and the
conversation diverged into comparison of plans and experi-
ences. Lilly had been in Europe nearly a year, and had seen
'almost everything', as she phrased it. She and her mother
had spent the previous winter in Italy, had taken a run into
Russia, 'done' Switzerland and the Tyrol thoroughly and
France and Germany, and were soon going into Spain, and
from there to Paris, to shop, in preparation for their return
home in the spring.

'Of course we shall want quantities of things,' she said.
'No one will believe that we have been abroad unless we
bring home a lot of clothes. The lingerie and all that is
ordered already; but the dresses must be made at the last
moment, and we shall have a horrid time of it, I suppose.
Worth has promised to make me two walking-suits and two
ball-dresses, but he's very bad about keeping his word. Did
you do much when you were in Paris, Katy?'

'We went to the Louvre three times, and to Versailles and
St Cloud,' said Katy, wilfully misunderstanding her.

'Oh, I didn't mean that kind of stupid thing! I meant
gowns. What did you buy?'

'One tailor-made suit of dark-blue cloth.'

'My! what moderation!'

Shopping played a large part in Lilly's reminiscences. She
recollected places, not from their situation or beauty or
historical associations, or because of the works of art which
they contained, but as the places where she had bought this
or that.

'Oh, that dear Piazza di Spagna!' she would say; 'that was
where I found my rococo necklace, the loveliest thing you
ever saw, Katy.' Or, 'Prague – oh yes! Mother got the most
enchanting old silver chatelaine there, with all kinds of
things hanging to it – needle-cases and watches and scent-

bottles, all solid, and so beautifully chased.' Or again, 'Berlin was horrid, we thought; but the amber is better and cheaper than anywhere else – great strings of beads, of the largest size and that beautiful pale yellow, for a hundred francs. You must get yourself one, Katy.'

Poor Lilly! Europe to her was all 'things'. She had collected trunks full of objects to carry home, but of the other collections, which do not go into trunks, she had little or none. Her mind was as empty, her heart as untouched as ever; the beauty and the glory and the pathos of art and history and Nature had been poured out in vain before her closed and indifferent eyes.

Life soon dropped into a peaceful routine at the Pension Suisse, which was at the same time restful and stimulating. Katy's first act in the morning, as soon as she opened her eyes, was to hurry to the window in hopes of getting a glimpse of Corsica. She had discovered that this elusive island could almost always be seen from Nice at the dawning, but that as soon as the sun was fairly up, it vanished, to appear no more for the rest of the day. There was something fascinating to her imagination in the hovering mountain outline between sea and sky. She felt as if she were under an engagement to be there to meet it, and she rarely missed the appointment. Then, after Corsica had pulled the bright mists over its face and melted from view, she would hurry with her dressing, and as soon as was practicable set to work to make the *salon* look bright before the coffee and rolls should appear, a little after eight o'clock. Mrs Ashe always found the fire lit, the little meal cosily set out beside it, and Katy's happy, untroubled face to welcome her when she emerged from her room; and the cheer of these morning repasts made a good beginning to the day.

Then came walking and a French lesson, and a long sitting on the beach, while Katy worked at her home letters and Amy raced up and down in the sun; and then toward noon

Lieutenant Ned generally appeared, and some scheme of pleasure was set on foot. Mrs Ashe ignored his evident *penchant* for Lilly Page and claimed his time and attentions as hers by right. Young Worthington was a good deal 'taken' with the pretty Lilly; still, he had an old-time devotion for his sister and the habit of doing what she desired, and he yielded to her behests with no audible objections. He made a fourth in the carriage while they drove over the lovely hills which encircle Nice toward the north, to Cimiers and the Val de St André, or down the coast toward Ventimiglia. He went with them to Monte-Carlo and Mentone, and was their escort again and again when they visited the great warships as they lay at anchor in a bay which in its translucent blue was like an enormous sapphire.

Mrs Page and her daughter were included in these parties more than once; but there was something in Mrs Ashe's cool appropriation of her brother which was infinitely vexatious to Lilly, who before her arrival had rather looked upon Lieutenant Worthington as her own especial property.

'I wish *that* Mrs Ashe had stayed at home,' she told her mother. 'She quite spoils everything. Mr Worthington isn't half so nice as he was before she came. I do believe she has a plan for making him fall in love with Katy; but there she makes a miss of it, for he doesn't seem to care anything about her.'

'Katy is a nice girl enough,' pronounced her mother, 'but not the sort to attract a gay young man, I should fancy. I don't believe *she* is thinking of any such thing. You needn't be afraid, Lilly.'

'I'm not afraid,' said Lilly, with a pout; 'only it's so provoking!'

Mrs Page was quite right. Katy was not thinking of any such thing. She liked Ned Worthington's frank manners; she owned, quite honestly, that she thought him handsome, and she particularly admired the sort of deferential affection which he showed to Mrs Ashe, and his nice ways with Amy. For herself, she was aware that he scarcely noticed her except as politeness demanded that he should be civil to his sister's friend: but the knowledge did not trouble her particularly. Her head was full of interesting things, plans, ideas. She was not accustomed to being made the object of admiration, and experienced none of the vexations of a neglected belle. If Lieutenant Worthington happened to talk to her, she responded frankly and freely; if he did not, she occupied herself with something else; in either case she was quite unembarrassed both in feeling and manner, and had none of the awkwardness which comes from disappointed vanity and baffled expectations, and the need for concealing them.

Toward the close of December the officers of the flagship gave a ball, which was the great event of the season to the gay world of Nice. Americans were naturally in the ascendant on an American frigate; and of all the American girls present, Lilly Page was unquestionably the prettiest. Exquisitely dressed in white lace, with bands of turquoises on her neck and arms and in her hair, she had more partners than she knew what to do with, more bouquets than she could well carry, and compliments enough to turn any girl's head. Thrown off her guard by her triumphs, she indulged a little vindictive feeling which had been growing in her mind of late on account of what she chose to consider certain derelictions of duty on the part of Lieutenant Worthington, and treated him to a taste of neglect. She was engaged three deep when he asked her to dance; she did not hear when he invited her to walk; she turned a cold shoulder when he tried to talk, and seemed absorbed by the other cavaliers, naval and otherwise, who crowded about her.

Piqued and surprised, Ned Worthington turned to Katy. She did not dance, saying frankly that she did not know how, and was too tall; and she was rather simply dressed in a pearl-grey silk, which had been her best gown the winter before in Burnet, with a bunch of red roses in the white lace of the tucker, and another in her hand, both the gifts of little Amy; but she looked pleasant and serene, and there was something about her which somehow soothed his disturbed mind as he offered her his arm for a walk on the decks.

For a while they said little, and Katy was quite content to pace up and down in silence, enjoying the really beautiful scene – the moonlight on the bay, the deep, wavering reflections of the dark hulls and slender spars, the fairy effect of the coloured lamps and lanterns, and the brilliant moving maze of the dancers.

'Do you care for this sort of thing?' he suddenly asked.

'What sort of thing do you mean?'

'Oh, all this jigging and waltzing and amusement!'

'I don't know how to "jig", but it's delightful to look on,' she answered merrily. 'I never saw anything so pretty in my life.'

The happy tone of her voice, and the unruffled face which she turned upon him, quieted his irritation.

'I really believe you mean it,' he said; 'and yet, if you won't think me rude to say so, most girls would consider the thing dull enough if they were only getting out of it what you are – if they were not dancing, I mean, and nobody in particular was trying to entertain them.'

'But everything *is* being done to entertain me,' cried Katy. 'I can't imagine what makes you think that it could seem dull. I am in it all, don't you see – I have my share – Oh, I am stupid, I can't make you understand!'

'Yes, you do. I understand perfectly, I think; only it is such a different point of view from what girls in general would take.' (By girls he meant Lilly!) 'Please do not think me uncivil.'

'You are not uncivil at all; but don't let us talk any more about me. Look at the lights between the shadows of the masts on the water. How they quiver! I never saw anything so beautiful, I think. And how warm it is! I can't believe that we are in December and that it is nearly Christmas.'

'How is Polly going to celebrate her Christmas? Have you decided?'

'Amy is to have a Christmas tree for her dolls, and two other dolls are coming. We went out this morning to buy things for it – tiny little toys and candles fit for Lilliput. And that reminds me, do you suppose one can get any Christmas greens here?'

'Why not? The place seems full of green.'

'That's just it; the summer look makes it unnatural. But I should like some to dress the parlour with, if they could be had.'

'I'll see what I can find, and send you a load.'

I don't know why this very simple little talk should have made an impression on Lieutenant Worthington's mind, but somehow he did not forget it.

' "Don't let us talk any more about me," ' he said to himself, that night when alone in his cabin. 'I wonder how long it would be before the other one did anything to divert the talk from herself. Some time, I fancy.' He smiled rather grimly as he unbuckled his sword-belt. It is unlucky for a girl when she starts a train of reflection like this. Lilly's little attempt to pique her admirer had somehow missed its mark.

The next afternoon Katy, in her favourite place on the beach, was at work on the long weekly letter which she never failed to send home to Burnet. She held her portfolio in her lap, and her pen ran rapidly over the paper, as rapidly almost as her tongue would have run could her correspondents have been brought nearer.

Nice, December 22

DEAR PAPA AND EVERYBODY – Amy and I are sitting on my old purple cloak, which is spread over the sand just where it was spread the last time I wrote you. We are playing the following game: I am a fairy and she is a little girl. Another fairy – not sitting on the cloak at present – has enchanted the little girl, and I am telling her various ways by which she can work out her deliverance. At present the task is to find twenty-four dull red pebbles of the same colour, failing to do which she is to be changed into an owl. When we began to play, I was the wicked fairy; but Amy objected to that because I am "so nice", so we changed the characters. I wish you could see the glee in her pretty grey eyes over this infantile game, into which she has thrown herself so thoroughly that she half believes in it. "But I needn't really be changed into an owl?" she says, with a good deal of anxiety in her voice.

To think that you are shivering in the first snowstorm, or sending the children out with their sleds and india-rubbers to slide! How I wish instead that you were sharing the purple cloak with Amy and me, and could sit all this warm, balmy afternoon close to the surf-line which fringes this bluest of blue seas! There is plenty of room for you all. Not many people come down to this end of the beach, and if you were very good we would let you play.

Our life here goes on as delightfully as ever. Nice is very full of people, and there seem to be some pleasant ones among them. Here, at the Pension Suisse, we do not see a great many Americans. The fellow-boarders are principally Germans and Austrians, with a sprinkling of French. (Amy has found her twenty-four red pebbles, so she is let off from being an owl. She is now engaged in throwing them one by one into the sea. Each must hit the water under penalty of her being turned into a muscovy duck. She doesn't know exactly what a muscovy duck is, which makes her all the more particular about her shots.) But, as I was saying, our little *suite* in the round tower is so on one side of the rest of the Pension that it is as good as having a house of our own. The *salon* is very bright and sunny; we have two sofas, and a square table, and a round table, and a sort of what-not, and two easy-chairs, and two uneasy chairs, and a lamp of our own, and a clock. There is also a sofa-pillow. There's richness for you! We have pinned up all our photographs on the walls, including Papa's and Clovy's, and that bad one of Phil and Johnnie making faces at each other, and three lovely red-and-yellow Japanese pictures on muslin which Rose Red put in my trunk the last thing, for a spot of colour. There are some autumn leaves too; and we always have flowers, and in the mornings and evenings a fire.

Amy is now finding fifty snow-white pebbles, which, when found, are to be interred in one common grave among the shingle. If she fails to do this, she is to be changed to an electrical eel. The chief difficulty is that she loses her heart to particular pebbles. 'I can't bury you,' I hear her saying.

To return – we have jolly little breakfasts together in the *salon*. They consist of coffee and rolls, and are served by a droll, snappish little *garçon* with no teeth, and an Italian–French patois which is very hard to understand when he sputters. He told me the other day that he had been a *garçon* for forty-six years, which seemed rather a long boyhood.

The company, as we meet them at table, are rather entertaining. Cousin Olivia and Lilly are on their best behaviour to me because I am travelling with Mrs Ashe, and Mrs Ashe is Lieutenant Worthington's sister, and Lieutenant Worthington is Lilly's admirer, and they like him very much. In fact, Lilly has intimated confidentially that she is all but engaged to him; but I am not sure about it, or if that was what she meant; and I fear, if it proves true, that dear Polly will not like it at all. She is quite unmanageable, and snubs Lilly continually in a polite way, which makes me fidgety for fear Lilly will be offended; but she never seems to notice it. Cousin Olivia looks very handsome and gorgeous. She quite takes the colour out of the little Russian countess who sits next to her, and who is as dowdy and meek as if she came from Akron or Binghampton, or any other place where countesses are unknown. Then there are two charming, well-bred young Austrians. The one who sits nearest to me is a 'candidat' for a doctorate of laws, and speaks eight languages well. He has only studied English for the past six weeks, but has made wonderful progress. I wish my French were half as good as his English is already.

There is a very gossiping young woman on the storey beneath ours, whom I meet sometimes in the garden, and from her I hear all manner of romantic tales about people in the house. One little French girl is dying of consumption and a broken heart, because of a quarrel with her lover, who is a courier; and the *padrona*, who is young and pretty, and has only been married a few months to our elderly landlord, has a story also. I forget some of the details; but there was a stern parent and an admirer, and a cup of cold poison, and now she says she wishes she were dying of consumption like poor Alphonsine. For all that, she looks quite fat and rosy, and I often see her in her best gown with a great deal of Roman scarf and mosaic jewellery, stationed in the doorway, 'making the Pension look attractive to the passers-by'. So she has a sense of duty, though she is unhappy.

Amy has buried all her pebbles, and says she is tired of playing fairy. She is now sitting with her head on my shoulder, and professedly studying her French verb for tomorrow, but in reality, I am sorry to say, she is conversing with me about beheadings – a subject which, since her visit to the Tower, has exercised a horrible fascination over her mind. 'Do people die right away?'

she asks. 'Don't they feel one minute and doesn't it feel awfully?' There is a good deal of blood, she supposes, because there was so much straw laid about the block in the picture of Lady Jane Gray's execution which enlivened our walls in Paris. On the whole, I am rather glad that a fat little white dog has come waddling down the beach and taken off her attention.

Speaking of Paris seems to renew the sense of fog which we had there. Oh, how enchanting sunshine is after weeks of gloom! I shall never forget how the Mediterranean looked when we saw it first – all blue, and such a lovely colour! There ought, according to Morse's *Atlas*, to have been a big red letter T on the water about where we were, but I didn't see any. Perhaps they letter it so far out from shore that only people in boats notice it.

Now the dusk is fading, and the odd chill which hides under these warm afternoons begins to be felt. Amy has received a message written on a mysterious white pebble to the effect –

Katy was interrupted at this point by a crunching step on the gravel behind her.

'Good-afternoon!' said a voice. 'Polly has sent me to fetch you and Amy in. She says it is growing cool.'

'We were just coming,' said Katy, beginning to put away her papers.

Ned Worthington sat down on the cloak beside her. The distance was now steel grey against the sky; then came a stripe of violet, and then a broad sheet of the vivid iridescent blue which one sees on the necks of peacocks, which again melted into the long line of flashing surf.

'See that gull,' he said, 'how it drops plump into the sea, as if bound to go through to China!'

'Mrs Hawthorne calls skylarks "little raptures",' replied Katy. 'Seagulls seem to me like grown-up raptures.'

'Are you going?' said Lieutenant Worthington in a tone of surprise, as she rose.

'Didn't you say that Polly wanted us to come in?'

'Why, yes; but it seems too good to leave, doesn't it? Oh, by the way, Miss Carr, I came across a man today and ordered your greens! They will be sent on Christmas Eve. Is that right?'

'Quite right, and we are ever so much obliged to you.' She turned for a last look at the sea, and, unseen by Ned Worthington, formed her lips into a 'good-night'. Katy had made great friends with the Mediterranean.

The promised 'greens' appeared on the afternoon before Christmas Day, in the shape of an enormous faggot of laurel and laurustinus and holly and box, orange and lemon boughs with ripe fruit hanging from them, thick ivy tendrils whole yards long, arbutus, pepper tree, and great branches of acacia, covered with feathery yellow bloom. The man apologised for bringing so little. The gentleman had ordered two francs' worth, he said, but this was all he could carry; he would fetch some more if the young lady wished. But Katy, exclaiming with delight over her wealth, wished no more; so the man departed, and the three friends proceeded to turn the little *salon* into a fairy bower. Every photograph and picture was wreathed in ivy, long garlands hung on either side the windows, and the chimney-piece and doorframes became clustering banks of leaf and blossom. A great box of flowers had come with the greens, and bowls of fresh roses and heliotrope and carnations were set everywhere; violets and primroses, gold-hearted brown auriculas, spikes of veronica, all the zones and all the seasons combining to make the Christmastide sweet, and to turn winter topsy-turvy in the little parlour.

Mabel and Maria Matilda, with their two doll visitors, sat gravely round the table, in the laps of their little mistresses; and Katy, putting on an apron and an improvised cap, and speaking Irish very fast, served them with a repast of rolls and cocoa, raspberry jam and delicious little almond cakes. The fun waxed fast and furious, and Lieutenant Worthington, coming in with his hands full of parcels for the Christmas tree, was just in time to hear Katy remark in a strong County Kerry brogue: 'Och, thin indade, Miss Amy, and it's no more cake you'll be getting out of me the night. That's four pieces you've ate, and it's little shlape your poor mother'll git with you a-tossin' and tumblin' forenenst her all night long because of your big appetite.'

'Oh, Miss Katy, talk Irish some more!' cried the delighted children.

'Is it Irish you'd be afther having me talk, when it's me own langwidge, and sorrow a bit of another do I know?' demanded Katy. Then she caught sight of the new arrival, and stopped short with a blush and a laugh.

'Come in, Mr Worthington,' she said; 'we're at supper, as you see, and I am acting as waitress.'

'Oh, Uncle Ned, please go away,' pleaded Amy, 'or Katy will be polite, and not talk Irish any more!'

'Indade, and the less ye say about politeness the bether, when ye're afther ordering the jantleman out of the room in that fashion!' said the waitress. Then she pulled off her cap and untied her apron. 'Now for the Christmas tree,' she said.

It was a very little tree, but it bore some remarkable fruits, for in addition to the 'tiny toys and candles fit for Lilliput', various parcels were found to have been hastily added at the last moment for various people. The *Natchitoches* had lately come from the Levant, and delightful Oriental confections now appeared for Amy and Mrs Ashe; Turkish slippers, all gold embroidery; towels, with richly decorated ends in silks and tinsel – all the pretty superfluities which the East holds out to charm gold from the pockets of her Western visitors. A pretty little dagger in agate and silver fell to Katy's share out of what Lieutenant Worthington called his 'loot'; and beside, a most beautiful specimen of the inlaid work for which Nice is famous – a looking-glass with a stand and little doors to close it in – which was a present from Mrs Ashe. It was quite unlike a Christmas Eve at home, but altogether delightful; and as Katy sat next morning on the sand, after the service in the English church, to finish her home letter, and felt the sun warm on her cheek, and the perfumed air blow past as softly as in June, she had to remind herself that Christmas is not necessarily synonymous with snow and winter, but means the great central heat and warmth of the advent of Him who came to lighten the whole earth.

A few days after this pleasant Christmas they left Nice. All of them felt a reluctance to move, and Amy loudly bewailed the necessity.

'If I could stay here till it is time to go home, I shouldn't be homesick at all,' she declared.

'But what a pity it would be not to see Italy!' said her mother. 'Think of Naples and Rome and Venice!'

'I don't want to think about them. It makes me feel as if I was studying a great long geography lesson, and it tires me so to learn it.'

'Amy, dear, you're not well.'

'Yes, I am – quite well; only I don't want to go away from Nice.'

'You only have to learn a little bit at a time of your geography lesson, you know,' suggested Katy; 'and it's a great deal nicer way to study it than out of a book.' But though she spoke cheerfully she was conscious that she shared Amy's reluctance.

'It's all laziness,' she told herself. 'Nice has been so pleasant that it has spoiled me.'

It was a consolation, and made going easier, that they were to drive over the famous Corniche Road as far as San Remo, instead of going to Genoa by rail as most travellers nowadays do. They departed from the Pension Suisse early on an exquisite morning, fair and balmy as June, but with a little zest and sparkle of coolness in the air which made it additionally delightful. The Mediterranean was of the deepest violet-blue; a sort of bloom of colour seemed to lie upon it. The sky was like an arch of turquoise; every cape and headland shone jewel-like in the golden sunshine. The carriage, as it followed the windings of the road cut shelf-like on the cliffs, seemed poised between earth and heaven; the sea below, the mountain summits above, with a fairy world of verdure between. The journey was like a dream of enchantment and rapidly changing surprises; and when it ended in a quaint hostelry at San Remo, with palm trees feathering the Bordighera Point and Corsica, for once seen by day, lying in bold, clear outlines against the sunset, Katy had to admit to herself that Nice, much as she loved it, was not the only, not even the most beautiful place in Europe. Already she felt her horizon growing, her convictions changing; and who should say what lay beyond?

The next day brought them to Genoa, to a hotel once the stately palace of an archbishop, where they were lodged, all three together, in an enormous room, so high and broad and long that their three little curtained beds, set behind a screen of carved wood, made no impression on the space. There were not less than four sofas and double that number of armchairs in the room, besides a couple of monumental wardrobes; but, as Katy remarked, several grand pianos could still have been moved in without anybody's feeling crowded. On one side of them lay the port of Genoa, filled with craft from all parts of the world flying the flags of a dozen different nations. From the other they caught glimpses of the magnificent old city, rising in tier over tier of churches and palaces and gardens; while nearer still were narrow streets, which glittered with gold filigree and the shops of jewel-workers.

And while they went in and out, and gazed and wondered, Lilly Page, at the Pension Suisse, was saying: 'I am so glad that Katy and *that* Mrs Ashe are gone! Nothing has been so pleasant since they came. Lieutenant Worthington is dreadfully stiff and stupid, and seems quite different from what he used to be. But now that we have got rid of them it will all come right again.'

'I really don't think that Katy was to blame,' said Mrs Page. 'She never seemed to me to be making any effort to attract him.'

'Oh, Katy is sly,' responded Lilly vindictively. 'She never *seems* to do anything, but somehow she always gets her own way. I suppose she thought I didn't see her keeping him down there on the beach the other day when he was coming in to call on us, but I did. It was just out of spite, and because she wanted to vex me; I know it was.'

'Well, dear, she's gone now, and you won't be worried with her again,' said her mother soothingly. 'Don't pout so, Lilly, and wrinkle up your forehead. It's very unbecoming.'

'Yes, she's gone,' snapped Lilly; 'and as she's bound for the east, and we for the west, we are not likely to meet again, for which I am devoutly thankful.'

CHAPTER EIGHT

On the Track of Ulysses

'We are going to follow the track of Ulysses,' said Katy, with her eyes fixed on the little travelling-map in her guidebook. 'Do you realise that, Polly dear? He and his companions sailed these very seas before us and we shall see the sights they saw – Circe's Cape and the Isles of the Sirens, and Polyphemus himself, perhaps – who knows?'

The *Marco Polo* had just cast off her moorings, and was slowly steaming out of the crowded port of Genoa into the heart of a still rosy sunset. The water was perfectly smooth; no motion could be felt but the engine's throb. The trembling foam of the long wake showed glancing points of phosphorescence here and there while low on the eastern sky a great silver planet burned like a signal-lamp.

'Polyphemus was a horrible giant. I read about him once, and I don't want to see him,' observed Amy, from her safe protected perch in her mother's lap.

'He may not be so bad now as he was in those old times. Some missionary may have come across him and converted him. If he were good, you wouldn't mind his being big, would you?' suggested Kate.

'N–o,' replied Amy doubtfully; 'but it would take a great lot of missionaries to make *him* good, I should think. One all alone would be afraid to speak to him. We shan't really see him, shall we?'

'I don't believe we shall; and if we stuff cotton in our ears, and look the other way, we need not hear the sirens sing,' said Katy, who was in the highest spirits. 'And oh, Polly dear, there is one delightful thing I forgot to tell you about! The captain says he shall stay in Leghorn all day tomorrow taking on freight, and we shall have plenty of time to run up to Pisa and see the cathedral and the Leaning Tower and everything else. Now, that is something Ulysses didn't do! I am so glad I didn't die of measles when I was little, as Rose Red used to say!' She gave her book a toss into the air as she spoke, and caught it again as it fell, very much as the Katy Carr of twelve years ago might have done.

'What a child you are!' said Mrs Ashe approvingly; 'you never seem out of sorts or tired of things.'

'Out of sorts! I should think not! And pray why should I be, Polly dear?'

Katy had taken to calling her friend 'Polly dear' of late – a trick picked up half-unconsciously from Lieutenant Ned. Mrs Ashe liked it; it was sisterly and intimate, she said, and made her feel nearer Katy's age.

'Does the tower really lean?' questioned Amy – 'far over, I mean, so that we can see it?'

'We shall know tomorrow,' replied Katy. 'If it doesn't, I shall lose all my confidence in human nature.'

Katy's confidence in human nature was not doomed to be impaired. There stood the famous tower, when they reached the Place del Duomo in Pisa next morning, looking all aslant, exactly as it does in the pictures and the alabaster models, and seeming as if in another moment it must topple over, from its own weight, upon their heads. Mrs Ashe declared that it was so unnatural that it made her flesh creep; and when she was coaxed up the winding staircase to the top, she turned so giddy that they were all thankful to get her safely down to firm ground again. She turned her back upon the tower, as they crossed the grassy space to the majestic old cathedral, saying that if she thought about it any more, she should become a disbeliever in the attraction of gravitation, which she had always been told all respectable people *must* believe in.

The guide showed them the lamp, swinging by a long, slender chain, before which Galileo is said to have sat and pondered while he worked out his theory of the pendulum. This lamp seemed a sort of own cousin to the attraction of gravitation, and they gazed upon it with respect. Then they went to the Baptistery to see Niccolo Pisano's magnificent pulpit of creamy marble, a mass of sculpture supported on the backs of lions, and the equally lovely font, and to admire the extraordinary sound which their guide evoked from a mysterious echo, with which he seemed to be on intimate terms, for he made it say whatever he would, and almost 'answer back'.

It was in coming out of the Baptistery that they met with an adventure which Amy could never quite forget. Pisa is the mendicant city of Italy, and her streets are infested with a band of religious beggars who call themselves the Brethren of the Order of Mercy. They wear loose black gowns, sandals laced over their bare feet and black cambric masks with holes, through which their eyes glare awfully; and they carry tin cups, for the reception of offerings, which they thrust into the faces of all strangers visiting the city, whom they look upon as their lawful prey.

As our party emerged from the Baptistery, two of these brethren espied them, and like great human bats came swooping down upon them with long strides, their black garments flying in the wind and their eyes rolling strangely behind their masks, brandishing their alms-cups, which had 'Pour les Pauvres' lettered upon them and gave forth a clapping sound like a watchman's rattle. There was something terrible in their appearance and the rushing speed of their movements. Amy screamed and ran behind her mother, who visibly shrank. Katy stood her ground; but the bat-winged fiends in Doré's illustrations to Dante occurred to her, and her fingers trembled as she dropped some money in their cups.

Even mendicant friars are human. Katy ceased to tremble as she observed that one of them, as he retreated, walked backward for some distance in order to gaze longer at Mrs Ashe, whose cheeks were flushed with bright pink and who was looking particularly handsome. She began to laugh instead, and Mrs Ashe laughed too; but Amy could not get over the impression of having been attacked by demons, and often afterward recurred with a shudder to the time when those awful black *things* flew at her and she hid behind Mamma. The ghastly pictures of the Triumph of Death, which were presently exhibited to them on the walls of the Campo Santo, did not tend to reassure her, and it was with quite a pale, scared little face that she walked toward the hotel where they were to lunch, and she held fast to Katy's hand.

Their way led them through a narrow street inhabited by the poorer classes – a dusty street with high shabby buildings on either side and wide doorways giving glimpses of interior courtyards, where empty hogsheads and barrels and rusty cauldrons lay, and great wooden trays of macaroni were spread out in the sun to dry. Some of the macaroni was grey, some white, some yellow: none of it looked at all desirable to eat, as it lay exposed to the dust, with long lines of ill-washed clothes flapping above on wires stretched from one house to another. As is usual in poor streets, there were swarms of children; and the appearance of little Amy, with her long bright hair falling over her shoulders and Mabel clasped in her arms, created a great sensation. The children in the street shouted and exclaimed, and other children within the houses heard the sounds and came trooping out, while mothers and older sisters peeped from the doorways. The very air seemed full of eager faces and little brown and curly heads bobbing up and down with excitement, and black eyes fixed upon big beautiful Mabel, who with her thick wig of flaxen hair, her blue velvet dress and jacket, feathered hat and little muff, seemed to them like some strange small marvel from another world. They could not decide whether she was a living child or a make-believe one, and they dared not come near enough to find out; so they clustered at a little distance, pointed with their fingers and whispered and giggled, while Amy, much pleased with the admiration shown for her darling, lifted Mabel up to view.

At last one droll little girl with a white cap on her round head seemed to make up her mind, and, darting indoors, returned with *her* doll – a poor little image of wood, its only garment a coarse shirt of red cotton. This she held out for Amy to see. Amy smiled for the first time since her encounter with the bat-like friars and Katy, taking Mabel from her, made signs that the two dolls should kiss each other. But though the little Italian screamed with laughter at the idea of a *bacio* between two dolls, she would by no means allow it, and hid her treasure behind her back, blushing and giggling, and saying something very fast which none of them understood, while she waved two fingers at them with a curious gesture.

'I do believe she is afraid Mabel will cast the evil eye on her doll,' said Katy at last, with a sudden understanding as to what this pantomime meant.

'Why, you silly thing,' cried the outraged Amy; 'do you suppose for one moment that my child could hurt your dirty old dolly? You ought to be glad to have her noticed at all by anybody that's clean.'

The sound of the foreign tongue completed the discomfiture of the little Italian. With a shriek she fled, and all the other children after her; pausing at a distance to look back at the alarming creatures who didn't speak the familiar language. Katy, wishing to leave a pleasant impression, made Mabel kiss her waxen fingers toward them. This sent the children off into another fit of laughter and chatter, and they followed our friends for quite a distance as they proceeded on their way to the hotel.

All that night, over a sea as smooth as glass, the *Marco Polo* slipped along the coasts past which the ships of Ulysses sailed in those old legendary days which wear so charmed a light to our modern eyes. Katy roused at three in the morning, and, looking from her cabin window, had a glimpse of an island, which her map showed her must be Elba, where that war-eagle, Napoleon, was chained for a while. Then she fell asleep again, and when she roused in full daylight the steamer was off the coast of Ostia and nearing the mouth of the Tiber. Dreamy mountain-shapes rose beyond the faraway Campagna, and every curve and every indentation of the coast bore a name which recalled some interesting thing.

About eleven a dim-drawn bubble appeared on the horizon, which the captain assured them was the dome of St Peter's, nearly thirty miles distant. This was one of the 'moments' which Clover had been fond of speculating about; and Katy, contrasting the real with the imaginary moment, could not help smiling. Neither she nor Clover had ever supposed that her first glimpse of the great dome was to be so little impressive.

On and on they went till the air-hung bubble disappeared; and Amy, grown very tired of scenery with which she had no associations, and grown-up raptures which she did not comprehend, squeezed herself into the end of the long wooden settee on which Katy sat and began to beg for another story concerning Violet and Emma.

'Just a tiny little chapter, you know, Miss Katy, about what they did on New Year's Day or something. It's so dull to keep sailing and sailing all day and have nothing to do, and it's ever so long since you told me anything about them, really and truly it is!'

Now, Violet and Emma, if the truth is to be told, had grown to be the bane of Katy's existence. She had rung the changes on their uneventful adventures, and racked her brains to invent more and more details, till her imagination felt like a dry sponge from which every possible drop of moisture had been squeezed. Amy was insatiable. Her interest in the tale never flagged, and when her exhausted friend explained that she really could not think of another word to say on the subject, she would turn the tables by asking, 'Then, Miss Katy, mayn't I tell *you* a chapter?' whereupon she would proceed somewhat in this fashion: 'It was the day before Christmas – no, we won't have it the day before Christmas; it shall be three days before Thanksgiving. Violet and Emma got up in the morning, and – well, they didn't do anything in particular that day. They just had their breakfasts and dinners, and played and studied a little, and went to bed early, you know, and the next morning – well, there didn't much happen that day, either; they just had their breakfasts and dinners and played.'

Listening to Amy's stories was so much worse than telling them to her that Katy in self-defence was driven to recommence her narrations, but she had grown to hate Violet and Emma with a deadly hatred. So when Amy made this appeal on the steamer's deck, a sudden resolution took possession of her, and she decided to put an end to these dreadful children once and for all.

'Yes, Amy,' she said, 'I will tell you one more story about Violet and Emma; but this is positively the last.'

So Amy cuddled close to her friend, and listened with rapt attention as Katy told how, on a certain day just before the New Year, Violet and Emma started by themselves in a little sleigh drawn by a pony, to carry to a poor woman who lived in a lonely house high up on a mountain slope a basket containing a turkey, a mould of cranberry jelly, a bunch of celery and a mince-pie.

'They were so pleased at having all these nice things to take to poor widow Simpson, and in thinking how glad she would be to see them,' proceeded the naughty Katy, 'that they never noticed how black the sky was getting to be, or how the wind howled through the bare boughs of the trees. They had to go slowly, for the road was uphill all the way, and it was hard work for the poor pony. But he was a stout little fellow, and tugged away up the slippery track, and Violet and Emma talked and laughed, and never thought what was going to happen. Just halfway up the mountain there was a rocky cliff which overhung the road, and on this cliff grew an enormous hemlock tree. The branches were loaded with snow, which made them much heavier than usual. Just as the sleigh passed slowly underneath the cliff, a violent blast of wind blew up from the ravine, struck the hemlock, and tore it out of the ground, roots and all. It fell directly across the sleigh, and Violet and Emma and the pony and the basket with the turkey and the other things in it were all crushed as flat as pancakes!'

'Well,' said Amy, as Katy stopped, 'go on! what happened then?'

'Nothing happened then,' replied Katy, in a tone of awful solemnity; 'nothing could happen! Violet and Emma were dead, the pony was dead, the things in the basket were broken all to little bits, and a great snowstorm began and covered them up, and no one knew where they were or what had become of them till the snow melted in the spring.'

With a loud shriek Amy jumped up from the bench.

'No! no! no!' she cried; 'they aren't dead! I won't let them be dead!' Then she burst into tears, ran down the stairs, locked herself into her mother's stateroom, and did not appear again for several hours.

Katy laughed heartily at first over this outburst, but presently she began to repent and to think that she had treated her pet unkindly. She went down and knocked at the stateroom door; but Amy would not answer. She called her softly through the keyhole, and coaxed and pleaded, but it was all in vain. Amy remained invisible till late in the afternoon; and when she finally crept up again to the deck, her eyes were red with crying, and her little face as pale and miserable as if she had been attending the funeral of her dearest friend.

Katy's heart smote her.

'Come here, my darling,' she said, holding out her hand; 'come and sit in my lap and forgive me. Violet and Emma shall not be dead. They shall go on living, since you care so much for them, and I will tell stories about them to the end of the chapter.'

'No,' said Amy shaking her head mournfully; 'you can't. They're dead, and they won't come to life again ever. It's all over, and I'm so so–o–rry.'

All Katy's apologies and efforts to resuscitate the story were useless. Violet and Emma were dead to Amy's imagination, and she could not make herself believe in them any more.

She was too woebegone to care for the fables of Circe and her swine which Katy told as they rounded the magnificent Cape Circello, and the isles where the sirens used to sing appealed to her in vain. The sun set, the stars came out; and under the beams of their countless lamps, and the beckonings of a slender new moon, the *Marco Polo* sailed into the Bay of Naples, past Vesuvius, whose dusky curl of smoke could be seen outlined against the luminous sky, and brought her passengers to their landing-place.

They woke next morning to a summer atmosphere full of yellow sunshine and true July warmth. Flower-venders stood on every corner, and pursued each newcomer with their fragrant wares. Katy could not stop exclaiming over the cheapness of the flowers, which were thrust in at the carriage windows as they drove slowly up and down the streets. They were tied into flat nosegays, whose centre was a white camellia, encircled with concentric rows of pink tea-rosebuds, ring after ring, till the whole was the size of an ordinary milk-pan; all to be had for the sum of ten cents! But after they had bought two or three of these enormous bouquets, and had discovered that not a single rose boasted an inch of stem, and that all were pierced with long wires through their very hearts, she ceased to care for them.

'I would rather have one Souvenir or General Jacquerminot, with a long stem and plenty of leaves, than a dozen of these stiff platters of bouquets,' Katy told Mrs Ashe. But when they drove beyond the city gates, and the coachman came to anchor beneath walls overhung with the same roses, and she found that she might stand on the seat and pull down as many branches of the lovely flowers as she desired, and gather wallflowers for herself out of the clefts in the masonry, she was entirely satisfied.

'This is the Italy of my dreams,' she said.

With all its beauty there was an underlying sense of danger about Naples, which interfered with their enjoyment of it. Evil smells came in at the windows, or confronted them as they went about the city. There seemed something deadly in the air. Whispered reports met their ears of cases of fever, which the landlords of the hotels were doing their best to hush up. An American gentleman was said to be lying very ill at one house. A lady had died the week before at another. Mrs Ashe grew nervous.

'We will just take a rapid look at a few of the principal things,' she told Katy, 'and then get away as fast as we can. Amy is so on my mind that I have no peace of my life. I keep feeling her pulse and imagining that she does not look right; and though I know it is all my fancy, I am impatient to be off. You won't mind, will you, Katy?'

After that everything they did was done in a hurry. Katy felt as if she were being driven about by a cyclone, as they rushed from one sight to another, filling up all the chinks between with shopping, which was irresistible where everything was so pretty and so wonderfully cheap. She herself purchased a tortoiseshell fan and chain for Rose Red, and had her monogram carved upon it; a coral locket for Elsie; some studs for Dorry; and for her father, a small, beautiful vase of bronze, copied from one of the Pompeian antiques.

'How charming it is to have money to spend in such a place as this!' she said to herself, with a sigh of satisfaction, as she surveyed these delightful buyings. 'I only wish I could get ten times as many things and take them to ten times as many people. Papa was so wise about it! I can't think how it is that he always knows beforehand exactly how people are going to feel, and what they will want!'

Mrs Ashe also bought a great many things for herself and Amy and to take home as presents; and it was all very pleasant and satisfactory, except for that subtle sense of danger from which they could not escape and which made them glad to go. 'See Naples and die,' says the old adage; and the saying has proved sadly true in the case of many an American traveller.

Beside the talk of fever there was also a good deal of gossip about brigands going about, as is generally the case in Naples and its vicinity. Something was said to have happened to a party on one of the heights above Sorrento; and though nobody knew exactly what the something was, or was willing to vouch for the story, Mrs Ashe and Katy felt a good deal of trepidation as they entered the carriage which was to take them to the neighbourhood where the mysterious 'something' had occurred.

The drive between Castellamare and Sorrento is in reality as safe as that between Boston and Brookline; but as our party did not know this fact till afterward, it did them no good. It is also one of the most beautiful drives in the world, following the windings of the exquisite coast mile after mile, in long links of perfectly made road, carved on the face of sharp cliffs, with groves of oranges and lemons and olive orchards above, and the Bay of Naples beneath, stretching away like a solid sheet of lapis-lazuli, and gemmed with islands of the most picturesque form.

It is a pity that so much beauty should have been wasted on Mrs Ashe and Katy, but they were too frightened to half enjoy it. Their carriage was driven by a shaggy young savage, who looked quite wild enough to be a bandit himself. He cracked his whip loudly as they rolled along, and every now and then gave a long shrill whistle. Mrs Ashe was sure that these were signals to his band, who were lurking somewhere on the olive-hung hillsides. She thought she detected him once or twice making signs to certain questionable-looking characters as they passed; and she fancied that the people they met gazed at them with an air of commiseration, as upon victims who were being carried to execution. Her fears affected Katy; so, though they talked and laughed, and made jokes to amuse Amy, who must not be scared or led to suppose that anything was amiss, and to the outward view seemed a very merry party, they were privately quaking in their shoes all the way, and enjoying a deal of highly superfluous misery. And after all they reached Sorrento in perfect safety; and the driver, who looked so dangerous, turned out to be a respectable young man enough, with a wife and family to support, who considered a plateful of macaroni and a glass of sour red wine as the height of luxury, and was grateful for a small gratuity of thirty cents or so which would enable him to purchase these dainties. Mrs Ashe had a very bad headache next day, to pay for her fright; and she and Katy agreed that they had been very foolish, and resolved to pay no more attention to unaccredited rumours or allow them to spoil their enjoyment, which was a sensible resolution to make.

Their hotel was perched directly over the sea. From the balcony of their sitting-room they looked down a sheer cliff, some sixty feet high, into the water; their bedrooms opened on a garden of roses, with an orange grove beyond. Not far from them was the great gorge which cuts the little town of Sorrento almost in two, and whose seaward end makes the harbour of the place. Katy was never tired of peering down into this strange and beautiful cleft, whose sides, two hundred feet in depth, are hung with vines and trailing growths of all sorts, and seem all a-tremble with the fairy fronds of maidenhair ferns growing out of every chink and crevice. She and Amy took walks along the coast towards Massa, to look off at the lovely island shapes in the bay, and admire the great clumps of cactus and Spanish bayonet which grew by the roadside; and they always came back loaded with orange-flowers, which could be picked as freely as apple-blossoms from New England orchards in the spring. The oranges themselves at that time of the year were very sour, but they answered as well for a romantic date, 'From an orange grove', as if they had been the sweetest in the world.

They made two different excursions to Pompeii, which is within easy distance of Sorrento. They scrambled on donkeys over the hills, and had glimpses of the faraway Calabrian shore, of the natural arch, and the temples of Paestum shining in the sun many miles distant. On Katy's birthday, which fell toward the end of January, Mrs Ashe let her have her choice of a treat; and she elected to go to the island of Capri, which none of them had seen. It turned out a perfect day, with sea and wind exactly right for the sail, and to allow of getting into the famous 'Blue Grotto', which can only be entered under particular conditions of tide and weather. And they climbed the great cliff-rise at the island's end, and saw the ruins of the villa built by the wicked emperor Tiberius, and the awful place known as his 'Leap', down which, it is said, he made his victims throw themselves; and they lunched at a hotel which bore his name, then just at sunset pushed off again for the row home over the charmed sea. This return voyage was almost the pleasantest thing of all the day. The water was smooth, the moon at its full. It was larger and more brilliant than American moons are, and seemed to possess an actual warmth and colour. The boatmen timed their oar-strokes to the cadence of Neapolitan *barcaroles* and folk-songs, full of rhythmic movement, which seemed caught from the pulsing tides. And when at last the bow grated on the sands of the Sorrento landing-place, Katy drew a long, regretful breath, and declared that this was her best birthday gift of all, better than Amy's flowers, or the pretty tortoiseshell locket that Mrs Ashe had given her, better even than the letter from home, which, timed by happy accident, had arrived by the morning's post to make a bright opening for the day.

All pleasant things must come to ending.

'Katy,' said Mrs Ashe, one afternoon in early February, 'I heard some ladies talking just now in the *salon*, and they said that Rome is filling up very fast. The Carnival begins in less than two weeks, and everybody wants to be there then. If we don't make haste we shall not be able to get any rooms.'

'Oh dear!' said Katy, 'it is very trying not to be able to be in two places at once. I want to see Rome dreadfully, and yet I cannot bear to leave Sorrento. We have been very happy here, haven't we?'

So they took up their wandering staves again, and departed for Rome, like the Apostle, 'not knowing what should befall them there'.

CHAPTER NINE

A Roman Holiday

'Oh dear!' said Mrs Ashe, as she folded her letters and laid them aside, 'I wish those Pages would go away from Nice, or else that the frigates were not there.'

'Why! what's the matter?' asked Katy, looking up from the many-leaved journal from Clover over which she was poring.

'Nothing is the matter except that those everlasting people haven't gone to Spain yet, as they said they would, and Ned seems to keep on seeing them,' replied Mrs Ashe petulantly.

'But, dear Polly, what difference does it make? And they never did promise you to go at any particular time, did they?'

'N–o, they didn't; but I wish they would, all the same. Not that Ned is such a goose as really to care anything for that foolish Lilly!' Then she gave a little laugh at her own inconsistency, and added: 'But I oughtn't to abuse her when she is your cousin.'

'Don't mention it,' said Katy cheerfully. 'But, really, I don't see why poor Lilly need worry you so, Polly dear.'

The room in which this conversation took place was on the very topmost floor of the Hotel del Mondo in Rome. It was large and many-windowed; and though there was a little bed in one corner half-hidden behind a calico screen, with a bureau and washing-stand, and a sort of stout mahogany hat tree on which Katy's dresses and jackets were hanging, the remaining space, with a sofa and easy-chairs grouped round a fire, and a round table furnished with books and a lamp, was

ample enough to make a good substitute for the private
sitting-room which Mrs Ashe had not been able to procure
on account of the near approach of the Carnival and the
consequent crowding of strangers to Rome. In fact, she was
assured that under the circumstances she was lucky in
finding rooms as good as these; and she made the most of the
assurance as a consolation for the somewhat unsatisfactory
food and service of the hotel, and the four long flights of
stairs which must be passed every time they needed to reach
the dining-room or the street door.

The party had been in Rome only four days, but already
they had seen a host of interesting things. They had stood
in the strange sunken space with its marble floor and
broken columns, which is all that is left of the great Roman
Forum. They had visited the Coliseum, at that period still
overhung with ivy garlands and trailing greeneries, and
not, as now, scraped clean and bare and 'tidied' out of much
of its picturesqueness. They had seen the Baths of
Caracalla and the Temple of Janus and St Peter's and the
Vatican marbles, and had driven out on the Campagna
and to the Pamphili-Doria Villa to gather purple and red
anemones, and to the English cemetery to see the grave of
Keats. They had also peeped into certain shops, and
attended a reception at the American minister's – in short,
like most unwarned travellers, they had done about twice as
much as prudence and experience would have permitted,
had those worthies been consulted.

All the romance of Katy's nature responded to the
fascination of the ancient city – the capital of the world, as
it may truly be called. The shortest drive or walk brought
them face to face with innumerable and unexpected delights. Now it was a wonderful fountain, with plunging
horses and colossal nymphs and Tritons, holding cups and
horns from which showers of white foam rose high in the air
to fall like rushing rain into an immense marble basin. Now

it was an arched doorway with traceries as fine as lace – sole remaining fragment of a heathen temple, flung and stranded as it were by the waves of time on the squalid shore of the present. Now it was a shrine at the meeting of three streets, where a dim lamp burned beneath the effigy of the Madonna, with always a fresh rose beside it in a vase, and at its foot a peasant woman kneeling in red bodice and blue petticoat, with a lace-trimmed towel folded over her hair. Or again, it would be a sunlit terrace lifted high on a hillside, and crowded with carriages full of beautifully-dressed people, while below all Rome seemed spread out like a panorama, dim, mighty, majestic, and bounded by the blue wavy line of the Campagna and the Alban Hills. Or perhaps it might be a wonderful double flight of steps with massive balustrades and pillars with urns, on which sat a crowd of figures in strange costumes and attitudes, who all looked as though they had stepped out of pictures, but who were in reality models waiting for artists to come by and engage them. No matter what it was – a bit of oddly-tinted masonry with a tuft of brown and orange wallflowers hanging upon it, or a vegetable stall where endive and chicory and curly lettuces were arranged in wreaths with tiny orange gourds and scarlet peppers for points of colour, it was all Rome, and, by virtue of that word, different from any other place – more suggestive, more interesting, ten times more mysterious than any other could possibly be, so Katy thought.

This fact consoled her for everything and anything – for the fleas, the dirt, for the queer things they had to eat and the still queerer odours they were forced to smell! Nothing seemed of any particular consequence except the deep sense of enjoyment, and the newly-discovered world of thought and sensation of which she had become suddenly conscious.

The only drawback to her happiness, as the days went on, was that little Amy did not seem quite well or like herself.

She had taken a cold on the journey from Naples, and though it did not seem serious, that, or something, made her look pale and thin. Her mother said she was growing fast; but the explanation did not quite account for the wistful look in the child's eyes and the tired feeling of which she continually complained. Mrs Ashe, with vague uneasiness, began to talk of cutting short their Roman stay and getting Amy off to the more bracing air of Florence. But meanwhile there was the Carnival close at hand, which they must by no means lose; and the feeling that their opportunity might be a brief one made her and Katy all the more anxious to make the very most of their time. So they filled the days full with sights to see and things to do, and came and went; sometimes taking Amy with them, but more often leaving her at the hotel under the care of a kind German chambermaid, who spoke pretty good English and to whom Amy had taken a fancy.

'The marble things are so cold, and the old broken things make me so sorry,' she explained; 'and I hate beggars because they are dirty, and the stairs make my back ache; and I'd a great deal rather stay with Maria and go up on the roof, if you don't mind, Mamma.'

This roof, which Amy had chosen as a play-place, covered the whole of the great hotel, and had been turned into a sort of upper-air garden by the simple process of gravelling it all over, placing trellises of ivy here and there, and setting tubs of oranges and oleanders and boxes of gay geraniums and stock-gillyflowers on the balustrades. A tame fawn was tethered there. Amy adopted him as a playmate; and what with his company and that of the flowers, the times when her mother and Katy were absent from her passed not unhappily.

Katy always repaired to the roof as soon as they came in from their long mornings and afternoons of sightseeing. Years afterward, she would remember with contrition how

pathetically glad Amy always was to see her. She would put
her little head on Katy's breast and hold her tight for many
minutes without saying a word. When she did speak it was
always about the house and the garden that she talked. She
never asked any questions as to where Katy had been, or
what she had done; it seemed to tire her to think about it.

'I should be very lonely sometimes if it were not for my
dear little fawn,' she told Katy once. 'He is so sweet that I
don't miss you and Mamma very much while I have him to
play with. I call him Florio – don't you think that is a pretty
name? I like to stay with him a great deal better than to go
about with you to those nasty-smelling old churches, with
fleas hopping all over them!'

So Amy was left in peace with her fawn, and the others
made haste to see all they could before the time came to go
to Florence.

Katy realised one of the 'moments' for which she had
come to Europe when she stood for the first time on the
balcony, overhanging the Corso, which Mrs Ashe had hired
in company with some acquaintances made at the hotel, and
looked down at the ebb and surge of the just-begun
Carnival. The narrow street seemed humming with people
of all sorts and conditions. Some were masked, some were
not. There were ladies and gentlemen in fashionable
clothes, peasants in the gayest costumes, surprised-looking
tourists in tall hats and linen dusters, harlequins, clowns,
devils, nuns, dominoes of every colour – red, white, blue,
black; while above, the balconies bloomed like a rose garden
with pretty faces framed in lace veils or picturesque hats.
Flowers were everywhere wreathed along the house-fronts,
tied to the horses' ears, in ladies' hands and gentlemen's
buttonholes, while venders went up and down the street
bearing great trays of violets and carnations and camellias
for sale. The air was full of cries and laughter, and the shrill
calls of merchants advertising their wares – candy, fruit,

birds, lanterns and *confetti*, the latter being merely lumps of lime, large or small, with a pea or a bean embedded in each lump to give it weight. Boxes full of this unpleasant confection were suspended in front of each balcony, with tin scoops to use in ladling it out and flinging it about. Everybody wore or carried a wire mask as protection against this white, incessant shower, and before long the air became full of a fine dust, which hung above the Corso like a mist, and filled the eyes and noses and clothes of all present with irritating particles.

Pasquino's Car was passing underneath just as Katy and Mrs Ashe arrived – a gorgeous affair, hung with silken draperies, and bearing as symbol an enormous egg in which the Carnival was supposed to be in act of incubation. A huge wagon followed in its wake, on which was a house some sixteen feet square, whose sole occupant was a gentleman attended by five servants, who kept him supplied with *confetti*, which he showered liberally on the heads of the crowd. Then came a car in the shape of a steamboat, with a smoke-pipe and sails, over which flew the Union Jack, and which was manned by a party wearing the dress of British tars. The next wagon bore a company of jolly maskers equipped with many-coloured bladders, which they banged and rattled as they went along. Following this was a troupe of beautiful circus-horses, cream-coloured with scarlet trappings, or sorrel with blue, ridden by ladies in pale-green velvet laced with silver, or blue velvet and gold. Another car bore a birdcage which was an exact imitation of St Peter's, within which perched a lonely old parrot. This device evidently had a political signification, for it was alternately hissed and applauded as it went along. The whole scene was like a brilliant, rapidly shifting dream; and Katy, as she stood with lips apart and eyes wide open with wonderment and pleasure, forgot whether she was in the body or not – forgot everything except what was passing before her gaze.

She was roused by a stinging shower of lime-dust. An Englishman in the next balcony had taken courteous advantage of her preoccupation, and had flung a scoopful of *confetti* in her undefended face! It is generally Anglo-Saxons of the less refined class, English or Americans, who do these things at Carnival times. The national love of a rough joke comes to the surface encouraged by the licence of the moment, and all the grace and prettiness of the festival vanish. Katy laughed and dusted herself as well as she could, and took refuge behind her mask; while a nimble American boy of the party changed places with her, and thenceforward made that particular Englishman his special target, plying such a lively and adroit shovel as to make Katy's assailant rue the hour when he evoked this national reprisal. His powdered head and rather clumsy efforts to retaliate excited shouts of laughter from the adjoining balconies. The young American, fresh from tennis and college athletics, darted about and dodged with an agility impossible for his heavily-built foe; and each effective shot and parry on his side was greeted with little cries of applause and the clapping of hands on the part of those who were watching the contest.

Exactly opposite them was a balcony hung with white silk, in which sat a lady who seemed to be of some distinction; for every now and then an officer in brilliant uniform, or some official covered with orders and stars, would be shown in by her servants, bow before her with the utmost deference, and after a little conversation retire, kissing her gloved hand as he went. The lady was a beautiful person, with lustrous black eyes and dark hair, over which a lace mantilla was fastened with diamond stars. She wore pale-blue with white flowers, and altogether, as Katy afterwards wrote to Clover, reminded her exactly of one of those beautiful princesses whom they used to play about in their childhood and quarrel over, because every one of them wanted to be the princess and nobody else.

'I wonder who she is,' said Mrs Ashe in a low tone. 'She might be almost anybody from her looks. She keeps glancing across to us, Katy. Do you know, I think she has taken a fancy to you.'

Perhaps the lady had; for just then she turned her head and said a word to one of her footmen, who immediately placed something in her hand. It was a little shining *bonbonnière*, and, rising, she threw it straight at Katy. Alas! it struck the edge of the balcony and fell into the street below, where it was picked up by a ragged little peasant girl in a red jacket, who raised a pair of astonished eyes to the heavens, as if sure that the gift must have fallen straight from thence. Katy bent forward to watch its fate, and went through a little panto-mime of regret and despair for the benefit of the opposite lady, who only laughed, and, taking another from her servant, flung with better aim, so that it fell exactly at Katy's feet. This was a gilded box in the shape of a mandolin, with sugar-plums tucked cunningly away inside. Katy kissed both her hands in acknowledgment for the pretty toy, and tossed back a bunch of roses which she happened to be wearing in her dress. After that it seemed the chief amusement of the fair unknown to throw bonbons at Katy. Some went straight and some did not; but before the afternoon ended, Katy had quite a lapful of confections and trifles – roses, sugared almonds, a satin casket, a silvered box in the shape of a horseshoe, a tiny cage with orange blossoms for birds on the perches, a minute gondola with a *marron glacée* by way of passenger, and, prettiest of all, a little ivory harp strung with enamelled violets instead of wires. For all these favours she had nothing better to offer, in return, than a few long-tailed bonbons with gay streamers of ribbon. These the lady opposite caught very cleverly, rarely missing one and kissing her hand in thanks each time.

'Isn't she exquisite?' demanded Katy, her eyes shining with excitement. 'Did you ever see anyone so lovely in your life, Polly dear? I never did. There, now! she is buying those birds to set them free, I do believe.'

It was indeed so. A vender of larks had, by the aid of a long staff, thrust a cage full of wretched little prisoners up into the balcony; and 'Katy's lady', as Mrs Ashe called her, was paying for the whole. As they watched she opened the cage door, and with the sweetest look on her face encouraged the birds to fly away. The poor little creatures cowered and hesitated, not knowing at first what use to make of their new liberty; but at last one, the boldest of the company, hopped to the door, and with a glad, exultant chirp flew straight upward. Then the others, taking courage from his example, followed, and all were lost to view in the twinkling of an eye.

'Oh, you angel!' cried Katy, leaning over the edge of the balcony and kissing both hands impulsively, 'I never saw anyone so sweet as you are in my life. Polly dear, I think carnivals are the most perfectly bewitching things in the world. How glad I am that this lasts a week, and that we can come every day! Won't Amy be delighted with these bonbons! I do hope my lady will be here tomorrow.'

How little she dreamed that she was never to enter that balcony again! How little can any of us see what lies before us till it comes so near that we cannot help seeing it, or shut our eyes, or turn away!

The next morning, almost as soon as it was light, Mrs Ashe tapped at Katy's door. She was in her dressing-gown, and her eyes looked large and frightened

'Amy is ill,' she cried. 'She has been hot and feverish all night, and she says that her head aches dreadfully. What shall I do, Katy? We ought to have a doctor at once, but I don't know the name even of any doctor here.'

Katy sat up in bed, and for one bewildered moment did not speak. Her brain felt in a whirl of confusion; but presently it cleared, and she saw what to do.

'I will write a note to Mrs Sands,' she said. Mrs Sands was

the wife of the American minister, and one of the few acquaintances they had made since they came to Rome. 'You remember how nice she was the other day, and how we liked her; and she has lived here so long that of course she must know all about the doctors. Don't you think that is the best thing to do?'

'The very best,' said Mrs Ashe, looking relieved. 'I wonder I did not think of it myself, but I am so confused that I can't think. Write the note at once, please, dear Katy. I will ring your bell for you, and then I must hurry back to Amy.'

Katy made haste with the note. The answer came promptly in half an hour, and by ten o'clock the physician recommended appeared. Dr Hilary was a dark little Italian to all appearance; but his mother had been a Scotchwoman, and he spoke English very well – a great comfort to poor Mrs Ashe, who knew not a word of Italian and not a great deal of French. He felt Amy's pulse for a long time, and tested her temperature; but he gave no positive opinion, only left a prescription, and said that he would call later in the day, and should then be able to judge more clearly what the attack was likely to prove.

Katy augured ill from this reserve. There was no talk of going to the Carnival that afternoon; no one had any heart for it. Instead, Katy spent the time in trying to recollect all she had ever heard about the care of sick people – what was to be done first and what next – and in searching the shops for a feather pillow, which luxury Amy was imperiously demanding. The pillows of Roman hotels are, as a general thing, stuffed with wool, and very hard.

'I won't have this horrid pillow any longer,' poor Amy was screaming. 'It's got bricks in it. It hurts the back of my neck. Take it away, Mamma, and give me a nice soft American pillow. I won't have this a minute longer. Don't you hear me, Mamma? Take it away!'

So, while Mrs Ashe pacified Amy to the best of her ability,

Katy hurried out in quest of the desired pillow. It proved almost an unattainable luxury; but at last, after a long search, she secured an air-cushion, a down cushion about twelve inches square, and one old feather pillow which had come from some auction, and had apparently lain for years in the corner of the shop. When this was encased in a fresh cover of Canton flannel, it did very well, and stilled Amy's complaints a little; but all night she grew worse, and when Dr Hilary came next day, he was forced to utter plainly the dreaded words 'Roman fever'. Amy was in for an attack – a light one he hoped it might be – but they had better know the truth and make ready for it.

Mrs Ashe was utterly overwhelmed by this verdict, and for the first bewildered moments did not know which way to turn. Katy, happily, kept a steadier head. She had the advantage of a little preparation of thought, and had decided beforehand what it would be necessary to do 'in case'. Oh, that fateful 'in case'! The doctor and she consulted together, and the result was that Katy sought out the *padrona* of the establishment, and without hinting at the nature of Amy's attack, secured some rooms just vacated, which were at the end of a corridor, and a little removed from the rooms of other people. There was a large room with corner windows, a smaller one opening from it, and another, still smaller, close by, which would serve as a storeroom or might do for the use of a nurse.

These rooms, without much consultation with Mrs Ashe – who seemed stunned, and sat with her eyes fixed on Amy, just answering, 'Certainly, dear, anything you say,' when applied to – Katy had arranged according to her own ideas of comfort and hygienic necessity, as learned from Miss Nightingale's excellent little book on nursing. From the larger room she had the carpet, curtains, and nearly all the furniture taken away, the floor scrubbed with hot soapsuds, and the bed pulled out from the wall to allow of a free circulation of air all around it. The smaller one she made as comfortable as possible for the use of Mrs Ashe, choosing for it the softest sofa and the best mattresses that were obtainable; for she knew that her friend's strength was likely to be severely tried if Amy's illness proved serious. When all was ready, Amy, well wrapped in her coverings, was carried down the entry and laid in the fresh bed with the soft pillows about her; and Katy, as she went to and fro, conveying clothes and books and filling drawers, felt that they were perhaps making arrangements for a long, hard trial of faith and spirits.

By the next day the necessity of a nurse became apparent, and in the afternoon Katy started out in a little hired carriage in search of one. She had a list of names, and went first to the English nurses; but, finding them all engaged, she ordered the coachman to drive to a convent where there was hope that a nursing-sister might be procured.

Their route lay across the Corso. So utterly had the Carnival with all its gay follies vanished from her mind that she was for a moment astonished at finding herself entangled in a motley crowd, so dense that the coachman was obliged to rein in his horses and stand still for some time.

There were the same masks and dominoes, the same picturesque peasant costumes which had struck her as so gay and pretty only three days before. The same jests and merry laughter filled the air, but somehow it all seemed out of tune. The sense of cold, lonely fear that had taken possession of her killed all capacity for merriment; the apprehension and solicitude of which her heart was full made the gay chattering and squeaking of the crowd sound harsh and unfeeling. The bright colours affronted her dejection; she did not want to see them. She lay back in the carriage, trying to be patient under the detention, and half shut her eyes.

A shower of lime-dust aroused her. It came from a party of burly figures in white cotton dominoes, whose carriage had been stayed by the crowd close to her own. She signified by gestures that she had no *confetti* and no protection, that she 'was not playing', in fact; but her appeal made no difference. The maskers kept on shovelling lime all over her hair and person and the carriage, and never tired of the sport till an opportune break in the procession enabled their vehicle to move on.

Katy was shaking their largesse from her dress and parasol as well as she could, when an odd gibbering sound, close to her ear, and the laughter of the crowd attracted her attention to the back of the carriage. A masker attired as a scarlet devil had climbed into the hood, and was now perched close behind her. She shook her head at him; but he only shook his in return, and chattered and grimaced, and bent over till his fiery mask almost grazed her shoulder. There was no hope but in good-humour, as she speedily realised; and, recollecting that in her shopping-bag one or two of the Carnival bonbons still remained, she took these out and offered them in the hope of propitiating him. The fiend bit one to ensure that it was made of sugar and not lime, while the crowd laughed more than ever; then, seeming satisfied, he made Katy a little speech in rapid Italian, of which she did not comprehend a word, kissed her hand, jumped down from the carriage, and disappeared in the crowd to her great relief.

Presently after that the driver spied an opening, of which he took advantage. They were across the Corso now, the roar and rush of the Carnival dying into silence as they drove rapidly on; and Katy, as she finished wiping away the last of the lime-dust, wiped some tears from her cheeks as well.

'How hateful it all was!' she said to herself. Then she remembered a sentence read somewhere: 'How heavily roll the wheels of other people's joys when your heart is sorrowful!' and she realised that it is true.

The convent was propitious, and promised to send a sister

next morning, with the proviso that every second day she was to come back to sleep and rest. Katy was too thankful for any aid to make objections, and drove home with visions of saintly nuns with pure, pale faces full of peace and resignation, such as she had read of in books, floating before her eyes.

Sister Ambrogia, when she appeared next day, did not exactly realise these imaginations. She was a plump little person, with rosy cheeks, a pair of demure black eyes, and a very obstinate mouth and chin. It soon appeared that natural inclination, combined with the rules of her convent, made her theory of a nurse's duties a very limited one.

If Mrs Ashe wished her to go down to the office with an order, she was told: 'We sisters care for the sick; we are not allowed to converse with porters and hotel people.'

If Katy suggested that on the way home she should leave a prescription at the chemist's, it was: 'We sisters are for nursing only; we do not visit shops.' And when she was asked if she could make beef-tea, she replied calmly but decisively: 'We sisters are not cooks.'

In fact, all that Sister Ambrogia seemed able or willing to do, beyond the bathing of Amy's face and brushing her hair, which she accomplished handily, was to sit by the bedside telling her rosary, or plying a little ebony shuttle in the manufacture of a long strip of tatting. Even this amount of usefulness was interfered with by the fact that Amy, who by this time was in a semi-delirious condition, had taken an aversion to her at the first glance, and was not willing to be left with her for a single moment.

'I won't stay here alone with Sister Embroidery,' she would cry, if her mother and Katy went into the next room for a moment's rest or a private consultation; 'I hate Sister Embroidery! Come back, Mamma, come back this moment! She's making faces at me and chattering just like an old parrot, and I don't understand a word she says. Take Sister

Embroidery away, Mamma, I tell you! Don't you hear me?
Come back, I say!'

  The little voice would be raised to a shrill scream; and Mrs
Ashe and Katy, hurrying back, would find Amy sitting up on
her pillow with wet, scarlet-flushed cheeks and eyes bright
with fever, ready to throw herself out of bed; while, calm as
Mabel, whose curly head lay on the pillow beside her little
mistress, Sister Ambrogia, unaware of the intricacies of
the English language, was placidly telling her beads and
muttering prayers to herself. Some of these prayers, I do not
doubt, related to Amy's recovery, if not to her conversion,
and were well meant; but they were rather irritating under
the circumstances!

CHAPTER TEN

Clear Shining after Rain

When the first shock is over and the inevitable realised and accepted, those who tend a long illness are apt to fall into a routine of life which helps to make the days seem short. The apparatus of nursing is got together. Every day the same things need to be done at the same hours and in the same way. Each little appliance is kept at hand; and, sad and tired as the watchers may be, the very monotony and regularity of their proceedings give a certain stay for their thoughts to rest upon.

But there was little of this monotony to help Mrs Ashe and Katy through with Amy's illness. Small chance was there for regularity or exact system, for something unexpected was always turning up, and needful things were often lacking. The most ordinary comforts of the sickroom, or what are considered so in America, were hard to come by, and much of Katy's time was spent in devising substitutes to take their places.

Was ice needed? A pailful of dirty snow would be brought in, full of straws, sticks and other refuse, which had apparently been scraped from the surface of the street after a frosty night. Not a particle of it could be put into milk or water; all that could be done was to make the pail serve the purpose of a refrigerator, and set bowls and tumblers in it to chill.

Was a feeding-cup wanted? It came of a cumbrous and antiquated pattern, which the infant Hercules may have enjoyed, but which the modern Amy abominated and rejected. Such a thing as a glass tube could not be found in all Rome. Bed-rests were unknown. Katy searched in vain for an india-rubber hot-water bag.

But the greatest trial of all was the beef-tea. It was Amy's sole food, and almost her only medicine; for Dr Hilary believed in leaving Nature pretty much to herself in cases of fever. The kitchen of the hotel sent up, under that name, a mixture of grease and hot water, which could not be given to Amy at all. In vain Katy remonstrated and explained the process. In vain did she go to the kitchen herself to translate a carefully written recipe to the cook, and to slip a shining five-franc piece in his hand, which, it was hoped, would quicken his energies and soften his heart. In vain did she order private supplies of the best of beef from a separate market. The cooks stole the beef and ignored the recipe; and day after day the same bottleful of greasy liquid came upstairs, which Amy would not touch, and which would have done her no good had she swallowed it all. At last, driven to desperation, Katy procured a couple of stout bottles, and every morning slowly and carefully cut up two pounds of meat into small pieces, sealed the bottle with her own seal ring, and sent it down to be boiled for a specified time. This answered better, for the thieving cook dared not tamper with her seal; but it was a long and toilsome process, and consumed more time than she well knew how to spare – for there were continual errands to be done which no one could attend to but herself, and the interminable flights of stairs taxed her strength painfully, and seemed to grow longer and harder every day.

At last a good Samaritan turned up in the shape of an American lady with a house of her own who, hearing of their plight from Mrs Sands, undertook to send each day a supply of strong, perfectly-made beef-tea from her own kitchen for Amy's use. It was an inexpressible relief, and the lightening of this one particular care made all the rest seem easier of endurance.

Another great relief came, when, after some delay, Dr Hilary succeeded in getting an English nurse to take the places of the unsatisfactory Sister Ambrogia and her substitute, Sister Agatha, whom Amy, in her half-comprehending condition, persisted in calling 'Sister Nutmeg-Grater'. Mrs Swift was a tall, wiry, angular person, who seemed made of equal parts of iron and whalebone. She was never tired; she could lift anybody, do anything; and for sleep she seemed to have a sort of antipathy, preferring to sit in an easy-chair and drop off into little dozes, whenever it was convenient, to going regularly to bed for a night's rest.

Amy took to her from the first, and the new nurse managed her beautifully. No one else could soothe her half so well during the delirious period, when the little shrill voice seemed never to be still, and went on all day and all night in alternate raving or screaming, or, what was saddest of all to hear, low pitiful moans. There was no shutting in these sounds. People moved out of the rooms below and on either side, because they could get no sleep; and till the arrival of Nurse Swift, there was no rest for poor Mrs Ashe, who could not keep away from her darling for a moment while that mournful wailing sounded in her ears.

Somehow the long, dry Englishwoman seemed to have a mesmeric effect on Amy, who was never quite so violent after she arrived. Katy was more thankful for this than can well be told; for her great underlying dread – a dread she dared not whisper plainly even to herself – was that 'Polly dear' might break down before Amy was better, and then what *should* they do.

She took every care that was possible of her friend. She made her eat; she made her lie down. She forced daily doses of quinine and port-wine down her throat, and saved her every possible step. But no one, however affectionate and willing, could do much to lift the crushing burden of care which was changing Mrs Ashe's rosy fairness to wan pallor and laying such dark shadows under the pretty grey eyes. She had taken small thought of looks since Amy's illness. All the little touches which had made her toilette becoming, all the crimps and fluffs, had disappeared; yet somehow never had she seemed to Katy half so lovely as now in the plain black gown which she wore all day long, with her hair tucked into a knot behind her ears. Her real beauty of feature and outline seemed only enhanced by the rigid plainness of her attire, and the charm of true expression grew in her face. Never had Katy admired and loved her friend so well as during those days of fatigue and wearing suspense, or realised so strongly the worth of her sweetness of temper, her unselfishness and power of devoting herself to other people.

'Polly bears it wonderfully,' she wrote her father; 'she was all broken down for the first day or two, but now her courage and patience are surprising. When I think how precious Amy is to her, and how lonely her life would be if she were to die, I can hardly keep the tears out of my eyes. But Polly does not cry. She is quiet and brave and almost cheerful all the time, keeping herself busy with what needs to be done; she never complains, and she looks – oh, so pretty! I think I never knew how much she had in her before.'

All this time no word had come from Lieutenant Worthington. His sister had written him as soon as Amy was taken ill, and had twice telegraphed since, but no answer had been received, and this strange silence added to the sense of lonely isolation and distance from home and help which those who encounter illness in a foreign land have to bear.

So, first one week and then another wore themselves away somehow. The fever did not break on the fourteenth day, as had been hoped, and must run for another period, the doctor said; but its force was lessened, and he considered that a favourable sign. Amy was quieter now and did not rave so constantly, but she was very weak. All her pretty hair had been shorn away, which made her little face look tiny and sharp. Mabel's golden wig was sacrificed at the same time. Amy had insisted upon it, and they dared not cross her.

'She has got a fever too, and it's a great deal badder than mine is,' she protested. 'Her cheeks are as hot as fire. She ought to have ice on her head, and how can she when her bang is so thick? Cut it all off, every bit, and then I will let you cut mine.'

'You had better give ze child her way,' said Dr Hilary. 'She's in no state to be fretted with triffles' (trifles, the doctor meant), 'and in ze end it will be well; for ze fever infection might harbour in zat doll's head as well as elsewhere, and I should have to disinfect it which would be bad for ze skin of her.'

'She isn't a doll,' cried Amy, overhearing him; 'she's my child, and you shan't call her names.' She hugged Mabel tight in her arms, and glared at Dr Hilary defiantly.

So Katy, with pitiful fingers, slashed away at Mabel's blond wig till her head was as bare as a billiard-ball and Amy, quite content, patted her child while her own locks were being cut, and murmured, 'Perhaps your hair will all come out in little round curls, darling, as Johnnie Carr's did;' then she fell into one of the quietest sleeps she had yet had.

It was the day after this that Katy, coming in from a round of errands, found Mrs Ashe standing erect and pale, with a frightened look in her eyes and her back against Amy's door, as if defending it from somebody. Confronting her was Madame Frulini, the *padrona* of the hotel. Madame's cheeks were red, and her eyes bright and fierce; she was evidently in a rage about something, and was pouring out a torrent of excited Italian, with now and then a French or English word slipped in by way of punctuation, and all so rapidly that only a trained ear could have followed or grasped her meaning.

'What is the matter?' asked Katy, in amazement.

'Oh, Katy, I am so glad you have come!' cried poor Mrs Ashe. 'I can hardly understand a word that this horrible woman says, but I think she wants to turn us out of the hotel, and that we shall take Amy to some other place. It would be the death of her – I know it would. I never, never will go, unless the doctor says it is safe. I oughtn't to – I couldn't; she can't make me, can she, Katy?'

'Madame,' said Katy – and there was a flash in her eyes before which the landlady rather shrank – 'what is all this? Why do you come to trouble madame while her child is so ill?'

Then came another torrent of explanation which didn't explain; but Katy gathered enough of the meaning to make out that Mrs Ashe was quite correct in her guess, and that Madame Frulini was requesting, nay, insisting, that they should remove Amy from the hotel at once. There were plenty of apartments to be had now that the Carnival was over, she said – her own cousin had rooms close by – it could easily be arranged; and people were going away from the Del Mondo every day because there was fever in the house. Such a thing could not be, it should not be – the landlady's voice rose to a shriek, 'the child must go!'

'You are a cruel woman,' said Katy indignantly, when she had grasped the meaning of the outburst. 'It is wicked, it is cowardly, to come thus and attack a poor lady under your roof who has so much already to bear. It is her only child who is lying in there – her only one, do you understand, madame? – and she is a widow. What you ask might kill the child. I shall not permit you or any of your people to enter that door till the doctor comes, and then I shall tell him how you have behaved, and we shall see what he will say.' As she spoke she turned the key of Amy's door, took it out and put it in her pocket, then faced the *padrona* steadily, looking her straight in the eyes.

'Mademoiselle,' stormed the landlady, 'I give you my

word, four people have left this house already because of the noises made by little miss. More will go. I shall lose my winter's profit – all of it – all; it will be said there is fever at the Del Mondo – no one will hereafter come to me. There are lodgings plenty, comfortable – oh, so comfortable! I will not have my season ruined by a sickness; no, I will not!'

Madame Frulini's voice was again rising to a scream.

'Be silent!' said Katy sternly; 'you will frighten the child. I am sorry that you should lose any customers, madame, but the fever is here and we are here and here we must stay till it is safe to go. The child shall not be moved till the doctor gives permission. Money is not the only thing in the world! Mrs Ashe will pay anything that is fair to make up your losses to you, but you must leave this room now, and not return till Dr Hilary is here.'

Where Katy found French for all these long coherent speeches, she could never afterward imagine. She tried to explain it by saying that excitement inspired her for the moment, but that as soon as the moment was over the inspiration died away and left her as speechless and confused as ever. Clover said it made her think of the miracle of Balaam; and Katy merrily rejoined that it might be so, and that no donkey in any age of the world could possibly have been more grateful than was she for the sudden gift of speech.

'But it is not the money – it is my prestige,' declared the landlady.

'Thank Heaven! here is the doctor now,' cried Mrs Ashe.

The doctor had, in fact, been standing in the doorway for several moments before they noticed him, and had over-heard part of the colloquy with Madame Frulini. With him was someone else, at the sight of whom Mrs Ashe gave a great sob of relief. It was her brother at last.

When Italian meets Italian then comes the tug of expletive. It did not seem to take one second for Dr Hilary to whirl the *padrona* out into the entry, where they could be heard going at each other like two furious cats. Hiss, roll, sputter, recrimination, objurgation! In five minutes Madame Frulini was, metaphorically speaking, on her knees, and the doctor standing over her with drawn sword, making her take back every word she had said and every threat she had uttered.

'Prestige of thy miserable hotel!' he thundered; 'where will that be when I go and tell the English and Americans – all of whom I know, every one! – how thou hast served a countrywoman of theirs in thy house! Dost thou think thy prestige will help thee much when Dr Hilary has fixed a black mark on thy door? I tell thee no; not a stranger shalt thou have next year to eat so much as a plate of macaroni under thy base roof! I will advertise thy behaviour in all the foreign papers – in *Figaro*, in *Galignani*, in the *Swiss Times* and the English one, which is read by all the nobility, and the *Heraldo* of New York, which all Americans peruse – '

'Oh, doctor – pardon me – I regret what I said – I am afflicted – !'

'I will post thee in the railroad-stations,' continued the doctor implacably; 'I will bid my patients to write letters to all their friends, warning them against thy flea-ridden Del Mondo; I will apprise the steamboat companies at Genoa and Naples. Thou shalt see what comes of it – truly, thou shalt see.'

Having thus reduced Madame Frulini to powder, the doctor now condescended to take breath and listen to her appeals for mercy; and presently he brought her in with her mouth full of protestations and apologies, and assurances that the ladies had mistaken her meaning, she had only spoken for the good of all; nothing was further from her intention than that they should be disturbed or offended in any way, and she and all her household were at the service of 'the little sick angel of God'. After which the doctor dismissed her with an air of contemptuous tolerance, and laid his hand on the door of Amy's room. Behold, it was locked!

'Oh, I forgot!' cried Katy, laughing, and she pulled the key out of her pocket.

'You are a hee–roine, mademoiselle,' said Dr Hilary. 'I watched you as you faced that tigress, and your eyes were like a swordsman's as he regards his enemy's rapier.'

'Oh, she was so brave, and such a help!' said Mrs Ashe, kissing her impulsively. 'You can't think how she has stood by me all through, Ned, or what a comfort she has been.'

'Yes, I can,' said Ned Worthington, with a warm, grateful look at Katy. 'I can believe anything good of Miss Carr.'

'But where have *you* been all this time!' said Katy, who felt this flood of compliment to be embarrassing; 'we have so wondered at not hearing from you.'

'I have been off on a ten days' leave to Corsica for moufflon-shooting,' replied Mr Worthington. 'I only got Polly's telegrams and letters the day before yesterday, and I came away as soon as I could get my leave extended. It was a most unlucky absence. I shall always regret it.'

'Oh, it is all right now that you have come!' his sister said, leaning her head on his arm with a look of relief and rest which was good to see. 'Everything will go better now, I am sure.'

'Katy Carr has behaved like a perfect angel,' she told her brother when they were alone.

'She is a trump of a girl. I came in time for part of that scene with the landlady, and upon my word she was glorious! I didn't suppose she could look so handsome.'

'Have the Pages left Nice yet?' asked his sister, rather irrelevantly.

'No – at least they were there on Thursday, but I think that they were to start today.'

Mr Worthington answered carelessly, but his face darkened as he spoke. There had been a little scene in Nice which he could not forget. He was sitting in the English garden with Lilly and her mother when his sister's telegrams were brought to him; and he had read them aloud, partly as an explanation for the immediate departure which they made necessary and which broke up an excursion just arranged with the ladies for the afternoon. It is not pleasant to have plans interfered with; and as neither Mrs Page nor her daughter cared personally for little Amy, it is not strange that disappointment at the interruption of their pleasure should have been the first impulse with them. Still, this did not excuse Lilly's unstudied exclamation of, 'Oh, bother!' and though she speedily repented it as an indiscretion, and was properly sympathetic, and 'hoped the poor little thing would soon be better', Amy's uncle could not forget the jarring impression. It completed a process of disenchant-ment which had long been going on; and as hearts are sometimes caught at the rebound, Mrs Ashe was not so far astray when she built certain little dim sisterly hopes on his evident admiration for Katy's courage and this sudden awakening to a sense of her good looks.

But no space was left for sentiment or matchmaking while still Amy's fate hung in the balance, and all three of them found plenty to do during the next fortnight. The fever did not turn on the twenty-first day, and another weary week of suspense set in, each day bringing a decrease of the dangerous symptoms, but each day as well marking a lessening in the childish strength which had been so long and severely tested. Amy was quite conscious now, and lay quietly, sleeping a great deal and speaking seldom. There was not much to do but to wait and hope; but the flame of hope burned low at times as the little life flickered in its socket and seemed likely to go out like a windblown torch.

Now and then Lieutenant Worthington would persuade his sister to go with him for a few minutes' drive or walk in the fresh air, from which she had so long been debarred, and once or twice he prevailed on Katy to do the same; but neither of them could bear to be away long from Amy's bedside.

Intimacy grows fast when people are thus united by a common anxiety, sharing the same hopes and fears day after day, speaking and thinking of the same thing. The gay young officer at Nice, who had counted so little in Katy's world, seemed to have disappeared, and the gentle, considerate, tender-hearted fellow who now filled his place was quite a different person in her eyes. Katy began to count on Ned Worthington as a friend who could be trusted for help and sympathy and comprehension, and appealed to and relied upon in all emergencies. She was quite at ease with him now, and asked him to do this and that, to come and help her, or to absent himself, as freely as if he had been Dorry or Phil.

He, on his part, found this easy intimacy charming. In the reaction of his temporary glamour for the pretty Lilly, Katy's very difference from her was an added attraction. This difference consisted, as much as anything else, in the fact that she was so truly in earnest in what she said and did. Had Lilly been in Katy's place, she would probably have been helpful to Mrs Ashe and kind to Amy so far as in her lay; but the thought of self would have tinctured all that she did and said, and the need of keeping to what was tasteful and becoming would have influenced her in every emergency, and never have been absent from her mind.

Katy, on the contrary, absorbed in the needs of the moment, gave little heed to how she looked or that anyone was thinking about her. Her habit of neatness made her take time for the one thorough daily dressing – the brushing of hair and freshening of clothes, which were customary with her; but, this tax paid to personal comfort, she gave little further heed to appearances. She wore an old grey gown, day in and day out, which Lilly would not have put on for half an hour without a large bribe, so unbecoming was it;

but somehow Lieutenant Worthington grew to like the grey gown as a part of Katy herself. And if by chance he brought a rose in to cheer the dim stillness of the sickroom, and she tucked it into her buttonhole, immediately it was as though she were decked for conquest. Pretty dresses are very pretty on pretty people – they certainly play an important part in this queer little world of ours; but depend upon it, dear girls, no woman ever has established so distinct and clear a claim on the regard of her lover as when he has ceased to notice or analyse what she wears, and just accepts it unquestioningly, whatever it is, as a bit of the dear human life which has grown or is growing to be the best and most delightful thing in the world to him.

The grey gown played its part during the long anxious night when they all sat watching breathlessly to see which way the tide would turn with dear little Amy. The doctor came at midnight, and went away to come again at dawn. Mrs Swift sat grim and watchful beside the pillow of her charge, rising now and then to feel pulse and skin, or to put a spoonful of something between Amy's lips. The doors and windows stood open to admit the air. In the outer room all was hushed. A dim Roman lamp, fed with olive-oil, burned in one corner behind a screen. Mrs Ashe lay on the sofa with her eyes closed, bearing the strain of suspense in absolute silence. Her brother sat beside her, holding in his one of the hot hands whose nervous twitches alone told of the surgings of hope and fear within. Katy was resting in a big chair near by, her wistful eyes fixed on Amy's little figure seen in the dim distance, her ears alert for every sound from the sickroom.

So they watched and waited. Now and then Ned Worthington or Katy would rise softly, steal on tiptoe to the bedside, and come back to whisper to Mrs Ashe that Amy had stirred or that she seemed to be asleep. It was one of the nights which do not come often in a lifetime, and which people never forget. The darkness seems full of meaning, the hush, of sound. God is beyond, holding the sunrise in his right hand, holding the sun of our earthly hopes as well – will it dawn in sorrow or in joy? We dare not ask, we can only wait.

A faint stir of wind and a little broadening of the light roused Katy from a trance of half-understood thoughts. She crept once more into Amy's room. Mrs Swift laid a warning finger on her lips; Amy was sleeping, she said with a gesture. Katy whispered the news to the still figure on the sofa, then she went noiselessly out of the room. The great hotel was fast asleep; not a sound stirred the profound silence of the dark halls. A longing for fresh air led her to the roof.

There was the dawn just tingeing the east. The sky, even thus early, wore the deep, mysterious blue of Italy. A fresh *tramontana* was blowing, and made Katy glad to draw her shawl about her.

Far away in the distance rose the Alban Hills above the dim Campagna, with the more lofty Sabines beyond, and Soracte, clear cut against the sky like a wave frozen in the moment of breaking. Below lay the ancient city, with its strange mingling of the old and the new, of past things embedded in the present; or is it the present thinly veiling the rich and mighty past – who shall say?

Faint rumblings of wheels, and here and there a curl of smoke, showed that Rome was waking up. The light insensibly grew upon the darkness. A pink flush lit up the horizon. Florio stirred in his lair, stretched his dappled limbs, and as the first sun-ray glinted on the roof, raised himself, crossed the gravelled tiles with soundless feet, and ran his soft nose into Katy's hand. She fondled him for Amy's sake as she stood bent over the flower-boxes, inhaling the scent of the mignonette and gillyflowers, with her eyes fixed on the distance; but her heart was at home with the sleepers there, and a rush of strong desire stirred her.

Would this dreary time come to an end presently, and should they be set at liberty to go their ways with no heavy sorrow to press them down, to be carefree and happy again in their own land?

A footstep startled her. Ned Worthington was coming over the roof on tiptoe, as if fearful of disturbing somebody. His face looked resolute and excited.

'I wanted to tell you,' he said in a hushed voice, 'that the doctor is here, and he says Amy has no fever, and with care may be considered out of danger.'

'Thank God!' cried Katy, bursting into tears. The long fatigue, the fears kept in check so resolutely, the sleepless night just passed, had their revenge now, and she cried and cried as if she could never stop, but with all the time such joy and gratitude in her heart! She was conscious that Ned had his arm round her and was holding both her hands tight; but they were so one in the emotion of the moment that it did not seem strange.

'How sweet the sun looks!' she said presently, releasing herself, with a happy smile flashing through her tears; 'it hasn't seemed really bright for ever so long. How silly I was to cry! Where is dear Polly? I must go down to her at once. Oh, what does she say?'

CHAPTER ELEVEN

Next

Lieutenant Worthington's leave had nearly expired. He must rejoin his ship; but he waited till the last possible moment in order to help his sister through the move to Albano, where it had been decided that Amy should go for a few days of hill air before undertaking the longer journey to Florence.

It was a perfect morning in late March when the pale little invalid was carried in her uncle's strong arms, and placed in the carriage which was to take them to the old town on the mountain slopes which they had seen shining from far away for so many weeks past. Spring had come in her fairest shape to Italy. The Campagna had lost its brown and tawny hues and taken on a tinge of fresh colour. The olive orchards were budding thickly. Almond boughs extended their dazzling shapes across the blue sky. Arums and acanthus and ivy filled every hollow, roses nodded from over every gate, while a carpet of violets and cyclamen and primroses stretched over the fields and freighted every wandering wind with fragrance.

When once the Campagna, with its long line of aqueducts, arches, and hoary tombs, was left behind, and the carriage slowly began to mount the gradual rises of the hill, Amy revived. With every breath of the fresher air her eyes seemed to brighten and her voice to grow stronger. She held Mabel up to look at the view; and the sound of her laugh, faint and feeble as it was, was like music to her mother's ears.

Amy wore a droll little silk-lined cap on her head over which a downy growth of pale-brown fuzz was gradually thickening. Already it showed a tendency to form into tiny rings, which to Amy, who had always hankered for curls, was an extreme satisfaction. Strange to say, the same thing exactly had happened to Mabel: her hair had grown out into soft little round curls also; Uncle Ned and Katy had ransacked Rome for this baby-wig, which filled and realised all Amy's hopes for her child. On the same excursion they had bought the materials for the pretty spring suit which Mabel wore, for it had been deemed necessary to sacrifice most of her wardrobe as a concession to possible fever-germs. Amy admired the pearl-coloured dress and hat, the fringed jacket and little lace-trimmed parasol, so much that she was quite consoled for the loss of the blue velvet costume and ermine muff which had been the pride of her heart ever since they left Paris, and whose destruction they had scarcely dared to confess to her.

So up, up, up they climbed till the gateway of that old town was passed, and the carriage stopped before a quaint building, once the residence of the Bishop of Albano but now known as the Hôtel de la Poste. Here they alighted, and were shown up a wide and lofty staircase to their rooms, which were on the sunny side of the house, and looked across a walled garden, where roses and lemon trees grew beside old fountains guarded by sculptured lions and heathen divinities with broken noses and a scant supply of fingers and toes, to the Campagna, purple with distance, and stretching miles and miles away to where Rome sat on her seven hills, lifting high the Dome of St Peter's into the illumined air.

Nurse Swift said that Amy must go to bed at once and have a long rest. But Amy nearly wept at the proposal and declared that she was not a bit tired, and couldn't sleep if she went to bed ever so much. The change of air had done her good already and she looked more like herself than for many weeks past. They compromised their dispute on a sofa, where Amy, well wrapped up, was laid, and where, in spite of her protestations, she presently fell asleep, leaving the others free to examine and arrange their new quarters.

Such enormous rooms as they were! It was quite a journey to go from one side of them to another. The floors were of stone, with squares of carpet laid down over them which looked absurdly small for the great spaces they were supposed to cover. The beds and tables were of the usual size, but they seemed almost like doll furniture because the chambers were so big. A quaint old paper, with an enormous pattern of banyan trees and pagodas, covered the walls, and every now and then betrayed, by an oblong of regular cracks, the existence of a hidden door, papered to look exactly like the rest of the wall.

These mysterious doors made Katy nervous, and she never rested till she had opened every one of them and explored the places they led to. One gave access to a queer little bathroom. Another led, through a narrow dark passage, to a sort of balcony or loggia overhanging the garden. A third ended in a dusty closet with an artful chink in it from which you could peep into what had been the bishop's drawing-room but which was now turned into the dining-room of the hotel. It seemed made for purposes of espial; and Katy had visions of a long line of reverend prelates with their ears glued to the chink, overhearing what was being said about them in the apartment beyond.

The most surprising of all she did not discover till she was going to bed on the second night after their arrival, when she thought she knew all about the mysterious doors and what they led to. A little unexplained draught of wind made her candle flicker, and betrayed the existence of still another door, so cunningly hidden in the wall pattern that she had failed to notice it. She had quite a creepy feeling as she drew her dressing-gown about her, took a light, and entered the narrow passage into which it opened. It was not

a long passage, and ended presently in a tiny oratory. There
was a little marble altar, with a kneeling-step and candlesticks and a great crucifix above. Ends of wax candles still
remained in the candlesticks, and bunches of dusty paper
flowers filled the vases which stood on either side of them.
A faded silk cushion lay on the step. Doubtless the bishop
had often knelt there. Katy felt as if she were the first
person to enter the place since he went away. Her common
sense told her that in a hotel bedroom, constantly occupied
by strangers for years past, someone *must* have discovered
the door and found the little oratory before her; but
common sense is sometimes less satisfactory than romance.
Katy liked to think that she was the first, and to 'make
believe' that no one else knew about it; so she did so, and
invented legends about the place which Amy considered
better than any fairy story.

Before he left them Lieutenant Worthington had a talk
with his sister in the garden. She rather forced this talk upon
him, for various things were lying at her heart about which
she longed for explanation; but he yielded so easily to her
wiles that it was evident he was not averse to the idea.

'Come, Polly, don't beat about the bush any longer,' he
said at last, amused and a little irritated at her half-hints and
little feminine *finesses*. 'I know what you want to ask; and as
there's no use making a secret of it, I will take my turn in
asking. Have I any chance, do you think?'

'Any chance! – about Katy, do you mean? Oh, Ned, you
make me so happy!'

'Yes; about her, of course.'

'I don't see why you should say "of course",' remarked his
sister, with the perversity of her sex, 'when it's only five or
six weeks ago that I was lying awake at night for fear you
were being gobbled up by that Lilly Page.'

'There was a little risk of it,' replied her brother seriously.
'She's awfully pretty and she dances beautifully, and the

other fellows were all wild about her, and – well, you know yourself how such things go. I can't see now what it was that I fancied so much about her; I don't suppose I could have told exactly at the time; but I can tell without the smallest trouble what it is in – the other.'

'In Katy? I should think so,' cried Mrs Ashe emphatically; 'the two are no more to be compared than – than – well, bread and syllabub! You can live on one and you can't live on the other.'

'Come, now, Miss Page isn't so bad as that. She is a nice girl enough, and a pretty girl too – prettier than Katy; I'm not so far gone that I can't see that. But we won't talk about her, she's not in the present question at all; very likely she'd have had nothing to say to me in any case. I was only one out of a dozen, and she never gave me reason to suppose that she cared more for me than the rest. Let us talk about this friend of yours; have I any chance at all, do you think, Polly?'

'Ned, you are the dearest boy! I would rather have Katy for a sister than anyone else I know. She's so nice all through – so true and sweet and satisfactory.'

'She is all that and more; she's a woman to tie to for life, to be perfectly sure of always. She would make a splendid wife for any man. I'm not half good enough for her; but the question is – and you haven't answered it yet, Polly – what's my chance?'

'I don't know,' said his sister slowly.

'Then I must ask her herself; and I shall do so today.'

'I don't know,' repeated Mrs Ashe. ' "She is a woman, therefore to be won" – and I don't think there is anyone ahead of you; that is the best hope I have to offer, Ned. Katy never talks of such things; and though she's so frank, I can't guess whether or not she ever thinks about them. She likes you, however, I am sure of that. But, Ned, it will not be wise to say anything to her yet.'

'Not say anything! Why not?'

'No. Recollect that it is only a little while since she looked upon you as the admirer of another girl, and a girl she doesn't like very much, though they are cousins. You must give her time to get over that impression. Wait awhile; that's my advice, Ned.'

'I'll wait any time if only she will say yes in the end. But it's hard to go away without a word of hope, and it's more like a man to speak out, it seems to me.'

'It's too soon,' persisted his sister. 'You don't want her to think you a fickle fellow, falling in love with a fresh girl every time you go into port, and falling out again when the ship sails. Sailors have a bad reputation for that sort of thing. No woman cares to win a man like that.'

'Great Scott! I should think not! Do you mean to say that is the way my conduct appears to her, Polly?'

'No, I don't mean just that: but wait, dear Ned, I am sure it is better.'

Fortified by this sage counsel, Lieutenant Worthington went away next morning, without saying anything to Katy in words, though perhaps eyes and tones may have been less discreet. He made them promise that someone should send a letter every day about Amy; and as Mrs Ashe frequently devolved the writing of these bulletins upon Katy, and the replies came in the shape of long letters, she found herself conducting a pretty regular correspondence without quite intending it. Ned Worthington wrote particularly nice letters. He had the knack, more often found in women than men, of giving a picture with a few graphic touches, and indicating what was droll or what was characteristic with a single happy phrase. His letters grew to be one of Katy's pleasures; and sometimes, as Mrs Ashe watched the colour deepen in her cheeks while she read, her heart would bound hopefully within her. But she was a wise woman in her way, and she wanted Katy for a sister very much; so she never said a word or looked a look to startle or surprise her, but left the thing to work itself out, which is the best course always in love affairs.

Little Amy's improvement at Albano was something remarkable. Mrs Swift watched over her like a lynx. Her vigilance never relaxed. Amy was made to eat and sleep and walk and rest with the regularity of a machine; and this exact system, combined with the good air, worked like a charm. The little one gained hour by hour. They could absolutely see her growing fat, her mother declared. Fevers, when they do not kill, operate sometimes as spring bonfires do in gardens, burning up all the refuse and leaving the soil free for the growth of fairer things; and Amy promised in time to be only the better and stronger for her hard experience.

She had gained so much before the time came to start for Florence that they scarcely dreaded the journey; but it proved worse than their expectations. They had not been able to secure a carriage to themselves, and were obliged to share their compartment with two English ladies and three Roman Catholic priests, one old, the others young. The older priest seemed to be a person of some consequence, for quite a number of people came to see him off, and knelt for his blessing devoutly as the train moved away. The younger ones Katy guessed to be seminary students under his charge. Her chief amusement through the long dusty journey was in watching the terrible time that one of these young men was having with his own hat. It was a large three-cornered black affair, with sharp angles and excessively stiff; and a perpetual struggle seemed to be going on between it and its owner, who was evidently unhappy when it was on his head, and still more unhappy when it was anywhere else. If he perched it on his knees it was sure to slide away from him and fall with a thump on the floor, whereupon he would pick it up, blushing furiously as he did so. Then he would lay it on the seat when the train stopped at a station, and jump out with an air of relief; but he invariably forgot, and sat down upon it when he returned, and sprang up with a look of horror at the loud crackle it made; after which he would tuck it into the baggage rack overhead, from which it would presently descend, generally into the lap of one of the staid English ladies, who would hand it back to him with an air of deep offence, remarking to her companion: 'I never knew anything like it. Fancy! that makes four times that hat has fallen on me. The young man is a feedgit! He's the most feedgitty creature I ever saw in my life.'

The young *seminariat* did not understand a word she said; but the tone needed no interpreter, and set him to blushing more painfully than ever. Altogether the hat was never off his mind for a moment. Katy could see that he was thinking about it, even when he was thumbing his breviary and making believe to read.

At last the train, steaming down the valley of the Arno, revealed fair Florence sitting among olive-clad hills, with Giotto's beautiful belltower, and the great, many-coloured, soft-hued cathedral, and the square tower of the old palace, and the quaint bridges over the river, looking exactly as they do in the photographs; and Katy would have felt delighted, in spite of dust and fatigue, had not Amy looked so worn out and exhausted. They were seriously troubled about her, and for the moment could think of nothing else. Happily the fatigue did no permanent harm, and a day or two of rest made her all right again. By good fortune, a nice little apartment in the modern quarter of the city had been vacated by its winter occupants the very day of their arrival, and Mrs Ashe secured it for a month, with all its conveniences and advantages, including a maid named Maria, who had been servant to the just-departed tenants.

Maria was a very tall woman, at least six feet two, and had a splendid contralto voice, which she occasionally exercised while busy over her pots and pans. It was so remarkable to hear these grand arias and recitatives proceeding from a kitchen some eight feet square that Katy was at great pains to satisfy her curiosity about it. By aid of the dictionary and much persistent questioning, she made out that Maria in her youth had received a partial training for the opera; but in the end it was decided that she was too big and heavy for the stage, and the poor 'giantess', as Amy named her, had been forced to abandon her career, and gradually had sunk to the position of a maid-of-all-work. Katy suspected that heaviness of mind as well as of body must have stood in her way; for Maria, though a good-natured giantess, was by no means quick of intelligence.

'I do think that the manner in which people over here can make homes for themselves at five minutes' notice is perfectly delightful,' cried Katy, at the end of their first day's housekeeping. 'I wish we could do the same in America. How cosy it looks here already!'

It was indeed cosy. Their new domain consisted of a parlour in a corner, furnished in bright yellow brocade, with windows to south and west; a nice little dining-room; three bedrooms, with dimity-curtained beds; a square entrance-hall, lighted at night by a tall slender brass lamp whose double wicks were fed with olive-oil; and the aforesaid tiny kitchen, behind which was a sleeping cubby, quite too small to be a good fit for the giantess. The rooms were full of conveniences – easy-chairs, sofas, plenty of bureaux and dressing-tables and corner fireplaces like Franklin stoves, in which odd little fires burned on cool days, made of pine cones, cakes of pressed sawdust exactly like Boston brown bread cut into slices, and a few sticks of wood thriftily adjusted, for fuel is worth its weight in gold in Florence. Katy's was the smallest of the bedrooms, but she liked it best of all for the reason that its one big window opened on an iron balcony over which grew a Banksia rose-vine with a stem as thick as her wrist. It was covered just now with masses of tiny white blossoms, whose fragrance was inexpressibly delicious and made every breath drawn in their neighbourhood a delight. The sun streamed in on all sides of the little apartment, which filled a narrowing angle at the union of three streets; and from one window and another, glimpses could be caught of the distant heights about the city – San Miniato in one direction, Bello Sguardo in another, and for the third the long olive-hung ascent of Fiesole, crowned by its grey cathedral towers.

It was astonishing how easily everything fell into train about the little establishment. Every morning at six the English baker left two small sweet brown loaves and a dozen rolls at the door. Then followed the dairyman with a supply of tiny leaf-shaped pats of freshly-churned butter, a big flask of milk, and two small bottles of thick cream, with a twist of vine leaf in each by way of a cork. Next came a *contadino* with a flask of red Chianti wine, a film of oil floating on top to keep it sweet. People in Florence must drink wine, whether they like it or not, because the lime-impregnated water is unsafe for use without some admixture.

Dinner came from a *trattoria*, in a tin box, with a pan of coals inside to keep it warm, which box was carried on a man's head. It was furnished at a fixed price per day – a soup, two dishes of meat, two vegetables and a sweet dish; and the supply was so generous as always to leave something toward next day's luncheon. Salad, fruit and fresh eggs Maria bought for them in the old market. From the confectioner's came loaves of *pane santo*, a sort of light cake made with arrowroot instead of flour; and sometimes, by way of treat, a square of *pan forte da Siena*, compounded of honey, almonds and chocolate – a mixture as pernicious as it is delicious, and which might take a medal anywhere for the sure production of nightmares.

Amy soon learned to know the shops from which these delicacies came. She had her favourites, too, among the strolling merchants who sold oranges and those little sweet native figs dried in the sun without sugar, which are among the specialities of Florence. They, in their turn, learned to know her and to watch for the appearance of her little capped head and Mabel's blonde wig at the window, lingering about till she came, then advertising their wares with musical modulations so appealing that Amy was always running to Katy, who acted as housekeeper, to beg her to please buy this or that, 'because it is my old man, and he wants me to so much'.

'But, chicken, we have plenty of figs for today.'

'No matter; get some more, please do. I'll eat them all; really, I will.'

And Amy was as good as her word. Her convalescent appetite was something prodigious.

There was another branch of shopping in which they all took equal delight. The beauty and the cheapness of the Florence flowers are a continual surprise to a stranger. Every morning after breakfast an old man came creaking up the two long flights of stairs which led to Mrs Ashe's apartment, tapped at the door, and, as soon as it opened, inserted a shabby elbow and a large flat basket full of flowers. Such flowers! Great masses of scarlet and cream-coloured tulips, and white and gold narcissus, knots of roses of all shades, carnations, heavy-headed trails of wistaria, wild hyacinths violets, deep crimson and orange ranunculus, *giglios* or wild irises – the Florence emblem, so deeply purple as to be almost black – anemones, spring-beauties, faintly tinted wood-blooms tied in large loose nosegays, ivy, fruit blossoms – everything that can be thought of that is fair and sweet. These enticing wares the old man would tip out on the table. Mrs Ashe and Katy would select what they wanted, and then the process of bargaining would begin, without which no sale is complete in Italy. The old man would name an enormous price, five times as much as he hoped to get. Katy would offer a very small one, considerably less than she expected to give. The old man would dance with dismay, wring his hands, assure them that he should die of hunger, and all his family with him, if he took less than the price named; he would then come down half a franc in his demand. So it would go on for five minutes, ten, sometimes for a quarter of an hour, the old man's price gradually descending, and Katy's terms very slowly going up, a cent or two at a time. Next the giantess would mingle with the fray. She would bounce out of her kitchen, berate the flower-vender, snatch up his flowers, declare that they smelt badly, fling them down again, pouring out all the while a voluble tirade of reproaches and revilings, and looking so enormous in her excitement that Katy wondered that the old man dared to answer her at all. Finally, there would be a sudden lull. The old man would shrug his shoulders, and, remarking that he and his wife and his aged grandmother must go without bread that day since it was the signora's will, take the money offered and depart, leaving such a mass of flowers behind him that Katy would begin to think that they had paid an unfair price for them and to feel a little rueful, till she observed that the old man was absolutely dancing downstairs with rapture over the good bargain he had made, and that Maria was black with indignation over the extravagance of her ladies!

'The Americani are a nation of spendthrifts,' she would mutter to herself, as she quickened the charcoal in her droll little range by fanning it with a palm-leaf fan; 'they squander money like water. Well, all the better for us Italians!' with a shrug of her shoulders.

'But, Maria, it was only sixteen cents that we paid, and look at those flowers! There are at least half a bushel of them.'

'Sixteen cents for garbage like that! The signorina would better let me make her bargains for her. *Già! Già!* No Italian lady would have paid more than eleven sous for such useless *roba*. It is evident that the signorina's countrymen eat gold when at home, they think so little of casting it away!'

Altogether, what with the comfort and quiet of this little home, the numberless delightful things that there were to do and to see, and Viessieux's great library, from which they could draw books at will to make the doing and seeing more intelligible, the month at Florence passed only too quickly, and was one of the times to which they afterward looked back with most pleasure. Amy grew steadily stronger, and the freedom from anxiety about her after their long strain of apprehension was restful and healing beyond expression to both mind and body.

Their very last excursion of all, and one of the pleasantest, was to the old amphitheatre at Fiesole, and it was while they sat there in the soft glow of the late afternoon, tying into bunches the violets which they had gathered from under walls whose foundations antedate Rome itself, that a cheery call sounded from above, and an unexpected surprise descended upon them in the shape of Lieutenant Worthington, who, having secured another fifteen days' furlough, had come to take his sister on to Venice.

'I didn't write you that I had applied for leave,' he explained, 'because there seemed so little chance of my getting off again so soon; but as luck had it, Carruthers, whose turn it was, sprained his ankle and was laid up, and the commodore let us exchange. I made all the capital I could out of Amy's fever; but upon my word, I felt like a humbug when I came upon her and Mrs Swift in the Cascine just now, as I was hunting for you. How she has picked up! I should never have known her for the same child.'

'Yes, she seems perfectly well again, and as strong as before she had the fever, though that dear old Goody Swift is just as careful of her as ever. She would not let us bring her here this afternoon, for fear we should stay out till the dew fell. Ned, it is perfectly delightful that you were able to come. It makes going to Venice seem quite a different thing, doesn't it, Katy?'

'I don't want it to seem quite different, because going to Venice was always one of my dreams,' replied Katy, with a little laugh.

'I hope at least it doesn't make it seem less pleasant,' said Mr Worthington, as his sister stopped to pick a violet.

'No, indeed, I am glad,' said Katy; 'we shall all be seeing it for the first time, too, shall we not? I think you said you had never been there.' She spoke simply and frankly, but she was conscious of an odd shyness.

'I simply couldn't stand it any longer,' Ned Worthington confided to his sister when they were alone. 'My head is so full of her that I can't attend to my work, and it came to me all of a sudden that this might be my last chance. You'll be getting north before long, you know, to Switzerland and so on, where I cannot follow you. So I made a clean breast of it to the commodore; and the good old fellow, who has a soft spot in his heart for a love story, behaved like a brick, and made it all straight for me to come away.'

Mrs Ashe did not join in these commendations of the commodore; her attention was fixed on another part of her brother's discourse.

'Then you won't be able to come to me again? I shan't see you again after this!' she exclaimed. 'Dear me! I never realised that before. What shall I do without you?'

'You will have Miss Carr. She is a host in herself,' suggested Ned Worthington. His sister shook her head.

'Katy is a jewel,' she remarked presently; 'but somehow one wants a man to call upon. I shall feel lost without you, Ned.'

The month's housekeeping wound up that night with a 'thick tea' in honour of Lieutenant Worthington's arrival, which taxed all the resources of the little establishment. Maria was sent out hastily to buy *pan forte da Siena* and *vino d'Asti*, and fresh eggs for an omelette, and chickens' breasts smothered in cream from the restaurant, and artichokes for a salad, and flowers to garnish all; and the guest ate and praised and admired; and Amy and Mabel sat on his knee and explained everything to him, and they were all very happy together. Their merriment was so infectious that it extended to the poor giantess, who had been very pensive all day at the prospect of losing her good place, and who now raised her voice in the grand aria from *Orfeo*, and made the kitchen ring with the passionate demand 'Che faro senza, Eurydice?' The splendid notes, full of fire and lamentation, rang out across the saucepans as effectively as if they had been footlights; and Katy, rising softly, opened the kitchen door a little way that they might not lose a sound.

The next day brought them to Venice. It was a 'moment', indeed, as Katy seated herself for the first time in a gondola, and looked from beneath its black hood at the palace walls on the Grand Canal past which they were gliding. Some were creamy white and black, some orange-tawny, others of a dull delicious ruddy colour, half-pink, half-red; but all, in build and ornament, were unlike palaces elsewhere. High on the prow before her stood the gondolier, his form defined in dark outline against the sky, as he swayed and bent to his long oar, raising his head now and again to give a wild musical cry, as warning to other approaching gondolas. It was all like a dream. Ned Worthington sat beside her, looking more at the changes in her expressive face than at the palaces. Venice was as new to him as to Katy; but she was a new feature in his life also, and even more interesting than Venice.

They seemed to float on pleasures for the next ten days. Their arrival had been happily timed to coincide with a great popular festival which for nearly a week kept Venice in a state of continual brilliant gala. All the days were spent on the water, only landing now and then to look at some famous building or picture, or to eat ices in the Piazza with the lovely façade of St Mark's before them. Dining or sleeping seemed a sheer waste of time! The evenings were spent on the water too; for every night, immediately after sunset, a beautiful drifting pageant started from the front of the Doge's Palace to make the tour of the Grand Canal, and our friends always took a part in it. In its centre went a barge hung with embroideries and filled with orange trees and musicians. This was surrounded by a great convoy of skiffs and gondolas bearing coloured lanterns and pennons and gay awnings, and managed by gondoliers in picturesque uniforms. All these floated and shifted and swept on together with a sort of rhythmic undulation, as if keeping time to the music, while across their path dazzling showers and arches of coloured fire poured from the palace fronts and the hotels. Every movement of the fairy flotilla was repeated in the illuminated water, every torch-tip and scarlet lantern and flake of green or rosy fire; above all the bright full moon looked down as if surprised. It was magically beautiful in effect. Katy felt as if her previous sober ideas about life and things had melted away. For the moment the world was turned topsy-turvy. There was nothing hard or real or sordid left in it; it was just a fairy tale, and she was in the middle of it as she had longed to be in her childhood. She was the princess, encircled by delights, as when she and Clover and Elsie played in 'Paradise' – only, this was better; and, dear me! who was this prince who seemed to belong to the story and to grow more important to it every day?

Fairy tales must come to ending. Katy's last chapter closed with a sudden turn-over of the leaf when, toward the end of this happy fortnight, Mrs Ashe came into her room with the face of one who has unpleasant news to communicate.

'Katy,' she began, 'should you be *awfully* disappointed, should you consider me a perfect wretch, if I went home now instead of in the autumn?'

Katy was too much astonished to reply.

'I am grown such a coward, I am so knocked up and weakened by what I suffered in Rome, that I find I cannot face the idea of going on to Germany and Switzerland alone, without Ned to take care of me. You are a perfect angel, dear, and I know that you would do all you could to make it easy for me, but I am such a fool that I do not dare. I think my nerves must have given way,' she continued half-tearfully, 'but the very idea of shifting for myself for five months longer makes me so miserably homesick that I cannot endure it. I dare say I shall repent afterward, and I tell myself now how silly it is; but it's no use – I shall never know another easy moment till I have Amy safe again in America and under your father's care.

'I find,' she continued, after another little pause, 'that we can go down with Ned to Genoa and take a steamer there which will carry us straight to New York without any stops. I hate to disappoint you dreadfully, Katy, but I have almost decided to do it. Shall you mind very much? Can you ever forgive me?' She was fairly crying now.

Katy had to swallow hard before she could answer, the sense of disappointment was so sharp; and with all her efforts there was almost a sob in her voice as she said: 'Why, yes, indeed, dear Polly, there is nothing to forgive. You are perfectly right to go home if you feel so.' Then with another swallow she added: 'You have given me the loveliest six months' treat that ever was, and I should be a greedy girl indeed if I found fault because it is cut off a little sooner then we expected.'

'You are so dear and good not to be vexed,' said her friend, embracing her. 'It makes me feel doubly sorry about disappointing you. Indeed I wouldn't if I could help it, but I simply can't. I *must* go home. Perhaps we'll come back someday when Amy is grown up, or safely married to somebody who will take good care of her!'

This distant prospect was but a poor consolation for the immediate disappointment. The more Katy thought about it the sorrier did she feel. It was not only losing the chance – very likely the only one she would ever have – of seeing Switzerland and Germany; it was all sorts of other little things besides. They must go home in a strange ship with a captain they did not know, instead of in the *Spartacus*, as they had planned, and they should land in New York, where no one would be waiting for them, and not have the fun of sailing into Boston Bay and seeing Rose on the wharf, where she had promised to be. Furthermore, they must pass the hot summer in Burnet instead of in the cool Alpine valleys; and Polly's house was let till October. She and Amy would have to shift for themselves elsewhere. Perhaps they would not be in Burnet at all. Oh dear, what a pity it was! what a dreadful pity!

Then, the first shock of surprise and discomfiture over, other ideas asserted themselves; and as she realised that in three weeks more, or four at the longest, she was to see Papa and Clover and all her dear people at home, she began to feel so very glad that she could hardly wait for the time to come. After all there was nothing in Europe quite so good as that.

'No, I'm not sorry,' she told herself; 'I am glad. Poor Polly! it's no wonder she feels nervous after all she has gone through. I hope I wasn't cross to her! And it will be *very* nice to have Lieutenant Worthington to take care of us as far as Genoa.'

The next three days were full of work. There was no more floating in gondolas, except in the way of business. All the shopping which they had put off must be done, and the trunks packed for the voyage. Everyone recollected last errands and commissions; there was continual coming and going and confusion, and Amy, wild with excitement, popping up every other moment in the midst of it all to demand of everybody if they were not glad that they were going back to America?

Katy had never yet bought her gift from old Mrs Redding. She had waited, thinking continually that she should see something more tempting still in the next place they went to; but now, with the sense that there were to be no more 'next places', she resolved to wait no longer, and with a hundred francs in her pocket, set forth to choose something from among the many tempting things for sale in the Piazza. A bracelet of old Roman coins had caught her fancy one day in a bric-à-brac shop, and she walked straight toward it, only pausing by the way to buy a pale-blue iridescent pitcher at Salviate's for Cecy Slack, and see it carefully rolled in seaweed and soft paper.

The price of the bracelet was a little more than she expected, and quite a long process of bargaining was necessary to reduce it to the sum she had to spend. She had just succeeded, and was counting out the money, when Mrs Ashe and her brother appeared, having spied her from the opposite side of the Piazza, where they were choosing last photographs at Naga's. Katy showed her purchase and explained that it was a present; 'for of course I should never walk out in cold blood and buy a bracelet for myself,' she said, with a laugh.

'This is a fascinating little shop,' said Mrs Ashe. 'I wonder what is the price of that queer old chatelaine with the bottles hanging from it.'

The price was high; but Mrs Ashe was now tolerably conversant with shopping Italian, which consists chiefly of a few words repeated many times over, and it lowered rapidly under the influence of her *troppo*'s and *è molto caro*'s, accompanied with telling little shrugs and looks of surprise. In the end she bought it for less than two-thirds of what had been originally asked for it. As she put the parcel in her pocket, her brother said: 'If you have done your shopping now, Polly, can't you come out for a last row?'

'Katy may, but I can't,' replied Mrs Ashe. 'The man

promised to bring me gloves at six o'clock, and I must be there to pay for them. Take her down to the Lido, Ned. It's an exquisite evening for the water, and the sunset promises to be delirious. You can take the time, can't you, Katy?'

Katy could.

Mrs Ashe turned to leave them, but suddenly stopped short.

'Katy, look! Isn't that a picture?'

The 'picture' was Amy, who had come to the Piazza with Mrs Swift to feed the doves of St Mark's, which was one of her favourite amusements. These pretty birds are the pets of all Venice, and so accustomed to being fondled and made much of by strangers that they are perfectly tame. Amy, when her mother caught sight of her, was sitting on the marble pavement, with one on her shoulder, two perched on the edge of her lap, which was full of crumbs, and a flight of others circling round her head. She was looking up and calling them in soft tones. The sunlight caught the little downy curls on her head and made them glitter. The flying doves lit on the pavement, and crowded round her, their pearl and grey and rose-tinted and white feathers, their scarlet feet and gold-ringed eyes, making a shifting confusion of colours, as they hopped and fluttered and cooed about the little maid, unstartled even by her clear laughter. Close by stood Nurse Swift, observant and grimly pleased.

The mother looked on with happy tears in her eyes. 'Oh, Katy, think what she was a few weeks ago, and look at her now! Can I ever be thankful enough?'

She squeezed Katy's hand convulsively and walked away, turning her head now and then for another glance at Amy and the doves, while Ned and Katy silently crossed to the landing and got into a gondola. It was the perfection of a Venice evening, with silver waves lapping and lulling under a rose and opal sky; and the sense that it was their last row on those enchanted waters made every moment seem doubly precious.

I cannot tell you exactly what it was that Ned Worthington said to Katy during that row, or why it took so long to say it that they did not get in till after the sun was set, and the stars had come out to peep at their bright, glinting faces reflected in the Grand Canal. In fact, no one can tell; for no one overheard, except Giacomo, the brown yellow-jacketed gondolier, and as he did not understand a word of English, he could not repeat the conversation. Venetian boatmen, however, know pretty well what it means when a gentleman and lady, both young, find so much to say in low tones to each other under the gondola hood, and are so long about giving the order to return; and Giacomo, deeply sympathetic, rowed as softly and made himself as imperceptible as he could – a display of tact which merited the big silver piece with which Lieutenant Worthington 'crossed his palm' on landing.

Mrs Ashe had begun to look for them long before they appeared, but I think she was neither surprised nor sorry that they were so late. Katy kissed her hastily and went away at once – 'to pack', she said – and Ned was equally undemonstrative; but they looked so happy, both of them, that 'Polly dear' was quite satisfied and asked no questions.

Five days later the parting came, when the *Florio* steamer put into the port of Genoa for passengers. It was not an easy goodbye to say. Mrs Ashe and Amy both cried, and Mabel was said to be in deep affliction also. But there were alleviations. The squadron was coming home in the autumn, and the officers would have leave to see their friends, and of course Lieutenant Worthington must come to Burnet – to visit his sister. Five months would soon go, he declared; but, for all the cheerful assurance, his face was rueful enough as he held Katy's hand in a long tight clasp while the little boat waited to take him ashore.

After that it was just a waiting to be got through with till they sighted Sandy Hook and the Neversinks – a waiting varied with peeps at Marseilles and Gibraltar, and the sight of a whale or two and one distant iceberg. The weather was fair all the way, and the ocean smooth. Amy was never weary of lamenting her own stupidity in not having taken Maria Matilda out of confinement before they left Venice.

'That child has hardly been out of the trunk since we started,' she said. 'She hasn't seen anything except a little bit of Nice. I shall really be ashamed when the other children ask her about it. I think I shall play that she was left at boarding-school and didn't come to Europe at all! Don't you think that would be the best way, Mamma?'

'You might play that she was left in the state prison for having done something naughty,' suggested Katy; but Amy scouted this idea.

'She never does naughty things,' she said, 'because she never does anything at all. She's just stupid, poor child! It's not her fault.'

The thirty-six hours between New York and Burnet seemed longer than all the rest of the journey put together, Katy thought. But they ended at last, as the *Lake Queen* swung to her moorings at the familiar wharf, where Dr Carr stood surrounded with all his boys and girls just as they had stood the previous October, only that now there were no clouds on anybody's face, and Johnnie was skipping up and down for joy instead of grief. It was a long moment while the plank was being lowered from the gangway; but the moment it was in place, Katy darted across, first ashore of all the passengers, and was in her father's arms.

Mrs Ashe and Amy spent two or three days with them, while looking up temporary quarters elsewhere; and so long as they stayed all seemed a happy confusion of talking and embracing and exclaiming and distributing of gifts. After they went away things fell into their customary train, and a certain flatness became apparent. Everything had happened that could happen. The long-talked-of European journey was over. Here was Katy at home again, months sooner than they expected; yet she looked remarkably cheerful and content! Clover could not understand it: she was likewise puzzled to account for one or two private conversations between Katy and Papa in which she had not been invited to take part, and the occasional arrival of a letter from 'foreign parts' about whose contents nothing was said.

'It seems a dreadful pity that you had to come so soon,' she said one day when they were alone in their bedroom. 'It's delightful to have you, of course; but we had braced ourselves to do without you till October, and there are such lots of delightful things that you could have been doing and seeing at this moment.'

'Oh, yes, indeed!' replied Katy, but not at all as if she were particularly disappointed.

'Katy Carr, I don't understand you,' persisted Clover. 'Why don't you feel worse about it? Here you have lost five months of the most splendid time you ever had, and you don't seem to mind it a bit! Why, if I were in your place my heart would be perfectly broken. And you needn't have come, either; that's the worst of it. It was just a whim of Polly's. Papa says Amy might have stayed as well as not. Why aren't you sorrier, Katy?'

'Oh, I don't know! Perhaps because I had so much as it was – enough to last all my life, I think, though I *should* like to go again. You can't imagine what beautiful pictures are put away in my memory.'

'I don't see that you had so awfully much,' said the aggravated Clover; 'you were there only a little more than six months – for I don't count the sea – and ever so much of that time was taken up with nursing Amy. You can't have any pleasant pictures of *that* part of it.'

'Yes, I have, some.'

'Well, I should really like to know what. There you were in a dark room, frightened to death and tired to death, with only Mrs Ashe and the old nurse to keep you company – Oh, yes, that brother was there part of the time! I forgot him – '

Clover stopped short in sudden amazement. Katy was standing with her back toward her, smoothing her hair, but her face was reflected in the glass. At Clover's words a sudden deep flush had mounted in Katy's cheeks. Deeper and deeper it burned as she became conscious of Clover's astonished gaze, till even the back of her neck was pink. Then, as if she could not bear it any longer, she put the brush down, turned, and fled out of the room; while Clover, looking after her, exclaimed in a tone of sudden comical dismay: 'What does it mean? Oh, dear me! is *that* what Katy is going to do next?'